BECAUSE of YOU

Sara Marx Mitchell

Sunstar
PUBLISHING LTD.

Because of You
by Sara Marx Mitchell
United States, 2001
Sunstar Publishing, Ltd.
204 South 20th Street
Fairfield, Iowa 52556

First Edition 2001

Printed in the United States of America

Library of Congress Catalog Card Number: 2001093936

ISBN: 1-887472-86-X

This novel is a work of fiction and any resemblance of the characters, names, events, dialogue or plot to actual persons or events is coincidental. They are the exclusive product of the author's imagination and are fictitious.

Cover and book design by Irene Archer, Fairfield, Iowa

Readers interested in obtaining further information on the subject matter of this book are invited to correspond with:

The Secretary, Sunstar Publishing, Ltd.
P.O. Box 2211, Fairfield, Iowa 52556
More Sunstar books at: http://www.newagepage.com

To My Family.
I am the luckiest girl.
I love you.

To Kim V.
Thanks for teaching me
what a real friend is.
By the way, could you do me a favor?

This book is for Jackie Joudo in Oz,
aka: Noel.
My first editor and one pushy chic,
your enthusiasm inspires me.
XOXO
You are the best—
No, you are!
No, you are!
No, you are!

Chapter One

" **A** spine-tingling thriller. Another fine specimen of what we have come to from Melody Pittoff, best-selling horror novelist."

Meghan Laine smoothed the wrinkled newspaper that was nearly transparent with wetness. Little chunks of Iowa snow had scattered the countertop when she shook it out, and were melting into tiny pools all around. Folding it again, she took a better look at the weekly syndicated book review.

"That this rugged work, written from a first person male perspective, could actually be from the pen of a woman, only adds to the intrigue of this novel. There is incredible "ballsiness" that proves masculinity cannot be judged by the writer's gender."

A few blond hairs had worked their way out of her braid, softly framing her face, tickling her eyelashes. She blinked and hastily shoved the hairs out of her cobalt eyes.

"Ballsiness. How charming."

Gibson Porter was a man who would likely never write a book himself, yet, felt qualified to direct the masses as to where to best invest their seven bucks for a paperback or twenty-five for a hardbound. And the masses paid loyal attention.

Unimpressed with the business of books and reviews, Boo, her tan Labrador, sighed from his place in the corner. Meg smiled at him before her eyes roved down the kitchen countertop to her laptop computer. It was her own novel in the works, one in an unpublished series of dozens, untouched so far this morning.

Meg stretched, arching her back as she yawned. Her rumpled plaid pajama pants were warm and cozy, topped off with a navy sweatshirt and a pair of oversized socks that actually belonged to her fiancee. The bulkiness guarded her feet from the icy hardwood floor, as December in Jasper Falls was maybe all of eight degrees above zero. Still, that was better than winter in her hometown, Lacross, Wisconsin, where winter daytime temperatures would peak at ten below on the worst days. But she was used to it, having lived there all her life. It was the only thing she'd known before becoming engaged to Marcus St. John, which called for a move to Iowa.

Meg knew that she and the farm boy couldn't be more different. But he adored her, and she appreciated his intended sweetness, despite his sometimes unconventional way of showing it. Finding a moral, single, self-supporting man in this day and age was a luxury that some never knew. In her young thirties, Meg felt fortunate to have him.

He was barely tolerant of her passion for writing, however, citing far more useful ways that she could spend her days. There were rooms to fill with St. John babies, after all, a project that she was admittedly less enthusiastic about than he. But theirs was a comfortable relationship. She considered it a work in progress.

A blast of northern air pummeled the room as the door swung open, ramming the doorstop with a loud *twang!* Meg turned to see Marcus' solid frame nearly filling the doorway. Even he was battling with the wind gusts this bitter day.

She looked next at the snow that had invited itself in, all over the place.

"Oops." Marcus offered her his trademark little-boy grin, fumbling with his stocking cap. He pulled it off altogether, revealing a mess of dark hair that he shook like a wet dog, flipping little chunks of ice about.

Meg heaved a small sigh of annoyance, but gave him an indulgent smile, watching as Marcus brushed off his coveralls with his wool gloves.

It only took him a few long strides to get to the other side of the cozy kitchen. He smiled at her over rosy cheeks as he poured steaming coffee into his thermos and screwed the lid back on.

"Look at my floor, *you.*" She pretended to smack him with the tea towel, and sidled over, wrapping herself in as close a hug as she could manage over his tan Carharts. The coveralls were cold from having spent so much time in the barn, and little chilly blasts of breath emitted through his apologetic laughter. Meg planted a kiss on his cool cheek.

"Creative juices flowing?" The welcome warmth of the oven filled the room, and he gazed over the paper stacks that lined the countertop as they always did whenever she was working. Clumsily, he tousled her hair, causing a few more tendrils to droop into her eyes. She drew back and smirked at her computer, still sitting there, lonely. He nodded. "Having a little writer's block?"

"Yeah, all the publishers are blocking me from writing. It's depressing. I just read a review for the new Melanie Pittoff thriller and it was disgusting." She wriggled out of his hold, flailing her arms hopelessly. "Absolutely gushing—*she's the best,* blah blah . . ." Meg was all over it now. "I read her last book, and I can't say it's any better than anything I've turned out so far only to have it rejected."

Meg paused in her ranting, looking bewildered. She sighed, as she stood in the middle of the floor in her pajamas, her arms folded. When her eyes met his again, her voice was entirely serious.

"Am I making too much of this? Do I like my stuff because it's *mine* or am I crazy?"

"You are crazy," he said, chuckling. Marcus stroked the back of her hair with his damp glove. He found her dramatic performances charming. "But that's besides the point, now. You already know that I think your stuff is good."

Meg shrugged her shoulders and mouthed *good?* Marcus shuffled past her, back to the door. He shook out his stocking cap before putting it back on, adding crystally flakes to the nearly melted pool he'd created earlier. He looked at her through squinted eyes and shook his head.

"But you know I don't get all that publishing business in the first place. I know this much though. I took a look at that last book of hers too, and I'll tell you what I think." Marcus paused, looking right, then left, as if to be sure that no one else would hear. His voice was a whisper. "I'm thinkin' she's a man."

"Marcus, *you* are crazy." Meg said, laughing. She playfully kissed his nose, standing on her tiptoes to reach him.

"Hey, you never can be too certain these days. I have a cousin who lives in the big city who picked up a woman from a bar one night. Turned out that she had a little secret hiding under those control tops." He wiggled his eyebrows, nodding vigorously.

Meg rolled her eyes. She went back to the neat stacks of paper.

"You do *not* have a cousin that lives in a big city, and they don't have bars there anyway—they have *clubs*." She shot him a playful grin. "In any case, this book's not going to sell itself. I better get back to it."

Marcus plunged his hand back into his glove, his tone becoming more serious. "You know, Meg, I wish you were half as committed to having a family with me as you are to frittering away your time on that computer all day."

It was started.

What Meg called independence, Marcus called stubbornness. Refusing to marry a man who was absolutely head over heels for her for the simple reason that there was no book yet.

And she would airily defend herself, waving her hands with her usual wide-eyed expression and soft, reassuring smile that told him not to take it personally.

"Marcus," She prepared her typical defense.

"There's that look again," Marcus said, narrowing his eyes.

"What look?"

"The one that says *really honey, it's not you*." He rubbed his forehead. "I was okay with that in the beginning, but it's getting harder and harder to buy."

"Honey, it's *not* you. You know how important this book is to me." Her eyes softened. "These things take time."

"You know how important having a big family is to me and those things take time. You can't just decide one day that *that's* the day and squeeze out four or five healthy tots for an instant family."

The same conversation was played out at least every few days. His thirty-six year-old patience was wearing thin, this she knew. But she couldn't quit now, not when she felt so close.

She went to him, encircling his waist with her smallish arms, and kissed him.

"Give it just a little more time," she whispered.

"Well, that's fine, Meg, but too much more time and you'll be ordering a specimen for fertilization off that computer too, because *this* old body will be bedridden, watching Lawrence Welk reruns and imbibing a steady diet of Geritol." The distraught look on his face said that he was trying to be understanding. Her lips formed a thin, consoling smile while he continued: "Besides, I thought you were going to get yourself an agent—I mean that's what them publishers keep tellin' you."

"Inside the confines of a rejection letter, what else are they going to say? You *stink*, hang it up?"

"They're writers, Meg, I think they'd say it better than *that*." Marcus grinned at her as he pulled his muffler tighter around his neck and turned to go.

"I should just face facts. I'm destined to be the Queen of Rejection, perched high upon an ever mounting throne of returned post and *sorry-but* letters."

"So long as you remain the Queen of My Heart, I don't reckon I care much what else you do." Marcus winked at her, grinning sheepishly. Meg softened some.

"I know, honey. You know, I should probably beg for my job back at the Gazette and just call *that* my writing career." She rubbed her forehead with the backside of her hand. Her eyes turned dreamy before going on. "I just had this notion that it would be so nice to see *Meghan Laine* on the cover of some thick, wonderful novel."

"The only thing I can think that would be nicer would be to see Mrs. Marcus St. John on one."

"Soon, soon." Her defense was weakening.

"Come on Meg."

"If the rejection count hits two hundred I'll give in." She turned toward her work again and pretended to busy herself, restacking papers randomly.

Meg, I'd like to toss a football around with my kids without relying on the use of a cane."

"Please, Marcus, you know how I feel." Her tone said she was done talking about it.

"Tick, tick, tick—"

"Go to work." It came out in the form of an order as she pointed toward the door. The subject was changed. Unsatisfied with her answer, he left, his hands raised in surrender.

Meg slumped over her laptop.

The water-wrinkled newspaper seemed to mock her as it lay there. She tossed it into the garbage.

Get an agent.

"This is crazy," she muttered.

Ballsy.

She mulled over the review. *Who was Gibson Porter to say what was ballsy anyway?*

Her eyes roved over a pile of freshly-returned manuscripts still in their envelopes. She grabbed one and tore it open.

"Dear Author, I don't care what your name is. *Thank you for think - ing of our company for your manuscript,* now think of someone else. *Unfortunately at this time, it doesn't fit our publishing needs*--—we hate it, take it away. *Good luck with your future endeavors,* take it away very quick-ly—in fact if you plan to send us anything else, please enclose express postage for the most expedient return possible."

Meg added it to the box where the others were: The rejection collection. Her eyes fixed upon three hundred pages of her most recently returned labor.

I'm thinkin' she's a man.

Suddenly, she grabbed a fresh manila mailer and shoved the same story into it. Meg flipped through her schedule of publishing companies.

"Hm, let's see. Oswell House. I haven't received a rejection letter from them for a few weeks."

Addressing the mailer in thick black marker, she revised her cover let-ter a bit and snatched the freshly printed sheet from the Epson.

Sincerely, Mr. Marcus St. John.

Smiling, Meg plunked the letter into the envelope along with the recycled story, and sealed it shut.

Chapter Two

Nick Carter heaved his briefcase upon the desktop in his office. The thing seemed to be growing heavier as the day wore on. Carter spent his morning bouncing back and forth between a star client's office and his own. Being a human Ping-Pong ball was nothing new, he was accommodating to the busy writers he represented, and if they couldn't get to the mountain, well, then, the mountain would go to them.

He hastily loosened his tie and popped the button of his collar. Once again, the day had gotten warmer than the leggy weather forecaster had predicted on the locals the night before.

A partner in his own literary agency, Bankson, Laughton and Carter, Nick Carter was worn out from a week of shuffling a manuscript between a writer and the editor handling the piece, who, apparently, had no like ideas about the direction of the work whatsoever. He was about to miss a major deadline, which meant no bonus for him, and possibly putting off publication until next season.

He sighed dejectedly and slumped into his leather chair.

An electrifying buzzing sound jolted him abruptly, and he slammed his finger onto the return call button to answer it.

"Yes?"

"Boss?"

He rubbed his throbbing temple, squeezing his eyes shut. It was Jan, his secretary.

"Yes?"

"Mr. Kelsey is here to speak with you."

Nick opened one eye suddenly and arched an eyebrow. Without disturbing his slump, he slid the rollers of his chair closer to his desk, scanning his oversized calendar. "Kelsey, Kelsey." He didn't find it and hit the button again. "Mr. Kelsey doesn't have an appointment this morning."

"I am *aware* of that." Jan's voice hinted her impatience, something he was familiar with, and he knew that he'd best handle it before she lost her temper completely.

"Send him in, then."

Before he could finish the sentence, the man was standing before his desk, the office door closing behind him. Nick cupped his hands around his mouth and called to his secretary sarcastically. "Thanks!"

The agent offered his client half a forced smile and stood from his place there, extending a handshake.

"How are you, Lou?"

Lou Kelsey bypassed the handshake and approached his agent's desk, intensity burning in his eyes.

"I'm not well, but thanks for your concern." The man's voice trailed off and Nick nodded, attempting to emulate concern, but was cut off before he could verbally respond. "I have Wheaton House on me like a rash on my ass. How am I supposed to work with that diversion?"

"Well, you *are* five months over deadline—" Nick began, but was cut off a second time.

"It's not a wonder!" Lou exclaimed loudly. The middle-aged man's balding head reddened with anger, his brow furrowing in white creases. "Who can work with all that hounding going on! And now they're telling me that they're going to start penalizing me for being late by deducting from my residuals!"

Nick Carter stared at the man, mild amusement flickering in his eyes. He wondered if America knew that one of its best loved authors was a sniveling, greedy whiner. He smiled.

"Lou, did you or did you not sign an agreement that stated that your book would be completed before summer?" Nick waited but Lou only stared at him. "And, is it, or is it not, December? And did you, indeed, accept a fat advance from the company in keeping with this agreement?"

"That's not the point," Lou started in again, angrily.

Nick rose and quickly strode over to the door of his office. He opened it, examining the plaque with his name on it. "One more thing, does this say Nick Carter, counselor and baby-sitter?"

Lou had never been addressed by his agent in such a manner, and only looked at him blankly, suspicious that the man was about to crack. Nick smiled as he continued.

"No. No it doesn't. It says Nick Carter, *Literary Agent*. And, Mr. Kelsey, if we were to make such a plaque for you, it would say Lou Kelsey, *Writer*." He pointed toward the door. "Go, write."

"See here, Carter—"

"Hep! Ho!" Carter held his hands like a shield, halting the man, as if the very voice of Lou Kelsey might harm his precious ears. He squinted his eyes shut and smiled, restating the order, quiet but firm: "Go. *Write*."

The gentleman stormed out of his office, past the pointing arm that directed him to do so, and the door slammed shut. Nick Carter shook his head as he went back to his chair, plopping into it.

"I think that went well. Who says I can't communicate?" He was referring to his girlfriend who had allowed him only two hours of sleep the night before, insisting that *that* was the night they would hash out every single facet of their lives. He yawned as he leaned back comfortably, and stretched his legs onto his desktop, crossing them at his ankles.

"That's what you get when you live with a shrink." He closed his eyes, mocking her in a quiet voice now that he was in the privacy of his office. "*Nick* doesn't know how to communicate. *Nick* can't express himself. *Nick* likes to sleep on the couch."

The buzzer sounded a second time, jarring him out of his rambling. Opening only one eye, he uncrossed his legs, using one foot to scoot the intercom across the desk and into the garbage.

Chapter Three

N oel O'Dell dug through a pile of rubber bands in the top drawer of her desk in her office at the *Jasper Falls Gazette*. With the telephone wedged between her ear and her shoulder, she listened carelessly to the person on the other end, her chestnut shoulder-length hair lopping across her forehead and into her round face as she extracted the widest band she could find. Unable to get a word in edgewise, she rolled her eyes and nodded, as if the speaker could actually see her doing so.

Pulling the rubber band tightly around the L of her hand, she aimed toward the oversized picture of an old woman hanging on the far wall.

Snap—Smack!

She smiled triumphantly at the perfect hit, raising her arms to an imaginary cheering crowd. Meg Laine entered her office and sat down.

"Uh-huh. Yes." Noel clicked her fingers and thumb together in a jabbering motion that said the person on the line had entirely too much to say. Meg smiled at her best friend's impatient antics as Noel rolled her eyes for the millionth time.

"You know—I'm swamped, absolutely swamped. Sounds good. We'll do." Noel's voice squeaked sarcastically as she added: "Buh-bye."

She slammed the receiver down and glared at Meg.

"What the hell do you want?"

Meg watched Noel assume a pseudo yoga stance. She began to hum.

"Stressful day?" Meg asked sympathetically.

"I'm going to meditate it all away now, hold on."

"Mother O'Dell?"

At this, Noel briefly opened her eyes and closed them tightly again, humming louder.

"I swear t' Gawd, Meggie, the woman's gonna drive me to an early grave." Noel's accent, left over from her earlier life in New York, rang through her words thickly as she rubbed her temple, finding her focus. "I'm sorry—let's start over. How are you?"

Meg sighed loudly.

"I'm not published." She started. She took the jar of holiday ribbon candy from the desk and twisted the top off. Selecting a red and green mixed piece, she popped it into her mouth. "I've been figuring. Do you know that at closest count, I have spent *nine hundred fifty-eight dollars* on postage, copying, and paper—only to be rejected over and over and over . . ."

She rolled her hand in the air as she recounted.

"Not to mention the countless hours that I have *wasted*—"

"Invested," Noel corrected.

Meg made a face and spit the bitter candy out of her mouth, looking around for someplace to put it. Her friend promptly offered up a tissue and discarded it for her.

"Invested, *wasted*. What's the difference?" Meg shook her head. "I'm thinking of giving it up. Take *all* that money I save and go on a little vacation or something. That's what smokers do with the money they save when they quit their habit."

Noel's mannerisms were curt and predominantly emotionless, the husky New York girl that she was. She narrowed her dark eyes, speaking to her best friend in a no-nonsense tone.

"Last time I knew, writing wasn't hazardous to your health."

"Hazardous to my *heart*."

It was worse than Noel had suspected. Meg continued, her dramatic voice softening. "I had just hoped my life would be doing so much more at this stage in the game—that one of these books would be a reality. What happened? I'm a good Catholic girl. I go to church semi-regularly. I give to the poor and hold doors open for little old ladies."

"Good Catholic girls don't live with their boyfriends, and skipping church ever is a Cardinal sin." Her friend bit off another section of the candy as she spoke in her monotone voice. "I think it goes deeper than that, Meg."

"Deeper than what?"

"Than the book."

"It's the book."

"It's not the book."

"You think it's *me*?"

"I think it's you and whatshisname."

"His name," Meg straightened her posture and smoothed her hair, speaking with forced confidence. "His name is *Marcus.*"

If you were happy with your life, you wouldn't have a need to weave these tales of yours—to write yourself into the kind of life you *really* want."

"You think that's what I'm doing?" Meg's eyes widened with surprise.

"Of course it's what you're doing."

"Then you don't believe my writing's worthy of publication?"

"Of *course* it is—I published it every week myself! For the love of the gawds." Noel rolled her eyes and leaned forward onto her desk, looking into Meg's eyes. "You *will* get published someday, Meg, I don't doubt that for a second. I'm just saying, it wouldn't bother you so darned much if you had a little side dish of happiness to fall back on. Instead you keep holding out for this all-encompassing book that you think is going to come along and save you—*rescuing* you away from whatshisname."

"I certainly do not," Meg defended.

"Yes, you do."

"No, I don't."

"Yes."

"No."

"Do."

"Don't." Meg rose from her place in her chair and looked out the glass window at the offices around them. "I'm thinking of coming back to the Gazette."

"Why would you wanna do a dumb thing like that?" Noel's voice raised an octave. "If this wasn't Mother O'Dell's stupid paper, I would have been out of this editorial gig ages ago. Just because I'm destined to spend my life correcting stories about bean prices and Farmer Bo's butter cow at the state fair, doesn't mean I think it's the greatest."

"So why do you do it? For love?" It was Meg's turn to laugh, recalling the ever-stormy relationship between Noel and her husband, Everett. "Is *that* the kind of thing you think I'm missing?"

That's just what you're headed for sister." Noel waved a finger at her. "You'll marry whatshisname—"

"Marcus."

"You'll start popping out kids like kittens and start slacking off the writing—saving it for naptime or bedtime or in between microwaving bowls of spaghettios. Or those little disgusting things that kids like. Those gushy little things that my Jeremy is always eating—"

"Ravioli."

"That's it—except it'll be in the shape of dinosaurs and space cowboys. The next thing you know there's soccer and 4-H and then, before you know it, you're drivin' a mini van and you're super mom and *that's* your job." Noel paused to sip her coffee. "Don't go there, Meg. Don't give up. Personal happiness, Meg. It's not easy to achieve."

"Personal happiness?" Meg sat back down, shaking her head. "You make it sound like a chore rather than what it is."

"What do you think it *is*, Meg? Like in the movies?"

Meg shrugged sheepishly, looking away.

"Yes, you do." Noel helped her out. "I've read your stuff. I know that you think that all lovers just naturally come together—that fate puts people in the right place at the right time, and everyone always lives happily ever after on some wonderful, exotic beach or something."

"Well, I don't think too many housewives want to read a book for escape that resolves itself in the dead of winter in Iowa, microwaving bowls of dinosaur-shaped raviolis for her seven kids." Meg rubbed her eyes. "That's why it's called *romance*."

"Romance *shomance*—there is no such thing as everything coming together out of nowhere just like that." Noel snapped her fingers to get her friend's attention. "You need to face the real issues here. You need more excitement than this little newspaper, town—or even what *whatshisname* can give you. You need a life, Meg."

"I have a life."

"As your editor, I'm ordering a rewrite."

"Rewrite my life?" Meg looked at her as if she'd gone insane.

"Well, except for the part that says I'm your best friend." Noel smiled.

"As if it could be that simple."

"As for your job, you can't have it back. I will not let you compromise your integrity by having this little corn-shuckin' press on your resume." She stood abruptly and motioned for her friend to do the same. Raising her hand in a salute position she shouted her command: "Go! *Write!*"

"Yes ma'am." She marched out of the office but poked her head back in suddenly. "You having lunch with Mother O'Dell?"

"Please! And listen about the pros and cons of fried versus baked, vinegar versus ranch, and plain versus *I'll have everything on it?* I'm never *that* desperate for a lunch partner."

"Brugle's Bagels at noon then."

"Deal."

Chapter Four

Nick Carter's intercom buzzed loudly a second time, its echo resounding in the metal trash container.

Buzz!

Buzzzzzzz!

The fourth buzz was bound to go on indefinitely unless he answered the blessed thing.

Nick, whining about being interrupted again from the only rest he might get that day, cursed under his breath as he leaned over and dug the device out of the trash can. He slammed it onto the desk before him, and, bent at the waist, glared at the thing eye level as it continued to buzz.

He looked thoughtful as he depressed the button at last, forcing a smile onto his lips, in an attempt to convey the same through his speaking. "Yes, Jan? How can I help you?"

"You wanna take a call from the *squirrel?*" Her flippant tone told him immediately who was holding the line. He sighed.

"Got it." He muttered, and then twirled his finger above the keypad, landing on the blinking light. He picked up the receiver. "Hello, J.T."

"Carter—I've been trying to get a hold of you all morning! Didn't you get any of my messages?"

Nick looked at the overflowing stack before him and smirked.

"Yeah."

"And the package. What did you think of the package?" J.T. Oswell, publishing house extraordinaire, sounded like an excited child as he rambled on while Nick pushed through the heap of mailers and letters on his desk. He half-listened, his eyebrow raised, scoping the stacks for whatever he was supposed to be finding. At last he spied something that had fallen, lying next to the garbage. He picked it up and pulled off the attached note: *Carter—Received this Wednesday but as you know, we do not accept unagent - ed material. Interested? You may enjoy the twist. -J.T.*

"I've got it here." He tore open the envelope and pulled out the manuscript, flipping through it. He read the title out loud. *"Just Around the Corner."*

"Pretty good stuff, don't you think?" Oswell interrupted.

Carter leaned back in his chair as he glanced through the manuscript briefly. No doubt that it was a well constructed script, but he got thousands of decent book queries every year.

"A romance. Where's the twist?" And then, as if to answer his own question, his eyes narrowed as they landed on a single line of scribble.

Mr. Marcus St. John.

"A sappy romance in first person female written by a man? That's different, I'll give you that." He restacked the story and tossed it back on his desktop, rubbing his eyes tiredly.

"Now *there's* a guy whose really in touch with his feminine side!"

"Not that I have anything against the gay community, but is this guy—"

"I doubt it, it's from Iowa. They don't have gay people in Iowa."

"You don't say?"

They all live on farms and shop at the general store and have kids named Mary and John," the publishing mogul went on.

"So, what's the seller?"

"What's the *seller*? Carter, women will go nuts to see their feelings in print—and from the pen of a man, no less. I see it as killing two birds with one stone—women are always bitching about a man's inability to connect on a personal level. What gets more personal than one of us writing *this* intimate crap?"

I'm not sure this guy's one of us." Carter raised an eyebrow as he read a few excerpts of the manuscript as it lay there. "Quite frankly, some of this stuff scares the hell out of me. What's your second bird?"

"That it gets men off the hook a little. Makes us look like a more of sensitive bunch as opposed to the ball-scratching assholes all the women writers are doing books on these days. Plus, you being the agent to this guy and me being your publishing connection, makes us sort of *in* on it—

the good guys."

Carter fell silent as he scanned the manuscript.   Finally, J.T. spoke again.

"This could be the big ticket—orders from all bookstores across the country. You haven't *witnessed* power until you've seen a woman wield a Mastercard at a Barnes & Noble."

"How would you know?"

My wife used to wrack up a fortune on ours buying that crap."

"Which wife would that be? Three or four?"

"Very funny, Carter." J.T. mimicked his friend. "I just think these lovestruck broads with the notion that the perfect man still exists out there, *somewhere*, would flock to the shelves for this kind of trash."

"Maybe you should read the book instead of trying to sell it." Nick put in, dryly. His sentiment was ignored.

"What do you say?"

"Your press doesn't even *do* romances."

"They'd do this kind of romance."

Nick Carter was contemplative in his silence. He finally spoke again.

"What kind would that be?"

"The kind that sells millions."

Chapter Five

The sound of shoes shushing across the tiled floor of the shopping mall alerted Meg that her tardy friend had, at last, arrived for their lunch date. Noel's face popped around the corner and smiled broadly. Meg shook her head and waved her to join her at the table for two inside the little bagel bakery.

"I could hear you all the way down the hall—those shoes sound like a train."

"You know how graceful I am in heels." Noel answered with no apology. She whipped open the menu, making a little tent before her.

"Those are flats."

"They're flat *heels*. What of it?" Her best friend shrugged and Meg only rolled her eyes.

Noel tore open a package of sugar and sprinkled it into the iced tea that was already waiting for her. Their young waitress, wearing a gingham checked apron, approached them for their order.

"I'll have the goat cheese and bean sprouts on a wheat bagel, lite mayo and baked Chips." Meg's order was well rehearsed, her usual, prompting the same old response from Noel. She wrinkled her nose and stuck out her tongue.

"How can you eat that stuff? I think it's safe to say that our position is secure at the top of the food chain. What kind of a farm woman orders cheese from a goat? *Whatshisname* would have your head on a platter." Noel cast her a dirty look as she spoke, and quickly scanned the menu. "Gimme a fajita pita, extra sauce, no lettuce. I can't stand ruffage this early in the day."

The waitress nodded, taking both of the menus.

Noel didn't waste a precious second of their time together, leaning forward over clasped hands, leering into Meg's eyes.

"So, what'd ya decide?" Her eyes sparkled.

About what?"

The sudden sound of a male's trilly voice from the entryway of the eatery saved her from having to pursue it. Both women promptly whipped their heads to its source.

"There's my *gir-rels!*" The impeccably dressed man with buzzed short hair smiled from ear to ear, flickering his fingers playfully in the air. He promptly ran to join them, drawing another chair up to the small table.

"Hey Reed," Meg offered a little smile to her strange but dear, friend.

"Hey girl! You look good! All a-*glimmer!*" He planted a little kiss on each of their cheeks. Noel was nonchalant about his loudness and antics, both of which she was long used to. "Noel."

"Hello Reed. How is my fairy nice friend today?" she asked with little emotion, dumping a second sugar into her tea. Reed playfully smacked her arm and fluttered his eyelashes. His flawless olive skin was rosy about the cheeks as he teased her.

"Gay pride sister! *Loud* and *proud!*" He lept to his feet beside his seat in the little eatery and Noel lept up to join him in a little dance. He sang loudly in his best Sister Sledge voice: *"We are family! I got all my sisters with me!* Yeah! Whew! Uh-huh—you go on!"

This action attracted the attention of the few patrons in the cafe, including the waitress, who eyed them in an unamused manner. Noel picked right up on this and called out to her.

"Hey! *He's* here and *he's* queer—get over it."

"Sit down!" Meg ordered, shielding her eyes with the back of her hand. They obeyed. Reed was blotting invisible beads of sweat from his forehead, feigning breathlessness toward an imaginary audience.

"Thank you. You've been great." He folded his napkin on his lap and turned in his seat, calling to the waitress once again. "I'll have a French Vanilla Slim Fast and croissant."

"That poor girl." Meg muttered, changing the subject quickly. "How's the Picture Palace, Reed? Busy today?"

"Girl, I have been coughed on, spit on, and sneezed on by more

preschoolers than I care to ever see again—at least not until next X-mas."
He cocked his head with attitude, drawing an imaginary X in midair with
his index finger.

"At least you didn't say *peed* on." Noel comforted.

"That's the fat man in a red suit's job. The almighty powerful
Mississippi can't hold a candle to the liquid that man's got in his lap as we
speak." He unwrapped a straw and plunged it into the can of diet drink
the waitress placed before him. "You made a wise decision girl, not havin'
any of those little germ infested, snot-sprayin', Rug-Rat wearin', punk-ass
spoiled brats."

His last comment was directed toward Meg who shrugged.

"I didn't exactly *decide* to not have any of the little carriers."

"Well, you surely aren't going to wait much longer! You'll be the old-
est mama in progressive school P.T.O." He looked surprised. "I guess I
didn't even know you were *considerin'* it—thought you were going to
write some book and make us both relative to the rich and famous. I did-
n't know you were interested in dolin' out the three B's all day long."

"The three B's?"

"Bathin', burpin' beatin'."

"Of course." Meg nodded, her eyes wide as she took him in.

Their waitress returned once again to set their lunch before them.
Meg lifted the top of her sandwich to see that the mayo was satisfactory,
not too globby, and then watched as Reed eyeballed Noel's pita, oozing
with fried strips of chicken and cheese.

"That looks so delicious." He licked his lips and cast a glance at his
own sorry, barren plate.

"Doesn't that violate some pita code of ethics—all that fat and all?"
Meg shivered as she watched the grease run down Noel's fingers upon taking her first bite.

"Meggie, you're starting to sound like Mother O'Dell. It's a pita, for
the love of the gawds."

"If once you just tried the pita with a little, say, tunafish or ranch
dressing or something, you might be surprised to find that you actually
like the way it tastes underneath all that extracurricular crap you load it
with."

"There is not a single low fat item that I can't jazz up. You might as well forget it. Man, or woman, cannot live on celery and rice cakes alone. That is, unless the celery is stuffed with that cream cheese and pimento spread."

"Rice cakes are good with an inch or so of peanut butter on them," Reed was nodding in agreement now.

"Well, I'm glad you two have your way mapped around it all."

"Reed, you're looking like a pleasantly plump Ethiopian staring at me eating my pita. Stop it."

"Quite frankly, that croissant has as many calories in it as a bagel with turkey and low fat mayo on it, you could have splurged and . . . " Meg changed her mind as she took another bite. She mumbled before swallowing. "Oh, nevermind."

"So what's the hot gossip about today?" Reed tore off a little piece of his croissant and popped it into his mouth.

"About how Meggie needs to strike out on her own. Get the heck out of the cornbelt." Noel licked the grease off her fingers and nodded at Reed. "We know that she could get on at some big magazine or better quality newspaper, right? What's the hold up?"

It's not that simple."

"Sure it is. Naturally I'll give you a glowing reference, and your work speaks for itself."

"It might as well, everyone else is speaking for me—except *me*."

"She doesn't want to leave Farmer St. John." Noel's comment was directed toward Reed. He made an *eeks* mouth and shrugged.

"He's not the person you think he is," Meg defended.

"I think he's a farmer with no aspirations beyond working the fields or having a zillion or so children."

"Okay, so he is who you think he is." Meg wiped her hands and threw her napkin aside, looking at her friend. Reed watched with silent growing interest. "But what's so wrong with that? I mean, we'll raise a little family in a cozy little home in a wholesome setting—"

"You've confused cozy with boring, Meg."

"How many kids does he want?" Reed finally put in.

"Oh, a few."

"Four, at least." Noel looked so smug. "I heard him say it at last years Farmer's Banquet. Don't deny it."

"*Four?* They say you don't lose the weight after two."

"That's insane." Meg shook her head again.

"Insane that you'd want to."

"Of course if he's stuck on the idea you could adopt after the second." Reed looked thoughtful.

"*Stop it!*" Meg's voice rose suddenly. "Can I tell you what I want for a change?"

Both friends fell silent and offered the petite blonde woman their undivided attention, sitting upright, not even moving to blink.

"And as soon as I decide what that is, I'll get back to you." She flicked her hair out of her eyes, frustrated that she couldn't come up with something.

They munched in silence for a few minutes and finally Reed spoke.

"He's not so bad I suppose. But his taste is so ugh."

"Thanks," Meg nodded, sarcastically.

"I mean the way he *dresses*. Those flannel shirts and all. You two are opposites down to your Hanes. Is he a boxer or briefs kind of man?"

"What?"

"My Elliot is boxers all the way," Noel lamented. "He used to at least wear these cute silky ones when we were dating. Now it's all cotton all the time."

"What was the appeal of Elliot? I mean, was there romance or a throw-caution-to-the-wind spontaneity that caught you?" Meg pushed her plate aside and looked at her friend with a certain romantic curiosity in her eyes.

"I liked his name, and the fact that he had a good car."

"His *name?*" Reed burst out laughing slapping his hands on the table.

"Turned out the car belonged to his mother." She smirked. "And the name was bogus. I went for *three* months thinking that I was about to become Mrs. Noel Von Freesia."

"Von Freesia?"

"Yeah. You sure as heck didn't think I'd actually chose to become *Noel O'Dell*, did you? Please."

"Well, I for one think that we should let our little Meggie make her own decisions about who she wants to marry or what-how, simply offering her our loving support, no questions asked."

"Thank you, Reed," Meg nodded at him. She ran her finger along the rim of her coffee cup and looked away for a minute. "Are you boxers or briefs, Reed?"

Reed laid a few bills on the table and stood to go with a confident smile.

"I'm all string, sister!" He high-fived Noel and wagged his behind in a teasing way. Meg only smiled with minor embarrassment. He glanced at his watch and made a surprised round mouth. "Oh child, I have got to get back to the studio. The fat man's probably damp with pneumonia by now. Don't you worry your pretty little head, Meggie. You just follow the signs. They won't lead you wrong."

"Unfortunately I keep running into a succession of *stops* and *do not enters.*" Meg smiled at him.

"Ta for now, my sisters! Glimmer on! Peace out!"

The waitress poured more iced tea in Noel's nearly empty glass and she tore open two more sugars to sweeten it. She raised her eyes to her best friend when she was satisfied.

"What's with you? This isn't like you. You don't act the same lately."

"I don't feel the same lately. You know how you read in the papers about the feeling that some people get before they board a plane and then all of the sudden they decide not to go? Then later they find out that the plane went down in flames and they say that they just knew somehow that something wasn't right? No, that's a bad example." Meg slumped a little in her seat. "I just feel it *close*—the book I mean. I can't explain why."

"Intuition."

"Yes! *Intuition.* That's what I'm trying to say."

"I have a powerful intuition about the status of your relationship with whatshisname should you continue to pursue it."

"Not that." Meg waved her hand lightly in frustration. Her friend clearly wasn't on her wavelength today. "The book, Noel. I feel it close to something, and suddenly, I'm really nervous about it."

"So why are you all weird then? That's a good thing."

"It's just—it's just that I have never been wrong about these things. These *feelings* of something pending. If I'm wrong, I'll never trust myself again."

"That's my point Meg. You put so much stock in this book—too much. You need other things too. It's not too late. There's no ring yet."

"How come this always comes back to Marcus?"

Noel leaned forward now and spoke with quiet sincerity.

"Because I've heard him say it before. You *could* as easily pen the thing as Meghan St. John instead of Meghan Laine. Because you know that, too. And because if you haven't done anything about it by this time, there's a reason why which goes way beyond some independent need of yours." She tipped her head, gazing into her her friend's eyes. "For all the sappy, happy romances you write, you have to know what you want. The question is, is that what you have now?"

Meg stared at her quietly, considering her words.

"I think if you start there, Meggie, you'll discover the true meaning behind those weird feelings and they won't have *squat* to do with intuition or this crazy book."

Chapter Six

Meg pulled open the top of yet another cardboard box, pulling out a long red and green garland snake. She whirled around the living room with it playfully, wrapping it around her shoulders and neck like an extravagant boa. The sounds of "Surfin' Santa" were playing in the background and she danced in circles now, tossing her head back with a little laugh. Marcus watched this action from where he was squatted near the floor, working steadily at a maze of cords. He shook his head.

"You're like a child, Meg." He pulled a screwdriver out of his back jeans pocket and made a few more adjustments. "A little giddy tonight, aren't we? What's the occasion?"

She swirled around again and stopped to get her focus.

"It's nearly Christmas! Of course I'm giddy! It's my favorite time." She frowned dramatically, pushing the stray hairs out of her eyes. "Why don't you stop that and help me deck these here halls?"

"I'm doing something right now." He didn't look at her as he continued what he was working on. "If I can splice these two ends together, all of our lights can be turned on with a simple switch every night."

"Indoors and out?"

"Meg, I'm not putting lights outdoors. We go through this every year."

"Why not?" She pouted. "I love lights in the winter time!"

"Because clear out here no one will see them to enjoy them. It's pointless."

"I'll see them. I would definitely enjoy them." She rubbed her garland boa under his nose and he blew the little silvery pieces away from his lips with a hint of annoyance that he stifled nicely.

"Then maybe you want to get out there and scale the house putting them on only to take them off in two weeks in sub-zero weather."

Meg wrinkled her forehead. She watched as he continued to work with the cords in his lap.

"You know, they have an all-encompassing cord you can buy that does the same thing."

"Why pay for it when I am perfectly capable of creating it right here?" He paused and looked at her for a moment. Finally Marcus smiled and nodded toward the box. "There's white lights in that box I just brought in over there and my grandmother's little glass ornaments in the smaller one."

"Do you think that next year we could do colored lights? I know how you feel about them, but they're so pretty."

"My grandmother always used white on our trees when I was a kid. I like that memory. Didn't your family have any traditions like that?"

"We used colored lights. And we didn't have such a uniform way of putting things together. We made some of the decorations or threw handfuls of tinsel on the branches over blinking lights. It was a whole family effort, not just one person."

Marcus looked at her with an expression that she immediately recognized as hurt.

"Not that your grandmother's trees weren't absolutely stunning honey, I didn't mean it that way." She smiled at him apologetically. "If it's white lights and little glass ornaments and little red bows every year, so be it. It will be beautiful every year then! Sort of timeless."

"Monotonous," he said quietly.

"No! No! Not monotonous at all! Classic and traditional. That's exactly what it is. I'd have it no other way. Who needs anything else when you've got tradition! Don't be silly!"

She turned away raising her eyebrows as she did where he wouldn't see her. Meg stuffed the red garland reluctantly into the box where she'd found in and instead turned toward the same three smaller boxes from which they'd decorated for the past four years. She quietly began to tie the perfect little bows all over the branches.

"You missed a little spot, right there."

"Thanks, honey."

He finished what he was doing and flipped the switch to test it out. Four strings of white lights turned on simultaneously and Meg stepped back, clapping her hands together.

"It's beautiful."

"It sure is." He stood beside her looking at the glowing tree before them, squeezing her shoulder lovingly as he admired it. They stood there in silence. Finally Marcus spoke again, his words slow and well thought out. "So, you know, you seem different lately, and I was just wondering what's up?"

Meg stepped away from him a bit with raised eyebrows and wide, surprised eyes.

"Me? How so?"

"Um, just sort of . . . aloof. Quiet. Just wondering if there was something that I needed to know about. Something troubling you?"

"No, no." She shook her head reassuringly. "It's probably just the season. I have been doing a little reflecting as I do this time each year— thinking about the things that are important to me, that kind of thing."

"I thought maybe you were having second thoughts about being with me, maybe."

Meg couldn't understand why he would be asking her such things, and her conversation with Noel and Reed came to mind.

Just follow the signs.

A sign?

No, probably not.

"As long as you're sure that's all it is."

"I'm absolutely certain."

"Then you still want to marry me?"

"Of course I do . . . when you ask me to, anyway."

"Ask you to?" He laughed out loud. "I beg you to almost every day!"

Meg was growing a bit nervous as she continued. She looked into his eyes to gather her strength there before going on.

"Well, Marcus, you've never really *officially* asked me for my hand in marriage."

"Well, sure I have. What kind of an invitation do you need?"

"The old fashioned kind. The romantic kind."

"What? You want me to get down on one knee and clasp your hand

and plead with you to marry me?"

"Not plead, just ask."

"That's crazy."

"That's romantic, sensitive—the way it should be done! You don't want to get married more than once, do you?"

"Of course not." He wasn't sure where this was leading exactly as he studied her with a furrowed brow.

"Then if you're only going to ask one time, you might as well do it right."

"Are you stringing me along?"

At this Meg dropped his hand with a little anger and perhaps some hurt in her voice.

"I'm doing no such thing, Marcus St. John. I'm simply saying that if you want my hand in marriage, you're going to have to ask for it and make it good. The end!" She stacked the three empty boxes together and pushed them toward the corner of the room, picked up a book she'd been reading and stormed down the hallway. He could hear her going up the stairs of the old farmhouse.

"Are you going to bed, honey?"

Yes, *honey*, I am."

"Good night then."

"Good night!"

Chapter Seven

"**S**o he threw a baby fit and wouldn't propose to you on bended knee."

Noel stirred her coffee and dumped some more sugar into it.

"Yes!"

"And that surprises you?" Noel wrinkled her nose. "Do you have any cappuccino?"

"Yes that surprises me, and no, I don't have any cappuccino." She waved her hands airily as she pulled her stool up to the breakfast bar of her kitchen taking a seat next to her friend. "I mean, he's the one all in a rush to get married and wouldn't you think that he'd want to do it the right way?"

I wouldn't think that it would have taken four years for you to be asking these questions." She sipped the coffee, making a face. "Do you have any chocolate chips? Sometimes if you put enough chocolate chips in this stuff it tastes like a double chocolate latte from Starbucks."

Meg tilted her head, squinting.

"What the hell's *Starbucks?*"

"Meggie, such language." She feigned shock. "Precisely another reason you should get out of Oz and get a real life. *Starbucks*, my city challenged friend, is the only place on earth that you can walk into wielding three bucks and be the center of attention for the thirty seconds it takes you to order one of fifteen different flavored coffees that make you sound like a cuppa joe connoisseur. You walk out feeling revitalized, invigorated, *smarter.*"

"All for a cup of coffee?"

"Not just a *cup of coffee.* It's more like a religious experience."

"Religion with cream or sugar."

"Or high fat, low fat, no fat, chocolate, vanilla, raspberry . . . "

"I get the picture. How did we get started on this?"

"We were talking about whatshisname but the subject of coffee came up and won out as the more interesting topic of the two." She took another sip and added more sugar.

"Why don't you just dump the entire bowl of sugar in that cup and get it over with?"

"See? It won out again. So what are you going to do?"

"What do you mean what am I going to do?"

There was a knock on the door.

"I'm going to wait until he proves that he cares enough to ask me in a way that I see fit."

The mailman poked his head through the door once Meg had opened it. He smiled and handed her a stack of mail.

"Here ya go, Meggie! Looks like the snow plow buried your mailbox out there so I just came up the way a bit to bring yours today."

"Thanks, Fred. Do you want some coffee?"

"No thanks! You have a nice holiday if I don't see you again before!"

"Merry Christmas, Fred." Meg shut the door behind him and dropped the stack of mail on the countertop. "That was nice of him."

"Yeah, in New York they would have cussed you out and thrown your mail in the snow bank where you probably wouldn't have gotten it until the first big thaw in spring after all the mudsplash froze all over it." Noel took a bite of one of the poppyseed muffins she'd brought for them. She sighed. "Gawd, I loved that place."

Meg watched her for a second before she began to shuffle through the mail. All of it was for Marcus. She set it aside.

"Meg, you know that your demanding that Marcus propose to you formally only means that you can't think of a better excuse for the time being to tell him that you don't want to marry him."

"That's insanity."

"I agree."

"I mean it's insanity that you would think that I'd need an excuse to tell him what's on my mind. When Elliot proposed to you, how did he do it?"

"I proposed to him."

"You never told me that."

"Yeah, I told him that I was pregnant and proposed that he'd better marry me or I was going to pop him. He was a little afraid. Elliot's not a real big guy you know."

"So then what?"

"We eloped."

"That's so romantic!" Meg's eyes sparkled. "What did you do? Climb out the window and run off to Vegas?"

"I was five months pregnant, for the love of the gawds—ain't no way I was climbin' out the window! You're forgettin' that it was my house, too. I could use the front door freely to come and go as I pleased." Noel looked at Meg oddly before continuing. "And no, I just took off work early that day and the Justice of the Peace at the county courthouse married us. The end."

"Oh."

"See, that's your problem, Meg. You are overly romantically inclined! You think that everything has a happy ending! Lassie always comes home, the good-looking doctor always saves the dying kind on *ER*—Mulder and Scully always get the mutant just before it wipes out the population of the Earth, and the friends on Friends always stay . . . *friends.*"

"Oh, I love the tension between Mulder and Scully." Meg looked dreamy, suddenly ignoring her friend.

"Only you could find the *X-Files* romantic. You're sick Meg, you have an illness. Romanticitus, or something like that. You are a hopeless romantic—a quality that you inflict upon your books in an effort to mask the fact that there is very little true-to-life romance between you and whatshisname."

Meg's eyes wandered across the countertop to the pile of mail again, and she noticed the post mark on the top envelope. She studied it as Noel went on.

"It's too late for me, but you—you've still got your whole unattached life ahead of you."

Meg picked up the envelope and read the return address.

Bankson, Laughton and Carter Literary Agency.

Quickly, she slid her fingernail under the flap of the envelope and sliced it open, dumping the letter onto the countertop before her. She unfolded it and began to read.

"You need excitement, Meg, more than anything you could hope to find around this place. The last time I saw genuine excitement in this house was when that mouse came in with the Schwaan Man in October." Noel suddenly burst out laughing at the recollection. "Oh! And you were chasing it with a flyswatter and Reed jumped up on top of the counter screaming with every pass you made around the kitchen! Ah, Gawd, Meggie! I nearly peed my pants that day—I never saw such a look on a man's face before. Why would you make a flyswatter your weapon of choice?"

Suddenly Meg screamed at the top of her lungs. She jumped down from her place at the breakfast bar. Noel screamed and jumped down as well.

"What? What is it?" Noel looked panicked. "Shall I get the flyswatter?"

"Oh my God, Noel! Omigod! Omigod! Omigod! Omigod!"

"Omigod!" Noel echoed.

"Omigod! Omigod!"

Both women jumped in place there in the kitchen. Meg's eyes were wide with disbelief while Noel's were with wonder.

"Omigod! What are we omigodding?"

"Omigod—this is the big one!" Meg tried to calm herself down. She grabbed her best friend's hands tightly in hers and looked her square in the eyes. "I am so glad that you are here to share this moment with me."

"Me too." Noel nodded with encouragement for her to continue.

"This letter is from an agent who wants to help me get my book published!"

"*Eeeks!*" Noel shrieked.

"*Eeeks*! I know!"

The jumping continued frantically all around the kitchen and lasted for several minutes accompanied by screaming. Finally, both women regained their composure and sat back down..

"Okay—" Noel raised her hands in a calming manner. "*Eeeks!* There, I just had one last one."

"Oh God, Oh God ... " Meg's eyes sparkled and her cheeks were rosy with excitement. "I think I *am* glimmering!"

"Reed would be so proud!" Noel couldn't let go of her friend. "What now? What do you do now?"

"He writes here—"

"Who writes?"

"This, Nick Carter. Apparently some publisher sent my manuscript to him. He says that he would like to have me sign on with his agency and that he will hook me up with an editor to work out a few glitches, which is normal, and that he already has a publisher in mind for *Just Around the Corner.*"

"Oh my Gawd! I can't believe it! I'm finally going to see little Maggie's name on the cover of a big, fat book! I was her first publisher! I was her boss and her best friend—I was there from the start."

"Not exactly . . ."

"Whaddaya mean? I was too." Noel's expression changed as she looked curiously at her friend. Meg forced a little smile.

"I mean, this letter isn't exactly for me. It's for Marcus."

"What?"

Oh, Noel, I was so sick of getting rejected from the same companies over and over and over—"

"Get to the point."

"I resubmitted it to the same company and signed Marcus' name to it. I had this idea that my name might be becoming tiresome to them. So I just changed it to his. That's all. Put a little spin on things."

"That's a spin, I'll give you that much. Now what?"

"I'm sure that once I talk to Mr. Carter and explain the whole silly thing that he will just laugh about it. I mean, the manuscript is the same, only the name is different."

"I hope so."

"I'm sure."

"You better be—you know how weird some publishers are. You read that critique from Gibson about that woman that wrote those twisted books, what was her name? Anyway, he was all turned on by the fact that a woman had such a sick and perverse mind."

"It's not like that. Don't worry."

Noel's expression changed to a lighter one and she raised her coffee mug to her friend now with a smile. Meg did the same.

"To the birth of my author friend's career. May she have a long and prosperous career and write herself straight into happiness and out of the arms of . . . whatshisname."

"Noel—"

"Whatever! Here here!"

Meg rolled her eyes with a smile and clinked mugs with her friend.

"Here here."

Chapter Eight

When Marcus arrived home that night from his day of working in the barn and helping some neighbors with their stock,he found Meg to be in a mood quite contrary to that he'd witnessed over the past few days. Ever since the decorating festivities, she'd been different—angry, and her new attitude was a pleasant surprise. Seeing him,she bounced across the floor and planted a kiss on his chilly cheek. Meg leaned back with sparkling eyes and a new zest about her.

"Get cleaned right up. We're having a special dinner! Hurry now!" She pushed him toward the hallway once he'd slipped out of his boots.

"What's going on?"

"I love you, that's what's going on!" She kissed him again. Marcus smiled warmly with a hint of wonder in his eyes. He nodded and kissed her back before making his way to the bathroom. She could hear him whistling a little tune as he went, a good sign that his mood,like hers, had been restored properly.

When he returned ten minutes later, he was clean shaven, dressed in a good shirt and pants and smiling sneakily. Marcus took his seat across from her at the little table for two that their kitchen space allowed for, and waited for her to sit.

"Wine." He nodded in an approving manner. "This *is* a celebration."

"Yes, it is."

Meg finally took her own seat and faced him, her hands clasped on the table before her. She was smiling, barely able to contain her news.

"I have something to tell you."

"No, me first," He interrupted. "I'm sorry about the other night, decorating the tree and all."

"No, heavens!" Meg flipped her hand as if it were long in the past.

"No, you were right, as usual. I don't plan to get married more than once, and that in itself is cause for celebration. A good enough reason to do it the right way the first time." He scooted his chair back from the table and, with his gaze never leaving hers, leaned onto one knee, taking her hand. Meg's eyes grew wide with disbelief. "Meghan Laine, would you do me the honor of becoming my beautiful wife, Mrs. Marcus St. John?"

"Oh God . . ." She laughed softly as he held her hand firmly.

Marcus pulled something out of his pocket and slipped it carefully onto her finger. He looked at her again, clasping her hand and smiling.

"Marry me."

Meg raised her hand to see the traditional half karat diamond on its thin band. It was simple and beautiful, not probably what Meg herself would have chosen, but stunning and sparkling nonetheless. She admired it with misty eyes.

"It's perfect! It's wonderful, Marcus."

They embraced as she laughed, happily.

"I'm glad you like it." He was pleased to have been responsible for her capricious behavior. She stepped back and squeezed his hands tightly. "You didn't answer."

"I have something too." She motioned for him to sit. "You're going to have to sit down for this one."

When they were both sitting, she leaned forward and spoke carefully.

"There was a letter today in the mail. An agent in Florida wants to try to get my book published!" Her voice was rising as she spoke. "Can you believe it!"

"You're kidding me!"

"No!" She shrieked.

"That's wonderful honey!"

"I know—isn't it!"

"It is, it is." He looked rather uncertain of himself. "Looks like your news sorta took the air out of mine."

"What was yours?"

"Um, the ring."

"Oh! No! Of course it didn't!"She shook her head quickly to reassure him. "I'm *crazy* about the ring Who wouldn't be? What's not to be crazy about!"

Marcus smiled and watched her go on.

"So what happens now?"

"Well, the manuscript goes to an editor who will help change a few things, gear the work toward the market, and then we'll try to get it in print! Fate takes it from there."

Where Marcus had actually been questioning the timeline on their engagement and marriage, he'd nodded and smiled at the answer anyway. There would be time to pursue it later.

"So when do you speak with the agent?"

"His name's Nick Carter, and the letter said to call as soon as I received the information."

"You called then?"

"Well, not yet."

"What's the hold up?"

"Well, there's a little issue that needs to be resolved first."

"Which is?"

"A little question of identity."

"I'm not following you."

"Well, he's *kind of* under the impression that you wrote the book."

"Kind of?"

"It's just a little technicality that can be worked out."

"Why would he be under that impression?"

"I signed your name to the manuscript."

Marcus squinted, wrinkling his forehead.

"Why on earth would you do that?"

"I thought that if there were a man's name on a romance novel which is *different*, you have to admit, that it might be a bite." She shrugged confidently with a smile. "And it worked—I mean, someone bit!"

"You signed my name to a romance novel?"

"All in the name of fate."

"So, I assume you'll straighten this whole matter out ASAP?"

"I will. I will." Her voice grew serious. "But I need you to do me a little favor first."

"Which is?"

"I need you to call Nick Carter and carry out this masquerade just a little longer until we've earned his trust."

"*Trust?* Earning trust through deception. What a concept." He looked away, sighing impatiently.

"Okay, his *confidence*. We need to gain his confidence in my ability as a writer before we go telling him that I'm the actual author." She got on her knees before him. "I know it sounds crazy, Marcus, but just in case it wasn't just a bite. Let him see what I'm capable of and then I'll come clean with him."

"Like the guy with the big nose? Cicero?"

"Cyrano."

"Who cares. You want me to carry on like some bigtime writer while you do all the behind the scenes work?"

"Just for now."

"This is crazy."

"This *is* crazy, Marcus . . . " She giggled, smiling triumphantly. "But it could just work."

There was silence.

"It's a good thing I love you."

Chapter Nine

J.T. Oswell walked into the office of Bankson, Laughton and Carter. He bypassed the other appointments sitting in the waiting area and put his hand on the doorknob of Carter's office, preparing to barge in as usual. Jan, the receptionist, bolted across the floor immediately, wedging herself between the publishing mogul and the door.

"Uh-uh! Not so fast, Mr. Moneybags. You have no appointment and there are others in line to see Mr. Carter."

Jan was an attractive woman in her mid-thirties, with bronzed healthy Florida-sunned skin, green eyes and a stunning crown of dark ringlets that framed her face. She had been Carter's faithful secretary since he'd begun this partnership five years earlier, and for five years she'd been handling the childish antics of J.T. Oswell with great skill, dealing him regular doses of sarcasm to combat his arrogance. Today, as usual, her words backed by her East coast accent were no-nonsense and her eyes said that there was no chance he was getting into Carter's office without adversary.

"Come on Jan! It's important!" Oswell tried to save himself by adding: "Incidentally, that's a nice dress."

"Save it, Pinocchio, because you ain't gettin' in."

"I have business with Carter."

Jan nodded toward the four others in the small room.

"And so do these folks here."

"These folks here are probably here to see about getting published at *my publishing house!* I think we can make the exception."

"What makes you think that you can just walk in here and—"

"Let me save you the speech," he interrupted her, rolling his eyes.

Oswell ran his fingers through his sandy blonde hair smiling in his devil-ish way as he mimicked her. *"You can't just walk in here, flapping your gums, having your way with everyone!"*

"You have never had your way with me." She immediately corrected, dancing her head with her rigid words and accompanying glare.

"But if I had, you'd never forget it."

"But I'd try."

"Listen here sister, these are good genetics! I wouldn't share them with you any day—anyway!"

"Looks like the gene pool could use a little chlorine."

Those waiting in their seats watched on with growing amusement. Carter, hearing the escalating voices,pushed the door open, nearly knock-ing them both over. Oswell fell into Jan a little and immediately pulled himself away, brushing his sleeve with a disgusted look about him. She returned the sentiment.

"That was a cheap attempt." She smirked walking back to her desk. "Your clients are waiting, Mr. Carter, and then there's a matter of *this* lit-tle annoyance here."

"I'll see the annoyance first."

Oswell smiled smugly as if to say ha-ha and followed Carter into his office, shutting the door behind them.

"Hmph," Jan muttered as she rearranged the items on her desk mechanically. "Somebody shoulda' stepped on him before he got away."

"So, you talked to our next best-selling author?"

Carter suspected that the conversation would start this way and he smiled at J.T. as he sat down across from him.

"No, he hasn't gotten back to me yet."

"What the hell's the hold up? I'll bet he went with someone else." J.T. sat back in his seat and began to gnaw at his fingernail nervously. "Did you send the letter FedEx?"

"No, I sent it second day mail. Trust me, he'll call."

"Things like this don't just come floating across the desk everyday. Someone else got him."

"J.T., is there another reason why you're here, or is it just to stew and fret in the comfort of my office?" Carter opened his appointment book and began to cross a few things out. "If you thought it was so *wonderful,* why didn't you grab right up on it?"

"My father has very strict policies on what we will and won't publish. One of them being we won't publish anything that is unagented."

"You should have done it without telling him then."

"He'd kill me when he found out. That's the Oswell Publishing Group tradition—if we did it for one we'd have to do it for the rest. Period."

"Kill you?" Carter laughed. "Your father is seventy-six."

"A very keen seventy-six."

"I doubt he can even track down a date on the calendar let alone track you down to kill you."

"You doubt the power of a man who is a pillar in the Jewish Community?" J.T.'s tone of voice changed to a lighter one. "Besides, pal I'm offering you a chance to profit off this as well. You should be *thank-ing* me, but instead you're telling me that you're not even the least concerned with what could be one of the hottest selling collections of all times. You do suppose there's more where that came from, don't you?"

"I don't know."

"I mean, what good would a one hit wonder be to us, am I right?"

"I don't know."

J.T. glanced at his watch impatiently.

"He's gone with someone else."

"Why don't you go out for coffee?"

"No thanks, I don't want any."

"That wasn't a request, really. I have clients waiting."

"I didn't notice any potential Hemmingways out there."

"How could you? Carrying on with my secretary that way." Carter stifled the smile that begged to emerge upon his lips.

"Carrying on,nothin' doin'!" J.T. sat up, alert. "Carter, that woman's a *beast*!"

"Really?"

I'd be willin' to bet that if you did a thorough background check on her you'd find she was related to one of those prehistoric dog women they discovered in the Himalayas!"

"Some men find that kind of thing charming."

"And some men find that kind of thing scary as hell."

"Get out of here, J.T. I'll tell you as soon as I learn anything."

"Oh—"

"Get."

" . . .Okay." The publisher rose from where he'd been squirming about and wandered over to the window. He examined the ledge carefully and then looked down at the ground four stories below. "

"What are you doing?" Carter eyed him suspiciously.

"Just wondering how bad a jump like that would hurt as opposed to walking through your lobby past the jaws of death."

"Be a man." Carter lowered his eyes back to the paper he was reviewing.

"Isn't it illegal to not have a fire escape?"

"Oswell—"

"All right! All right! Geesh!" His shoulders slumped as he made his exit. Carter only shook his head after he was gone.

Chapter Ten

"So exactly what am I supposed to say to Mister, Mister . . . "

"Carter. Nick Carter. But don't call him by his first name, definitely call him Mister."

Meg and Marcus had dragged the speaker phone across the countertop in the kitchen of the farmhouse and were now sitting perched over it as they discussed the all important call.

"Mr. Carter. All right. Then what do I say to him?"

You got the letter! Ask him what he needs from you now."

"But I don't know all that writer speak that you're always going on about."

"Like what?

"Like query or rewrite, whatever."

"You won't need to talk query because he already has the manuscript. A query is just something you send to see if the company is interested, and we already know they are."

"Okay, so . . . " Marcus stopped suddenly, rubbing his forehead with worry. "This is never going to work."

"Of course it is, Marcus. Honey, you're making too big a deal over it." Meg touched his shoulder with that pleading look in her eye that she knew he couldn't resist. "Just ask him for the changes and ask when they need them back. Ask about the fees associated with soliciting to a publisher, the percentage he's taking for his representation, and the timeframe on the whole project. Oh, and ask him if I—if *you* can send in some more stuff that you have, but don't tell him that any other company has seen it and rejected it a million or so times."

"Oh God . . "

"You'll do great honey!" Meg patted his shoulder again with an excited little smile. "Don't give it another thought."

She pressed the speaker phone button and dialed the number she was directed to per the letter from Carter. She punched in the last digit, speaking as she waited for the ringing tone.

"Just sound, you know, romantic."

"Romantic?"

"You know." She shrugged as it rang a second time.

"This will never work."

"Of course it will!" she whispered.

"Good afternoon, Bankson, Laughton and Carter."

"Hello—hello." Marcus was already stumbling. They could hear the secretary sighing impatiently, and Meg waved for him to continue. "I'm . . . er, this is Marcus St. John. I've been asked to call and speak with Nick. Mr. Nick Carter."

"One moment."

Jan rolled her eyes and set her magazine aside.

"This one sounds like a winner," she muttered, pressing the buzzer. "Nick, there's a call on line one for you. A doof called Marcus St. John. Says you're expecting him."

Carter snapped to attention and closed the portfolio before him. He pressed the intercom buzzer and picked up the telephone receiver at the same time.

"Jan, get Oswell back here for me, would you? I don't think he's had time to leave the building yet."

"Do I have to?"

"I would like you to."

"It's Christmas and all, everyone *ho-ho-ho-ing* and the works, and what do I get to do but track down the Jewish grinch in person? Some present."

"Consider it a gift to me."

She glared at the button before finally pressing the one for the elevator intercom. She knew he'd not had time to reach the lobby yet.

"Pondscum, get your lily white butt back up here. Carter wants you." She took her finger off the button and picked up the magazine again. "I need a raise."

"Hello? Mr. St. John?"

"Yes, it's me," came the shaky voice.

"How do you do, Mr. St. John? Can I call you Marcus?"

"Yes, that would be fine, Nick." Marcus flinched as Meg slapped his arm and he immediately amended his statement. "Er, Mr. Carter, that is."

"You can call me Nick."

Marcus looked at Meg who was still shaking her head frantically with wide eyes. Marcus was losing every ounce of confidence as he noted her look that said he was an idiot.

"No, I can't. Thank you, Mr. Carter."

Meg slumped in her seat and let out a long sigh. She rolled her eyes and pursed her lips. This was not going as planned. Marcus was mouthing "what?" to her and the agent on the other line was quiet. *Probably laughing.* She thought. She nodded that he should continue, despite the rocky start.

J.T. Oswell came running back across the lobby, babbling all the way to Jan.

"You should really watch what you're saying on that thing—there was some poor old gray-haired dame on the elevator with me who'd just had her corns removed upstairs at the podiatrist's office! She about had a heart attack when your booming voice sounded with all those insults!"

"Good thing there's a cardiologist on the second floor, now isn't it?" Jan wasn't impressed as she the page in her magazine waving him on in.

J.T. hurried through the door, and, seeing him, Carter pressed the speaker phone as he gently set the receiver back in its place.

"So how is Iowa, Marcus?"

"Cold."

Carter nodded as he shot a glance at the publisher who was seated before him again, listening intently.

"The weather's pretty good here. About seventy-eight today. Don't see too many of those days in the Heartland, I imagine, do you?"

The agent laughed lightly in an effort to ease the obvious tension. The line was quiet and he made a little face.

Meg tapped the list of things she'd wanted Marcus to ask the agent. He squinted to read it in that he might have something to say.

"So, how much money are we gonna to make and how much are you gonna take?"

Meg slapped her forehead with frustration at the question posed kamikaze-style. She sat at the countertop looking at her feet, hopelessly.

Carter made a face at the question, but J.T. only nodded with wide eyes and then touched his temple to signal that they were on the same wavelength. The agent shook his head thinking that if they were on the same wavelength, he needed a better life. He proceeded anyway.

"You're a man of few words, Marcus. You get right to the point. You apparently know what you want and don't mess around discussing it. Standard agent fee is fifteen percent domestic, twenty percent foreign."

"Foreign?"

"You know, if your book is published outside of the United States."

"Oh, yeah."

"In any case, Marcus, I'll forward your manuscript to an editor this afternoon who will fax you with any changes or rewrites within a few days. Does that sound reasonable?"

"Sounds fine."

"Good. As well, I have a publishing house who is more than eager to handle your work." Carter trailed off a bit as he watched the hand signals being played out before him by the publisher. J.T. surrendered the sign language when he saw the puzzled look on his colleague's face, and he hurriedly scribbled him a note. Carter studied it briefly before going on. "It's Oswell House and they have an idea that involves a special format for your particular book. It will have a different shape, it will be square, setting it apart from the others."

"Different typeface too. Don't forget that," J.T. whispered. Carter motioned for him to stay quiet.

"The words will look a little different as well. It will be an attractive package that will really draw the buyer to it."

"Sounds fine."

"And we'd like to make it happen immediately per the publisher's wishes. That's pretty rare, Marcus, I hope you can appreciate that. The publisher feels that the market is there for this type of thing and doesn't want to waste any time."

J.T. was brushing his fingers together in the money sign and smiling foolishly.

"Sounds fine." Marcus said again. His voice was steady and monctonal and Meg immediately pointed back to her list. "I was wondering if you'd like any more submissions of, um, *mine*, as well."

The agent and publisher looked at each other with mutual approval. J.T. raised an open palm to his friend, slapping Carter a silent high five.

"Certainly, I think that would be good. Do it right away."

"Sounds fine."

"Is there anything you can think of, Marcus, that we haven't covered?"

"Nope."

"Then I think we'll get started on this writing endeavor quickly and hopefully have a profitable relationship. I'll be anxiously waiting to hear back from the editor when that process is complete."

"Sounds fine."

"I'll be in touch, Marcus. Take care."

"You too, now."

Carter punched the telephone button off and sat back in his chair, his hands clasped before him, an amused but puzzled look on his face.

"What? What is it? We're about to make a million bucks here!" J.T. nearly leaped out of his seat.

"Nothing, I just . . ." Carter shook his head with a little smile. "I was just wondering how a man of such few words could write an entire book chock full of them, that's all."

"Who cares how he did it? He did it!"

"It just seems that someone who just cranked out a three hundred page manuscript would have more to say than *sounds fine* repeatedly."

J.T. hurriedly stood up and leaned onto the agent's desk.

"Give me that precious, precious manuscript! I'm going to take it to editing myself!"

Carter sighed, tossing the mailer onto the desk toward him. J.T. snatched it up and went to the door, opening it. He bellowed his excitement as he stood in the threshold.

"I'm taking this right over! *Right* over! Oh, you just wait pal—this is one for the bank! Women will *flock* to this thing like flies on—" He noticed the audience he had now of the waiting clientele thanks to his loud voice. He changed his intended statement. "Flytape."

"Oh, I'm sure you can attract plenty of flies without flytape." Jan mumbled loud enough for him to hear. But his mood would not be dampened as he glanced at her before practically skipping out of the waiting area toward the elevators.

Meg threw her arms around Marcus once the call was over. He smiled with relief.

"Was I poetry?" He grinned from ear to ear. Meg ruffled his hair with her hand as she contemplated the question.

"Well, *Sanskrit*, but poetry nonetheless." She planted a kiss on his cheek with a loud smack and jumped down from her place at the breakfast bar. "I've gotta get my other stuff together—send it out first thing tomorrow."

"You gonna be printing for a while, then?" He looked disappointed, having been hoping to spend some time with her.

"No, don't worry, honey. I've got enough copies in my rejection stack to fill a small library."

She bounded out of the room leaving him alone. Then,as if she realized she were forgetting something, she slunk back in with an impish grin and hugged him in the middle of the floor where they were standing.

"Thank you, honey."

"Anything for you, Meg."

Chapter Eleven

"I sent them four more," Meg said in between bites of zucchini pasta as she and Noel ate lunch at Louie's Italian Eatery.

"You mean *Marcus* sent four more." Noel looked at her friend rather disapprovingly, speaking in her normal monotone. She gave up trying to swizzle the fettucini noodles around her fork and plunged it into the bowl in a barbaric fashion. "I don't have a good feeling about this."

"What's not to feel good about? My life's dream is coming true—and with *Oswell Publishing House* nonetheless." She stopped eating and looked at her friend, her eyes sparkling. "You know, *they* are the ones who print those Rachal Stone detective books. Or that post war series, what is that called?"

"*The Rebel.*"

"Yes! *The Rebel!* How's *that* for a first time writer? To land in their same company? Wow!" She looked at her watch. "Where's Reed?"

"He couldn't make it. The mall was swamped this morning. But Gawd, Meggie, you should have heard him when I told him. He started crying for the love of the gawds—I swear! He kept pulling tissues out of the sleeve of his sweater like my grandmother used to do. It was like a freaky flashback."

"Oh, Reed is so wonderful."

"Well, his eye makeup was all running and everything from those nonstop waterfalls. The Santa had to lend him an eyeliner."

"The Santa, is he . . . ?"

"Well I can't say, but he did have a fabulous little Mary Kay bag in his locker."

"Really?"

"Yeah, and that gold body sparkle they're selling for the holidays that's like fifteen bucks a tube? He had that."

"I wanted to order that."

"Me too." Noel shoved another forkful of pasta into her mouth and chomped away, waiting impatiently to be able to speak again. "So Marcus made the call."

"He did."

Suddenly, when her mouth was clear, and as if she'd had a moment to think about the possible hilarity of the situation, Noel burst out laughing.

"What did he sound like?"

"What do you mean?"

"I mean, did he go—*So, d'ya wanna sell my book Mr. Agent?*" She dissolved into a fit of giggles after imitating Marcus with the best hick accent that she could muster.

"Noel O'Dell."

Suddenly her friend was serious again as she sat up straight, speaking curtly.

"You know I hate it when you call me that."

"Well, you know I hate it when you make fun of the man that I love."

"You don't *love* him."

"I most certainly do, I'm *terribly* in love with him, in fact."

"Are not."

"Am."

"Are not."

"Am!"

"Can't be! The love that you have for Marcus is just, just *brother* love. I've seen it before."

"*Brother* love?"

"Yeah, you know, comfortable, easy brother love. It's kind of like an oven. It's warm enough, but there's no fire burning inside."

"An oven, Noel?"

"Yeah. An oven."

"How do you feel you can compare my love life to a major appliance?"

"How do you feel you can compare everything else in life to a

Christmas movie?"

Meg set her fork down and looked at Noel with a puzzled expression. "What do you mean?"

Noel set her fork aside, too, and returned the look.

"I mean, everything you say is like a line quoted from a sappy Christmas movie." She said, smugly. "For example, when Reed broke up with that one—that *Ronald* fellow, and you said it wasn't real love but that it was like the caring kind of love like what George Bailey had for Violet. Kind of infatuation. But that Ronald was certainly no Mary Hatch."

"Did I say that?"

"Well, not in those words, but something like that."

"Well, that's just because I happen to find Christmas movies very insightful, moving, and incredibly romantic."

"There's that word again."

"What's wrong with that word?"

"It's not so much the word as it is *you*." Noel sipped her tea and blotted her chin with her napkin. The waitress took their plates away and she leaned forward now to speak quietly across the table in the crowded restaurant. "I'm just saying you should practice what you preach."

"You're calling me a hypocrite?"

"I'm doing no such thing. Well, okay, I am." Noel waved her hand airily. "But I'm only doing it out of love for my best friend. It's just that I thought I was getting somewhere convincing you that Marcus wasn't *the* one for you, and incidentally, my position hasn't budged, but then *you* and *him*, and this book? And now four more? Meggie, I'm worried. You're locking yourself in tight."

There was silence until Meg finally spoke.

"I know you mean well. But these things have a way of taking care of themselves. It's like in *White Christmas*, the part where it looks like Betty and Bob will never get it together, and she gets on that train and he goes to New York and they're so bitter. Then suddenly, fate steps in and she goes back to Vermont and it snows finally and it's so, *so* beautiful!"

"Oh Gawd, here we go with the Christmas shows again." Noel rolled her eyes. "Okay, then here's one for ya. It's like in "*Christmas in Connecticut*" where that old time Martha Stewart chic has to have that soldier into her home with her family for the holidays."

"I don't think I've seen that one."

"Well, everything is fine, except for there's no home and no family—she'd made it all up for this magazine column she writes. So she *borrows* a friend, who happens to love her, and fabricates the whole thing, and all for the sake of her career. Sound familiar? And then she falls in love with the soldier, yet she's still tied to this other guy—this friend who she's promised she will marry when this is all over."

"So what happens?"

"So, finally she realizes that she can't keep up this charade." Noel's eyes glossed over, and she looked away dreamily as she told the story. "And she tells the soldier that she is a big fake and that she loves him, and it's *so* beautiful how they end up together."

"What happens with the magazine?"

Noel snapped out of her haze and looked at her friend, speaking matter-of-factly.

"She gets fired."

"Oh great."

"But that's just *it*! It doesn't matter that she gets fired! Because she has found the *true love* in her life!" Noel's voice was rising and a few patrons seated nearby began to stare. "You just don't get it, do ya? You just can't settle for hamburger when you might have a chance at steak."

"What's so wrong with hamburger?"

"There's nothing wrong with it at first. But then it starts getting old, and you have to continually try to jazz it up. You make it with onions one night and then peppers and before you know it, you're mixing it into taco salads and Hamburger Helper and all sorts of stuff to make it taste a little better. But the fact remains, it's *hamburger*. Now steak, steak you might dip in a little *57 Sauce* from time to time, but it stays pretty delicious without it."

"What if you like hamburger though?"

"Who in their right mind would have *hamburger* when you could have a delicious, juicy, mouth watering *steak*!"

Meg was silent for a moment as she thought about this.

"What if you give up hamburger and you never ever find steak?"

Noel looked at her seriously.

"Worse. What if you settle for hamburger and steak walks through the door one day. And you're thinking, that looks pretty damn good to me. And you're *hungry* for it." Noel practically growled "You think you'll go crazy if you can't have that steak. But here's this perfectly nice pile of hamburger sitting right before you, and *that's* whatchya have to eat. And yet, having seen steak, you never quite feel the same about the hamburger again."

"So, apart from the food metaphors, what are you saying?"

"I'm saying, believe me, by saying you'll wait for a steak and pass on the hamburger, you're only actually doing the hamburger a favor. Nobody wants to play second fiddle, and who knows, maybe there's a Miss Mary Farmer out there who will see that hamburger and think it's a steak."

"And I'm the weird one?" Meg finally took her eyes away from her friend, glancing at her watch. She stood and picked up her purse. "I've got to run. I want to be there if that fax comes across this afternoon. I'm buying this one. It's a celebration."

Meg picked up the check and planted a hurried kiss on her friend's cheek.

"Fine, fine go on." Noel waved her napkin, carelessly. "Go home to your pile of reprocessed cow product."

"I'll call you."

"You call me."

Chapter Twelve

"There's a message for you, well, for *me*, on the machine."

Marcus was hunting through the cabinets for something to eat when Meg walked into the kitchen. She stared at him for a moment before slowly removing her plaid neckscarf and wriggling out of her coat. She looked concerned.

"Oh God, it's all been a dream and they decided not to publish me—you."

"No, quite the contrary actually. Go ahead, listen to it."

Meg walked over to the countertop and pressed the button on the answering machine, waiting nervously.

"Marcus St. John, Carter here. There will be no fax for rewrites because there are no rewrites. Amazingly enough, the editor and publisher both believe that you have an intuition about the market you've written for and only made a few minor changes. Some general structural corrections were made and Claire's name is now Zayra because Suzanne Dryfuss' lead char - acter in her latest book also had a daughter named Claire. No biggy, just words. I'm faxing the contract tomorrow at noon that's ours—yours and mine. I'm already well into negotiations with Oswell Publishing House and I'll let you know how that goes. Take care now."

Meg slapped the counter with her hand and turned to face Marcus, beaming from ear to ear.

"Oh my God!" She shook her head in disbelief. "Can you *believe* it!"

"It's hard to believe." His words were soft and held a note of uncertainty.

Meg walked toward him, her eyes hinting concern.

"What is it Marcus?"

"You've waited so long for this and now you don't get the limelight for any of it." He held her look for a few moments, finally shaking his head with an apologetic smile. "Doesn't seem quite right, that's all."

"Nonsense! No, no." She wrapped her arms around his waist. Meg leaned back and looked into his eyes with a reassuring smile. "It's not about limelight, Marcus. It's about personal satisfaction. I've been doing this for so long, it's just rewarding knowing that someone wants to read it and thinks others might too."

"I hope that will be a good enough return on your hard work, because I don't feel good about it."

"Come here." She lead him to a chair nodding for him to sit. She squatted before him looking in his face with earnest eyes. "You and I are in this for the long haul—we're not keeping track of points to see who's got what. So, I write the books and you get the credit for now. That's not so terrible. The money belongs to *both* of us and I get that personal satis-faction that I'm always going on about. Consider it an adventure!"

"An adventure, huh?" He smiled at her.

"Yes, an adventure!"

"Do you think we can pull it off?"

We already have!"

"But sooner or later—"

"Shhh."

She stifled his protests with a kiss. Marcus looked at her with won-der. She kissed him again and again until he finally gave in and returned her embrace.

Chapter Thirteen

J.T. Oswell peeked cautiously around the corner of the lobby toward Nick Carter's office. He drew back and mentally analyzed the situation. Jan was reading quietly at the reception desk and only one person was seated in the waiting area. With a look of new confidence, J.T. dropped onto all fours and quickly scooted across the floor, pausing behind a waiting room chair. He waited.

Glimpse up.

Eyes down.

He crawled frantically while Jan's eyes were averted, stopping directly in front of her desk where she wouldn't be able to see him. J.T. held his breath. When his eyes met those of the only waiting client, he smiled quickly and then looked away. The client, an older woman who'd been flipping through a magazine, smirked, unfazed by the quirky actions of the man in his expensive business suit. She went back to reading.

The next move wouldn't be so easily pulled off in the situation he'd put himself in. He couldn't glance upward for fear of looking directly into her face. J.T. waited until he suspected she wasn't watching and charged toward Carter's office door violently on all fours.

Jan watched as the door opened and then shut quickly. She immediately rose and strode to the door, swinging it back eagerly. The woman stood there, her arms crossed before her, glaring at J.T.

"*Out*, whipper snapper. You can't get past me that easily."

"I just did! You didn't even see me!" The whining voice easily grated her nerves today.

"Oh, I suppose I was to think the invisible man was walking through the door," she said. "I saw you wallering all over my rug out there like some kind of an animal. Now get out before I beat you like the dog that you are."

J.T. looked over to Carter. He was smiling. He didn't attempt to help him out.

"I need to speak to Carter."

"Then you *need* to make an appointment."

"Oh come on, why can't you ever cut me a break?"

"Why can't you be normal?"

"I *am* normal, I was just playing a little joke there, that's all. Women can never take a joke."

"The very essence of your existence is proof enough that women can take a joke."

"Come on! You're killing me here!"

"Unfortunately, my powers of ESP aren't that strong." She looked at Carter. "Boss, shall I call animal control, again?"

Carter was amused.

"I'll let him state his case and he'll be on his way."

"Hmph, you are seriously *not* okay." She stared at the blonde publisher once again before leaving muttering all the way. "I'm checking the rug out there and if there's anything not altogether *natural*, I'm sending you the cleaning bill."

"I did share that dog woman theory about her didn't I?"

"Yes, I believe you did."

"God, what a shame—those looks wasted on that personality." J.T. shook his head.

"It's the strangest relationship we have here, J.T. Isn't it usually customary for the agent to visit the publisher?" Carter was finishing up a stack of paperwork before him, stacking them neatly.

"That's the only way you look at our relationship, Carter?" He looked wounded. "I think of us more like, like *family*. Isn't that how you see us?"

Suddenly Jan's voice called through the door which had been left slightly ajar. "Only before he wakes up screaming in a cold sweat!"

J.T. didn't waste anytime as he bolted to the door and slammed it.

"I believe this is what you're here for, am I right?" The agent held out several stacks of paper held together by a few large rubberbands. Carter sprang away from the door, snatching them away promptly. "Where's my contract?"

J.T. opened his jacket, removing a few sheets from his inside pocket, turning them over in exchange. "You sign this and he—"

"I'm aware."

"Well, of course." J.T. briefly flipped through some of the papers and smiled greedily. "This man is a veritable gold mine of feminine oddities."

"Is that so?"

"He didn't sound, you know, did you think?"

"What?"

"You *know.*"

"No, I don't know."

"Did you think he sounded like a, you know, *less* than manly kind of guy?"

"Did I think he was gay?"

"Shh!" J.T. looked around him as if someone might hear.

"What would it matter as long as you were making residuals from his book?"

"No, no, of *course* it wouldn't matter—it wouldn't matter at all."

"If it wouldn't matter then why did you ask?"

"I was just curious."

"Why don't you go be curious in your own office for a while?"

"What are you trying to say? You don't enjoy my company?"

Carter pressed the button on his intercom.

"Jan, could you come in for a minute?"

"Oh come on, what did I do?" J.T.'s eyes were pleading. Instantly Jan was in the doorway, her hand on her hip, her look unmoving.

"You want dog-boy gone?"

"Come on! I thought we were friends here!" He started for the door but stopped as he looked at the tall woman standing there.

"I'll be in touch with the editor to see what you think about those manuscripts." Carter smiled cordially, ignoring the angry antics of the publisher. "Sound good?"

"See ya, wouldn't want to be ya." Jan waved toward the door.

"But you're in my way!" J.T. turned to Carter. "She's in my way."

"Be a man."

"Oh, God." He clenched his eyes shut.. "I'm getting you a fire escape for Christmas if it's the last thing I do."

"If you don't get out of here the last thing you'll see is my open palm headed straight for your funny little face." Jan stepped slightly to the side and waved him on. "But if you want to run, I'll blink."

"My *funny little face?* What kind of treatment is that for one of your best clients?"

"I'm one of your best clients." Carter corrected.

"Even worse!"

"Good-bye J.T."

"Geesh."

"Leave before I force you to exit the way that you entered—on your knees." Jan pointed in the direction of the elevators.

"Oh, I love it when you talk dirty to me." J.T.'s mood miraculously lightened and he grinned at her.

"Get!"

"Yahoo! Merry Christmas!" In an unexpected burst of jubilance, the publisher suddenly sprinted across the lobby and hurdled a chair. He disappeared down the hallway. Carter was standing next to his secretary as they watched the behavior of the quirky man. She shook her head and walked back to her desk.

"They say Tampa is gettin' more and more dangerous these days." She pulled her chair out and sat down shuffling through her folders there. "Your friend is a very disturbed little man. And I emphasize *very.*"

Chapter Fourteen

"**M**erry Christmas, Honey."

"Merry Christmas, Meg."

The clink of their wine glasses sounded over the lightly playing holiday music. Marcus leaned in to kiss her. He looked into her eyes as they sparkled with the reflection of the white Christmas tree lights. The dimly lit room was warmed by the crackling fireplace a few feet away. Meg snuggled her oversized sweater over her knees as she sat there nestled into his arms leaning against his chest enjoying the peacefulness of Christmas Eve.

"I want you to open my present," he urged after a few minutes.

"Oh, you shouldn't have, Marcus."

He pulled a little neatly wrapped box out the midst of a few tree branches and handed it over to her proudly. Meg kissed his lips again, smiling with gratitude.

"It's just a little something, but I think you'll like it."

"What could I like more than this?" She waved her ring before him. "You're too much Marcus, really you are *too much.*"

He leaned back as they sat on the floor together. Meg worked at the little bow and pulled the paper off the tiny box. She lifted the lid. Puzzled she glanced up at him and then back to the box.

"Take it out."

She gingerly pulled the little device out and looked at it carefully, smiling all the while.

"What is it, Marcus, honey?" She finally asked. He laughed lightly and turned it over in her hand where she could see something imprinted in black rubber on the bottom side.

"It's a stamper. I had them make it for you special with my signature on it." He pointed to the ridges with pride. "So you can sign your contracts and paperwork and fax them right back without my even being here."

"Ah." She nodded, raising an eyebrow with new understanding.

"What do you think?

"I think . . . that is a very *inventive* gift. Of course, only you would think of that, Marcus." She kissed his nose playfully. "You've always been so imaginative."

"I knew you'd like it. I figured you'd know better than I would about the agreements and rights and stuff, so there you have my trust, my signature, that you will make the best decisions for me—and you. Well, *both* of us." He was still smiling at her and put his finger to her lips to quiet her before she could say anything. "Do you hear that? This was always one of my favorite Christmas Carols. Dance with me. Come on."

He stood and pulled her to her feet as well wrapping her in his embrace. Meg leaned her head against his chest. The sounds of "I'll Be Home For Christmas" wafted softly through the room as they silently moved in slow circles. Meg's eyes went to the little pile of wrapping paper still strewn there near the tree, and to the shiny handle of the stamp. She gently gnawed on her lower lip as she continued to move with Marcus in time to the music, never letting his present out of her sight.

Chapter Fifteen

"**A** *stamper?* He got you a *stamper?* What kind of a present is that, for the love of the gawds."

Noel sipped her Absolut and cranberry juice, stirring it around with her finger. The women stood amidst the revelers at Jasper Falls Civic Center, home of the big central Iowa New Year's Bash. A healthy littering of confetti covered every inch of the floor. The band playing made it difficult to hear, coupled with the triumphant sounds of party horns.

Meg's eyes quickly scanned the room's expanse looking for Marcus. She moved closer to her friend who was trying desperately to hear her. Giving up, Meg pulled her friend like a train leading its caboose through the thick crowd, toward the back of the room. They sat down at a little table. A waitress quickly zeroed in on them for their drink order. They watched the party.

"It was a gesture, more so than a simple stamp." Meg finally started again.

"I'd have a gesture for any guy who tried to give *me* a stamper for my Christmas present." Noel rolled her eyes. "That's some big present there."

"That wasn't the only thing Marcus gave me."

Suddenly Meg felt extremely uncomfortable as she set her beaded bag on the tabletop. She slowly opened it and removed a tiny item from within, holding it firmly in her hand, her eyes never budging from Noel's.

"Oh, no . . . Oh, no—no—no . . . "

Meg unfolded her hand, revealing the ring.

"Oh, no—no—no . . . " Noel waved her hands and looked away. "No—no—no—no . . . "

"Would you stop saying that?"

"Oh Gawd."

"Don't you want to look at it?"

"I don't want to be a party to this action."

"Well, we knew it was going to happen—"

"Would you look at you?" Noel was disgusted. "You, you sitting here all dolled up, lookin' like a cool million-and-a-half in your silvery sequined thing, here! Look—do you see *anyone* in this joint with the class that you have? And yet, here you sit, alone, holding your future in the palm of your hand,and the best you can say is *we knew it was going to hap - pen?*"

"I'm not alone, you're here with me."

"Meggie . . ."

Suddenly Reed, dressed in his tuxedo with tails and a top hat flounced over to the girls' table and pulled up a chair. He dropped into a deep bow before sitting. "Ladies, may I?"

Meg smiled and nodded.

"You both look stunning! Whew! Meggie you are glimmering for *real* girlfriend! Check you out!" Reed's eyes danced atop his rosy cheeks and he motioned toward the waitress.

"Hey Reed, you're looking pretty dapper tonight." Noel eyeballed him approvingly.

"Thank you."

"Very GQ, very." Meg said.

The waitress brought three glasses of champagne back to their table.

"What gives?" he asked.

What?" Meg was innocently sipping her drink.

"The long faces."

"Meg got *the ring*."

"Oh my God. Well, we knew it was going to happen."

Meg set her glass aside and began her protest.

"You say that, *the ring*, like it's the plague or something."

"It might as well be at this rate—and your overall happiness will be its *first* victim."

"Oh come on!"

"You come on!"

Reed watched the two bicker, moving his head back and forth, as though he were watching a tennis match.

"Wait! Ladies! Yoo-hoo!" He clapped his hands softly at first and then louder when the squabbling duo ignored. "Ladies! Thank you. Now, Meg, the ring please?"

She reluctantly handed it over to him and Reed took it, studying it carefully. He turned it upside down and then held it to the light, squinting. Finally Meg snatched it out of his hand with some aggravation and set it back on the table.

"What are you? A jeweler?"

"I was checking the fire."

"The *what?*"

"You really should know more about the whole business of buying fine stones. You need to look for a lustrous fire and flawless center."

"Oh, and if a man offers me a ring for my hand in marriage I'm to look at the luster of it first to see that it's got enough fire." Meg shook her head at him as if he'd clearly lost his mind.

"They say the fire in a man's heart is reflected by the luster of the diamond he chooses."

Noel quickly pulled off her own ring and held it up to the light, squinting. Reed took it from her and whistled a low whistle.

"This rock has a fabulous luster." Reed looked surprised but not nearly as much as Noel who took it back from him again.

"Really?"

"Wonderful, stunning."

Meg studied the ring as it lay before her on the crimson tablecloth. Finally she asked.

"Okay, so did mine have *fire?*"

Reed widened his eyes and nodded a little.

"All diamonds have fire."

"Stunning fire, eh?" Noel smiled and slipped her ring back over her knuckle with a little force. She admired it, perched on her hand.

"Well? Was mine *stunning?*"

"It was very nice."

Reed patted the top of her hand reassuringly.

"Hers is stunning and mine is *very nice?* That doesn't seem quite fair."

"What's not fair," Noel's attention returned to the issue at hand.

"What's not fair is that you are knowingly depriving yourself of the opportunity to have a true and everlasting love and thereby depriving whatshisname of being number one for someone else."

"Uh oh. Is this the steak versus hamburger speech, again?" Reed asked.

"It's a matter of *security*." The woman went on, ignoring him. "Insecure people who are afraid of their own success—their own *happiness*—tend to cling to the first thing that comes along out of the fear that nothing else will present itself."

"Where does she get this stuff?" Meg looked helplessly at Reed who shrugged.

"You marry whatshisname and you'll regret it for the rest of your life."

"Ladies! Let's not fight about it! Come on!"

"He bought her a *rubber stamper* for Christmas, for the love of the gawds, Reed!"

"It is a stamp of his *signature*. It's a symbol that he trusts me to make decisions about the book on his behalf." Meg looked smugly at Reed.

"The book on *his* behalf!" Noel's voice was rising with near hysteria. "It's *your* book, sister! Not his! He? You? This . . . ? Oh no, this is *so* much not a good thing. If it's symbolic of *anything* it would be that you have willingly handed yourself over to him for him to consume you! Entirely! Your personality and now, even your *talent*!"

"Noel!

Reed signalled to the woman to calm down. He turned to Meg.

"It may not be either one of those things, but this we can be sure of It's symbolic at least of the fact that your relationship is now being externally controlled by a book—your life's *dream*! It's not altogether aboveboard, and that's not right anyway." Reed patted her shoulder. He swiftly moved to change the subject. "Come on ladies, it's nearly midnight. We're amongst good friends here—let's *enjoy* ourselves!"

No one moved. Reed thumped his top hat and smiled, dancing in his seat.

"Let's par-tay! Come on girlfriends! Shake your groove thangs!"

"You two go on ahead." Meg waved them on.

Still no one moved.

Finally, Reed stook her hands.

"Just ask yourself this, Meg, is he Mary Hatch? Or just Violet?" He smiled at her adoringly. She remembered making him ponder the same notion only months ago. Her eyes misted over and she looked away quickly.

"I don't know."

"Yes, you do," he continued in his soft way. "If he was your Mary Hatch, the ring would be on your finger instead of on the tablecloth."

The music around them seemed to grow louder and the celebration more frenzied as the band broke into a drum roll to prepare the count-down to the new year.

"Come on! Come on!" Reed changed the subject, pulling them both to their feet. "You have to dance in the New Year with the ones you love! Come on!"

The women followed him onto the dance floor. Reed's jumping and whooping antics soon lightened their somber moods.

Three! Two! One! Happy New Year!

The band burst into a round of Auld Lang Syne and the three best friends, oblivious to the whereabouts of their significant others, draped their arms lovingly around each other and began to move in time to the music.

"I love you, Noel. Reed."

"I love you both, too."

"Happy New Year girlfriends. Glimmer on."

Chapter Sixteen

M arcus,

Just a note to wish you a splendid holiday and joyous New Year! But alas, my associate at Oswell Publishing House believes that paper that has no bit of business attached to it is a mere waste of precious trees. So, I wish to arrange a meeting that will take place in two weeks during which we shall discuss our venture and proceed with a promotional plan. Until then,

Nick Carter

P.S. Could you bring along a professional picture of yourself for a possible jacket Oswell House is tossing around?—Thanks.

"We're really going to make this happen!" Meg squealed after reading the letter Marcus had handed to her. He was obviously a little less than enthusiastic. He sat at the kitchen table, staring off as she did a little dance across the floor in her sock feet. Noticing his look, she stopped and made a playful frown, and went to him. She blinked her blue eyes, widening them innocently. He said nothing, only reaching his hand out to brush a few hairs out of her lashes. She blew the remaining strands away from her face, shriveling her nose impatiently.

"Why do you do that?" He changed the subject, studying her there. "This hair used to fall in long waves clear down to your behind like Godiva. It was a heavenly sight, I swear. Then you cut a little, and a little more. It just kept creeping up your back, and now it's up to your shoulder blades. You have always had the most beautiful hair and you have always hated it."

"I don't *hate* it. Well, maybe a little." She'd danced around the idea of short hair over the years only to receive a boisterous *no* from Marcus.

She pursed her lips and wondered what her hair had to do with taking a trip to Bankson, Laughton and Carter Agency in Tampa. But she listened with a certain impatience anyway.

"Why do women do that?"

"Do what?"

"They wear their hair long and loose until they get into a relationship and then it starts inching its way up the ol' back, and the minute there's a ring on their finger, the hair just disappears," Marcus snapped his fingers. "Poof! I just don't understand it. I really don't."

Meg smiled, touching her blonde crown, lightly pulling at a few of the natural waves in the waterfall of tresses.

"There have been a million articles written about this very subject— don't you ever read?" She looked thoughtful. "Women see short hair as a symbol of security. I believe that's what they wrote. You see, a woman uses her beauty, her hair, as a lure. Then as she is reeling him in,she exercises his tolerance by lessening the lure. To be sure that he loves her unconditionally. It's sort of a preliminary measure to be sure that as the woman's appearance becomes less beautiful over the years, she will indeed be as attractive to her spouse as when he first met her."

"That is crazy."

"But true, but true. You see, when the fish is securely tucked away in the basket, women are compelled to act on their natural inclination."

"To look like Sinead O'Connor?"

To look however they *want*, and sometimes, they want to look a little . . . a little less *hairy*."

"You're making this up."

"I'm not, really." She straightened her posture and looked at him confidently. "It's kind of like what you men do, I suspect, the way you wear that little bit of scruff around your chin because you know that we think it's sexy. But then you all go off and get married and the scruff comes right off. Like you don't have time to fool with it."

"You think that's why?"

"I said I *suspect*."

"This here scruff is the offset of getting up at four o'clock in the morning everyday. By noon I'm already sporting a five o'clock shadow. It doesn't get any better than this."

"Well then—how lucky am I?" Meg brushed the tip of her nose across his bristly chin.

"So, women use their *hair* to reel in their catch and plop it into a, a holding basket."

"Sort of."

"So, dating and marriage compares nicely to fishing."

Meg considered it, then nodded.

"In a sense. Hair makes a much better lure than worms now, don't you think?"

"Tell that to Medusa."

"That was snakes."

"Snakes, worms. They're both squiggly." He shuddered jokingly. "So, when a woman cuts her hair what exactly is she trying to say?"

"She's saying that she feels secure enough in her relationship to take such a drastic chance as to cut her hair." Meg furrowed her brow, pondering the theory. "Or maybe it was that she feels the need to exercise her independence in overcoming feelings of oppression, I'm not sure."

She shook her head and flipped her hand nonchalantly.

"It doesn't matter anyway. So when do we go to Florida?"

"The twenty-fifth." He looked strange.

"What is it? What's wrong?"

"I'll have to see if I can get Cliff to give me a hand—feed the stock while I'm gone." Marcus rose from his chair and brushed his fingers across his chin stubble as he gazed out the window, thinking.

"While *we're* gone."

"He'll have to keep an eye on the sow, she's due along about the time they want me there."

"And me." Meg tiptoed along behind him as he moved about the kitchen, interjecting occasionally in her sing-song voice.

"I'll have to get Harve to go to the monthly Home Grown meeting for me. We need a representative from our quadrant, you know. I won't be here."

"Neither will I, right?"

Marcus turned to her finally, coming out of the one track thinking he'd fallen into, offering her a broad smile.

"I'm not going into that place alone, honey." He pulled her to him in an embrace. "I'm your eyes and ears, remember?"

Meg smiled,squeezing her eyes shut tightly, hugging him. She pulled away quickly and grabbed her purse off the countertop.

"Come on, we've got to go."

"Where to?"

"To the mall."

"It's the middle of the day, I have things to do still."

"It's ten thirty, you have all day." She sat on the floor, pulling her short suede boots over her socks, blindly fishing one arm into the closet for her coat. "It takes nearly two weeks to get a picture back. If we go to Picture Palace this morning, it will be here just in time."

"*Reed* is going to take it?" Marcus grimaced as he grabbed his coat. "No."

"No matter what you think about Reed, he is a great photographer. I'll grab you a sweater."

"What's wrong with what I'm wearing?"

"It's a flannel shirt. The authors on the covers of the books always wear sweaters. It's just, you know, more *scholarly* looking."

"I'm wearing this or I'm not doing it at all."

"Marcus, *please* honey!"

"That's my final word Meg, they can take this or nothing at all." And before she had a chance to protest or flash her wide eyed looks at him he clenched his own eyes firmly shut and shook his head. "That's my final word."

Meg arched an eyebrow. Blue, her big dog, quietly observed their conversation. She shrugged.

"All right. You win. Let's go."

Chapter Seventeen

The buzz of people at the Jasper Falls Shopping Center had diminished significantly now that the holidays were over. Exchanges had been made, gift certificates honored and returns completed, causing the shops to be staffed at bare minimum. The remaining employees appeared to be quite bored.

Meg lead Marcus along down the barren openness of the mall, their feet shuffling lightly on the tiled floor creating the only sounds around them. Looking rather out of place, he reluctantly succumbed to her towing, glancing now and again in either direction as if he might bump into someone he knew. He cleared his throat and unbuttoned the top button of his heavy coat as Meg pulled him into Picture Palace.

"Meggie!"

Reed immediately lept to his feet from his place behind the counter near the waiting area. He took a little pair of wire rimmed spectacles from his nose and set them aside. Meg glanced at him suspiciously. He promptly flung his arms around her and chirped gleefully into her ear.

"What a surprise, girl! You look wonderful as *always*!" He babbled on happily, then, noticing how she was still eyeing his glasses, he picked them back up and smiled broadly. "Do you love these or *what?*"

"You don't wear glasses, Reed."

"I know, but these were too cute to pass up! The new optometrist shop down the way had them in—you know, *Right Sight?* I loved them so bad I had them make me a pair with clear lenses! Am I *all that* and more in these things or what?" He shoved them back onto the bridge of his nose and struck a regal pose, glancing over the tops of the glasses. "I swear I even *feel* smarter!"

"They do! You know, they *really* do, don't they Marcus?" Meg turned toward her fiancée who was still standing near the door, warily. He nodded with a little smile that looked like it actually hurt. Meg waved him on in to join them but he pretended not to notice as he stared out at the quiet mall. "You need to do me a favor."

"Name it, girlfriend."

"I need you to take a picture of Marcus." Meg leaned toward him and spoke in a low voice. "It's for the jacket of my first *book!*"

Marcus' attention came back to her now as he narrowed his eyebrows with a questioning look upon his face. He shook his head but she only shrugged.

"Well, you know I would rather be taking a picture of *you* for your own book." Reed rolled his eyes at her as if he were contemplating the favor.

"And you *will*, in good time."

"Okay, let's do it then!" He clapped his hands in Marcus' direction. The decision was made. "Come come! Hop to!"

Meg nodded toward the back room where Reed had already disappeared.

"Come on, honey."

"I don't like it when he claps his hands at me."

"You don't like it when he does anything."

"I forgot," Marcus smirked. "Why are we here?"

"Because Reed's the best, that's why."

They walked into the brightly lit room where Reed was assembling a pedestal and draping it with a black cloth. He methodically pulled a black backdrop along behind it and straightened the seat once more.

"Come on over, Markie."

"It's Marcus."

"Of course it is." Reed smiled at him in a tolerating way and settled him into a position on the pedestal. "Now what are we going to wear?"

"*We* are wearing it." Marcus answered shortly.

"No, no, no, no. You can't wear *that*. That will never do." He stuck his finger onto his temple to signal that he was deep in thought. No one moved. "Well, we'll just have you wear one of my sweaters."

"No, we'll be just fine in this."

"No, I insist. You can't wear just *anything* for these types of pictures. The authors on the covers of books always wear sweaters. It makes them look smarter."

"Kind of like those phony glasses?" Marcus came back.

Reed stood back for a moment, studying the man before him, trying to decide whether or not he was offended. Meg held her breath until Reed suddenly clapped his hands and laughed. She sighed with relief and laughed along with him. When her friend turned to make a camera adjustment, she shot Marcus a look of death. Marcus rolled his eyes and sighed. Reed emerged from behind the camera.

"I have a perfectly fetching sweater back in my locker, let me get it for you. It's got bold geometric blocks on it and it will be a smash hit for sure on Meggie's bookcover. Be back!" Reed flitted into the next room and Marcus promptly glared at Meg who was standing off to the side.

"Why did you tell *Queenie* about our little deal? I thought this was supposed to be hush hush!" he whispered loudly.

"Don't call him that—it's impolite!"

"What? He can call himself that but I can't?"

"He calls himself a *queen*, there's a difference."

"Okay, okay whatever! Why did you tell him?"

"Because he's my best friend."

"I thought Noel was your best friend?"

"She is."

"What is the deal with women having so many best friends? You can only have one best friend or they wouldn't call it best."

"Noel's my best sister friend and Reed's my best fashion fun friend."

"That's ridiculous."

"It's perfectly understandable. Best school friends, best shopping friends, best *confidante*. These are titles not to be taken lightly." She peeked out the door to hear Reed chattering away to himself in the next room as he looked for the sweater. She stepped back in and looked at Marcus sitting there expectantly. "Get over it, it's a woman thing."

"Reed's not a woman. Not that I have investigated the matter."

"He's an honorary woman."

"Oh great," Marcus slapped his thigh as he sat there, nodding his head. "He's an honorary woman and I'm going to be wearing his sweater"

"Shh, here he comes. Don't hurt his feelings!"

"Here we go!" He handed the sweater to Marcus who was eyeing him,his lip curled. "I couldn't find that geometric one, but I love the waffle weave pattern in this one. Put it on and let me see."

Marcus grudgingly obliged, slipping the red and navy blue sweater over his head. Meg moved in,smoothing his dark hair back into place and straightening his collar. Marcus pulled his sleeves a little and brushed his chest with his hand, removing a few little pieces of lint.

"It looks great! What do you think, Reed?" Meg turned around when her friend didn't answer immediately and furrowed her brow when she caught his look. He had covered his lips with his hand and his eyes were glassed over. "What is it Reed? What's wrong?"

"Nothing," he lied, waving his hand a little as he gnawed at his lower lip.

Meg walked over and gently laid a hand on his shoulder. "Tell me what it is."

Reed gathered his words trying to remain collected. He failed miserably, sniffing and sobbing loudly.

"The last time I saw that sweater on, Ronald was wearing it," he blubbered. Meg put her arms around him to offer comfort. She closed her eyes and rocked him as he let it out. "Of course, it *looked* better on Ronald, but the memory is still so painful."

"Thanks," Marcus muttered looking away. Meg shot him a second warning look.

"Now, now, there. That's just terrible, Reed." Her words were soothing. "If you would like, Marcus will take it right off."

"Gladly," her fiancée put in.

"No, no." Reed took the tissue that Meg was offering him and blew his nose into it loudly. "That's okay. I can handle it."

"Moving forward now?" Meg asked softly.

"Moving forward now." One last sob made its escape and Reed revised the statement as he clenched his eyes shut and swallowed hard. "Okay, now."

Marcus rolled his eyes for the millionth time since he'd entered the photography studio and sat back a bit, trying to relax. Reed dabbed his eyes with a tissue and then pressed his lips together into a forced smile.

He approached Marcus and made a few adjustments, tipping his chin just so, repositioning his clasped hands and moving his pedestal ever so slightly. He backed up next and stared at his subject from behind the camera, selecting the right lens and preparing for his shot. He stood back and smiled at Marcus.

"Relax your forehead, chin down, eyes up. Relax your forehead," Reed instructed from behind the camera as Marcus made various expressions trying to follow along. He was growing frustrated and it was showing. "Forehead! That's gonna have to go."

"What the hell's wrong with this forehead? How in God's name am I supposed to relax my *forehead*!"

Reed thrust his hands onto his hips and looked over the top of his glasses at Meg who was standing off to the side. He shook his head and made a tsk-tsk sound with his tongue.

"I can't work like this," Reed stated matter-of-factly.

"Not a problem." Marcus stood.

"Marcus! Honey! *Please*! Reed?" Meg rushed to his side. "We need this. I told you Reed's the *best*. If he tells you to relax your forehead, do it in for the sake of . . .of . . . "

"Art." Reed helped her out.

"Yes. That's right." Her eyes were pleading. "Please?"

Marcus sighed loudly and sat back down. Reed walked over to him and readjusted his clothing and position, retreating to the camera once again.

"We're going for the serious look here, the smile thing isn't happening."

"I know how to smile."

"If that's what you want to call it," Reed's voice trilled as he adjusted his camera.

Meg immediately headed off the mounting slam war.

"Honey, just do what Reed asks. It will only take a minute."

Reed studied the man before him for a few moments and then suddenly pointed toward something on the ground.

"Look at that."

"What?" Marcus' eyes went right to the place and Reed snapped the picture, smiling triumphantly.

"All done!"

Marcus looked at him as if he'd lost his mind.

"What do you mean, all done?"

"I mean I got the shot I wanted."

"In one picture?"

"It only takes one when it's perfect."

"And you don't want a second for safety's sake?"

Reed pulled the film cartridge out of the camera and wrote on it, shoving it into a carton. He looked quite sure of himself. Marcus, never removing his rather sarcastic look from Reed, peeled the sweater off over his head and tossed it to him.

"That's an earthy scent," Reed smelled the sweater when he had it back. "What is that? Aspen?"

"Iowa," Marcus smirked. The photographer raised an eyebrow as he deposited the sweater onto a nearby chair. He followed the couple to the waiting area.

"Lunchtime." Reed clapped his hands together and pulled an *out to lunch* sign out of the cabinet, hanging it on the door. "Shall we?"

"No, Meg, I'm going back to get some work done."

"Pity," Reed said with little remorse. Meg glanced at her friend before she planted a kiss on Marcus' cheek.

"Okay, honey. I'll see you there this afternoon. Thanks for, you know, all that."

"It's a good thing I love you, Meg."

Chapter Eighteen

"So he got *the* official picture taken right in this here mall, huh?" Noel nodded approvingly. She took another bite of her gyro sandwich and blotted the grease that was starting to ooze down her chin. "What did he wear?"

"He borrowed something from Reed, this fabulous sweater."

"It *was* fabu." Reed looked melancholy all over again as he sighed deeply and set his salad fork aside. Meg patted his hand in quiet support.

"Did he look good? I mean, did he look like a *writer*?" Noel prodded for details. "Did he look intellectual and all?"

"He didn't look half bad." Meg said after giving it a little thought. She tried to steer the subject away from Reed's former love, knowing this was consuming him at the moment. "Speaking of intellect, did you get a load of Reed's new specs?"

"Not a news flash, sister. I saw those days ago." She sipped her iced tea and opened another packet of sugar, dumping it in, whitening the ice cubes on top. "So, did he look good in the sweater? I mean, I don't think I've ever seen Marcus in a sweater. He usually looks so, you know, *farmy*."

"I'll tell him you said so," Meg stabbed her fork into another bite of salad, stopping to pick out the carrot slivers that were tossed in with the greens. She made a face at the orange vegetables. "He took it reasonably well."

"He wore that beautiful sweater that I got Christmas before last." Reed was still on the last subject. "That beautiful waffle weave Ronald bought, *supposedly* for me, but then he had it on himself at every turn."

"That's the way it works, Reed, or at least that's the way it works for me. You Meggie?" Noel turned the floor over to her friend and waited.

"What do you mean?" She looked aloof curious.

"I mean when you buy a sweater or sweatshirt for Marcus, don't you look for something that you know you'll want to wear yourself?"

"Yes, yes I guess I have."

"You guess? That baby blue corduroy jacket that you bought for Marcus' birthday last year—like you picked that out for him! *Please!* The man wouldn't wear baby blue if it were the last stitch of clothing on earth!" Noel took another bite and talked through a mouthful of sandwich. "That's what he was doing, Reed. Ronald wanted it for himself."

"Maybe he knew I'd enjoy seeing him in it, which I did, you know."

Meg pushed her salad platter aside, leaning her elbows on the table top in the nearly vacant food court.

"So Reed, if you loved Ronald so much, and you obviously did, or *do*, why did you break up with him?"

"I had to."

"But you're crazy about him. I mean, what gives?"

"Meg, you know that I'm on a two-year cycle."

"Yeah, Meg," Noel stirred her tea and added a third sugar as she explained. "All life events work in shifts. Every so often we create or behold a radical change in our lives that literally alters our behavior for the next few years. I, personally, am on a seven-year cycle."

"How do you know?"

"Because at seven I got my front teeth in and kissed Ray Potter in the second grade; at fourteen I went on my first date to the Sadie Hawkin's dance where I asked Billy Winters out; at twenty-one I graduated college and at twenty-eight I met Elliot."

"So what will happen when you turn thirty-five in October?" Meg was intrigued and Noel only looked away and shrugged her shoulders.

"I'm not sure yet. I don't know what the future holds for Elliot and myself. Who knows."

"You're not leaving him, are you?"

"I don't have an appointment to, but it's not the most exotic life we're living here. He does his thing and I do mine. The end. That's why I feel like there's some kind of change in store and there's a new cycle on the horizon, so who knows."

"I have always thought that I could detect pretty major changes in my life about every four years. High school, college, grad school, starting my career, switching jobs." Meg looked wistful as she recalled the changes.

"Then you, my friend, are on the four-year cycle. And at thirty-two? You betcha sister! Times they are a-changin' for you! I'm jealous. Now Reed here, he's on the fast track. We've talked about it in great length."

Reed nodded and looked rather apologetic.

"I'm on the two-year cycle," he conceded. "Everything changes every two years, almost right on the nose. Which, don't get me wrong, change is admirable, but then when things are going good and it's time to change, *that* can be a killer too."

"Wait a minute,wait a minute!" Meg waved her hands stopping him. She squinted. "You mean to tell me that you alter your lifestyle every two years regardless of how things are going for you?"

"I have to."

"That's crazy! Reed! That is *insane*! You aren't on the two-year cycle—you're forcing it! It's one thing to say that it happens naturally! But is that the reason why you broke up with Ronald?"

Reed looked at her with a measure of reluctance and then nodded slowly.

"It's the way things work."

"No, no that's not the way things work, Reed. We talked about this! You said he wasn't the *one*—remember?"

"I did say that." He nodded, looking straight into Meg's eyes.

"And so. Did you *not* tell me everything?"

There was a moment of silence.

"I did tell you true at that time, but then I realized after he was gone that he could have truly been the one." Reed grew misty again as he quietly spoke, barely looking at his friends.

"So why didn't you go after him?"

He didn't answer her.

"You know what this reminds me of?" Meg snapped her fingers. "*Miracle on 34th Street*—you know where the lawyer keeps pursuing Susan's mother and she keeps rejecting him all because of her high rigid standards, kind of like your cycles, Reed, and then he stops one day and she realizes that maybe she felt a little more for him than she'd let on. And chances are that they would have never spoken again or been around each other if it weren't for the court case that forced them to. And then the Santa, and the house and the cane . . . See? Everything works itself out."

Reed and Noel both stared at her. Noel spoke up with a smirk. "That's much more touching than my parallel featuring Pepe Le Pew and that sexy little skunk-cat."

"My life is more like an episode of Roadrunner—when Wiley Coyote thinks he sees the love of his life, but really it's a little stack of dynamite covered with a blond wig and the whole thing explodes when he tries to get his hands on it." Reed looked depressed. "That's a more accurate account of how things usually go with me."

"Do you know what that tells me?" Meg smiled and nodded as if she had just figured it all out.

"That he should stay away from blondes just to be safe?" Noel looked at her mockingly.

"*No*, Noel. It tells me that Reed is afraid to get too close with any one person, therefore he creates this diversion to prevent himself from doing so. And then he seeks out support from his friends, which I *heartily* offered up, so that he can feel less to blame for the whole incident. You are using us for false support to help you overcome your own fear of loving. You are afraid to love."

"Well, coming from the future farm queen, that's good to know." Noel sneered in Meg's direction. She looked at her watch. "Well kids, this therapy session has been enlightening, but I can't afford more than forty minutes at a time."

Noel rose from her seat and discarded her plate in the nearby garbage bin, turning to wish her friends goodbye.

"Don't worry about it, Reed, farm queen's *sort* of right—if it was meant to work out you'll get the signs." She squeezed his shoulder lovingly. "Come on, Reed, lemme see ya glimmer for the love of the gawds."

Reed flashed her a small embarrassed smile.

"There we go. Uh huh! I see glimmering."

Meg smiled from across the table and took in the vision of the two of them together, thinking what an unusual and funny group of friends they formed, the three of them. So unlike in their beliefs but each similarly looking for their own purpose for existence. Meg locked the memory of them like that into her mind hoping she could draw on it later and remember the feeling.

"You know, love and I have never been good friends." Reed and Meg were alone after Noel had gone. He dabbed his glassy eyes and smiled at her, trying to keep his emotions in check. "In fact, I'm not even sure I've been properly acquainted with love in the first place."

"I *love* love." Meg looked at him dreamily. "It's wonderful in theory, isn't it?"

They both giggled and Reed grew serious and quiet again as he leaned toward her.

"God, in another life, wouldn't we be beautiful together? You and me?"

Meg smiled sweetly at their play.

"Our kids would have these dark curls and your blue eyes and this smooth peachy skin, and your hips and calves—"

"My hips and calves?" She laughed at her friend.

"Oh girl, you have the nicest little hips and drop dead shapely calves. I notice all that kind of stuff. Any man with any hormones at all does. And some jealous women." He sipped his drink and shook his head with a sigh. "God, it seems like a sin to deprive this ugly world of the gorgeous kids we could turn out. But alas, I wonder if I'll have any kids ever?"

"Sure you will, Reed. You know you can order your genetics right over the Internet these days—hook up with a surrogate mother, the whole works. Modern technology is . . . fabu."

Reed stopped staring off across the cafe and shot her a wink, bursting into a smile. He leaned across the table and tousled her hair planting a kiss on her forehead. When she saw his eyes again they were twinkling with wonder.

"You, my dear friend, are fabu." He looked at her straight on, clasping both of her hands in his. He lingered a moment longer before gathering his bag and standing to leave. Reed took a few steps away from the table and paused, speaking softly over his shoulder. "Don't just settle, Meggie."

Chapter Nineteen

"**S**o did you get the Amish boy to sign your contract?" Jan brought in the morning's mail and sat on the corner of Nick Carter's desk. He watched as she did so and sighed quietly.

"The Amish boy?"

"That St. John fella."

"Just because he's from Iowa doesn't mean he's Amish."

"Oh, that's Pennsylvania isn't it? Iowa is where they grow potatoes."

"Ohio is where they grow potatoes. In Iowa they grow . . . you know, other things." Carter waved his hand at the pile she was flipping through. "Any of that mail there for me?"

"All of it's for you." Jan slipped a sleek silver letter opener under the flap of the envelope and drew it across, slicing the paper open.

"Do you think I might have a *look* at it in that case, being that it's addressed to me and all?" He folded his arms before his as she dumped the contents of the letter onto the table.

"Here's another book proposal from some guy in . . . Toledo, hmmm, speaking of potatoes. It's about some guy who stumbles onto a blah, blah, blah—oh, another conspiracy theory. That's fresh."

Carter took the letter from her hand as she read from it. He shook his head.

"Who knows, it could have been an original when it was mailed. Tampa postal sucks." He set it in a pile to receive one of his standard returns. "The only way to be sure anyone gets anything here is to send it overnight. At least that way you know it'll get there in two to three days."

"I know what you mean," she nodded, slicing open yet another envelope. "I had a cousin once who sent her fiancée a letter to break it off. She lived in Plant City and he lived in Miami. So he never gets his *Dear Joan* and he shows up at our family Christmas Eve traditional dinner a month later just in time to meet her new husband."

"What an evil woman.   Breaking up with her fiancée in a letter? That's brutal."   He grabbed the letter from her hand before she had a chance to start it. She gave him a disgusted look. "She could have at least sprung for a phone call."

"The subject was *Tampa Postal Sucks*, not *My Cousin's a Bitch*."

"Well the second subject overwhelmed the first in the interesting category."

"You're not interested in love."

"You're right. But I am interested in a good story, and it had potential there for a few moments." He smiled at her before reading the next letter. "It was mildly amusing, but I'm over it now."

"Amusing?"

"Amusing."

Jan picked up a third letter and worked at it diligently with the letter opener.

"*You* are amusing, Nicholas Carter."

"In what way?"

"Hmph. A good lookin' guy like yourself here all the time, never goin' anywhere? You don't do social. You don't do parties. You don't do anything that might put you in the most *remote* contact with the opposite sex." She found that letter boring too, and promptly handed it off to her boss, diving into the stack for another. "I mean, how do you expect to ever settle down, get a little house and crank out the little Nicks? Surely you can't expect these things will happen along the way of the lifestyle you're leadin'."

"And what kind of lifestyle would that be?" He was barely interested, but kept the conversation up for some reason as he read over the letter she'd just passed off to him.

"That of a monk."

"Oh, *you* know religion?" He mused, absently.

"Hey pal, I know a lot of things. But mostly I know about love."

"Yeah, I see you have an abundance of it."

"I may not have love but at least I know what it is! I know where the land of plenty lies, I'm just routing a way to get there."

"What about the man? You plan to pick up a hitchhiker along that route?"

"MYOB."

"Mind *my* own business? And my love life is *your* business? You're the one who brought it all up." He shook his head as he gathered a few more envelopes to open.

"Hey, I have girlfriends who sit up way into the night with me discussing these very issues over turtle brownies and cappuccinos. I am *all* squared away with my ownself. Now, what are we gonna do about you? I know you men don't do that kind of stuff."

"No, we usually like to nosh peanuts and swig beers while throwing the shells at the television screen in some hole in the wall bar downtown. It's an effective means of bonding."

"This is about Susan, isn't it?"

"Who's Susan?" He shrugged raising his eyebrows at the same time. Pulling the rest of the mail from her grasp he smiled and waved her on. "I'll go through the rest of these. Thanks."

"Why don't you talk to me? I'm not going to go *blab* your intimate secrets to the world."

"What's intimate?"

"You just want to pretend we're not speakin' the same language here. But I assure you I'm quite fluent in man-speak. I grew up with four brothers, you know."

"At least you're acknowledging that I'm a man. Last time I knew you were still back there on that men-are-pondscum kick."

"I said Oswell is pondscum. Let me be a little more specific about that." She looked at Carter and rolled her eyes. "I don't know why that quirky little doof has to spend all of his days hanging out in the waiting room trying to get in here to see you about some of the most trivial stuff. I mean, in the age of E-mail, fax, and the old fashioned telephone, what's the point?"

Carter chuckled.

"Maybe he just enjoys the sport of trying to get past you. He is a man of very few hobbies."

"The *man* operates his own publishing company, for heaven's sakes. Why does he spend the better part of his time in this here office? And who's running that place while he's *here* being annoying?"

"Maybe Benny."

"Benny?"

"His dog." Carter looked at her and smiled. "Just an idea."

"Oswell has a dog? He *takes care* of something?" Jan stood up and stacked the mail into place preparing to leave. "Hmph."

"Will you do these letters here for me?" Carter handed her a few rough drafts that needed typing. She took them quietly and headed for the door. Jan paused before she made her exit and turned to see her boss again, a puzzled look on her face.

"I can't believe flaky boy has a dog. Of course I can't believe that God would put a body like that around such a scary personality. How cruel of a joke is that?" She shuddered and walked out the door.

Carter looked back at the paperwork on his desk and began to sort through it quietly. The buzzing of his desk intercom jarred him out of the daze he'd fallen into, and he pressed the receive button. It was Jan's sharp voice again.

"What kind of a dog is it?"

"Wha . . . ? I don't know," Carter looked up again and furrowed his brow. "Some terrier mix or something. Why?"

"I just wanted to know what to visualize when I picture that hilarity."

Carter smiled as he flipped the intercom switch to off.

Chapter Twenty

Meg plopped down upon the suitcase that she'd just crammed full of clothes and struggled as she yanked at the zipper to close the overstuffed thing. The pull was jammed and she cursed it silently as her fingers tugged at it.

"Meg?" Marcus entered the room unexpectedly causing her to emit a little surprised scream and topple from the top of the bulging suitcase, nearly onto the floor. She stood quickly brushing the hair from her eyes as she watched the lid of the case spring back open bursting in a spring loaded action. Meg sighed and looked at it with disgust.

"Yes, honey?"

"What are you doing?"

"What does it look like, honey?"

"We're only going to be gone for three days. Why are you taking all this, this *stuff*?" He waved his hand over the pile that was now loosely strewn across the bed.

"Well, I didn't know what the weather would be like."

"Why don't you just watch the weather channel and see?"

"Well, that's just it, the weather channel says that it's going to be one thing one day and another thing the next day so we'll likely need both shorts and pants, of course I'll wear skirts, but then I'll need a sweater for that in between day when it will be chillier and then there's a question of swimwear—"

"Honey, we're only going to be there three days! And if it will save you space, know that I'm not going to put these fleshy white legs in shorts or swim trunks. So that ought to make room for a few more of, of . . ." Marcus pulled out a continual succession of skirts and blouses until he got down to several pairs of shoes at the bottom of the bag. He turned to her with a puzzled look on his face. "I don't even see any of my stuff in here."

"It's in that bag over there."

Marcus looked at the smaller piece of luggage already neatly set before the doorway of the room and back at the fiasco on the bed that Meg was now trying to repack.

"Why all this? For three days?"

"Well, aside from the weather thing, I dress according to my mood and there is no channel that can forecast that."

"I'll go with that."

"If I'm in a playful mood perhaps I'll want something casual, like a little sweater or cap-sleeved shirt. You know." She talked casually as she folded the clothing items again and rearranged them in the suitcase, packing them together firmly. "Then if I'm in a more serious mood I might need this little dress here. Or maybe these dark pants for the evening. It all depends, everything is relative to my feelings that day."

"And what about these?" He picked up a pair of three quarter length white pants and looked at them oddly as he held them up. "What kind of mood would you be in to wear something like this?"

"Oh, that's body clothing, not mood related." She shrugged nonchalantly as she took them from him and folded them neatly, placing them in the bag. "You know, sometimes you have something that's flattering and you wear it only for that reason. That's all."

"Oh, I see." He sat on the edge of the bed. Meg glanced at him occasionally as he watched her finish the chore. He appeared to be deep in thought. "So, if this whole thing comes through the way you want it to, do you think we can expect to hear wedding bells in the next couple of months?"

Meg arched an eyebrow at him, swallowed hard and gave a little smile.

"Well, I don't know about the next few months . . . maybe in the next year though."

"I suppose I've waited this long." He smiled at her. Meg stopped what she was doing and came around to his side of the bed, and sat down. They were both quiet.

"Marcus, do you ever feel that all things happen for a reason? That fate plays a greater hand in all our lives than we credit it for?"

"What do you mean?"

"I mean with love and all."

"With love? I'm not following." He smiled, wondering what she was up to this time.

"I mean, do you think that love is based on chemistry or biology— or even astrology?" Her eyes met his now and he could see how serious she had become.

"Well, I suppose there are certain biological factors that cause people to behave the way they do. I think that chemistry is a nice idea."

"A nice *idea*?" She laughed. "I'm talking about *true love* here."

"True love is a nice idea too, honey, but too many people get the wrong idea about what true love really is." Marcus was careful. "As much as we would like to think that cupid determines our love destiny, in reality, whirlwind relationships believed to be contrived by fate statistically burn out over the course of the first three years after the honeymoon period is over—when they actually have to learn to *live* with each other. Fate is overrated. Practicality is where it's at."

"And astrology?"

"Nonexistent." He tousled her hair and smiled. "They're all nice ideas, Meg, but the truth is, lovestruck and dumbstruck are nearly synonymous. You can't believe everything you see in movies or read in books, because if you did, you'd just be setting yourself up for a world of hurt as the quest continued for the perfect mate."

"So you don't believe in happily ever after?"

"I wouldn't go that far. I mean, look at us. We've got staying power, that's what it's about. The maturity to enter into a relationship with no surprises, only honesty, and mutual caring. That's where the real stuff is."

Meg looked at him and then nodded slowly. She looked back at the suitcase to the last items she'd placed there. Finally she stood and removed a few things, pulled the zipper shut and lugged the bag over near the other.

Meg picked up the leftover items on the bed and began to hang them back into the closet. She stretched her arms high above her head, standing on her toes to reach the top bar. Her mind was still reeling with the events of the past few days, and she began to speak again.

"Do you look at calves?"

"Well, sure. At the spring market every year I buy new livestock, you know that."

Meg emerged from the closet and looked at him blankly.

"No, Marcus, I'm talking about these." She raised her flannel pantleg and held her bare leg up for him to see. "Do you like my *calves*—my *legs*?"

"Well, I do . . ." He was hesitant and maybe even a little afraid to answer, not knowing where she was going.

"How come you've never told me?"

"Well, why should I? There's nothing wrong with those legs—heck, there's nothing wrong with any part of you."

"Then why don't you say it?"

"I suppose I just figured that you knew." Marcus shrugged. "You know how I am, Meg, if you walked out and your skirt was tucked into the back of your pantyhose, I'd say something. Or if you had your shirt on backwards or inside out or something, I'd say so. I'm that kind of guy."

"So, you only point out what's wrong and never think to, oh say, throw out a random compliment? For just no reason. You know—nice hair Meg, nice dress Meg. Nice ass Meg."

"Meg? What's gotten into you lately?"

"I just want to understand these things, so that I can effectively communicate with you. And these are things I don't understand. I want to resolve these issues." She plopped down on the bed beside him again and waited for his reply.

"These were never issues before, Meg. Not last year, or two years ago—or three. Why now, all of a sudden?"

"I just want to know everything about the man who wants to spend the rest of his life with me, is that too much to ask?" Her voice was rising with growing impatience and she looked away quickly as to keep having him see the anger in her eyes. "Two people can live together, and yet, not really understand each other, know what the other needs, that kind of thing. I just want you to know that once in while, I would like it if you would just say, hey, nice outfit, you look great, you smell great, have I ever told you what great calves you have?"

Marcus burst into small laughter.

"What kind of man goes around telling his wife—"

"Fiancee," she interjected immediately.

"Okay, *fiancee.*" He shot her a look of bewilderment before he continued. "What kind of man goes around throwing out compliments like *hey—nice calves there* or *your calves look wonderful today.* I mean, what's this all about, really?"

"Maybe the kind of man who does that is the kind of man who cares to notice those things about the woman he loves, and cares enough to tell her so that she can get a little boost now and again. Maybe *that's* the kind of man. Don't you think?"

"Meg, I don't want to fight with you here. Do you want to fight with me?" He actually sounded scared.

"No, Marcus, *honey,* I don't want to fight with you." Her voice was stern. "I just want to hear something come out of your mouth regarding my appearance occasionally that's somewhat positive and not just that something is unusual about the way I look. Not just, you know—hey Meg, your arm is where your leg is supposed to be today—or, your feet are both hooked to the same ankle today, better take a look at that!"

"Meg—"

"Well, Marcus!" She stood and walked toward the hallway in a fashion resembling ranting. "I'm just saying, aside from this practicality business, the ho-hum soup might fare better when peppered with an occasional compliment! That's all!"

The door slammed behind her after she was gone, leaving Marcus sitting on the bed still, a stunned look upon his face. He waited to see if she would come back but she didn't. At last he persuaded himself to move to get ready for bed, a place that he would probably go alone that night after that unexpected outburst from his normally serene fiancée. He began to talk to himself as he pulled his pajamas from the dresser drawer. He mimicked her irate sing-song voice as he chastised himself aloud. "Marcus, you really put your head up your ass tonight."

Chapter Twenty-one

"So, your flight leaves at ten from Des Moines?" Noel took another bite of her breakfast omelet, and waited for her forlorn-looking friend to answer. She only nodded. "You should have ordered this, it's the best."

"It's oozing with all that cheese and stuff." Meg shuddered. "Besides, weren't you going to go on some big diet with Reed for the new year? That doesn't look terribly low fat."

"Hey, Miss Stick, I am on a diet." She nodded her head confidently. "I'll have you know that the bagel you're eating there is on the list of *no-nos* too, so before you go off giving me the *schpeel*, look at what you're doing to your ownself there."

"A bagel has four grams of fat and I'm eating it with lite cream cheese. It's a complex carbohydrate."

"It's a bad carbohydrate. Bagels promote water retention, so while the body is trying to flush toxins, it's grabbing all the things around it as fast as it can." Noel nodded. "It's a virtual little calorie sucker. It's in the book."

"Oh, please."

"Now proteins, proteins are where it's at. They work together to burn each other out and raise the metabolism. You'll note my selection—egg omelet with ham and a side of bacon. Proteins, sister."

Meg squinted at her and shook her head at the harebrained justification she was hearing.

"So how do you think you can actually lose weight eating like that—with all that fat and oil?"

"Well, I am going to suppose that the grease just lubes the whole system and the food just slips right on through unnoticed by the body. Huh? Sound good?" Noel smiled broadly and stabbed another large bite of the cheesy omelet.

"Sounds crazy."

"So you'll be gone for three days. Elliot said you dropped the dog by this morning. Naturally he'll be in good hands. My kid will be riding him like a horse by the time you get back."

"Thanks again."

"No problem." Noel chomped away and chased her food down with a long drink of iced tea.She swallowed and blotted her lips, looking at her friend now. "So why the long face? You and whatshisname get into an argument or something?"

"Not really an argument," Meg set her bagel down and looked at it carefully while she was thinking. "More like a little tiff."

"Oh, a *tiff.*"

"So to speak." Meg ran her finger along the rim of her coffee mug and raised her eyes finally. "Noel, do you believe that practical love has more staying power than romantic love?"

"Staying power, that's how he justifies his boring life huh? Well," Noel crunched into her bacon glancing upward, thoughtful, as she pondered her reply. "I don't think there's such a thing as practical love."

"How do you figure?" Meg eyed her wearily as she sighed deeply. She should have suspected that Noel and Marcus would, once again, be on opposite sides of the fence.

"I think if one can describe their relationship as being based on practical love, that it's not *true* love, but rather compromise. Don't get me wrong. Compromise is good, but compromise is *better* if it's dessert to a main course of romantic love."

"But what if one falls in love in a whirlwind sort of way and gets so caught up in it that they don't realize that they can't compromise where their differences are concerned?"

"You and whatshisname not seeing eye to eye these days about the everyday stuff?"

"The everyday stuff we have mastered. We get along fabulously—wonderfully. It's a very comfortable relationship not to be tampered with. I'm not necessarily asking these questions in relation to my own life.I just want your take on it, that's all."

"Um, sure." Noel rolled her eyes and handed her nearly empty break-fast platter to the waitress who'd returned with drink refills. She tore open a package of sugar and stirred it into her iced tea, looking at Meg again. "Okay, it's true that some people fall madly in love and never learn to get along, and it just plain old doesn't work out. Compromise is an art that not everyone gains the mastery to. It's a lot of work."

"So sometimes compromise is more valuable and practical than pas-sionate love?"

"More practical? Of course it is, but practical is for wimps! Valuable? Never. What value is there in practicality? No surprises. No fun.I mean—if you *value* that sort of thing, okay then, but that's not for you."

Meg sipped her coffee and listened, appearing a little confused.

"What about in *The Preacher's Wife*, you know, their practical love just needed a little zing to revive it and the outcome was just as wonderful."

"Marcus is a farmer, that's hardly a preacher."

"You know what I mean."

"So let's check the scoreboard—we have passionate love that works, whirlwind love that fizzles and then a third kind of love that I know about." Noel paused momentarily. "That would be the kind of relation-ship that is sturdy and long-lasting, but never really passionate. It's not that soul-gripping true love."

"I'm in love with Marcus."

"You're in *like* with Marcus." Noel corrected. "And I thought you said this wasn't about you and whatshisname?"

Meg shrugged as she glanced at her watch. She picked up her purse and began to search for her wallet.

"I better get going. It takes half an hour to get to the airport. I don't want Marcus to get nervous." She smiled.

"Wouldn't want to quake the steady." Noel shot her a look.

Meg handed the bill to the waitress and they put their coats on en route to the parking lot in silence. Noel caught Meg's arm before she'd reached her car.

"I want you to promise me that you're not going to do anything crazy like go to the big city and elope while you're there or something." She had a nervous look on her face as she spoke. Meg laughed.

"No fear."

"I'm *serious* Meg, and don't go getting any baby lust while you're there either. You're in the start of a new life cycle here, don't do anything funny to mess it up." Noel pulled her friend to her and they embraced in the blustery parking lot as little puffs of mist emitted from their mouths with their words.

"I won't."

"I'm serious."

"I'm okay."

"Well, you're working on it." Noel patted her shoulder and smiled. "Have a good trip and call me."

"I will." Meg smiled through chattering teeth. "I love you Noel."

"Love you too."

The friends clasped gloved hands.

"Who knows, maybe you'll go to the big city and find the one."

Meg was intrigued and for some reason found herself asking about it further.

"Describe him to me . . . the one, that is."

Her friend was quiet for a moment as she stood there studying Meg's eyes carefully. Finally she began.

"You think you'll know him when you see him, but you might not. You might suspect it's him, but then you'll know."

"How?"

"The touch of his hand, the look in his eye . . . Maybe he'll say something totally stupid or make a complete idiot out of himself." Noel chuckled softly. "But you'll know."

"I don't know if I understand that."

"Let me put it into your terminology. You know in *While You Were Sleeping*, that movie with Sandra Bullock? I know it wasn't exactly your standard Christmas fare, but it took place during that time of the year and that surely counts for something—so stay with me." Noel waved her hand airily. "So, you remember when Bill Pullman was walking Sandra Bullock home and he falls on the ice right in front of her apartment? I mean, she never even really had her sights set on this guy because she thought she was so head over heels with Bill Pullman's preppy comatose brother. But *then* when she goes to help him up and they touch . . . well, she just knew."

They were quiet for a moment as they stood there, trembling in the cold just outside of their cars in the lot still.

"You've heard that expression that says I'll probably be at the train station when my ship finally comes in? That's me." Meg chuckled now and Noel joined in a little.

"Take care, sweetie."

"You too."

Noel turned to go as her friend unlocked her own car door and got inside preparing to close it quickly. She impulsively called out, stopping her.

"Meggie." She paused. "It will happen."

Chapter Twenty-two

arcus St. John and Meghan Laine entered the offices of Bankson, Laughton and Carter Literary Associates a little after three o'clock that day. The exotic looking woman behind the desk took their names and asked them to be seated as she pressed the intercom to inform Carter that his appointment had arrived.

The duo had only waited seconds before the doors parted and the agent emerged, walking over to greet them, cordially. Meg stood beside Marcus as the introductions were being made.

Nick Carter seemed to Meg to be a businessman in every sense of the word. His naturally waving dark hair was worn conservatively short and he was clean shaven and stood with a posture that quietly stated confidence. Or maybe it was sternness, she couldn't tell right away. But clearly he was more interested in the book than the person behind the pencil as he breezed over the obligatory *how-do-you-dos* and *are-you-enjoying-the-weather* standards. His blue eyes lit on her own only briefly as he shook her hand, lingering perhaps a bit longer, or maybe that was in her mind too. Mr. Carter was simply talking in his easy, confident way, and just happened to be shaking her hand at the same time, and how rude would it be to just yank her hand back while he was doing so?

The agent averted his focus to the one he was surely most interested in, the talent behind a potential best selling book, and, in his eyes, Meg was just the other. Nothing more. How ironic that she'd waited for this very moment all her writing life and was now being asked to wait in the lobby while the men discussed the business aspects of the book before she was allowed to join them.

In her quiet haze, she obliged as Marcus shot her a look at the same time, perhaps internally begging her to protest the request. But she was powerless thanks to her nerves that suddenly directed that she do as she was asked. She took her seat, crossed her legs, and clasped her hands, watching as the two disappeared behind the solid double doors that had probably cost as much as her entire kitchen.

Jan looked up at her. "There's some magazines there on the table. It gets to be a long wait sometimes."

Meg nodded and picked up the closest one simply to have something to hide behind. She flipped it open as she waited there.

The telephone at the reception desk rang and Jan casually punched a single button to answer it, never removing her eyes from the magazine she was so engrossed in.

"Bankson, Laughton and Carter. Good afternoon." Her eyes raised after a few seconds of silence. "Hello?"

She pressed the button of the telephone headset. The telephone sounded again a few moments later and she answered a second time.

"Bankson, Laughton and Carter, good afternoon." She paused. "Did you call here a second ago? What do you mean there's a delivery? Bring it on up, then. I can barely hear you, can you *speak* up?"

Meg watched Jan tapping her pen on the desk before her, clearly growing frustrated.

"Well, you are the delivery boy, deliver it! I'm not walking downstairs to get it. No, no, no! You bring it up to me! That's how the system works." She rolled her eyes and looked at Meg, shaking her head. Meg smiled politely at the woman's manner and continued to pretend to read. "If I come down there, you better tip me! Mr. Carter is expecting it? Then perhaps I should put you through to him and he can come downstairs to get it. All right, all right. Cool your tool. I'll be right there."

The woman unplugged the telephone headset from the main telephone and twirled it coolly as she strode across the room and pressed herself against the wall, out of the view of anyone exiting the elevator. She waited and Meg watched on with anticipation and mild amusement.

A tall and rather handsome man with sandy hair and a wonderful Roman nose emerged from the elevator, and she watched as he carefully peered around the lobby. Quickly, in a fashion that contradicted his clearly expensive attire and suave demeanor, the man hiked across the way and through the chairs in the waiting area. The look on his face was one of triumph as he eagerly reached for the doorknob on the same double doors that Mr. Carter and Marcus had entered earlier. His optimistic look was sharply deflated by the terse sounding woman's voice as Jan stepped out of the shadow of the lobby and onto the rug that the well dressed man had practically sprinted over.

"Freeze, Joker!" She called to him. He obediently raised his hands in defeat, his shoulders slumping forward and chin lowering automatically to his chest. Sighing deeply, he turned to see her. "Just where do you think you're going, *delivery boy?*"

"I need to see Carter—it's vital to our future endeavors." He was almost whining.

"Well you aren't going to have a future when I finish robbing you of it should you try another lame stunt like that again." She was unflappable as she spoke to the man in a degrading manner that made Meg almost pity him. "Sit down, funny boy."

"Oh come on! You are *ice!*"

"And you are a pain in my ice. Sit down." She plugged her headset back into the system and casually sat behind the desk again, issuing a second order when it looked as though he were going to protest. "Sit!"

Looking defeated, the man took a seat a few down from Meg. She cast him a look of compassion and buried her nose once again in the magazine she was holding, wondering what the men inside were talking about and hoping that Marcus wasn't failing miserably in his effort to convince the agent that he was, indeed, a competent and capable writer.

The distinguished looking man seated there began to tap his toes in a rather annoying way and she looked at him quickly again. He nodded at her as he rested his forearms on his knees, sitting in a slump, continuing the annoyance until Jan finally called for him to cease.

"Stop your tap dancing."

He halted immediately, his eyes going right to the woman behind the desk who refused to look at him. He raised the toe of his sleek black dress shoes one last time and lowered it suddenly to the floor, emitting the echoing sound of a single loud slap. Her eyes raised into a hostile, low glare that she dealt straight at him.

"Do you *need* something?" She growled in her raspy voice.

"Yes, yes in fact I do! I need to speak to Carter!"

"I'm aware of that. It's a system we have here. This is a waiting room and you are waiting. See how that works?"

"Oh come on," He ran his fingers through his slightly wavy hair and stared at her with pleading eyes. "At least you can tell me if the client got here yet."

"What client?"

"Iowa boy, the bean farmer or whatever he is."

"Well, yes, in fact he did arrive."

"Then he's in there?"

"Yes, I believe he is."

The man sighed and shook his head impatiently.

"Listen here, woman, I need in that office."

"Don't try your boyhood fantasies out on me. I am your only means for getting into that coveted territory, and calling me *woman* isn't buying you any points here."

He sat back in his seat and nervously tapped his fingers on the arm of the chair looking around.

"You got a look at him, then?" He prodded.

"Yes, I did."

"And did he look, well, you know?"

"Could you be a little more specific?" Jan lead him on sneakily.

"You know—did he look, you *know*?" The man twinkled his fingers.

"You mean, did Mr. St. John look gay?" She smiled smugly at the man now and nodded toward Meg. "I don't know, why don't you ask Mrs. St. John?"

The man slapped his hands across his own face, hiding his eyes, barely having the nerve to look her in the eye. At the same time to office doors parted and Carter stepped into the lobby and motioned for Meg to join them. Along the way his eyes fell across the strange man sitting there with his hands across his eyes. He nearly grimaced.

"Mrs. St. John? Won't you join us?" He nodded at her and then looked at the only other waiting person and lowered his voice some. "And . . . Mr. Oswell, also."

Meg's eyes shot straight to the man sitting near her, widening with amusement and wonder. *Oswell? J.T. Oswell!* She pretended to not be overly impressed as she was as she stood to enter the office, Oswell following closely behind her. Meg cast an occasional glance in his red-cheeked direction but he stayed quiet.

Once inside, Meg looked around the luxurious office. Its high ceilings and impeccably restored antique arches that had been modernized beautifully. She was impressed as she scanned the tall vertical blinds that hung at the windows and the leather upholstered high back chairs. Carter touched one in an unspoken invitation for her to be seated. She smiled a little as she did as expected and waited patiently for someone to speak. J.T. Oswell sauntered over to the corner of Carter's desk and leaned against it.

"There are *seats*, Oswell," the agent hinted. The publishing mogul complied reluctantly and the meeting began. "I've outlined a plan of attack for the market we're aiming for. Also, Mr. Oswell would like to tell you a little more about the special press that your book is going to be published in. Mr. Oswell?"

Oswell rose from his place and eagerly shook Marcus' hand with a broad smile. "I'd like to welcome you on board. This venture of ours, I'm sure, will be both rewarding and profitable." He sat down again and nodded in Meg's direction lightly. "I already had the opportunity to *sort of* meet your lovely wife."

The publisher stopped briefly to clear his throat nervously before continuing. "As Carter mentioned to you before, your premier book will be published in a different format—it will be square as opposed to the traditional style. Hardcover as well, a beautiful jacket that I have waiting for you to see at the Publishing House—did you bring a picture, by the way?"

Marcus nodded.

"Good! Splendid! I think you'll be happy with the huge publicity push we're going to give this thing, Mr. St. John—book signings, workshops, reviews. You're in for quite a ride."

"I'm going to be doing all that?" Marcus looked aghast.

"All that and *more*! Your book is, well, very insightful in a way that a lot of women will appreciate. It's a rare talent to be able to probe the female mind in the way that you have, expressing their concerns, thoughts, fantasies. It's sensational!"

"It is a little sensational, isn't it?" Marcus smiled weakly.

"Indeed. Women will love the fact that such a mind exists. They will find you compassionate and wonderful. I have a feeling, Mr. St. John, that this is the next big thing. Do you feel good, Mr. St. John?"

"I do."

"Do you really?" Oswell pushed him.

"Oswell, he said he feels great." Carter looked embarrassed.

"I want to hear it from the next best seller!"

"I feel pretty good." Marcus said, the level of enthusiasm in his voice rising some.

"Do you?"

"I do."

"Then say it! Say *I feel great!* This book kicks some serious ass and we're going to push it in the way that it deserves! Through the glass ceiling!"

"I feel good!" Marcus was obediently following the crusader like a thoughtless cult member and Meg raised an eyebrow in a surprised way. "I feel *great!*"

"Okay, well, enough of that now," Meg heard her own voice suddenly and was a little startled that her mouth had overridden her common sense which told her to merely sit quietly. She smiled faintly.

"Yes, my thoughts exactly." Carter looked at the two men through narrow eyes. He opened the book before him and handed Marcus a pen, turning the papers toward him. "I need you to sign this here if you agree to this advance payment. Residual payments will follow, naturally."

Marcus' eyes lit up like a candle when he saw the patterned paper that lay before him, and instantly the pen was in his hand and he was signing away.

"Marcus, honey, did you *read* what you were signing there?" Meg inquired, meekly.

"Yes, yes I did, Meg, and it had quite a few zeros in it." Marcus set the pen aside after signing and tucked the check into his pocket. Meg's lips parted and she sat back in her seat waiting for whatever would happen next. "Where do we go from here, Carter?"

"Well, we finalize cover operations and get this thing up and running. We can be on the shelves by the end of next month and the push will begin."

"Oswell Publishing House has arranged to sponsor you on your own website that will allow the public to read portions of your sensational best seller. There are the Barnes & Noble book signings here in Miami, New York, Chicago, St. Louis, Dallas, LA, San Francisco. Are you up for it? We've got a lot of ground to cover in a little bit of time. Then when that two-week sweep is complete, we'll evaluate book sales and see if you have any interview requests. They will contact us."

"Interviews?"

"Yeah, you know, some local, some not. The author of the Rachel Stone mysteries did the *Today Show* last month. Who knows?"

"Who knows." Marcus echoed the sentiment. His eyes were twinkling and Meg wondered what was going through his mind. Probably fear, the poor soul. She smiled.

"Naturally you'll stop over to the publishing house today or tomorrow and sign some papers, see the spec, that kind of thing." J.T. rambled on.

"Naturally."

Carter glanced at his watch and stood up and clapped his hands together once.

"Great then, it's settled. Thank you for stopping in, Oswell." Carter nodded toward the door. "We'll get hold of you tomorrow for that tour."

Oswell stood there smiling.

"Thank you for stopping by. It's a shame you have to be going so soon." Carter tried a second time.

"I'm fine on time, Carter." He waved his hand with a smile.

Carter waved his finger through the air and spiraled it downward in an exaggerated motion that said it might be considering landing on the intercom button. Oswell immediately jumped to his feet.

"All-righty, well, I must be going." The publisher glared at the man behind the desk and turned next to Marcus. "It was a pleasure meeting you, Mr. St. John. We'll all do dinner tomorrow night, how would that be?"

"That sounds good." Marcus nodded with growing comfort.

"Great! Until then." Oswell paused at the door as if he were dreading entering the lobby area. Meg watched him carefully as he slowly opened the door and fled quickly. She turned back now toward the agent who was shrugging with a sigh.

"He's an eccentric fellow, great publisher though."

"I'm an avid reader of the material that his house puts out," Meg said politely.

"You're a big reader then, Mrs. St. John?" Carter sat back more comfortably in his seat now that the man was gone. "What kinds of things co you enjoy?"

"All sorts of things. I do read the Rachal Stone series, some thrillers. I like the romance, however—I just find them . . . "

"Compelling?" he prompted.

"Lacking, actually, is what I was going to say. Of course that's how I view a majority of the romance novels I read. So formulaic. Rigid in format. Typical, predictable." She looked off to the side as if she were deep in thought, speaking quietly.

"You should have this job. You can't believe the stuff I get here day in and day out, over and over. It's a nightmare."

"A lot of things come to your desk, then?"

"A lot of crap, mostly. Two to three hundred pages at a time."

"Two to three hundred pages that someone poured all their heart and soul into," she interjected, catching the agent by surprise. He smiled a little.

"Some of the stuff I read, Mrs. St. John, seems like it poured straight from a can of condensed soup as opposed to someone's *heart and soul*. It's the same old recipe but some fresh writer is always trying to make it their own homemade. It's pathetic."

"Trite?"

"Very much so."

"So you send them a standard letter offering them a bit of undeserved encouragement, but just enough to keep them hammering away at their typewriter for the next ten years to no avail?" She smirked softly. "*That's* a bit trite if you ask me."

Carter studied the woman before him carefully, listening as she spoke in a voice laced with sarcasm. Not many people outside of the business had the nerve to speak to him in such a way, particularly the wife of a man to whom he'd just offered a generous contract and a sizable advance check. Finally a little smile came to his lips and he actually looked rather apologetic.

"I'm sorry, Mr. Carter." She beat him to it. "I got carried away with myself. That was rude of me."

"That's quite all right. I was carried right along with you there for a moment. Where I don't recommend a career in politics, your lobbyist personality might lend a clear advantage where other people's concerns lay. Please take that as a . . . compliment, I think."

Meg's cheeks flushed and she said nothing else as she sat there, not really paying attention as the business meeting proceeded without her input. She wasn't sure that she liked Mr. Nick Carter. Not one little bit.

Chapter Twenty-three

"So was I good, or what?' Marcus jabbed his elbow playfully into Meg's side as she carefully hung her clothes on the closet rack of the lavish motel suite they'd been given. She shot him a smile and continued with the chore.

"Not too shabby, for a beanfarmer."

"A what?" He looked at her strangely for an explanation, but she turned suddenly and slid her arms around his waist, tucking her head under his chin. Instead of pursuing the comment, he took this opportunity to hold her there, one of the rare times recently that they weren't bickering about something trivial. Marcus sighed with relief and smiled. Finally he drew back to look into her eyes. "So what now?"

"Let's go to the beach." She grabbed his hand. "Come on!"

"It's getting late and we haven't eaten yet." He was whining and she pretended to slug his arm, a look of dejection gracing her face.

"We can eat in Iowa though! Lake Okaboji doesn't quite compare to the Atlantic Ocean."

"Meg, I don't want to wear swimming trunks, I already told you that."

"You don't have to! We're going for a walk along the beach, that's all."

"January in Florida, everyone dresses warmer than we are *now*. We'd stand out like sore touristy thumbs if we were to kick off our shoes and go for a walk in shorts along the shore!"

"Who cares, Marcus? We're in *Florida*! Let's enjoy it."

Marcus hesitated before finally conceding with a little smile that showed his annoyance at her persistence. He nodded slightly and she grabbed her purse and bounded out the door.

Forty minutes later, the couple found themselves on Clearwater Beach which was still buzzing with other vacationing couples like themselves, walking along the shore, dressed quite alike. Meg smugly gave Marcus that "I told you so" look as she clasped his hand and began to walk lazily through the sand.

Its fine, powdery whiteness seemed to disintegrate under each step, causing her to occasionally lose her balance as she marveled at its wonder. White sand and blue ocean melting into an even bluer sky. The tide was coming in and each wave made a peaceful sound as they journeyed toward the Big Pier. Meg stopped and looked out over it all, watching the seagull antics as they darted to the sand picking up anything left over from the tourists that might be edible. Salt air filled her head and she closed her eyes and breathed it all in, exhaling slowly, enjoying the sensation. She smiled at Marcus.

They stood there taking in the beauty of it all. Meg was quietly observing the others who were also enjoying the evening. A young couple clad in swimwear made their way along the water's edge, their hands melted together as they lost themselves in their own conversation. She enjoyed their laughter and watched them until they crossed paths with another couple who were leaning into each other as if they couldn't get close enough. A very small child went padding down the beach before them and the duo smiled at each other as they watched her run on. Then a slightly older couple walked along side by side, not touching each other, their arms perfectly content to swing idly at their sides, their hands never even brushing. They were dressed more formally, as if they'd just come from dinner and were going to make a concerted effort to be a little freer with themselves. They carried their shoes and walked rigidly. Meg's eyes roamed next to their faces, especially the woman's. Worn and tired. Humorless, with frown lines. And his, merely distant.

"Meg?" Marcus' voice startled her. He spoke quietly, smiling almost shyly. "Thank you for not correcting Mr. Carter today when he introduced you as Mrs. St. John. It felt nice."

Meg's eyes felt dry and tight and she wasn't sure she could blink them again. They stood beside each other gazing out over the ocean that had taken a navy blue cast as the sky darkened and the stars began to appear. The breeze had picked up as well and some of the other tourists had begun to leave. Meg focused on a couple sitting on the beach down the way. The sound of the woman's laughter rang out through the air as her silhouette nestled into the side of the one sitting next to her. An arm extended and draped itself around the woman's shoulders as they giggled on, sharing something that Meg could only guess to be terribly intimate.

It was a perfect night. Her skin was alive with goosebumps at the growing chill and she watched as a ship in the distance slid through the darkness.

Meg wiggled her fingers inside Marcus' grip and looked at him for a moment, watching as he stared off across the water and star-dotted sky. Suddenly she found herself fighting the empty feeling that had begun to consume her.

Chapter Twenty-four

Nick Carter checked his watch again. Eight fifteen PM. He sighed as he loosened his necktie that seemed to have grown tighter over the past few hours. He messed with it for only a moment before pulling it off altogether and chucking it into his briefcase. He glared again at the fax machine as it sat there quiet and still. He'd not gotten the forms he'd been waiting the better part of the evening for, and now, he was giving up.

He walked around the office flipping off the lights until the spacious office was lit only dimly by his desk lamp. He thumbed through a stack of messages that Jan had left for him before she'd gone home earlier in the day. Three were from J.T. but the fourth made him take a closer look. It had a silver key taped to it. Carter peeled it off and quickly recognized it to be that of his own apartment. As well, the handwriting was a rich large looping style that he immediately knew to be Kirstin's.

Nick—

Add me to the list as one of the ones that got away. I hope you find what you're looking for, though I'm not sure you know either. I sincerely wish you only the best.

Love, Kirstin

He stared at it stonily before he folded it into four quarters and tucked it into his jacket pocket. He stared at the key lying there on the desk until the phone rang and he shifted his focus to it.

Two rings. Three . . . four.

He was reluctant to answer it for fear that the day could actually manage to get worse, but finally did.

"Carter—Ted Bankson here. What's this I hear about Jay Steele's book being rejected by Parker Publishing? Why is this the first time I'm hearing anything about any trouble at all? What are you doing about it?"

It could still get worse, yes.

"I'm letting this one ride, Ted." Carter covered the mouthpiece and sighed loudly, waiting for his senior partner to blow a gasket, an experience he was well versed in by now.

"What the hell do you mean you're letting it *ride*? Eight of the last ten novels he cranked out hit the number one spot on the Times list—I think this deserves our complete attention! A publisher doesn't just reject a talent like Jay Steele! And his agent doesn't just let him take it in the—"

"They do when the book isn't quality." Carter cut off the man's potential string of swear words he was equally acquainted with.

"Quality? Explain what your idea of quality is then, Carter."

"Jay Steele's manuscript was unmoving, weak, not compelling, poorly constructed, had a plot about as strong as the back of a spineless jellyfish, and flat, underdeveloped characters with the intelligence level of nil and the allure of a case of head lice."

There was silence on the line.

"Thank you for that colorful review." The partner smirked. "Parker's editor could do nothing for it?"

"Only if he wanted to completely rewrite it, then there's a little issue of plagiarism, so I thought it best just to ride it out and forget about it."

"There are deadlines to be met. Jay Steele has an audience that needs to be fed."

"And our continually pumping him up about this starving audience has turned one of our glitzy pool of number one clients into a number one asshole." Carter's words were steady and firm. "Jay Steele thinks he doesn't need to try anymore. He thinks that he's made it now, paid his dues, and the publishing world can kiss his low rent, misspelling, foul mouthed, unmotivated ass. I wouldn't pay for it—and I wouldn't expect anyone else to do it either."

"Did you secure his advance?"

"He lost the advance," Carter mumbled.

"He has an advance coming, it's in his contract."

"When there's no book, there's no money. Period."

"Will this go to court? How are we going to handle it if Steele takes his representation elsewhere?"

"The man deserves what he gets. He deserves a good spanking and a long spell in a time out chair. That's the caliber of the spoiled clients we're dealing with these days, a characteristic of this firm that is about to make me run screaming madly through the streets pulling my hair out by the handfuls." Carter tried to calm his voice. He composed himself and continued. "If Steele walks, we let him. We've got exclusive rights to everything he has in print to this point, and I can tell you that if what I read from him last week was any indicator of what's to come, we've got the only goods on this guy."

There was a pause.

"I hope you know what you're doing, Carter," the older man grumbled in a less than enthusiastic way. The agent walked around his desk and snapped his briefcase shut, preparing to run for the door as soon as he could bring the conversation to an end.

"I think it's a safe bet at this point."

"How's everything else going?"

"Fine. How's Cancun?"

"It's the only place to be." Ted Bankson's voice sounded more relaxed suddenly and even held a hint of laughter in it.

And the only place you have been for the better part of the last five years.

Carter smiled and rolled his eyes knowingly. He'd been running the agency nearly single-handedly for quite some time now and it was wearing him down. "That's good to hear, old friend."

"And something else that's good to hear, but you didn't hear it from me." Ted's voice sounded sneaky in a most childlike way and Carter had to strain to hear as he continued in a secretive tone. "Judy Armando just split from Sanderson, her agent."

"Oh yeah? What for?" Parting ways with an agent was a serious matter that rarely occurred, and Carter listened with the first interest he'd had thus far.

"It's unclear at this point, but what's not unclear, my friend and dear, dear partner, is that she is in constant contact with her good friend Claire Sodey, who has only raved about her author-agent relationship with you. So you can guess what the rumor is there."

"I'm full-up over here. I can only take clients that can pull it off with minimal assistance. I've heard some things about Judy Armando's latest stuff—"

"Latest, schmatest! Nonsense! Judy Armando made Oprah's book list last year!"

"Yeah, but did you see her take that little white mutt on the show when they interviewed her? What's up with that? That's what I'm talking about here, what's wrong with these big name writers?"

"Carter, you've seen that woman and she's, well . . . Maybe she took the dog to have someone to upstage."

They both laughed lightly at the old man's humor.

"Well, I've about had my fill of big names with petty requests whenever they visit or interview or publish." Carter rattled on incessantly, waving his hand as if the old man could actually see him doing so. "They want only green M & Ms, or Pure Spring Bottled water—not to be confused with *distilled* bottled water. Or soft lights on camera to hide their big noses or little frown wrinkles. Why can't they spend some of those high dollar commercial book profits on a little laser surgery for that stuff instead of bugging the heck out of the rest of the world to bend to their whims? These things . . . are mysteries to me."

Now Bankson laughed heartily, something that caused Carter to smile broadly, as it was rare to get such a reaction from the senior partner.

"Pesky as they may be, it only takes a handful of their self centered sort to build an empire and ensure the comfortable retirement of ourselves and our own kids."

"Yeah, well, at the overtime rate I'm plugging away at I don't expect to squeeze in even a date in the near future let alone pencil in time to marry, conceive, and be a Lamaze partner for any little Carters." He thought about the note in his pocket and his mood turned unavoidably more serious. Carter hoped his partner didn't notice. "You know, Ted, I'm thinking about passing a few of the big names off to Frank and taking up a few of these new breeds that I'm getting now and again."

"Didn't you just pick up an unknown? Some St. John fellow?"

"Yeah, but he's headed down the same high dollar commercial road as the others. I can already detect the gleam in his eye."

"It's not so bad, my friend, that in the world of donuts you handle the eclairs."

"I've heard all the parallels—in the world of beautiful faces we handle the supermodels, blah, blah. But I do like that donut analogy." Carter ran his fingers over the smooth leather of his bag and contemplated aloud something he'd previously only thought about. "I'm just wondering where all the regular models went, that's all. You don't need a high dollar Tyra Banks when you've got a nice pretty face that will jump through all the hoops instead of demanding that *you* do so—oh and by the way, pick up a spring water on the way, *not* distilled water, of course."

"You sound distraught. Do you think you need a vacation?"

Bankson's voice had now came full circle to sympathetic and he waited quietly for his younger friend to continue.

"I need sanity, Ted. I need a handful of writers who actually write all of their own stuff and have their own ideas. Writers who *still* want to impress their audience, not just throw them a bone."

"What a concept."

"What a fantasy." Carter suddenly realized that he was having a near therapy session with his partner and immediately halted the subject. "In any case, of course I'll let you know if I hear anything from Claire Sodey or Judy Armando."

"I would appreciate that."

"Done. You take care Ted. Leave the cocktail waitresses alone."

"Surely you jest."

"And SPF, at least fifteen, you know." He could hear Ted Bankson chuckling on the other end which made him feel a little better. "Take care my friend."

Carter set the receiver back in its cradle and leaned over to turn out the light on his desk. He paused there in the darkened office, the only the moonlight streaming through the slits in the vertical blinds. It was late.

He slowly picked up his briefcase and headed for the door, giving himself a pep talk along the way.

"And now I'll just take myself to my half empty condo, sit on my half of the furniture, watch a movie on my television, minus the DVD, which *wasn't* my half. Get half undressed and have half a snack." He opened the door and continued mumbling to himself. "Maybe half a sandwich with a half a glass of milk—half and half, of course. Who knows, maybe I'll even take the dog for half a walk. Wait—do I even still *have* a dog? Surely she wouldn't be half-hearted to do that to a broken man. No, she wouldn't take Boo from me. I'd go half nuts."

Chapter Twenty-five

After making the rounds at the agency and at Oswell Publishing House, Marcus and Meg found themselves having dinner at a margarita bar called Mexican Bob's. Oswell had made the selection, bragging to the new author about his certainty that Iowan's would appreciate the down home atmosphere that this place possessed, much to Carter's embarrassment.

They entered the building which loosely resembled a large white tent that was noisy with revelers, some vacationing and some regulars. The mariachi band had dispersed from their place up front and was weaving in and around the crowd playing their various serenades. Meg strained to hear the waitress who lead them to a table near the bandstand. She looked at the floor and cocked her eyebrow, not realizing anyone was watching her and a little embarrassed to discover that Carter was. He smiled lightly and rolled his eyes.

"Yes, it is a dirt floor," he said in a voice that was barely audible in this place. Meg nodded with a small smile and began to look through the menu the serape-draped host had given them.

Taking her cue from the response she received upon issuing her opinion to the agent the day before, Meg stayed relatively quiet during the entire course of the conversation and the meal of sizzling fajitas and tortillas with garnishes. Only nodding in occasional agreement and laughing now and again when need dictated, she listened to the business, ignored the jokes and generally was quiet while the three men discussed their market strategy.

When the plates were cleared, Oswell smiled heartily and clapped his hands together with glee.

"Who's going to join me for a margarita at the bar?" He nudged Marcus' elbow.

"Not me." Carter raised his hands in objection immediately, hoping that everyone else would decline likewise and the business meeting would be wrapped up so that he could go home to the peacefulness of his own apartment.

Marcus, growing more and more at ease in his new position as the main attraction, barely hesitated before making his decision known. Impulsively, he nodded his head at Oswell and stood up, following him to the side bar where they made themselves comfortable on tall bar stools. Meg sighed loudly as she watched him go without even giving her a second look or prompting an invitation. She watched the men across the crowded, noisy restaurant and turned reluctantly to the man now seated across from her. Meg offered him an obligatory smile and raised her water to her lips, drinking, just to have something to do besides sit emotionless before him. She nodded.

Carter smiled in much the same way and sat there with his elbows propped upon the table top, drumming his fingers together. He was in no mood for casual conversation, especially with this woman who seemed to obviously dislike him. He made two mental notes, one, to never go to a business dinner with Oswell again, and two, to strangle Oswell after this just in case he forgot the first mental note.

He looked at the band and could see that they were winding down for a break and dreaded the notion that there would now be no music to support the barrier between them. He would now be forced to either make conversation of some type or let the uncomfortable silence fester between them. A waitress approached their table to check their drinks.

"Can I get ya somethin' else, people?" she asked in a short voice. Tampa seemed to be abundant with New York accents, constantly reminding her of Noel, and she instantly missed her friend.

"Water, please."

They spoke the words simultaneously and the young woman shot them a look, cracking the first little smile they'd seen of her all night. Mildly surprised at their synchronicity, Meg looked at Carter as he sat there and they both chuckled before looking away again.

Silence.

The waitress returned with two bottles of water and set them down on the table. Little crushed pieces of ice floated down the side of the smooth plastic and pooled in small puddles on the vinyl tablecloth.

"You two really know how to live it up." She finished scribbling on their check and set it back down again. "Not like your friends, there. I heard one of them say tequila when I walked past just now. It's always downhill from there."

Carter picked the bill up and glanced at it quickly, handing it back to the waitress and nodding in Oswell's direction.

"With that in mind, you can give this to the sandy-haired guy. Chances are he won't even notice."

The woman took it and left them alone. Carter took a gulp from his bottle and set it back, steadily drumming his fingertips on the checkered tablecloth.

"Good band, weren't they?" He forced himself to speak, surprised that he himself could take the silence no longer.

"Yes, I have no clue what they were singing about, but . . . "

He laughed at her attempt at a joke over the music which had all been in Spanish. He nodded again.

"You do that a lot."

"What's that?" He looked at her curiously, wondering what stream of nonsense she would spout off about now, having already been first-hand witness to her bold manner in his office.

"Nod like that. Are you really that agreeable of a person?"

"Yes, I am." He nodded again and then suddenly realized what he was saying. He furrowed his brow and began to shake his head. "No, actually I am not. Not at all."

"Okay."

More silence.

"So, what do you do . . . in Iowa?" He looked toward a table across the way where some people were whooping it up rather loudly. He smiled in their direction cordially.

"I'm a journalist, actually." She started slowly. "I work for the Jasper Falls Gazette."

"I see. I see." He was nodding again and a little smile came to Meg's lips upon seeing him do such. She stifled it immediately and sipped at her water. Now it was her turn to fill the silence. She sighed.

"So . . . how long have you been in this business?"

"I started with this company as an intern straight out of school fifteen years ago. Agent at twenty-five and partner at twenty-eight."

"I went to the University of Iowa." Her smile finally genuine, with the satisfaction that they might find a common interest that would relieve the tension in their conversation. "Where did you graduate from?"

"Yale."

Meg arched an eyebrow and made an "oh" mouth as she slumped ever so slightly in her seat.

"You liked the University, then?" Carter, realizing how arrogant his words had sounded as if they were just now reaching his own ears, actually seemed apologetic and tried to feign a level of interest.

"Sure. It's not *Ivy League*, but the football is good if you're into that sort of thing, which you probably aren't."

Carter smiled as her voice trailed off. He decided to change the subject immediately.

"So, I assume you've read Marcus' material."

"Yes, yes, I have. I guess I'm his original editor." Meg flipped the end of her hair nervously between her fingers and nodded at him.

"Good stuff, huh?" he went on. "Considering that he's a man and the viewpoint it's written in. Pretty insightful."

"Yeah." She nodded as she continued to scan the room. Meg looked up and saw Marcus laughing jovially with Oswell at the bar and could see the collection of shot glasses that was growing before them with each round they ordered. "It's almost like it's not even him . . . "

Carter looked at her inquisitively. She picked up on this immediately and smiled.

"Almost, you know."

"Right." Carter cleared his throat. "So you are a writer then too, I suppose."

"I suppose."

"And I suppose you're just waiting to burst into print like Marcus." The agent was clearly not interested in what she was waiting for, but rather felt that the silence between them was becoming a hole that needed immediate filling. Not a lot of thought was going into his words, a fact that was evident to Meg as well as she sat there now glaring at him.

"That's a cynical thing to say."

"It's a cynical world we live in, Mrs. St. John. You might as well thicken your skin to it now as opposed to letting them get you later." Marcus was even surprising himself at his own uncharacteristic honesty. Meg's mouth fell open and her eyes widened dramatically as she nodded her head looking for the best comeback. She could think of nothing, and what finally came out of her mouth didn't satisfy her need to crucify him somehow.

"You don't know so much."

"Oh, enlighten me, then," he said, hating himself for his cocky attitude that he knew this woman wasn't deserving of. He barely even knew her and she hated him already.

"That's not even my name."

"What?"

"I'm not *Mrs. St. John*. I have an identity! My name is Meghan Laine."

Her voice rose as she spoke and once the words were out, she felt foolish as she reviewed their childish content. Meg blinked once, never dismissing him from her look, however, and waited to see what he would say next.

"So, you kept your own name?"

"That's usually what single people do, unless they're in the witness protection program."

"You're not married?" He looked surprised.

"Did I stutter?"

"You are not betrothed to . . . to—"

"No. I am not married to—to whatshisname." Meg waved her hand angrily as she spoke, mad at herself for not thinking quickly enough.

"Oh. Oh I see. I get it now." He smiled and laughed out loud, nodding his head.

"You get what?"

"I get what the plan is. It's clear now." He continued. "You are the little girlfriend who tags along to the big city to get her feet wet in the publishing business thanks to her boyfriend whose just signed a big contract. Or maybe he's not your boyfriend. Maybe that's where he gets his spectacular insight because *he's* got a boyfriend and you are his cover! I see now—"

"Are you insane?"

"Yes, I am." He mocked her.

"Yes, you are! I am not using anyone for a free ride, and I assure you that, that whatshisname is all man!"

"All man, huh?"

"Yes, the real thing. The *all American boy*."

"Pure one hundred percent *ground beef*." Carter waved his hands as he played along now with a little smile, but his comment got Meg's attention immediately as she whipped her head toward him curiously.

"Why did you say that?"

"Say what? I was merely interjecting into your performance."

"Performance?"

"Yeah, you know, the hair flipping, eyelash batting, big wide blue eyed look and shocked expressions . . ." He laughed. "It's a good one—really convincing."

"You think I'm putting on an act for you?"

"It's okay, I've seen it a hundred times before. But the airy blinking thing—you might cut that down to a minimum, that's what gave you away."

"I have to blink! I don't choose to! I blink!"

"I blink. You blink . . ." Carter went on arrogantly and then caught the sleeve of their waitress as she passed by them. "Excuse me, Arlene. Do you blink?"

The waitress hesitated and then nodded, shooting him a look that said he was stupid as she kept her pace.

"See? We all blink." He smiled. "Some of us do it better than others, that's all."

Meg stared at him as she pursed her lips and narrowed her eyes. She breathed deeply, composing herself before continuing.

"Mr. Carter. I assure you that I have no intention of clinging to the coattails of *anyone*. Not him, not anyone! I guarantee this much, Mr. Personality, if I *wanted* to get published, I could do it on my own, and *without* your help!"

"Oh really?"

"Really."

"Yeah?"

"Yeah."

They sat there nodding at each other, defensively.

At that moment Marcus and Oswell returned to the table, laughing, half drunk, arms around each other's shoulders. Meg swallowed hard and stood, gathering her purse as she did so.

"Marcus, I'm very tired tonight."

"Meg, Meg—I *love* this guy!" He slapped Oswell on the back. Carter immediately shot her a smug look to which she snorted. She grabbed her fiancée's arm and motioned toward the door.

"Then I'll see you tomorrow?" Marcus continued to speak to the publisher.

"Sure thing. I'll meet you at Carter's office around noon before your flight. The editor finished looking through your some of your other stuff and there are some rewrites." Oswell sat down at the same time that Carter rose from his seat. "No big deal though. We're goin' all the way to the top baby!"

"To the top!" Marcus bellowed after his friend.

"Come on." Meg pulled his hand.

"Up and out, brother!"

"Up and out, my friend! Up and out!"

"It's been an interesting evening gentlemen. And lady." Carter shook Marcus' hand again. He hesitated as he took Meg's hand in his, looking into her eyes with a certain look that she couldn't quite distinguish between being apology or more arrogance yet. "Ms. Laine."

She decided that it was restrained arrogance. That was it, and she curtly drew her hand back, turning toward the door in a huff. Marcus shot the men a smile and shrugged his shoulders as he followed after her.

"Now there goes a hell of a guy." Oswell turned with a smile to his friend who was preparing to depart as he peeled a few bills from his money clip to tip the waitress. "I saw you were talking to his wife. She's hot."

"I was thinking the opposite actually. I found her a bit chilly." Carter pretended to shudder as he loosened his tie from his collar and looked at Oswell.

"A real popsicle huh?"

"Quite a deal."

"Is that a deal or a dill?" Oswell looked at him drunkenly.

"A dee-al," Carter reemphasized as he drew an "e" in the air with his finger as he stood there, his jacket draped over his arm.

"Oh, I thought you were going to say she was a pickle-sicle or something..." Oswell laughed at his own lame joke.

"Good night Oswell."

"Good night. God, I kill myself..." The publisher continued to giggle like a mere boy. "A *pickle-sicle.*"

Chapter Twenty-six

"**O**h, I feel *awful.*" Marcus was looking rather green as the elevator lurched to a stop on the floor of the literary agency. Meg looked at him quickly with minimal sympathy and then straight ahead again. She pursed her lips as he went on. "I mean, I feel like I could..."

He waved his hand as if she would fill in the blank at which point Meg recalled the last of the men's conversation the previous night.

"Up and out? Honey?" She had little kidding in her voice as she patted his arm, and he looked a bit shameful as he nodded. He began to knead the back of his neck with his right hand in an effort to relieve his pounding headache.

The doors parted and the two picked up their bags and headed for the lobby waiting area of the firm. Meg sat down quickly, making her intention known without words: she planned to stay there and he was on his own. In fact, she'd asked to stay in the cab and would have done so had it not been for his insistence that they lug all their suitcases to the agency and she wait for him there. She sighed and shot a polite smile at Jan who had pressed the button to inform Carter that his appointment was there.

"Mr. Carter's taking a call right now, but it will only be a minute or two. Take a seat."

Marcus joined her and a few seconds later the elevator doors opened again. Oswell stepped out and crossed the floor with a smile on his face. He shook Marcus' hand eagerly.

"How are you?"

"I've been better." Marcus looked rather pained.

"It takes training to drink like that. You need to get into shape."

Oswell smacked the man's back playfully and Marcus smiled faintly, lurching as the publisher's hand hit his shoulder.

"I guess a little training wouldn't hurt."

Carter's door opened and he stood there in an inviting manner waiting for the three to enter. Meg turned her attention suddenly to a magazine that was laying there. Marcus entered and Oswell began to follow as well before the receptionist stopped him short.

"Hold it there mister." She rose and walked coyly over to him eyeing him from head to toe.

"Not this time sister—I have an *appointment*." He smiled at her smugly.

"Well, aren't you the lucky one." She touched his arms as she stared at him straight on. "Raise your arms up."

He looked bewildered but did as the woman asked anyway. She began to lightly pat him down.

"What are you doing? Is this legal?"

She kept on until she reached his jacket pocket whereupon a sly smile came to her lips and she withdrew his cellular phone. Jan walked back to her desk and laid it aside as she took her seat again.

"What are you doing?" Oswell looked at her but she didn't answer. He turned to Carter. "What is she doing?"

Carter was mildly amused which showed through the little smile that danced across his pursed lips. He humored the publisher by posing the question for him. "Mr. Oswell wants to know what you're doing, Jan."

"Tell the little funny man that I'm taking this thing for safekeeping so that we don't have any more little phone tricks like the last time."

"But—" Oswell looked shocked.

"You can pick it up on the way back out Oswell." Carter hurried him.

"Well what about my calls? Are you going to answer them?"

"I'm his secretary, not yours."

"Well, how fair is that? *I* can't answer it, you *won't* answer it?"

"Maybe it will inspire you to expedite your visit with us here today." Jan glanced at him and then back down to her magazine. Everyone was quiet and finally Oswell conceded, walking in front of Carter and into the office, shaking his lowered head all the way. Carter looked next to Meg who was still sitting there.

"Ms. Laine, won't you be joining us?"

"No, I won't." She flipped through the pages rapidly.

"You might find it informative, due to the nature of your career."

She ignored him. He was trying desperately now to be civil, as apology didn't come to him easily. He sighed and tried again.

"I just thought that as we were talking about publishing a book—you, being a writer and all."

"Well, there's an article in here about tweezing that I want to check out—me, having eyebrows and all." She cast him a quick look and then returned her focus to the slick pages before her. Carter nodded slowly and backed into his office.

"Very well, then."

Once the door had shut, she tossed the magazine onto the table and crossed her arms. Meg saw Jan staring at her over the top of the magazine she was reading as she sat at her desk. Meg slumped a little in her seat offering the secretary a weak smile. Slowly, the magazine lowered.

"So, Meg—that's your name, right?" Jan had sudden interest for the first time in the woman sitting across from her. "So, tell me, what do you do there in Iowa?"

Chapter Twenty-seven

"So, this book is *actually* going to be published. After all the hoping. It's about time some agent or publisher got his head out of his hindquarters and realized your talent. I just can't believe that you got whatshisname to go with you to pitch the thing." Noel's eyes sparkled with amusement as her friend filled her in with the details of their trip to Florida. She paused to order from the man behind the counter of Cream Delight in the food court at the mall. "Double dip of chocolate cappuccino and pralines and cream in a sugar cone."

"Yes," Meg nodded. "The really strange thing is that I think he's actually enjoying himself! He was the hit of the office."

"Of course he was, men with dollar signs in their eyes will laugh at anything the money machine says. Even if it is dull."

"Did you want fat-free pralines and cream or traditional?" The man stood before them, ice cream scoop in hand, waiting for Noel's answer so that he could plop a second dip on the first. She responded by aiming her evil eye at him before speaking.

"Did I ask for fat-free? I don't think I asked for fat free."

"Well the fat-free pralines and cream tastes exactly like traditional. Just so you know." The man stood his ground, but politely.

"Who cares? It's ice cream, for the love of the gawds. Once inside it all turns to liquid anyway and you just pee it right out!" Noel waved her arm at the man who shrugged and readied his scoop. "Give me the fully loaded one with all the caramel and nuts you can cram in there. In fact—give me extra fat if you can manage it."

Meg looked at her silently as if her friend had quite lost her mind before she turned to face the now leery man. "I'll have raspberry ice milk."

The took their cones and walked to a bench in the center of the mall.

"What was that all about?" Meg asked as she sat down.

"I just don't like getting nutrition advice from a boy who makes five twenty-five an hour. I mean, what gives him the right to peddle his fat-free goods on me? He doesn't own the patent on rabbit food disguised as ice cream." She chomped away on the nutty ice cream. "If I wanted advice like that I'd go to that yuppy nutrition store down the way and pay through the nose for it."

"Okay," Meg nodded slowly. "Little edgy today, aren't we?"

Noel sighed and lowered her head defeatedly.

"It's Elliot and Mother O'Dell—they've been going around and around and it's about ready to drive me nuts! She called me crying this morning. Geesh already! It's not bad enough I move my whole life to this pathetic town and give up any aspirations for a career with a *real* newspaper. But to serve as mother, wife, counselor, servant, and editor to this rinky-dink press on a daily basis? It's just a little much."

"They're fighting again? Don't they usually wait at least two weeks in between brawls?"

"Now we're lucky if they can hold off two days." Noel shook her head. "Elliot wants to get out of here and make his degree work for him—something that we know isn't going to happen around this place. But Mother O'Dell goes 'I'm gonna sell the paper if you do.' So he goes 'Sell it' and she goes 'My mother started this paper fifty years ago—it's a Jasper Falls tradition.' Then he goes 'Then get Darrell to run it' and she goes 'All my other sons have big jobs in big cities and can't be expected to pick up and move to podunk Iowa'. Elliot goes 'But you find nothing wrong with keeping me around this soybean infested deadsville?' And Mother O'Dell starts crying."

Meg looked at her friend sympathetically and draped her arm around her shoulder, squeezing her tightly.

"I don't know how you do it. I honestly don't." She shook her head sympathetically. "You and Elliot will do the right thing."

"Well, that's just it." Noel continued. "I've been doing thinking of my own. I don't want my degree to disintegrate in this place either. I am in the process of creating a plan of escape."

"You're leaving Elliot?"

"I'm leaving." Noel looked at her sternly. "I'm not necessarily leaving Elliot. He has the option, and depending upon how much of a stand he wants to take against Mother O'Dell, he'll guide himself to make the best decision for himself. I'm going to set a timeline that will expire sometime after my birthday."

"The cycle," Meg's voice was soft as she spoke. "Oh wow. I didn't know it was so bad, Noel."

Noel turned to see her friend's sympathetic eyes and smiled to cheer her some.

"It's not that bad, Meg, but I have some talents too." She laughed lightly. "Maybe I'm not going to write a best-selling novel, but I think I can do better than editing this little paper."

"Of course you can."

"Well, you know when you have a family, the decisions that used to weigh heavily now weigh three times as much. But I think that's what's best for me. Who knows, maybe the next paper I work for will actually have sprung for a spell checker."

The friends both shrugged.

"Who knows, maybe once you and Elliot get out of here you'll rediscover each other." Meg nodded at her. "You know, when people are forced to rely upon each other, the bond almost inevitably strengthens. You might really be surprised."

Noel looked at Meg with a hopeless smile that she mustered only for her friend's benefit.

"Yeah, who knows." She took another bite of her ice cream and changed the subject. "So, tell me all about it. What does a bigtime literary agent's office look like? What did you talk about?"

Glad to be away from the subject of Mother O'Dell, Meg smiled and steadied her focus as she recalled the events.

"The agency was lavish, impressive," She squinted as she considered it. "And the book will hit the shelves next month."

"Next month!" Noel burst out. "These ventures usually take six, eight months—sometimes over a year!"

"Apparently they are basing it on timeliness of the material, and the time is now. I guess." She smiled and shrugged her shoulders.

"And, so?" Noel dipped her head, as she prompted her friend to detail the events.

"So, that's about it."

The women sat there in silence for a few minutes eating their ice cream, Noel looking on suspiciously as the mood continued. Finally she was unable to take it any longer.

"Meg! Did you tell them you wrote the damn book?"

"There will be time for these things."

"You didn't tell them that the newest John Steinbeck is really Judy Blume? Come on!"

"I couldn't. Noel, they were so impressed by the fact that Marcus possessed this incredible insight into the female persona, I just couldn't do it." Meg's eyes were wide as she continued. "And when it comes down to it, money is going to be made from the books, and you know, it's not like Marcus didn't support me for the most part while I was writing for the past four years. All is fair."

"All is crazy! *That* is crazy!" Her friend was ranting. "So Marcus is going to play your puppet at these upcoming events you were so excited to tell me about. The book signings and all."

"Yes."

"And he's going to leave the farm and run all over Billy-hell just like that? No questions asked?"

"Like everyone else around here, you know Marcus has been getting grants from the government because farming isn't what it used to be. It's not like he's growing the crops he once was anyway."

"Who cares about that? I'm talking about your work being exploited as that belonging to some man, a farmer, who knows nothing about the literary world except for what he reads in the Ann Landers column."

"You make him sound like an idiot." Meg pursed her lips momentarily.

"Did I? I'm sorry, I meant to make it sound like *you* were the idiot. Pardon me."

"I've said it before, these things will work themselves out. They just do. That's how it works." She tipped her head with certainty as she continued to lick at her cone. "You've got your problems with Elliot. No relationship is perfect."

"You've got a drip."

"Whatshisname is not a drip."

"I meant your ice cream, but my, the power of suggestion reveals a lot now, doesn't it?" Noel's voice droned on. "You've got to get a hold of that agent and come clean with him. You need to tell him who really wrote that stuff he's dying to get onto the press, and pronto."

"I have some corrections and rewrites for the next three that I'm to finish and get back to them ASAP as well."

"Hello? Are you hearing me?" Noel raised her voice some.

Meg tossed the rest of her ice cream into the nearby trash receptacle and blotted her lips with a paper napkin. She looked at Noel with worry in her eyes.

"I can't. Not right now anyway." She started slowly. "I guess you're just going to have to trust my judgment. I'll make that move when the time is right."

Noel studied her for a moment before deciding not to pursue it any further. Meg was clearly distraught and there was no need to make matters worse. She smiled finally and changed the subject to something lighter.

"So? How was the Sunshine State? The land of thongs—and I don't mean the ones you wear on your feet."

Meg giggled.

"It is January, regardless of where you live. Not too many thong bottoms running around the beach this time of year." She wrinkled her nose. "Besides, didn't they outlaw thong swimwear in Tampa? We ran an AP story on that once, remember?"

"I think they outlawed it in St. Petersburg but not in Tampa. Or maybe it was the other way around . . . Who knows. Really it's all for the best." Noel popped the last bite of her cone in her mouth and licked her fingers as she smiled sneakily. "I've never seen a guy yet that doesn't look repulsive in those things and who cares what the women look like in 'em when I ain't one of 'em."

They both laughed.

"So, did you meet any nice people while you were there? Any wealthy, clean men with a fondness for a sturdy woman who takes no crap and can stomach to see a chicken's head cut off?"

Meg made a face.

"Ewww, you make me sound so . . . womanly."

"I wasn't talking about you. I'm still breathing too, ya know." Noel elbowed her playfully. "No prospects, huh?"

"Well, it was only three days and it was all business," Meg started and then changed her attitude as she realized what she was saying. "And I'm engaged to Marcus and I wasn't looking anyway. I'm terribly in love with him."

"If you're going to keep saying that, at least change your tone of voice to a more believable one. It's not working anymore." Noel flipped her hand as she spoke. "It's a bad performance."

Hearing that last word, Meg was immediately reminded of the conversation she'd had with the agent at the restaurant and her stance changed as she slumped and narrowed her eyes.

"That just reminds me of the worst man I ever met!"

"When? What?" Her friend looked puzzled.

"On the trip, in Florida." Meg clenched her hands as she continued. "The most awful man ever—oh!"

"I thought you said you didn't have a chance to see anyone except for business people? When did *this* happen?"

"He was business people! Nick Carter—the rudest one of all, in fact." She steadied her voice and started again. "Marcus' agent."

"*Your* agent," Noel interjected.

"Oh, no! I could never have *this* man as an agent—that double talking, self centered, egotistical, narrow minded . . . "

"Horrific jerk? There, can I help you out?" Noel waved her hand when she saw that her friend was lacking for descriptive words. "Scum-sucking worm feed?"

"More!"

"Dim-witted fungi?"

"Exactly." Meg nodded eagerly. "He had the audacity to tell me that I was trying to soak off Marcus for publishing connections! Can you believe it?"

"No." Noel laughed a little. "Tell me more."

"He actually said that I was trying to put on a show for him—batting my eyelashes and making doey-eyed faces!"

"What a pig."

"Yes! *Exactly*!" Meg's eyes were wide as she expressed her insulted feelings. "It was all 'Marcus is a genius' and 'Marcus really knows a woman's feelings,' blah, blah, blah. Then he accuses me of trying to ride his publishing wave! Oh! Can you believe it!"

"What did he look like?"

Meg stopped suddenly and looked at her oddly.

"What? Why would you ask that?"

"I need a visual. Tell me."

She was quiet for a moment as she considered Nick Carter.

"He had this wavy, dark hair...these blue eyes and nice skin with this little dimple right about so—" She stopped when she noticed Noel looking at her strangely. "What?"

"I meant like, stance, evil looks—not the man's dermatology regime."

"Oh, well, he didn't look particularly evil...But his manners! *Oh!* I was so enraged!"

"What did Marcus say?"

"He wasn't there. He was at the margarita bar with the publisher. He just walked off and left me there with his agent."

"*Your* agent."

"*His* agent. And then the music stopped and suddenly we were forced to talk." Meg shook her head as her expression changed some. The angry wrinkles around her eyes softened some and her voice lowered a bit as if she were about to share something very intimate. "The funny thing is, when I first met him . . ."

Noel scooted closer to her friend, leaving her no personal space whatsoever as she nodded eagerly for her to continue.

"What? When you first met him what?"

Meg's eyes met hers and she smiled foolishly, shaking her head suddenly. She raised her hand in a halting motion.

"Nothing. Nothing at all."

"Nothing, huh?" Now it was Noel's turn to nod suspiciously. She refused to let it die. "Like I'm going to say anything. You already know how I feel. Come on—I'm your best friend, for the love of the gawds!"

Meg studied her for a few moments before reluctantly going on.

"Okay. I'm going to hate myself for saying this I know," She spoke quietly, glancing around to see that no one was near them. "When I first walked into his office and he shook my hand, I just thought that he, *lin -*

gered there, that's all."

"Lingered?"

"Yeah. Lingered."

"That's all?"

"That's all."

Noel nodded slowly, looking away as if she were mentally clicking the pieces together. She looked at Meg again.

"When you touched his hand, was there, you know."

"No, what?" Meg looked at her seriously.

"You know . . ." Noel waved her hand as if it would magically fill in the blanks. "Did you feel *light?*"

"Light?" Meg contemplated this for a second. "I felt light as soon as I entered the office as it was, Noel. We are embarking on a major project here."

"When you touched his hand, did you feel strangely different? *Twinkly?*"

"I don't think it was *twinkly*. I think it was nerves. In fact I'm sure now that it was nerves, thinking about it. I mean, I was a basket case the entire time!" Meg talked louder now as she smiled in a more relaxed way. Her confidence was growing as she spoke. "That's what it was, it was nerves."

"If it was nerves, then why did you mention it?"

"Mention what?"

"Mention meeting Nick Carter?"

"Because you asked."

"I asked if you met anyone interesting and you said that you met Nick Carter. Am I missing something here? Because the facts are in, and you think that Nick Carter is interesting, at least, and possibly *twinkly*, which the jury is still out on."

"I didn't say *twinkly*. That's not even a word I would use."

"But you don't deny that you were a bit, taken, by the likes of a man named Nick Carter." Noel wasn't going to let this one go either. Meg sighed deeply as she rolled her eyes.

"I wasn't *taken* by him. In fact, the entire idea is absurd. In fact, I wouldn't be taken by Nick Carter, not even across the street, because he is *seriously* disturbed! He has a very small capacity for human compassion.

A deranged outlook on the business that he's involved in, and the demeanor of a . . . a—"

"Weasel?"

"No, more like a *wolf.* He makes no apologies for his blatancy and he's not sneaky at all. He just comes right out with it. He's so annoying."

Noel raised one corner of her mouth in a half smirk and looked at her friend.

"Uh-huh."

"What? What's the *uh-huh* for?"

"Nothing, nothing at all." Noel feigned innocence now.

"Anyway," Meg switched her narrow focus away from her friend now and changed the subject. "I'm going to have to make this a short afternoon because I need to get one of those rewrites back to him by the week's end. They don't take their time on these things."

"Striking while the iron is hot, I hear ya."

"You know, the only thing I'm really going to hate about this whole deal is that I wanted to dedicate my first book to my friends. Now I won't be able to do that." Meg looked suddenly sad.

Noel softened her composure and patted her friend's shoulder.

"Those aren't important things, Meg." She soothed her. "That you are honest with yourself is what's important. Your happiness is more important to me than seeing my name in the front of some silly book."

Meg laughed and the two women leaned toward each other, their foreheads touching.

"Naming your first child after me will be an honor enough."

They both giggled.

Chapter Twenty-eight

Nick Carter opened a mutilated cardboard mailer sitting atop the stack of the day's mail that covered his desk. The contents had gotten wet and the ink was smeared on the letter and manuscript inside. He shook his head disgustedly.

"Tampa post," He looked at the date on the cancellation. "Well, this one only took a mere month to find its way here. Poor sap would have had a better chance should his mailer have decided to sprout wings itself and fly here."

He set it aside and looked at the next large envelope, tearing it open and briefly reading the cover letter.

"Dear Mr. Carter, blah, blah, blah. You might find interesting, blah blah, blah. A woman who's a housewife with ties to an international underground agency. As it turns out her husband is a *robot*." Carter raised his eyes to no one and arched an eyebrow, before continuing reading the letter. "That's one for the pile. Next?"

He pulled open another mailer and briefly looked at the letter that accompanied the next manuscript.

"A manual on training your pet hamster in fifteen minutes or less." He threw it aside immediately and smirked. "It's a *rodent* for God's sake, what could you teach it? A more effective means of running its *wheel?* Perhaps you could harness that energy and run the clothes dryer with it. Or maybe power the housewife's robot husband with it, just an idea. Now *there's* something I'd like to see come across my desk."

The rejection stack was quickly growing already this morning. He reached for another and another before finding something he read a little more carefully.

"Groups of inner city students who discover that the forces terrorizing their neighborhood aren't gang related, but alien derived." He nodded with a look that didn't promise much. He set it down and scanned the desk for another, his eyes briefly fell across a sticky note pressed on his pencil holder near his telephone. He narrowed his eyes curiously for a moment, trying to recognize the area code before he recalled that the number belonged to Marcus St. John. Oh yes, their newest commercial discovery bound for the promised land.

Mr. St. John certainly seemed to have hit it off with Oswell, in fact, his security with the man seemed to have cut Oswell's frequent visits to his office in about half. At least that was one thing he had to thank the Iowa boy for, if nothing else. It wasn't that he didn't *like* Marcus St. John, no that wasn't it. But there was just something about the man that gave him a feeling that resembled a touch of heartburn. Maybe it was that the man didn't seem to have any working knowledge as to how the whole publishing enterprise operated. That was a *little* unusual, but not really unacceptable. Maybe it was that he wasn't much of a conversationalist, which made for several lulls in their exchange. Quiet made Carter uncomfortable. He tried to avoid it.

His thoughts then went to the night at the restaurant, another thing on the list of things he tried to avoid thinking about. The night he'd made such a smashing impression on the writer's supposed wife-to-be. He'd been tired and maybe a bit impatient, but that couldn't account for the reasons why he'd said all the things he had said. After all, Meghan Laine wasn't truly deserving of all that he'd thrown her way, *or was she?* They had been at each others' throats since the start, nearly, maybe it was a bit of a sport with her. He nodded as he picked up another mailer and casually walked toward the window speaking quietly to himself.

"Sure, that's what it is—*I'm a writer.* Didn't take long for her to pop *that* one off." He laughed as he flipped through a manuscript he was holding, not really reading it. "*Performance? What performance? My eyes really are wide as golfballs! How can you be so trite?* Hmph. And that's another thing, what kind of a word is that? Trite is *trite!* For heaven's—"

Carter's exchange with himself was interrupted by the sound of a woman clearing her throat from the threshold of his office door. He turned quickly and touched his chin innocently, waiting to see what Jan wanted, wondering how much she'd heard. He stood still wearing no particular expression as she watched him curiously. Jan entered the office all the way, finally, shutting the door behind her as she did so.

"Am I interrupting something?"

"Like what?"

"Like whatever *all that* was."

"*All that* was nothing. I was just reading this particular manuscript aloud to hear how it sounded."

Jan approached him and took the papers from his grasp, eyeing them with a little nod.

"*Llamas: The Alternative Livestock.* Yeah, I can see it's a pretty compelling piece. You want me to finish reading it out loud so you can make up your mind?"

"Thanks anyway."

She set the packet on the desk and sighed deeply.

"You *know* this is my favorite part of the day. Why didn't you wait for me?" She waved her hand over the already opened portion of the mail.

"Don't worry, there's plenty where that came from to open and slaughter, so sharpen your ax." He looked back out the window again.

"Investing. Boring." Jan flipped through another one and set it aside. She ran the opener along the flap of a large yellow envelope. "Here's one, supposed to be a true story about the lovers of Louis XIV. Who would know? They're all dead."

"Hmph," Carter smiled a little as he continued to zone off out the window.

"So, who were you talking about when I came in?" Jan had been waiting to ask, yet approached the subject with her best nonchalant voice.

"No one."

"Someone."

"Not a someone you would know." He turned toward her now as if he were switching back into his business mode. "Did Oswell bring those papers back from St. John? They were overnighted three nights ago, I was supposed to get them sometime this afternoon by courier."

"If he'd have been here you would have heard my cutting comments and his whimpering. But no, that's another reason I came to talk to you. He lost it and is going to have to work the whole transaction by fax."

"Lost it?" Carter wrinkled his nose and pulled a chair up beside his desk,as Jan was already sitting in his own chair and looking quite at home doing such. "What do you mean?"

"I mean it arrived at his office and he lost it in the shuffle. You know how badly organized that little weirdo is. He insists he can do it all and then it ends up in Neverland with the rest of everything he's lost over the years."

"Well I want you to get hold of Jeannie in the mailroom at Oswell House and have her forward anything that comes from St. John's address straight to this office immediately from now on. We can't afford to be losing important paperwork—it's not like we can run across the street and get a second copy. The next thing you know, deadlines are being missed and money is being lost, or worst of all, someone else has beat us to the punch on the shelves. There's no excuse for that."

Jan scribbled herself a note and sat back again, looking at her boss.

"So, who were you talking about when I came in?"

"We already breezed over that and decided it wasn't worth talking about."

"Did we? I don't recall having said that." She cocked her head sideways, little curls springing around her face as she did so. "Is this about the note with the key on it?"

"No—this has nothing to do with Kirstin." He finally conceded, realizing that Jan wasn't going to let it go or get out of his office until he leveled with her. "It was about that woman that St. John brought with him the other day . . . whatsername—."

"Oh, Meggie, yeah, she's a peach isn't she?" Jan's expression softened some as she continued to work away at opening the remaining letters in the pile.

"A *peach*? I was thinking more along the lines of a lemon—sourish. Or an onion, surprisingly hot, but not in a good way." He waved his hands as he talked with an angry look about him. "She was perfectly dreadful. Ms. *I'm-Independent*, Ms. I'm-for-the-underdog. Ms. Batt-my-eyelashes-because I-want-my-way—but how dare you accuse me of doing such a thing? After all, I'm *Ms. Independent!*"

"Struck a chord, huh?" Jan smiled at him.

"She struck a whole symphony! If I never see that woman again, it will be too soon."

Jan gathered the mailers and envelopes and stood to leave the office finally.

"Another batch of the standard issue?" She asked as she headed for the door. Carter followed her quickly and examined the stack she was holding.

"Give me that one about the neighborhood gangs turned aliens, I might be bored this afternoon. The name and address on it are clear but write him and tell him that the rest looked like it was side routed by a hurricane and would he send it again."

Jan looked at him with an odd expression.

"Every day I come into the office and we pick through these letters and manuscripts and have a few laughs and stuff, and every day you send me out, and every day I make up a batch of standard replies. You're not going weird on me now, are you?" Jan laughed lightly. "I mean, alien neighbors isn't your standard fare."

"I just think that the man went through all the trouble to send it, we can at least take a look at it."

"He's a no-namer."

"All the more reason." Carter sat down behind his desk and began to rifle through some paperwork that was mounting before him. He raised his eyes to her once he felt her staring at him still. "Is there anything else?"

"No, no that's just not like you, that's all. In fact, you are just not like you today."

"Of course I am."

"No, you're different." She pushed the doorknob and the door to the lobby swung open to let her out. Jan looked at him one last time. "Different can be good, don't get me wrong."

As Carter sat at his desk his mind wouldn't dismiss the animosity that was ever growing for the woman he knew to be Meghan Laine. He tapped the desk with the eraser end of his pencil, an action that was becoming more and more harried as if he were tapping out an emergency SOS. Jan reentered the office in the midst of this action as she recalled something else that she'd needed to speak with him about. She paused before him and raised her eyebrows. He began to speak to the secretary without missing a beat as if she'd never left the room in the first place.

"No, you know, I was wrong about that onion thing. She was more like a . . . a *pepper*. That's right, because you see a pepper can be pretty, but then you bite into it and it's so deceiving, it's either really bitter or really hot and you run for a glass of water and swear you'll never be stupid enough to fall for such a pretty fixation again." He rattled on about the subject as if Jan had never left, avoiding looking directly at her. "An onion, is just, you know . . . oniony. But this woman's got—"

"Spice?" Jan furrowed her brow as she tried to help him out.

"Yes!" He nodded with a bit of an evil smile, then he quickly changed his expression. "No! Not spice as in *yeah, I like that*, but the bad kind that just leaves a burning sensation."

"Okay." Jan nodded slowly, humoring her boss. She looked thoughtful. "Too bad it's such a tempting looking vegetable though, huh?"

"I wouldn't say Ms. Laine was *tempting*. I wouldn't say that at all." Carter looked at his secretary for reassurance on the subject, but she only watched him with a level of growing interest. Jan wasn't sure she'd ever seen her boss so worked up in the four years she'd been in his employment. "I wouldn't say she was *un-tempting*. I'm sure she tempts *somebody*, just not me, that's all. And not any red blooded American man that values his self esteem anyhow!"

"Right."

"She uses that part of her to abuse men."

"What part?"

"You know, that big blue eyed thing she's got working for her, and that long blonde hair—that's just a gimmick, you know."

"In what way?"

"*In what way?*" Carter's voice raised dramatically and he laughed at the woman standing before her. "There's practically a million articles written about it! The long hair, symbolizing innocence and youth and vulnerability. Vixens blessed with a mane of such, reel in those poor unsuspecting imbeciles with their charm and symbolic *I need taken care of* line of crap and then devour them whole once they have them in their clutches! Kind of like that one spider who attracts the male and mates with him and then she eats him alive! What kind of a mating ritual is that?"

Jan shifted her weight to one foot and thrust her hand on her hip as she glared at him.

"You suspect that's why I have long hair? Surely you jest."

"Yes, I do."

"Oh, you do?"

"Yes, I do. I wouldn't date any woman with long hair. I'd take that defense shield away from her just like that!" Carter snapped his fingers and his eyes gleamed as he spoke of it. "I'd be like *ah-hah*! No, not this guy. This guy doesn't go for that helpless act. No how."

"You've been reading too much again, Carter."

"No, I've been studying up. I want you to think about the women you know who have gotten married and settled down. What's the *first* thing to go?"

"Their sanity?"

"No, the *hair*. And you know it and I know it. It's the hair. That princess crown is overthrown and she turns into the Queen to rule all in their domain!"

"I rule this domain and it ain't a wig, honey."

"Well, well then." Carter's voice lowered as he nodded at his secretary. "Then God help the man that you finally wed."

"Carter, you're missing the point. Men are like works in progress. I am like,the patent." She began to move her hands in a descriptive manner as if she were modeling something. "I work with them, mold them, shape them into the masterpiece that they can be, then I seal it with the patent and they're mine."

"Yeah, probably squeezing the life right out of them in the process."

"There are a few casualties along the way." Jan shrugged confidently with no apologies.

"Well, not this man, sister. I will not succumb to the whims of some flaxen long haired maiden . . . not some creamy skinned dame who is going to bat her blue eyes at me and make me beg and roll over."

Jan walked out of the door as her boss continued in a low tone.

"No wide-eyed, impish-smiling, dimple-showing, rosy apple-cheeked woman is going to inflict her wily wanton ways on *me*." He shook his head. "No how . . ."

Chapter Twenty-nine

Meg slammed a stack of nearly one hundred pages onto the counter with an angry thud. She sighed and pushed the hair out of her eyes, rereading the editor's notes once again, shaking her head.

"How? How can he think that Monica would possibly say something as stupid as that? Did he even read this story? Because if he *had*, he'd realize that Monica is a poignant character with a certain vulnerability and caring that exceeds beyond the norm and supersedes the type of shallow personality that would use *that* type of profanity that—well, I'm not even going to *say* it!"

Meg's faithful dog looked at her from his place in the corner and emitted a little whine. He stood up slowly and stretched and trundled over to where she was sitting at the breakfast bar and laid down again below her stool, offering her the reassurance that only Boo could. She smiled at him and impulsively leaned over, roughly patting the top of his head.

"What are we gonna do with these big time editors, Boo? Huh? What are they thinking?" She looked back at the computer before her and finally popped the disc into her laptop, calling up the story in its original form. She blew a few pieces of hair away from her eyes impatiently and then started making a few minor adjustments. Meg flipped to the second portion of the revised outline and her eyes widened with horror.

"*Trina*? They want me to change Jaqueline's name to *Trina*? That's a *bimbo* name." She read on a bit and then nodded dramatically with a sarcastic laugh. "Well, I see, that's because Trina's now a prostitute instead of a newspaper editor! Well! That makes *perfectly* good sense."

Meg marched into the dining room and jammed her finger onto the power button of the stereo that had been sending the sounds of Billy Holiday wafting throughout the house softly. The music came to an abrupt halt as she continued to leaf through the pages of the manuscript rewrite. Meg threw it on the countertop and pulled her small sling-back purse from the floor, spilling its contents all over. She quickly shuffled through the strewn mess until she came upon a small business card.

Bankson, Laughton & Carter
Literary Associates
Nick Carter

Meg scanned the card until her eyes fell upon the number listed there. She picked up the cordless telephone and hurriedly punched in the number.

After ten rings she glanced at the kitchen clock and rolled her eyes. It was 8:24 PM, 9:24 on the east coast. Why would she think anyone would answer this late at night? A farmer's hours and a business person's were two entirely different things, something she'd nearly forgotten about. Meg crossed the floor to hang the phone back up when suddenly someone answered.

"Bankson, Laughton and Carter. Carter, here."

Meg's eyes widened with surprise. It had been her intention to call and get the editor's telephone number from Jan at the front desk. She certainly hadn't expected anyone else to answer, and she *certainly* hadn't expected Carter, of all people, to be the one she would talk to.

"Hello? Can I help you?"

Meg sensed the annoyance in his voice and she swallowed hard, half wishing that she could merely slam the telephone down in his ear. But her eyes fell back upon the dissected manuscript laying there before her and she suddenly remembered why she had called in the first place. And that Nick Carter would answer was only his misfortune. So be it.

"Mr. Carter, this is Meghan Laine, Marcus St. John's . . . um—"

Oh, how confidently she'd started the attack only to be sidetracked by words that had unexpectedly gotten into the way. She regrouped immediately but Carter spoke before she had a chance to continue.

"Yes, yes, Ms. Laine, how could I possibly forget?" Carter rubbed his temple with vigor and squinted his eyes. And to think he almost hadn't answered. Now he wished he'd just kept his vigil in the quiet of his office, ignoring the incessant ringing. He sighed quietly. "How can I help you?"

"It's about these rewrites—they're *horrible*! They take away from the content of the story completely."

"Which rewrite are you referring to, Ms. Laine?"

"I am referring specifically to *An Event at Juniper Hill*, if you recall, a love story about a woman and her professor, who of course, is now a tramp and a horse trainer."

"Calm down, calm down. I haven't read the manuscript you're referring to, but if the editor has outlined some changes, well—"

"Well what? It's not even the same story with all the changes! What's the point? Why not just have the editor write the *entire* thing then? What do you need writers for?" Meg walked along the countertop, pulling various small stacks up to see for better evaluation. She slapped it back on the countertop and shook her head with a little laugh of disbelief.

"Ms. Laine, is this why you are calling me at this hour?"

She was quiet for a moment before answering.

"Yes. Yes it is. Although I had only planned to get a number for the editor from the woman at the front desk, but then I realized what time it was and then I saw that it was so late so I thought I'd leave a message and then you answered." She rambled without taking a single breath. She paused to think over what she'd said. "Why are you in the office this late anyway?"

Carter broke out of the stare he'd been keeping on the bulletin board on the far wall across the room. He'd been throwing little darts at the state map posted there, trying to hit Tampa square on, having decided that he would go home right after that feat was accomplished. So far he'd been working at it for an hour. He breathed out deeply and rolled his eyes.

"I was working on something." Carter took his feet down from their comfortable position on his desktop and leaned forward now in his seat. "Why are you calling at this hour anyway? And why is it *you* instead of Mr. St. John—and why do *you* care if there are a few changes to be made in a manuscript that you have nothing to do with? You told me yourself you work at the local newspaper—shouldn't you be writing an article about a 4-H event or something?"

There was silence as Meg's mouth dropped open in shock. She nodded her head slowly as though he could actually see her horror at his rudeness.

"Well, I'll be—"

"You'll be what?" He laughed smartly at her sudden lack of insult ammunition.

"*You*, Mr. Carter, are a *very* rude person! I would hate to be the one you come home to every day! To have to brush my teeth alongside you! To have to make your dinner every night! *You* would probably taste it and critique it—and then if you couldn't decide exactly what is wrong with it, you'd probably have it packed on ice and shipped off to one of your fancy-shmancy editors—who, by the time they were done with it, would have your turkey tetrazzini turned all the way into corn beef hash! *Oh!*"

"You ridicule me?" He asked with his voice softening some with his growing amusement.

"You exasperate me!"

"You can think what you want, Ms. Laine, but I assure you that the editors that I commission have their finger right on the pulse of what is current, trendy, vital and necessary for the work that we publish. If an editor sees a few things he doesn't agree with, or think would sell better if this were here and this were there, then so be it! That's how it works. They're editors, Ms. Laine, they *edit*. The end."

There was silence for a moment.

"Well, the only thing that I see that the editor has left in this piece is a few ands *and* an occasional *but*. Otherwise I'm hard pressed to find any similarities between the original piece and the piece they want me to revise."

"*You* revise? You have nothing to do with this!"

Meg suddenly was very aware of what she'd just said. She swallowed hard and continued with as much self assurance as she could muster.

"Well, as I told you, I serve as the editor in *this* house, and I found the first manuscript moving and compelling, and this revision business . . . is just—just *crap!*"

Mr. Carter smiled, glad that she couldn't see him. He was actually pleased with himself to have reduced her to mud slinging, as he hated to be the only one to do as much—slinging was no fun when no one slung back.

"My, my, such language." He tsked his tongue. "Well, it's like this, Ms. Laine, Marcus will either do the revisions or he won't. But I can tell you that considering the money that Oswell Publishing House is spending to launch a full scale promotion for his material, I would certainly consider doing what they are asking, even if it means sacrificing some personal interest in a few fictitious characters to do such. But that's just me."

Meg was quiet as she listened.

"I would also advise that in the future, you avoid calling your fiancee's agent and reaming him in such a way, as it only jeopardizes the agent-writer relationship, and, really is, *truly* none of your business anyway."

"Goodbye, Mr. Carter."

Meg slammed the receiver back onto the phone and pushed it aside angrily.

"*Oh!*" She clenched her hands.

Nick Carter flinched away from the receiver at the sound of the other end slamming in his ear. He looked at it curiously.

"Good night," he said into the empty phone. He picked up another dart and threw it across the way. It landed on Orlando.

"I swear to God that woman has balls of *steel*! Imagine calling your husband's or boyfriend's or whatever-the-hell he is—his *agent*! The one who has a vested interest in the whole publishing venture, and telling him where to get off. Hmph!"

He threw another dart at the board only to strike close to Georgia...Gulf Breeze to be exact. He picked up another.

"My editor! Turning tetrazzini into hash or spam or whatever . . ." He sent another dart sailing across the room.

Smack!

"Tampa!" He stood and raised his arms in a slow motion Olympic move, looking in all directions around him as if he were surrounded by millions. "*Augh . . . and the crowd goes wild!*"

He continued his play until he glanced again at the clock on his desk and saw that it was just past ten. He stood and gathered his briefcase and a few things to go.

"Tetrazzini." He pondered it quietly, knowing that it had been ages since he'd had a home cooked meal. Kirsten hadn't liked to cook and he didn't have the time or patience to learn. He walked toward the door, turning out the last light as he reached it. He hesitated before leaving. "I wonder if Lean Cuisine has a good tetrazzini?"

Chapter Thirty

"Can you direct me to the mailroom?" Jan leaned across the main reception desk at Oswell Publishing House, where an overweight after-hours guard was reading a detective book. He simply motioned down a particular hallway, never raising his eyes to see her. Jan nodded anyway and was on her way.

Her eyes roamed over the glass doors of the expansive hallway which were all darkened now. One light shown down the hall and she followed it, quickening her pace. The bold lettering across the doors read what she'd hoped. Mailroom. She pushed it open and tapped the countertop with her car keys as she waited. The room was quieter now, but was manned at all hours, as this particular house was one of the largest in the country. A short, plump woman with long dark hair waddled to the front to gaze at the woman standing there now through thick pop bottle glasses. She smiled showing her nearly buck teeth now, a rather horrid sight that made Jan cringe internally. She hoped it wasn't obvious.

"Can I help you, miss?"

"Yes, I'm Jan, Nick Carter's secretary."

The woman stared at her, bewildered.

"Carter, of Bankson, Laughton & Carter, the literary agents."

"How can I help you, miss?"

"I have this address here and you are to direct any incoming mail from it to Mr. Carter by courier. Can we arrange that?"

"I suppose. But you'll have to have J.T. Oswell sign a waiver to allow that transaction. I'll file it with him in the morning."

Recalling quite clearly how very unorganized Oswell was and realizing that mankind would likely never see any such waiver once it left the confines of the mailroom, Jan thought quickly.

"Well, I'm going to see Mr. Oswell after this. How would it be if I took the waiver to him and brought it back here for you to approve in say, the next ten minutes?" Jan's eyes brightened as she dealt the proposal.

"Well," The woman looked befuddled as she glanced away, unsure that she should let such a form out of her sight.

"It will only be a short bit. You are here until when?"

"Midnight."

"Splendid, then I will have it back here long before then."

Jan took the slip from the woman's grip and trotted out of the mail-room. She walked down the vacant hallway, her heels echoing on the tile floor as she went, speaking quietly to herself and blessing the young woman for her gullibility. She pushed open the door of the women's room and entered.

Jan flipped on the light and laid the form on the sink countertop, smoothing it as she withdrew a pen from her pocketbook. Carefully she scrawled a signature quite similar to the scribbled trademark one belonging to Oswell. She leaned back and admired her handiwork before folding the letter into thirds and tucking it into her jacket pocket. Jan turned out the light and slipped back down the hallway and into the mailroom.

"There, see? He was happy to oblige." Jan turned the paperwork over to the little woman who looked at it curiously. "What, you don't trust me?"

"Well, I suppose this will suffice."

"So I can be assured that all the mailers and envelopes that come from this address will be forwarded immediately to Mr. Carter's office?"

"Will do."

"Thank you very much." Jan made her exit and once in the hallway rolled her eyes when she was sure no one was around. She walked down the dark hallway back toward the front. "If that woman were any dumb-er you'd have to set her in a windowsill and water her."

"What?"

The sudden voice startled Jan who nearly lost her balance. She clutched her chest. It was J.T. Oswell.

"I thought I was alone."

"I noticed." He smiled at her brilliantly with a hint of smugness about him. "I see that you have no problem getting past our front desk."

"Hardly. Fat boy there was all wrapped up in some trash detective book or something. The challenge wasn't great." Catching her breath, she restored her trek toward the front of the building. Oswell tried to keep up with her business pace.

"So, what brings you to Oswell Publishing House?"

"I had something to drop off for Mr. Carter."

"I see. So what do you think?" He smiled almost shyly.

"What do I think about what?"

"About this place? Do you like it?"

Jan stopped walking and looked around at the modernized building that was lavishly decorated, complete with restored woodwork, modern high ceiling and marble floor. She nodded approvingly.

"Yeah, it's not too shabby. Not like what I would have expected from you." She began to walk again. "Makes me wonder why you don't spend a little more time here."

Oswell didn't say anything, only offering her a little shrug.

"I mean, you must have a *million* things to do here," She continued. "I just don't know why you'd want to hang out in some book agent's place all day."

"Well, it's just . . . big here, that's all."

Jan stopped again and looked at him strangely.

"Big?" She laughed. "Well, of course it is. It's a publishing metropolis. I mean, who oversees the entire operation while you're out and about?"

"The overseer."

"Okay . . . "

"Then there's an overseer who oversees the overseer." His voice was quieter now and he looked a little forlorn suddenly. "Things pretty much operate themselves in this building. It's on a giant auto pilot."

"I see, well then, what are you doing here tonight? I mean you must have something to do if you are here this late. Am I right?"

Oswell lowered his head with a little embarrassed laugh.

"Actually, I was watching finals in the Miss Hawaiian Tropic Swimwear competition on ESPN." He waved his hand as he spoke. "My father and his new wife, Bambi or Blinky or something were having another one of their fabulous cocktail parties. I told them I had to work. I needed an alibi. Here I am."

"I see." She nodded and then cast a glance at the large glass front of the building where she was about to make her exit. "I'm going to the cafe down the street for a big greasy cheeseburger and a malt."

"How do you eat things like that and keep a figure like *that?*" He laughed.

Jan smiled coyly at him.

"Nice line." She said sarcastically. "So, I guess I'll be going. Bother me later?"

"I live for it." He laughed lightly.

Jan walked past the heavyset man at the main desk again. He didn't even acknowledge her, and she put one hand against the handle on the large glass door. She stopped for a minute and turned to see Oswell standing there watching her go.

"You know, there's no law that says you can't eat at the same cafe just because I'm there. It is a free country."

Oswell practically lunged after her.

"Yeah, I mean we don't *have* to sit at the same table or anything. We could sort of sit and not really have to look like we're there together."

"Yeah, they do have that counter. That'd be best. We don't want to give anyone the wrong idea."

The duo kept a well guarded space between them as they made the three block journey to Speckler's Cafe which was relatively empty this time of the night. They sat at the counter, as planned,and ordered cheeseburgers and malts.

"How can you eat tartar sauce on your cheeseburger?" She eyed him suspiciously when their food came. Jan shuddered and took a big bite out of her own sandwich.

"You ordered mayo and pickles on yours—that's just what tartar sauce is. Mayo, pickles and a little vinegar. They're all relative."

"Well, then why didn't you just order pickles and mayo then—it sounds more normal than ordering tartar sauce on a cheeseburger. That sounds *disgusting.*"

"No." He started as if he were deep in thought. "Ordering mayo, pickle and *vinegar* on your cheeseburger is not normal. So I order tartar and cut right to the chase."

Jan stared at him for a minute and then smiled slowly.

"You are one strange man, J.T. Oswell."

He set his cheeseburger back on his plate and blotted the grease from his chin, looking at her with great surprise.

"That's the first time I've ever heard you call me that."

"What?"

"J.T. Oswell." He laughed. "You're always calling me anything but that. I have a little list of my favorite insults, you know."

"You really don't write that stuff down, do you?" She looked mildly impressed with herself but thought he was rather pathetic at the same time.

"No, mostly I just hold on to it here," He thunked his temple with a little smile. "It's like a steel trap. Like the time you told me not to stop to think or I might forget to start again. Or, when you asked if I could get in touch with my inner self and slap the hell out of him for you? Those were all good."

"Yeah, I liked those too." She nodded with a little smile as she licked the excess mayo off her fingers. "So, you've got your publishing house, which we know is in tip-top shape, and you've got this apparent extra time on your hands, why don't you join the rest of suburbia and settle down? Get yourself a wife and a couple of kids or something. What's up with that?"

Oswell shrugged and finished chewing his mouthful. He finally swallowed and spoke again.

"Guess I just haven't found that one yet."

"That one?"

"Yeah, you know. The one that makes it bearable to get up in the morning and face a day at home. I find myself in the office on Saturdays sometimes just to avoid having to stay in that house alone. Strange, huh?"

"Not strange." She looked suddenly sympathetic. "It's good to wait until you find that special person, as long as your expectations are realistic. Setting your standards too high can lead to letdown sometimes."

"I guess." He slowly nodded.

"I mean, what are you looking for in a woman? The one you want to have your kids? Lemme have it." She sipped her shake and set it aside, offering him her undivided attention. "And simply listing consciousness doesn't count."

"*A-ha!* That was funny!" He pointed at her and then turned thoughtful as he contemplated the subject at hand. "She should have a decent body—"

"I knew it!" Jan interrupted him immediately. "Why do men always list that first? I mean if someone asked me what I was looking for in a man and I said *well,he has to be well hung,* I would be considered a *tramp!* Now, if a man mentions that a woman blessed with a sizable set of knockers and a three inch waist would be worthy of wife material, then he's *the man!*"

"Okay." He started again as she calmed down. "She should be pretty—"

"There you go again! What is your *major malfunction?* You act like you're in a meat market feeling out the poultry!"

"You're getting so defensive!" He sputtered, trying to protect himself. "You shouldn't have to worry about that anyway! I mean you're a good looking chic—"

"Chic?" She bobbed her head with narrowed eyes. "I am no *chic,* nimrod!"

"Calm down, babe! I didn't mean to offend you! We were having a perfectly good time here—" Oswell raised his hands in a surrender motion.

"Oh my God, this is quickly going from bad to worse." Jan whipped her napkin from her lap and threw it up on the countertop before her, standing quickly. "You're right, Oswell, your mind is a steel trap. Oops! Looks like somebody caught a squirrel!"

She pulled her jacket on and grabbed her pocketbook.

"Come on! I didn't mean anything by it!"

"That's just your problem,Oswell, you really *don't* know you're doing anything wrong! Funny that you should say that you are looking for the one—what do you think you have to offer in the way of being the *one* for someone else? You've got green stuff, *babe,* and you better capitalize on that as much as possible because that's the only attraction you have to offer!"

Jan turned to leave and then faced him again, grabbing the rest of his malt from the counter before him, heading for the door.

"Jan!"

"Save it, Warbucks!"

Before he could say anything else, she stormed out and down the street. The waitress behind the counter looked at him with minor disgust as she set the bill down beside his plate.

"You really have the Midas touch there, friend."

"Yeah, everything I touch turns to cold."

Chapter Thirty-one

Nick Carter exited the elevator at seven twenty-two AM and walked across the vacant waiting area. He glanced up once and then a second time with surprise in his eyes when he noticed Jan at her desk already. She normally didn't make an appearance until around nine, something that he'd neglected to ever make Oswell aware of to ward off the possibility of regular early morning visits. He nodded to her.

"Jan?"

"Hey Boss! How's it goin'?" Her smile was uncharacteristically cheery. Carter look around suspiciously.

"I'm sorry, is this Bankson, Laughter and Carter . . . ? I could have the wrong—"

"Funny! You are *so funny* Boss! That's why I find you so adorable." She gushed, waving her hand at him. "Now I'm going to get right down to work. I am busy, busy, busy! I'll be buzzing around here like a little bee, so if you need anything, you just say the word!"

Carter stood there before her with his lips slightly parted, brow furrowed and eyes narrowed. Now he stared at her.

"This is not like you. Not like you at all."

"Like me?" She looked at him oddly.

"Yeah, you know, you're *flitting.*"

"Flitting? How so?"

Carter flipped his hand a few times as if to demonstrate before he finally merely shook his head and waved to her, entering his office.

"What's that smell?" He spoke quietly to himself as he walked to his desk and set his briefcase down. "*Fresh coffee?* Since when did fresh coffee come into this office and since when did it take on the aroma of daffodils?"

Carter turned slowly as if he were afraid of what he might discover as he followed the heavenly scent. There on a side table was a fresh bouquet of daffodils and lilies and he reflexively let out a little "ahh" when he discovered it. There was no card attached. He went to the door and opened it again.

"Why does my office smell like a floral case, next to a—a coffee shop?" His voice was quiet with concern.

"Oh, just thought you'd want your day brightened some. Isn't that nice for a change?"

Carter wasn't buying it.

"I didn't miss secretary's week or something and you're doing this to spite me, are you?"

"No."

"Death in the family that I'm not aware of yet?"

"No."

"Death of an associate at the firm here?"

"No."

Carter nodded and poked his head back into his office, retreating to his desk where he peeled the lid off his coffee cup.

"Hm ... Starbucks." He sipped its richness. "With almond, very nice. And the newspaper. Very nice. I've died and gone to good boss heaven, that's what it is." He opened the paper and laid it out on the desk. It was not in Carter's daily routine to read anything except messages when he first came in, but it was here and he decided to do that first this morning

It was only when he flipped through the first section, arriving upon the last page, that he noted his first clue that there might be a reason for the special treatment that he was receiving this morning, and not just that he was just a swell guy. Carter raised the paper before his face and peered through a cut out square of about three inches by five. He lowered it again and studied all around it, realizing it was the wedding announcements. He called to his secretary.

"Jan!"

She entered his office immediately.

"Yes, sir?" Jan's sickening smile was getting the better of him now.

"Cut the *sir* crap. What's this all about?" He raised the paper before him again, looking at her through the little window the cut out created.

"What's what about?" Her eyes were wide with innocence.

"You don't find anything unusual about this paper today? Or lack *thereof*?"

"Oh, you mean the little square there?"

Carter rolled his eyes and mouthed *yes, the little square.*

"Well." She cleared her throat.

"Never mind. Can I get another paper? The whole thing this time?"

"I have mine you can read." She was off and returned in a few minutes with her copy. Carter nodded thankfully, quickly flipped to the same page and caught her before she could make her harried exit from his office.

"Hah! Hold on!" He called to her. "Yours is the exact same way. What's going on?"

"Well, there was a coupon there."

"So you took it? *Both* of them?" He nodded suspiciously.

"It was a really good coupon."

Carter turned the paper over and smirked at his secretary as he read it.

"The Triple X Multiplex having a two for one admission offer?" He looked at her coyly.

"Well, sometimes a girl gets bored." She tried to cover her embarrassment.

"It's *not* the Triple X. But you have *no idea* what it is do you? Because you don't clip anything out of the paper unless it's something you don't want me to see."

Jan blinked a few times but held his stare finally nodding in concession.

"So, do you think I could have what I'm missing here? I'm a big boy. I can handle it."

Jan made her exit and reluctantly returned with the missing portion of the daily news, handing it over to her boss sheepishly. Carter took the crumpled section and studied it for a few moments.

"Susan got married." He looked at his secretary as if it were no big deal. "It was bound to happen, Jan, she was *engaged* after all, for a year. That's usually the finale to that prelude. Is this what you were trying to keep from me?"

Jan nodded slowly, looking rather sympathetic toward her boss.

"Well don't. It's good that she's married. It's good that she's gotten on with her life. We should be happy for her."

Jan nodded again with a puzzled look in her eye, but smiled a little nonetheless.

"I'm happy for her. She deserves the best."

"You're a good man, Boss."

"Don't be ridiculous. Now go on, *get*." He forced a little smile at her, his effort toward a meek reassurance. "Don't do this stuff anymore. I was worried something was really wrong."

"Lemme know if you need anything, Boss."

"I need nothing." He waved his hand nonchalantly as he flipped through a stack of new business that was waiting for him. Carter quickly raised his eyes again before she left. "Oh, but thank you for the flowers."

"I'm glad you liked them, I put them on your account."

Jan disappeared into the lobby and Carter looked sideways with a little sarcastic laugh.

"Well, thank me, then I guess." He walked over to his desk and took his seat again, still shuffling through papers. His gaze inadvertently drifted off until he realized it had landed on the little cut out picture that lay there now. Susan and her new husband, Conner Quinland, investment broker of the year. He silently observed their smiling faces. The way her white veil softly framed her peachy face and wide eyes. Those smooth lips curled into a perfectly charming smile, her hand clasped firmly to that of her newly betrothed. *Mr. and Mrs. Conner Quinland.* Funny that a Wall Street broker could make time to have a successful relationship flying madly between Florida and New York and yet *he* couldn't even make a go at it from a distance of forty minutes. Carter sighed and rubbed his eyes tiredly.

He recalled the many conversations they'd had during their time together. *It's all about everyday effort*, she'd tell him in her sweet, soft voice. Making the time to make the relationship work everyday—the little things. How she'd playfully scold him repeatedly about it. While he was busy planning three to four extravagant getaways a year for the couple, she was lamenting about the fact that he wouldn't take time to get a simple coffee with her during the midday, or get up a half an hour earlier to take a run with her. Simply going to the grocery store late at night with her would have meant something to Susan. She was a woman of simple means and he'd never been able to bridge the gap between the two of them.

Carter would explain the importance of all that he had to do each day over a quick breakfast, and promise that they would soon have time together when they made a jaunt down to Corpus Christi or Key West or wherever they were going to this time. And she would look forlorn as he left her there, sipping her orange juice after he'd chugged his so fast...that look that would haunt him all morning, sometimes all day. *You don't work at our relationship, you labor over it.* Susan's words droned on through his mind over and over again. Carter had always supposed love would walk into his life and change him into a better man. But he didn't feel that. He loved Susan with all his heart—probably *at least* as much as Conner Quinland had. Why were things so difficult for him? He nearly lost himself the day he came home to nothing, alone again, thus igniting a string of empty relationships whose purpose was to merely provide physical comfort with the weak hope of a second shot at feeling that old spark somewhere along the way again.

She called him a month or so after they'd parted ways to inquire about the dog and see how he was mending. Of course he told her he was fine and she said she was, too. When she asked if he'd gotten over her he'd forged ahead foolishly in his answer. *I've put it behind me.* She seemed happy for his confidence and he could almost hear her smiling through the telephone and wondered if she could as equally detect his brokenness. *Every minute of every hour of every day I put it behind me.* It wasn't entirely a lie. Then his life closed around him. He skipped breakfast entirely, now, never even bothering to sit at the table where they'd once shared orange juice over the newspaper and two minutes of conversation—something that the women since Susan didn't even seem to pay notice to. Emptiness begged to consume him, or maybe it already had.

First she'd left. Now she was gone.

The sound of the buzzing intercom broke him out of his growing slump and he half heartedly pushed the button to take the message.

"Yes?"

"Mr. Carter, Oswell House needs the St. John rewrites back by this weekend. Is that going to happen?"

"What?"

"Yes, their courier is here in the lobby right now." That was her unspoken cue for him to avoid saying anything stupid on the intercom, he knew. Suddenly he remembered the late evening telephone call he'd gotten from Meghan Laine only the previous night and he sighed. Carter depressed the button again.

"Jan, could you come into my office for a minute?"

In a moment the woman was standing there in the doorway and he motioned for her to come in and close the door.

"This *weekend?* I thought we had another week? How can they possibly need it by this weekend?" He rubbed his forehead roughly as he thought about it.

"They only need two of the four. Can it be done?"

"Well, that's just the thing. That wretched Iowa woman called me last night and told me that she and her fiancée didn't *agree* with any of the rewrites that Oswell's editor ordered. There could be a problem."

"I hate to say this, but you better think of something to tell them because apparently St. John signed an agreement that included the first two rewrites in full by this weekend." Jan looked a little worried as she went on. "I'm sure I don't need to tell you that if *he* reneges *you* renege.'

"Who in their right mind would order a total of three stories from one person within a month's time anyway?"

"The person who was told that there were at least three stories already complete."

Carter tapped his pencil on his desktop as he thought it through. He squinted as if he were in a certain amount of pain as he finally spoke.

"You know, on days like this, I would like to say to heck with it all. Maybe just wake up and find myself back in Wisconsin—little snow on the ground. Maybe take the dog for a walk. Come home to a warm house and a toasty fire. Maybe a nice quiche even." Carter turned to look at his secretary. "Do you know how long it's been since I had a good quiche? Do you make quiche, Jan?"

The woman never removed her curious stare from her boss even to blink. She shook her head now. "No, Boss. I don't do quiche."

"That's a shame." He flipped open his rolodex and pulled a little card out of it, handing it to her. "Would you please get me the soonest flight to

Des Moines and call Farmer St. John and his lovely whatever-she-is and tell them that gloom and doom is making a visit, please expect me?"

Jan listened carefully to Carter as he stood now and walked over to the flowers still sitting there. He plucked a lily from the mixture and tucked it into the button hole of his suit jacket. He turned to face her.

"Send word with the courier that Oswell House will have their rewrites by Friday."

Chapter Thirty-two

"Oh! Can you *believe* that man!" Meg snapped another crisp green bean and threw it into the strainer in the kitchen sink. She picked up another handful and continued with the mundane chore while Noel chopped onions for the casserole they were making. "To tell me to lay off and mind my own business!"

"Well," Noel sniffed as she attempted to rub her eyes with her shirtsleeve while working. "You gotta see that the man thinks that whatshisname is the author. I mean, from his viewpoint, you probably were being a bit *nosy.*"

"But to treat someone's wife—"

"Girlfriend."

"Live in girlfriend, which is *pretty* darn close! To treat someone's significant other that rudely is just...just *rude!*"

"So are you going to do the rewrites or what?"

"I did rewrite it, the way that *I* like it."

"And being that you are a big successful publishing house owner, I'm sure that's dandy." Noel shot her a sideways look as she chopped away, her voice dripping with sarcasm.

"They will get their rewrites, Noel. Never fear."

"But will they be what the editor told you he wanted?"

"Not exactly." Meg nodded a little with a sheepish look on her face. "But what do they know? I mean, if I make all the changes that they're calling for, it won't even be the same story. You might as well put someone else's name on it because it's no longer *mine.*"

"It's no longer yours anyway. I think you already put the fix to that." Noel sniffed more loudly as her eyes welled up with tears. "It's a shame too, after all that you've worked for."

Meg stopped snapping the beans and looked at her friend.

"I'm sure I can get everything straightened out." She softened her voice. "It's nothing to get upset about, Noel."

"I'm not, this is the strongest onion I've ever cut into." Noel looked upward and away from the onion as her friend rushed to get her a tissue, blotting her eyes for her. "I'm just saying, and I hate to sound like Mother O'Dell, but you made your bed, now it's time to *nap* a spell in it. That's the facts."

The ringing of the telephone jostled Meg from her thoughts as she considered what Noel had said. She picked it the receiver as she wiped her hands on a kitchen towel.

"Hello?"

"Hey Meggie. This is Jan from Bankson, Laughton and Carter. How are you?"

"I'm fine. You?"

"Just great. Say, I know this is unexpected, but Mr. Carter is flying into Des Moines this afternoon to give Marcus a little input about those rewrites. Apparently your fiancée signed into an agreement that said they would be complete by this weekend and Mr. Carter said you all were having a minor dispute."

"Yes, yes we were. The *agreement* said that?" Meg listened intently with wide eyes to the woman on the other end. She shot Noel a look.

"Honey, you know how men are. They never read anything." Jan smirked. "Unfortunately the lawyers are exempt from that habit—they read it all. Anyhow, Mr. Carter's staying on at a local hotel just for the night—hopefully he'll come back to Tampa with manuscripts in hand."

"Well, I'm afraid he's not going to find the accommodations around here that he's accustomed to. I'm sure it will be quite a step down."

"No biggy. Sounds like it's going to be all work anyway."

"Well, okay." Meg rolled her eyes as she surveyed her surroundings estimating the clean up that would be necessary before she could have any guests. "I'll make some reservations at a restaurant here."

"That won't be necessary either. I'd just throw together some sand-wiches or something. It really will be a quick trip."

"Well, I'm in the middle of making a casserole, so casserole it will be."

Suddenly Jan looked thoughtful as she twisted the telephone cord between her fingers. She looked around to be sure that no one was standing near enough to hear her. "Um, little FYI, Mr. Carter detests things like . . . *quiche*. He's allergic to egg products. Just so you know.'

"Thanks. I'll keep that in mind." Meg set the phone back down and stood quietly for a moment, a small smile coming to her lips. "Noel, check the pantry and see if I have any of those nice crusts left. We're having company. Oh, and while you're there, see if we need eggs."

Chapter Thirty-three

Carter entered his apartment in a hurry, throwing his coat aside and slamming the door. His faithful dog was there to greet him, likely curious as to why his master was home again so soon. He wagged his tail and followed him about loyally anyway, watching as the agent grabbed a bag from the top shelf of his closet and began punching it full of the things he'd need for an overnight excursion. He rambled on about the chore of having to do as much to his attentive pet, glancing at him now and again as he lay in the doorway.

"Your mother got married last week, and it wasn't to me in case you didn't notice." Carter muttered raising his eyebrows in a rather comedic fashion as he went on. "She's *Mrs. Stockbroker* now, chucking all plans for her initial intention of becoming *Mrs. Workaholic-can-have-no-joy-in-his-life*. Do you suppose she thought that was too much to write every time she signed a check?"

The dog sighed loudly as if on cue.

"Now, there's no reason for you to believe that you're the reason she left. Sometimes people can care for each other and just not be the marrying kind and it all goes to hell very fast." Carter grabbed his bag and trundled off to the bathroom where he began to empty the few contents of the medicine cabinet into it as well. Razor, deodorant, aftershave, cologne. "Why am I taking this? I don't need this, I'm not going on a date, I'm going to Iowa, for heaven's sake."

Carter removed the last item from his bag and set it upon the shelf again. He stared at it now.

"That's ridiculous. I can wear cologne, why wouldn't I? Do these cologne makers think that the only reason people wear cologne is so that you can draw women to you? Look at those stupid advertising gimmicks. Thank you Calvin Klein. Now I don't want to wear cologne because I don't want to send off the wrong impression." He took it down again and set it into his bag. Suddenly he pulled it back out of his bag a second time and set it back on the shelf, shaking his head. "No. I refuse to rub myself down with stinky bait like I'm *trout fishing* or something. I won't be a party to it. I'll be sporting that manly scent the next few days. What do they call that? Zest? Dial?"

Carter glanced down at his dog still standing there, mopey, sensing that he was about to be left behind. He knelt and roughly scrubbed his hand down the Labrador's back a few times with a smile.

"You're still depressed about your mother, aren't you? Well, don't you worry. I'll still be here to keep the dogchow on the table—keep the home-fires burning. Follow you around the courtyard with the poop scoop. Your old man won't bail on you."

Carter quickly scribbled a note for the cleaning woman who would be in that afternoon, asking her to let the dog out a few times before she left. He checked Boo's water and food and winked at him as he stood in the door.

"Don't mess the rugs up, stay away from Mrs. Swenson. You know how nervous you make her, she's got a heart condition. Oh—and I've sprinkled cayenne pepper all over the hibiscus in the living room so if you chew on it again, you're going to be in for a pleasant surprise." He stepped back inside again and quickly scratched behind the dog's ears once more. "Quality time when I get back—I promise."

Chapter Thirty-four

"Noel, clear a space on that countertop there! Quick!" Meg lunged forward to the clearing her friend has created and practically threw her laptop computer and a stack of mailers down. She stood back now, out of breath from the haul from her bedroom, pushed her hair out of her eyes and looked down at what she was wearing. "Would you look at me? I look like I just rolled out of bed."

"Well, a flight from Tampa is going to take a few hours, I think you have time to—*fix* yourself." Noel waved her hand as she spoke. She hurried around her friend's kitchen cramming things back into cupboards and picking up anything excess. She saw as Meg started toward the hallway closet, home to the vacuum cleaner, and she quickly grabbed the woman's arm and veered her back to the laptop. "No! *You write!*"

Meg sighed and rolled her eyes as Noel pulled out the vacuum and began to madly sweep it along the carpet in the living room and dining room. When she'd finished, she returned to the kitchen and peeled the wax paper from the thawing crust that she had set out earlier, shaking her head all the while.

"I don't get it. Vegetable tortellini is one of your best dishes. Why shelve it and go with a quiche?" Noel began to whip the eggs in a large glass bowl as she'd been instructed.

Meg only looked up with a sly smile from where she was seated. She hunched back over the computer and continued hammering away at the rewrites.

"I need to get enough of this done so that it looks like Marcus is doing the actual writing by the time Mr. Personality gets here." She shook her head. "I *told* him he needed to read what it was he was signing! Instead he saw dollar signs and his pen went on automatic pilot."

"Did you tell him not to sign it?"

"Yes, but you know how men are. The only think with their wallets and their, their, well *you know*." She never raised her eyes as she rambled on.

"That's all men, hon. Men are a simple race of egocentric Neanderthal creatures. I happen to be married to their king." Noel began to add finely chopped peppers, onions, and spices to the mixture. She poured it into the shell and looked up, wiping her hands on a towel as she went on. "Do you want me to put this in the oven already?"

"No, just the refrigerator. I'll add the cheese and finish it in a bit." Meg roughly tousled her hair in frustration. "*Oh!* I don't see how I can possibly get this stuff done in time to go back to press tomorrow! I need a magic wand. How can people rightfully put such rigid timelines on art? I mean, it doesn't just *happen!*"

Noel made a face to accompany her shrug as she started to gather her purse and slipped into her coat.

"In the real world they don't care about art. Finished product for retail, that's what it's all about." She droned on in her monotone way. Meg paused to see her friend standing there speaking so angrily.

"Well, reality bites then." Meg finally answered.

"Reality is not for wimps, that's for sure. Reality is a crutch for people who can't handle drugs."

Meg rose from her place at the counter, looking even more puzzled. She approached her friend and embraced her warmly.

"You sound like a perpetual string of bumper stickers," She smirked. "You sure you don't want to hang around and meet him?"

"No, I'll meet him someday."

Now Meg squinted at her curiously.

"How so?"

Noel smiled at her friend as she buttoned her navy blue down filled coat. She pulled her purple knit scarf around her neck tightly and took a step toward the door.

"I just will."

"You act like there's something you know that I don't."

"Oh, you *know* it Meggie." Noel ducked out the door calling one last time behind her. "Good luck, girl."

Meg had miraculously finished half of the required rewrite on the first story by the time that Marcus showed his face at the back door just before six. He was surprised to see her standing there, leaning over the computer perched on the countertop wearing a black skirt and a turtle-neck sweater. She was freshly made up and smelled of her vanilla bath crystals. He studied her before speaking.

"Well, there's no wakes, and it's not Sunday—and I know you don't go to church during the week." He started slowly as he took off his work gloves and stocking cap.

"Not true. I'm going to confession tomorrow." She said in a low voice before giving him her full attention. "We're having company here any time, something you would have known had you had your phone turned on."

"Company? Who?"

"Mr. Carter from the agency in Tampa is flying in to help prod you along on the rewrites that are to be finished by this *weekend*."

"Why this weekend?"

Meg glared at him.

"Because when you signed the agreement, the agreement that I encouraged you to read, I might add for the record, you signed yourself into a pact that said you would have these two rewrites completed by this weekend." She turned to the computer again, her fingers flying over the keyboard. "Next time you sign something without reading what it says, you *will* be the one doing the rewriting."

"I thought we were in this together?"

"We are in this together, but one of us is in it as a writer and the other as a signer, and your signing is saying that I'm writing faster than writers can write, something that as signer and not a writer, I'm sure you can't really appreciate." Clearly she was distraught and making little sense to him now. He let her words sink in for a few moments.

"You're mad."

"I'm not mad," she half-heartedly assured him.

"You are."

"I am not mad."

"I can sense your hostility, it's a gift I have."

Meg turned to see his seriousness and lowered her eyes a little, realizing that he wasn't going to laugh, and that indeed he did believe that he possessed an uncanny insight.

"Well, your gift is off a little because I am not mad." She looked away again. "However, in the future, let's just look over the paperwork together. If you're in a pinch and I'm not there for some reason, just tell them you need a lawyer to look it over and then I can see what we're getting into. Okay?"

"Okay." He nodded as he finished removing his heavy outdoor clothes. "So when will he be here? Carter?"

"Any time now."

"So how's the rewrites coming along? Will we make it?"

We?

"We might, honey, if you go and take a shower and let me do *our* work here." She followed him down the hallway. "I've laid out a pair of khakis and a sweater on the bed. But you'll need to know a little about the story that I'm on right now so that when he gets here we won't look like a couple of idiots—"

"I don't want to wear khakis, what's wrong with jeans?" He whined. "I hate sweaters, too."

"Well, khakis are a little more, more *whatever* than jeans. Wear the sweater. Okay, this book is the one about the three best friends who are growing as individuals and their lives take different turns. Their careers and families."

"Why can't I just wear a nice shirt? There's nothing wrong with that blue shirt over there."

"Marcus, are you listening to me?" Meg lightly grabbed his arm as she tried her best to continue. "This book is the one the editor is so hot to make all the changes too. You've *got* to understand the reasons why I don't feel those alterations are necessary. If you *don't* listen, you *can't* understand. And you *are* going to wear the sweater."

"That's an old man's sweater."

"Listen to me!" She found her own voice rising quickly and made herself stop suddenly. Meg took a few deep breaths before going on. "Marcus, this particular book is very important to me. It is the only thing that I've ever created that is based somewhat upon myself. It's about me and Noel and Reed."

"What about me?"

"What about you!" Her voice reached its pitch again as she rolled Noel's words back through her brain again believing now that bumper sticker cliché or not, she'd hit the nail on the head about the egocentrical part—or at least at that precise moment! "You wrote the book! That's *your* recognition! Why do you need to question my every motive behind the book that will bear *your* name and *your* image! How selfish can you be, Marcus?"

"Meg," he looked hurt all of a sudden. "We're fighting."

"We're not fighting!"

"Yes, yes we are. We never fight and we're having a fight. Right now."

"That's because I never disagree with you and *this* time I *do*. I'm entitled to that right under the Constitution of . . . of pre-matrimonial rights, or whatever it is." Meg shook her head helplessly. She took his hand, softening her tone. "I don't mean to fight with you, but you need to understand how important this book is to me. It has sentimental value and I think it will help others relate to the characters as well, because they can see themselves in it. I think that's important. I really do."

"I don't disagree. That sounds reasonable."

"Then you understand how I don't want to make all the changes that the editor ordered. You need to take a stand against it. Promise me you will."

Marcus stared at her blankly.

"This writing stuff is crazy. I'm not too good at it."

"*Please*, Marcus." She pleaded with wide eyes.

"I'll do what I can," he picked up a pair of socks and underwear lying there and headed for the bathroom to get ready. "But feel free to jump in anytime. I don't want to set myself up for a bunch of *Marcus you should haves.*"

"Never fear!" Meg flounced down the hallway with renewed optimism, and planted a kiss on his cheek before making a final sweep through the house picking up anything out of place.

Chapter Thirty-five

Nick Carter exited the airport with his single piece of carryon luggage and made his way to the lone taxi cab parked alongside the walkway outside. He shuddered as a blast of northern air blew through him, suddenly remembering how these winters were although it had been years since he was a first hand witness to their extreme chill. He nodded at the driver and got in, glancing at his watch. It was nearly seven o'clock now and he was disgusted that the better part of the working day had been spent in St. Louis on a layover due to a runway there which was sheeted with a thin layer of ice. He'd hoped to come into town and unwind a minute or two at his hotel and have this business wrapped up by late this evening, and now it was almost late this evening already. Carter sighed.

"Where would you like to go this evening?" The cabby asked politely. A little laugh escaped Carter. It was the first time he'd actually heard a cab driver speak in one complete, unbroken sentence. In Tampa if you were forced to take a cab, it was out of necessity. And if you were having a really lucky day you got a driver who spoke no English, thereby avoiding the a string of colorful curses bellowed out while stuck in traffic. Anyone who complained was told to rent a car or commission a limo. Cab riding wasn't a luxury. This cab, however, was clean and its driver looked as if he'd actually bathed in the past twenty-four hours, another refreshing thing he noted, together with the fact that there wasn't a ton of traffic.

"I need to get to Jasper Falls—how far is that?"

"It's about twenty minutes. You looking to go in town or the hills?"

"I have an address here," Carter dug it out of his jacket pocket and squinted to read in the darkened cab. "R. R. four."

"Rural Route. Yeah, you want the hills."

"Is the snow bad there? Can you make it in a cab?"

"I'll bet you're from the coast aren't you?" The driver smiled as he watched the man in the backseat nod in his rear view mirror. "Welcome to Iowa, home of steel belted radials. Don't leave home without 'em. You might get yourself a real coat, too, if you're going to be here any length of time at all."

Carter laughed lightly.

"I'm leaving tomorrow early afternoon. Hardly seems worth the trip, does it?"

"Might make you appreciate where you come from a little more." The cabby turned onto the uncrowded ramp that put the cab on the interstate that would take them to Jasper Falls.

The cab stopped in front of the little farmhouse about half an hour later. Carter got out and paid the man for his ride and tipped him generously.

He peeled the bills from his money clip dictating their purpose as he did so.

"Here's for getting me here minus whiplash or a panic attack. Here's for your courtesy. And here's for not cursing me out in Portuguese." He handed it over to the smiling driver who thanked him eagerly. Carter turned toward the quaint house and made his way to the back entry lit by a single light over the small deck there. He knocked on the door and waited.

"He's here!" Meg called to her fiancée. She skittered around the kitchen, wondering what was taking Marcus so long. He entered the room finally, quickly approaching the door. Meg expelled a deep disgusted breath as she discovered that he was wearing a navy blue polo and a pair of jeans. He didn't notice this as he pulled the door open, letting the agent inside and out of the piercing cold weather.

"Mr. Carter," Marcus shook the man's hand readily and took his bag from him, setting it aside. "How was your trip? I was starting to wonder about you. I heard it was nasty down south."

"Actually, yes, I got hung up in St. Louis. I've gotten here later than I would have liked, I'm afraid."

"Well, come on in then and let's get down to business." Marcus motioned for him to come away from the doorway. "Meg, will you take Mr. Carter's jacket?"

Meg couldn't help but stare with an odd expression as the agent removed his jacket to reveal his version of casual clothing. Khaki pants and a red sweater flecked with tan. She sighed and shot Marcus another look of disapproval, but he didn't seem to notice her for a second time.

Carter nodded a forced friendly hello to her and they went into the living room where Marcus had started a fire. She watched from there as they sat down in the overstuffed comfortable chairs positioned before the hearth and began to talk. Meg laid Carter's jacket over the back of a kitchen chair and entered the next room, following along like a small child. She took her seat on the couch, listening intently and quietly. Blue, perhaps taking the cue that she needed some reassurance, devotedly took his place at her feet. The dog sighed and laid his head across her knees as she sat there.

"I'm aware that you don't agree with all of the rewrites that Oswell's editor proposed. I talked with Ms. Laine about it a little the other night," Carter started. Hearing this, Marcus shot her a brief look of confusion but quickly averted his attention to the one before him again, nodding slightly. "As I told her, the editors play a vital role in the publishing business. It's their job to be current with what the market demands are. Whatever they deem important we take very seriously."

I understand that." Marcus started slowly. "I simply thought that the changes made were so radical that the story is barely what it was upon my submission. I just have to ask myself, what's the point of writing it then in the first place?"

"And I can understand your creative needs here too, Mr. St. John—"

"Call me Marcus," he interjected.

"Marcus, then. I do not wish to stifle your creative outlet or encourage you to allow anyone else to, but creating a book is an expensive process. The rising cost of paper coupled with the heavy promotion required to push the book before the noses of thousands of readers can really be overwhelming." Carter's words were free flowing and, Meg suspected, practiced a little too well. "That's what I was trying to explain to Ms. Laine. You see, being a new writer, you might not understand the unexpected push you are receiving and from a splendid publishing house as well. Some people try all their lives to get picked up by a group their size and never achieve it. You, my friend, are a very fortunate man."

"And I do appreciate that."

"I'm sure you do. And I'm sure that you can appreciate it when I tell you that, although I'm not at liberty to insist that you make the necessary rewrites, Oswell has made their decision about what they feel they need from that manuscript and the original one is not where it's at. It's not personal, it's strictly business."

"What about literary quality?" Meg couldn't keep to herself any longer. All eyes turned in her direction now as she continued wearily. "What about the fact that it appeals to women on a level that they can understand and appreciate? Mass appeal is the goal, am I right here?"

"You are right," Carter nodded quietly. "But, realize the editors are experienced in their field and know the market trends. They can virtually steer a new writer down the path to success. In fact, it's not unheard of that a literary producer would come up with an idea to hop on a trend and commission a writer to crank it out as soon as possible. That's along these lines. It's all about being in the right place at the right time."

Carter turned now to Marcus who was seated taking it all in carefully.

"You, Marcus, are in the right place at the right time. It is my recommendation that you make the changes and keep on your roll. You're about to be a very well known talent. Let's go with it." The agent watched him with a serious look. "What do you say?"

Marcus pondered the notion. Meg watched him, fearing what the turning wheels in his head would crank out next. Her faithful pet licked her fingers as she waited nervously.

"No, Boo."

Hearing this, Carter's head whipped around to see her, his brow furrowed and expression strange. She wondered what she could have done now.

"Did you say Boo?" He asked curiously.

Meg nodded softly, still waiting as the fate of her precious book hung in its delicate balance. The agent said nothing more as he turned to face Marcus now, waiting for the same thing. Finally the man spoke.

"Level with me, Mr. Carter." Marcus leaned forward. "What's the scope of this thing as we're looking at it now? What are the predictions?"

Carter thought carefully before speaking.

"Of course no one can know for certain—the first three weeks will give us a better idea. But with the promotion that Oswell House normally gives its big name clients, we're quite positive feeling about it."

"Big name clients?"

"Not to sound *trite*," Carter cast a quick glance in Meg's direction. "But you do appear to have all the right stuff."

"What about creative freedom on down the road?" Marcus continued. Meg could swear that his eyes were gleaming as she watched him with wonder.

"You get yourself established, get yourself an audience and they will hardly be able to tell you what they want to read because *you'll* be telling them what they want to read."

"Really?"

"Really."

Silence.

Marcus stood and clapped his hands together with a contented smile.

"Then it's settled. You want rewrites, you got 'em."

"Marcus!" Meg stood now suddenly.

"Good deal!" Carter shook the pseudo writer's hand heartily.

"Can I have a word with you, Marcus? In the kitchen?"

"Meg, I think that Mr. Carter—"

"Call me Nick."

"I think that Nick here has a very valid point. Maybe it's not where I want to be from a personal standpoint, but this a business decision as well as a creative one. I think it would be a very lucrative one, honey."

"Well, *honey*, maybe *you* don't believe in caving into the demands of others based solely on monetary motivation."

Marcus stood now, but dared not leave the safety of the room where the agent sat.

"*Honey*, the representation we have here is second to none. *I* believe that if *I* ride their wave initially, everything else will fall into place."

"Well *honey*, don't you think that if the company rejects your freedom of creativity right off the bat they'll be inclined to continue on after they own *you*?" Her voice was rising uncomfortably as she neared where Marcus was standing. He didn't flinch, his courage seemingly growing as was her anger.

"Well, *honey*, I just think that this is a practical decision to make—

financial and otherwise."

"Well, *honey*, I just think that perhaps sitting too near that fire has tweaked your brain a tad,causing you to become delusional, empowering you with a false sense of investment savvy, *Honey*!"

"You said honey two times there, sweetheart."

Meg flung her arms to her sides, attempting to restrain her anger as she walked out of the room in time with an unheard angry cadence.

"Well, *sweetheart*, I'm off to do my mundane housework before I turn in, leaving you to your *mentalk* or whatever bombastic conversation topics you may want to cover!"

Meg stormed down the hallway toward her room.

Chapter Thirty-six

When Marcus finally turned in for the night it was nearly midnight. He found Meg typing at her computer uncomfortably as she sat cross-legged on their bed. He was a bit sheepish about his entry as he smiled, settling himself next to her on the bed. She raised her eyes to him, issuing a glare that made him swallow hard.

"Honey?" he offered.

"I think we've honeyed and sweethearted each other enough for one night, don't you?" She gathered her notebooks and laptop standing to go. Her pencil fell off the bed and she quickly retrieved it, clamping it between her teeth as she juggled the armload trying to leave the room.

"Where are you going?"

"Well, where am I going?" She spit the pencil onto the bed and looked at him with pure disbelief. "Where am I going, you ask? Well, I'm going to do the rewrites, author! In fact, I'll probably spend the better part of the night rewriting a perfectly good story that will no longer have even an *iota* about it similar to its original form. That's where *I'm* going."

"Meg, we can't do this to ourselves."

"You're doing it to me!"

"And you're doing it to me! I wouldn't even be doing this if it weren't for your insistence that this book be printed come hell or high water! How can you blame me now?"

"I gave you the book—a perfectly good book that you should be honored to put your name on, and you decide to start throwing out those harebrained decisions of yours without even considering what *I* would like to do about it!"

"Let's not do this to each other."

Meg brushed the hair out of her eyes now and looked at him, trying to sort out what she would say.

"I just need some time to cool down, I'll be fine." She was restoring her composure and it was a real effort to do so. "I'm going to work in the guest room."

"Oh, you can't." Marcus rubbed his forehead and spoke in a low, apologetic tone. "It was so late I just told Carter to take that bed for the night. He's leaving in the morning anyway."

"*What?*" Her voice began to rise again. "He wants to leave and take your supposed rewrites with him tomorrow morning and you invite him to stay in this house? How do you expect that he'll think you had time to do such a thing? *Magic?*"

Marcus looked away and shrugged.

"I don't know. I just knew that it was late and I made the offer...and he stayed." He touched her arm. "Forgive me Meg if I've screwed it up too bad."

She looked at him for a moment. Slowly she backed out of the room with her stack, tiptoeing discreetly down the hallway, past the guest room, making her way to the kitchen.

She silently entered the kitchen nearly tripping over her big old dog as she did. Regaining her balance, Meg thrust the laptop and books onto the countertop. She flipped one dim light and turned toward her dog now.

"Well, Boo, whattaya think?"

He only stared at her and then glanced over to his dish in a way that he could use a bite to eat. Meg smiled and touched her own stomach remembering that she'd neglected to eat dinner that night as well. She first scooped out a helping of dog food for her loyal companion and then opened the refrigerator to survey her choices. There, top shelf and center, was the beautiful quiche she'd baked hours earlier, intending to serve it for the dinner than never happened due to the late arrival of their impromptu overnight guest. She pulled it out and cranked the oven on, setting it inside to warm it up. She settled back at the breakfast bar getting her papers in order to continue what had become a writing chore. She dove in full force anyway.

So wrapped up in her study of the editor's notes, she wasn't aware that anyone had entered the kitchen until a low voice sounded from the doorway.

"How you doing, Boo?"

Meg quickly raised her eyes to see Carter kneeling over her Labrador, roughly petting his neck. Her dog craned his head to enjoy it. *Hmph! Even the dog's on his side!* She looked at her computer, pretending not to notice him.

"Hi," he offered her. "Couldn't you sleep?"

"I have some work to take care of." She barely answered him. Carter nodded and raised his eyebrows. There was more quiet between them. After a second, he approached where she was sitting, causing her to hurriedly shove the editor's notes under one of the books lying beside her. She smirked. "Did you need something, Mr. Carter?"

"Not really. I just can't sleep very well in different places."

"I'm sorry, Marcus should have let you go into town and check into your hotel."

"It wouldn't matter, I couldn't sleep there either. Just one of those things."

"I see."

"I'm sorry if you find it uncomfortable, however, my staying here. I know you're not exactly *fond* of me."

"Where would you get that idea?"

"I think you told me."

"I see."

More silence.

"In any case, I'm sorry that we've gotten off to such a bad start. I'm really not that kind of a person."

"Really?" Meg still would not grant him even a glance as her fingers sped over the keys.

"Really, you know, that *bombastic* type." He laughed lightly now trying to stifle it by placing his fingers over his own lips. He looked away.

"Are you making fun of me, Mr. Carter?" Her fingers stopped moving but her gazed remained fixed on the screen of her computer. Finally she could contain herself no longer, emitting a little burst of laughter, cursing herself internally for not having the will to control it. At last Meg's eyes lifted and she looked at him with a hint of defeat.

"But it was a good word though. *Astute.*" He nodded as he smiled at her.

"I have others too."

"Well, I don't doubt that for a minute." He rubbed his chin thoughtfully. "Care to share?"

"Surreptitious."

"Good."

"Pretentious.

"Splendid." He continued to nod.

"Narcissistic."

"Go on."

"Sanctimonious." She rolled her eyes.

"Bank running dry?"

"There's plenty more where that came from, my contemptible acquaintance."

"Well, I don't think I've ever been called a self-centered, pig-headed, snooty bastard in so many highly intelligible words before. That was lovely. Pure poetry."

"That's that University of Iowa education for you."

They stared at each other for several long seconds. The smell of the quiche in the oven filled the room, reminding her that it was probably ready. She went to the oven and turned it off, suddenly feeling guilty about the scheme she devised.

"Are you hungry? I've probably got something around here I can whip up."

She walked to the pantry and scanned the shelves.

"I could make some tunafish salad or something."

"What's that delightful smell?" He sniffed the air in an exaggerated motion. "It smells like food, but I'm not quite familiar with anything beyond the Taco Bell drive through."

"What happened to that saying about it being lonely at the top but you eat better?" She leaned back from the pantry and looked at him.

"Whoever said that had a good cook in their kitchen." He smirked quietly. "I could be mistaken, it's been a while. But I would swear that you've got a quiche in there. Could it be?"

"Well, yes, but..." She looked bewildered, recalling Jan's warning about the egg allergy. "I didn't know if you would like quiche."

"Who, living and breathing, wouldn't like quiche? And you can't count coma victims."

Meg laughed as she shut the pantry doors, pulling an oven mitt over her hand. She slid the rack out of the oven and removed one perfect quiche, setting it aside.

Carter pushed a stool up to the breakfast bar and watched her as she gathered two plates and sliced through the pie, placing a piece on each. As she didn't seem to notice his watchful eye, he looked at her discreetly. Her petite figure was housed safely inside the confines of casual blue plaid pajama bottoms and a generous matching sweatshirt that brought out the same color in her eyes. His eyes roved over her tresses that cascaded haphazardly, ending somewhere above the middle of her back. Blonde with little highlighted portions here and there, probably reminiscent of the summer sun. Her feet were bare showing off pink tipped toes and slender ankles, and as she stretched to reach for two glasses from a high shelf in the cupboard, her small midriff was inadvertently revealed but only for a split second. He quickly looked away as she turned around, placing the plate before him. The heavenly aroma of the dish wafted through the air and he breathed it in deeply, catching the unexpected bonus of her vanilla musky smell along the way. Carter smiled politely and nodded.

"Thank you."

Meg didn't reply outside of a cordial smile as she poured him a glass of milk and set it down beside his plate. She then took her own dish and sat across from him. They ate in silence for a few minutes, she, waiting to see if he would actually eat the quiche. He did. She watched as he closed his eyes and chewed each bite slowly as if trying to decide if it were palatable or not. Finally she could take it no longer.

"Are you in pain?" she asked regarding his expressions.

"Pain? No. Heaven? Maybe." He took another bite. "This is better than sex. My God."

"Thank you, I think." She raised her eyebrows and took another bite of her own, chewing quietly.

"So," he muttered in between bites. "What are you working on here?"

"Work assignment, the Gazette...you know," she waved her fork as she spoke. "That all important writing job I have."

"Did I really sound like that much of a jerk about it?" His look resembled wounded. She only tipped her head sideways and continued to eat.

He shook his head. "I'm going to try this again. You know, we really got off to a bad start. I feel bad about it. Don't you feel bad about it? Do you think I could have another piece of this?"

"No and yes."

She took his plate and sliced another piece setting it down before him once again, reseating herself.

"You are content to just hate me then?"

"Why should you care, Mr. Carter?"

"Nick."

"Mr. Carter."

"Okay." He laughed nervously and looked away. Meg rolled her eyes.

"It's just that, you big city types are so involved in what you're cranking out for dollars in your ivory towers, you can't possibly think about the people you're creating these books for and their wants, let alone the poor saps beating their brains out on a typewriter trying to get published."

"We do the best we can based on the research we conduct."

"You base your decision-making abilities on facts and figures printed out by computers—nameless and faceless." She looked at him before going on. "What about the real people behind those numbers? What about human qualities that are discarded thanks to modern technology?"

"I see." He nodded his head. "And you think that book sales and figures aren't a good indicator of what everyone is buying and reading?"

"Just because they're buying it doesn't make it good."

"What do you suggest they're doing with the *good stuff* then that we don't have figures for? Stealing it? Do you think we can honestly conduct a poll where people are going to say, you know, I ripped that book off from the corner newsstand, it was poignant."

"Are you mocking me?"

"No, because what you're saying isn't even making enough sense to mock. It's business Ms. Laine, it certainly doesn't reflect upon the person behind the writing. It's not personal. *Period.*"

Meg stood from her place and took her plate to the sink. She quietly shut her laptop down and gathered her books together as he watched on.

"Oh come on, now you're mad again." He slumped in his seat. "Don't be that way. We were enjoying a good conversation here."

"Were we? I guess everyone is speaking for me these days."

"What does that mean?"

Meg glanced at his disturbed look momentarily, and then blew it off. She walked to the doorway with her things and looked down at her dog laying on his bed. As she prepared to bid her four legged friend good-night, Carter spoke again.

"I have a lab named Boo." He took another bite of his quiche.

"Is that a line?"

"What kind of a line is that? I do. I have a lab named Blue. I just thought that was odd, you know?"

She wasn't sure what to make of him.

"You know," he wouldn't stop trying to convince her. "Me and you and a—"

"Dog named Boo, I know the song." She wasn't as amused.

"Well, it was a little human interest, that's all."

"Since when are you concerned with human interest?" She laughed as she stood there. "I mean, where's your data? Figures—*sales sheets?*"

"Come on! You want me to tell you that everything Marcus creates is something unusual and perfect? Because that's not the way it works. Everyone thinks their work is up to par or better or they wouldn't submit it. In fact, Marcus' stuff is no better than a lot of stuff out there—but he happened to be in the right place at the right time. Timing. That's *it.*"

"Oh really?"

"Really." He nodded defensively. "As his agent, it's my job to represent him and help get these little editor-writer glitches ironed out so that pub-lication can *actually* happen. Otherwise I wouldn't be freezing my ass off here in Billy Hell."

"Thanks for the effort," she retorted sarcastically.

"You act like everything that flows from the man's pen is liquid gold!"

"You act like you're using him as a mouthpiece to pen your own ideas!"

"Well, many of those ideas have been bestsellers, and if he's making money along the way, who cares anyway!" Carter was irate. "What do you want me to say? That I've never seen such insightful material before? That I think it's top rate? Untouchable? Unique? I've seen these formulas a mil-lion times over! Nothing is unique when you reach my stage of the game."

"Maybe people are sending you stuff that is unique—but by the time the editors get done with it, it's like everyone else's! Why don't you take a chance?"

"You want unique?" He was whispering loudly now as their voices had become quite loud. "Congratulations! Marcus' work is unique! Just like everyone else's."

"You—you are entirely *imperious!*"

"And you—*presumptuous!*"

"Insolent!"

"Nonsensical!"

"Impetuous!" She shot back, her eyes wide now. She turned to leave, but stopped, glancing back once again before departing for her room. She was out of insult ammunition and nothing witty came to her mind either. "*You!*"

Carter raised his hands in defeat and in an effort to yield her name calling.

"Truce?"

"Not a chance." Meg glared at him. "You know what you are, Mr. Carter? And I'd rather be anything else but this. You are *jaded.*"

Her eyes were misty from anger and her trembling nearly evident as she stood there staring at him.

"Meghan—"

She cut him off with her exit.

Chapter Thirty-seven

The following morning, Nick Carter refused all offers from Marcus to take him to breakfast. He insisted that he needed to get to the airport in plenty of time for departure which wouldn't actually happen until after the noon hour. He did,however, make the pseudo author aware of the annual Oswell Publishing House party that would happen in four weeks and issued him a personal invitation. The agent went on to explain that the gala was formal and would be on the tail of the release of his first book,and that the others would be wanting to welcome him to the Oswell Family. Marcus agreed and shook the man's hand.

Carter wished them both well and left,hinting a trace of dejection as he got into the cab, armed with two manuscripts.

He sat back and attempted in vain to relax during the ride to the airport.

Mission accomplished. He sighed outloud feeling no better at having pulled off the feat. He slumped down a little looking out the window at the snow covered hills as the cab blew past them. Suddenly a phrase his secretary had coined to use against Oswell came to mind.

Congratulations, you're an idiot.

Chapter Thirty-eight

"So, what's the score here? Publishing house one, you zero?" Noel walked into a little cafe on the mall. Her friend smirked, narrowing her eyes.

"Marcus, zero."

"Trouble in paradise?"

Both women approached the glass front of the sandwich counter which had no line this afternoon, the lunch rush being long over. Noel quickly scanned the neon menu on the wall and shriveled her nose.

"I wouldn't necessarily say *trouble*." Meg's words were slowly forming. "In need of minor adjustment? Perhaps."

"I'll have the San Fran reubin on sourdough with avocado, a side of onion fries and an iced tea." Noel looked at her friend waiting for her to place her order so they could get their drinks and have a seat.

"I'll have the soup of the day and a bran muffin."

"Bleeck." Noel shuddered as she contemplated the order. "I don't do bran, or perhaps I should say, bran doesn't have an appreciation for my system."

"Your system seems to manage deep fried corned beef sandwiches rather efficiently, however." Meg shot her a knowing look as she pulled a bottled water out of the nearby cooler, walking over to their favorite table for two.

"I happen to have a very delicate system, if you must know. I'm on a stringent routine that includes oils and good fats." Noel sat down across from her friend and leaned onto the table as she continued. "I ingest one little bran flake or cracked wheat toast and the whole things goes out of whack. And you dare ask me to jeopardize such a delicate balance? Surely not."

"Good fats, sure."

"So what about the adjustment you were telling me about?" Noel moved her purse from the tabletop as the counterperson brought their lunch and placed it before them. She popped a fry into her mouth and waited.

"Wha—? Oh, that." Meg shrugged a little as she sipped her water. A little radio perched behind the counter was set to an oldies station and she was playing a little mental game of name that tune. "We just have conflicting ideas about how the book business works. I believe in retaining the creative force and Marcus believes that whatever sales research says should dictate what should be written—even if it means that the book ends up an uninspired,money driven,plot deprived and impersonal piece of crap. Um, I love this song."

"I see. So tell me about Nick Carter."

"What about him?"

"The man came and stayed overnight in your house, there must be *something* to tell."

"Well, I didn't succeed in poisoning him with my quiche." Meg didn't look up at Noel, who was wearing a questioning look. "He did, however manage to win Marcus over in a big way, bonded with my dog, and mutilated one perfectly good book before his departure. Not too bad for a visit that lasted a mere twelve hours."

"That must be a record."

"Oh chicken broccoli! My favorite!" Meg's eyes widened as she peeled the plastic lid from the Styrofoam container. She raised it up before her nose with a certain haziness about her as she breathed in its aroma deeply and smiled. "This could be a good day after all."

"You ordered soup of the day and you didn't ask what it was before they brought it?"

"I always do it that way—it's kind of like a little surprise."

"Like a fortune cookie."

"Yeah."

"What if they bring you something you hate?"

"They wouldn't."

"Ever the little optimist,aren't we?" Noel eyed her coyly. "So, will that change the day they bring you llama tortellini or something cruel?"

Meg shot her a look and her friend went on.

"Actually, I understand that, I really do. It's sort of along the principle that I have regarding a box of Whitman's Samplers." Noel took another bite of her sandwich as she contemplated the theory. "I like to discard that little insert that tells what's inside everything and take a chance. Just throw caution to the wind."

"Yeah, that's right," Meg nodded. "Like if you get a toffee or a pecan, or maybe even a caramel as opposed to a cream or a mint. They put way too many creams and mints into those things."

Noel considered this and her reply was entirely serious.

"All chocolates are good, Meg. There are no bad chocolates." She tipped her head to the side and squinted as she pondered the possibilities. "Of course, if I ever bite into one and llama tortellini soup comes gushing out, I'll reconsider the notion."

"He has a dog named Boo."

"Nick Carter has a dog named Boo?"

"Nick Carter has a dog named Boo. Is there an echo in here?" Meg plunged her spoon into the thick soup and stirred it around to cool it. "You know, me and you and—"

"A dog named Boo? Yeah, I know that." Noel nodded eagerly now as she gave her friend her undivided attention.

"That's exactly what he said."

"What did he say?"

"He said me and you and a and I said—"

"And a dog named Boo?"

"Yeah." Meg nodded nonchalantly.

"You finished his sentence?" Noel's voice rose now in minor excitement. "You finished his *sentence*?"

"It's a song, Noel, for heaven's sakes."

"That's on the checklist—you said you wanted someone who would finish your sentences, and then you tell me you finished *his* sentence, and that's *pretty* close! There ya go!"

"You finished my sentence too and I'm not convinced we are fate inspired soul mates."

"We're best friends though."

"True, but I can't even stomach the sight of that man! He makes

Marcus look like a saint!"

"Ewww. I can't imagine."

"Yes." Suddenly as if realizing what she was agreeing to, Meg sighed "No, you know what I mean, Noel. This was a very important book to me, and he butchered it and took the carcass back with him to Tampa."

"I'd love to be in Tampa right now." Noel seemed to be ignoring her as she gazed off as if considering a vision. "That beach, everywhere. Sunshine. You know just being tanned makes me feel better. It's strictly psychological, but I swear I feel more alive."

"You've been to Tampa?"

"Are you kidding? Every old fart in my family lives in and around Tampa, it's a New York thing. You spend your youth shuffling stocks and bonds and yelling at taxi drivers in New York, then you hop on the coast and slide all the way down to the New York retirement drop off: Tampa." She smiled at the notion. "It's great Meggie—people yellin' and honkin' their horns in traffic. Just like New York, but a lot warmer and you don't have those no parking tow away snow zones. I'd love to live there."

"You have a strange idea of happily ever after."

"Coming from the—" Noel was interrupted again.

"Queen of Happily Ever After. I know, I know..." Then, realizing that she'd finished Noel's sentence, she quietly added: "I better quit that or we'll end up married by dinner."

"The idea that you have a dog named Boo and that he has a dog named Boo," Noel suddenly leaned forward and began to quietly hum the theme to *The Twilight Zone*. "Tell me that's not fate inspired."

"That's not fate inspired."

"There's something here. Mysterious—like a little puzzle piece that's been left out."

"Yeah, the missing link." Meg shot her another sarcastic look. "I don't even know why I mentioned it. You, of course, making too big a deal of it. I knew you would."

"I just think that it's—you know what it's like?"

"You're going to tell me anyway."

Noel ignored her comment and rambled on.

"It's like in *Holiday Inn* where Betty goes to the lodge for buttermilk and sandwiches and—"

"That's *White Christmas*."

"Whatever. Bing Crosby anyway. So Bing is waiting for her sitting at the fireplace there and they start singing that song—"

"Noel, what does this have to do with me? This has absolutely nothing to do with me."

"Okay, well skip that. What about the part where Susan's mom explains to her about Santa Claus really being real—"

"That was *Miracle on 34th Street*. You're not very good at this." Meg shook her head with a little laugh.

"Well, pardon me for being Christmas movie challenged, unfortunately that's the only language my best friend happens to comprehend, and I'm doing the best that I can. Can I go on?" Noel waited for Meg to nod her head before finishing. "Okay, now where . . . ? All right. Anyway, so she's telling Susan that she was wrong, and that she should believe in Santa Claus after all. And then she says it: *Fate is believing in something when common sense tells you not to.* Now that is beautiful."

"What does this have to do with that? It makes no sense."

"No, it doesn't make sense at all, hence my example. Once in a while if you would take a chance on something that exists beyond the boundary of what you would normally consider *normal*, maybe your sought after ideas of fate would reward you."

Meg stared at her for a few moments, not really knowing how to answer that statement. Finally she looked away and sipped her water as she attempted to change the subject.

"So what do you think I should wear to this hoity-toity gala?"

"Don't think I don't recognize a blow off when I hear one." Noel glanced at her and then added. "Wear whatever you want—you look great in everything."

"I'd like to get my hair cut."

"Change is good."

"Cut off."

"That change would cause whatshisname to pee his pants. You are getting braver by the second! I'm so proud of you!"

"So you think that would be good?" Meg made an uncertain face and shrugged.

"I think that would be great. But don't do it until I have a day off. I wanna be there when he gets a load of that."

"You're cruel, Noel."

"It's a cruel world, you know I've always been a conformist."

The sounds of Johnny Mathis wafted through the little cafe, now only occupied by the two women and a handful of employees behind the counter. Meg tipped her head, a romantic glimmer in her eye as she sighed deeply. "I love this song."

"You love every song."

"No, I love this song. I have always loved this song."

Chances are cause I wear a funny grin the moment you come into view . . .

Noel snatched Meg's plastic spoon out of her soup bowl and raised it her to lips dramatically. Her voice sounded deep and she trilled the end of each word sung slightly off key.

"Chances are your chances are aw—fully goooood!"

"Noel." Meg covered her eyes with her hands.

"Oh come on! There's no one here. Sing with me." Her friend waved the spoon at her. "Chances are you think that *I'm* in love with *you.*"

Meg glanced around at the otherwise quiet cafe and shrugged. She joined in quietly, smiling. Together they sang.

"Just because my composure sort of slips, the moment that your lips meet mine . . ." Their voices were growing more confident. A boy mopping the floor behind the counter didn't even seem to notice anything out of the ordinary as they sang on. "Chances are you think my heart's your Valentine!"

Their singing went on, sprinkled with an occasional little burst of laughter. The sound of friendship wafted through the cafe and flowed lightly into the hallway of the mall.

Chapter Thirty-nine

*J*ust Around the Corner *is keen, witty, and luminous with creativity. That Marcus St. John, a newcomer in the literary world, would reveal himself to be the lead miner on a an archeological dig into the female psyche is incredible, to say the least. Who could imagine that one man could so capture the intuitive nature of a woman?*

Meg smirked a little as her eyes roved over the syndicated review written by the infamous Gibson Porter.

"The lead miner, huh?" She looked over to the dog who was lapping eagerly at his bowl of water. Boo sensed her stare and looked up at her, licking the wet fur around his mouth. Meg smiled. "And here comes the miner now."

"What?" Marcus smiled at her as he entered the kitchen, dressed and ready to catch their flight which would depart in a little over an hour. He walked around behind his fiancée and ran his fingers through her loosely hanging hair, pushing it aside slightly to plant a kiss on her cheek. "What are you reading?"

"Read for yourself, you—Mr. *Keen Intuition.*"

He took the article from her and squinted in the early morning light of the kitchen. Meg stood and stretched her arms out. She walked over to the coffee pot and refilled her mug, pouring a second one for Marcus. He took it gratefully.

"Well, what do you know, someone liked it." He remarked, sipping his steaming coffee as he set it aside.

"Someone?" She burst out. "That is not just someone—that some-one happens to be Gibson Porter, the most respected book critic there is! His reviews are syndicated in nearly every major newspaper in the country—when Gibson Porter speaks, people listen! Buyers listen."

"Okay." Marcus nodded his head with a dawning understanding.

"Yes, just so you understand the scope of things here. And should you be asked about it ever, Gibson Porter is *only* to be spoken of kindly. Never speak poorly of him, he can make or break a writer."

"Okay."

"*Never.* In fact, I've devised a list of some things that you should know before we go to this dinner and dance thing this weekend, or before you talk to anyone for that matter." She handed him an envelope before going on and Marcus marveled that is was stuffed full. He looked at her. "It's a little inside information about writing—what kinds of things inspired me when I wrote something particular. Might give you a little insight about how a writer feels when creating a piece of work."

"An acting lesson?"

"In essence," she waved her hand and started gathering her bags and purse. "You have to know the part before you can play it."

"I don't think all this is necessary."

"Of *course* it is!" Meg dropped her things back to the floor exasperated as she fumbled for words that would not make her sound like a nag. "When a person writes a book, they have to create believable characters—*create personalities.* You have to have some ability to get inside their mind—to feel what they feel in order to know what kinds of actions they would take in different situations. Think like they would think."

"Get inside the mind of someone who isn't real?" Marcus' expression was bordering on mockery.

"You *make* them real. And for as long as it takes to read the book, until the last page is read and the cover is closed, they *are* real! This is a very real process, Marcus, something that you need to understand if we are to pull this off."

"So, let me get this straight. I'm getting inside your mind who's getting inside the characters of some books mind?" He squinted one eye and smiled a little.

"*Some* book?" She looked utterly horrified. "*Some* book? Marcus! Have you even bothered to read the book Oswell House is spending tons of money on?"

He was quiet.

"Have you even a clue?"

He looked at her blankly.

"Oh, my God. You have no clue." She scampered out of the back doorway and into their bedroom closet where she'd stashed a few of the manuscripts that had been previously rejected when she had submitted them in her own name. She practically threw them at him when she re-entered the kitchen. "Here, your study guide. You've got twenty minutes to ride, half an hour to wait and a two and then a three hour flight to soak it up, big guy."

She fished her hand into his coat pocket as he stood there dumb-founded holding the manuscript and envelope. Finding his car keys, she forged ahead out the back door lugging her suitcase along behind her.

"Well, I can drive." He offered.

"I'm driving. You're reading. Come on."

Marcus tried to keep up with Meg as she strode steadily through the crowded little airport in Des Moines. They'd come across a traffic jam thanks to a fender bender just outside Jasper Falls and now they were running late. Still flipping through the manuscript, Marcus followed along, making an occasional expression of displeasure as he continued.

"What's wrong?" she asked, handing the woman at the counter their tickets. They were stamped and returned and the duo finished their trek down an extensive hall to the departure gate.

"Some of this stuff, it's so *girly.*"

"Well, of course it is. The romance market is aimed primarily at women. It's not sappy though."

"It's not?"

"No. Sap is not good. Realistic, contemporary romance is good."

"*Realistic?* This stuff isn't realistic." He waved his hand over the script as he walked through the metal detector. It buzzed loudly and he stopped to empty his pockets.

"What's so unrealistic about it?" Meg had already passed through and was waiting for him impatiently as he walked through the detector a second time. It buzzed again. Marcus rolled his eyes and pulled his wallet out of his pocket and removed his coat.

"I mean, it's full of fluff—sap. This couple has *their* song. They picnic on *their* hill—hell, they eat out of the same ice cream carton while watching old Cary Grant movies—*their* favorite flavor, of course."

"What's so sappy about that? It's romantic! It's sweet."

"It's *fiction*. Complete fiction." He tossed his wallet onto the conveyor belt that would run it through an X-ray. Marcus walked around and entered the detector only to be buzzed again. "Dammit!"

She watched on as he felt through his pockets for anything that he might possibly have on him that would set off the alarm. Meg folded her arms as she stood there waiting.

"What are you implying? That my work is second rate? That you don't like my writing style?"

"I'm saying it offers a fanciful outlook on what love really isn't—thus setting unrealistic relationship expectations for poor, unknowing lonely souls who have nothing to do that sit around and read stuff like this, this—"

"This what? What exactly do you think *this* is?" She stood there with her hand on her hip, waiting. Marcus removed his jacket and was standing there now in his T-shirt and jeans as the guard waved the wand around him.

"I'm just saying that stuff like that, this—*whatever*, only offers hope to women that the perfect one is out there somewhere and that when she finds him she'll recognize him because he'll be the one holding the broom with which to sweep her off her feet! That he'll romance her! Rendezvous with her in Paris under the stars over pasta and wine. That some magic feeling will transform her into some princess and she'll ride off into the sunset on horseback." He was ranting now. "Statistically speaking, the chances of a woman meeting a mate decrease with each year that passes. What you are doing is encouraging her to hold out and pass up anything good that may come her way just in case *Mr. Right* steps out of the shadows and saves the day! It's *insane!*'

"Try it again," the guard instructed Marcus and nodded toward the detector. Marcus gathered up his jacket, never removing his eyes from Meg's and walked around to the other side for a fourth time.

"I don't think there's anything wrong with encouragement. Or with love songs or romantic movies or finishing each other's sentences. I don't think that there's anything wrong with waiting for the one."

"The *one*? He laughed, his voice growing louder. "You are asking some poor old dame to hang on for some, some *fairy tale* knight to charge in—completely forgetting that knights usually charge right straight past the middle aged woman with a slightly crooked nose who still uses Clearisil now and again! That the knight, if there were such a creature, would likely head straight for the fair maiden—a busty waif, if you will—preferably one who did last season's Victoria Secret runway show. You are encouraging mere hopelessness, Meg!"

Marcus walked through the detector one last time and again the buzzer sounded loudly.

"What the hell's wrong with this thing?" The guard muttered as Marcus threw his bag aside in pure frustration. He was angry now. Meg leaned forward and spoke so that only Marcus and the guard could hear her words.

"It's that steel plate he's got in place of the lobal area that controls *humanity* and *compassion*!"

The guard patted him down and dismissed him to their gate at last. Marcus picked up the manuscript but Meg wasn't finished with their conversation yet.

"I don't offer false hopes to hopeless women. I want to inspire hopefulness to those who believe that true and long-lasting love *can* and *does* exist!" Her voice had risen. They reached the line and she pulled their boarding passes out, preparing to hand them to the man at the entry. "And if you expect to carry this charade off with any grace, you'll read the book, love the book and *live* the book!"

"Okay, calm down." Marcus noticed that a few people around them were eyeing them a little and he smiled and nodded politely in their direction as they continued to wait. "Just concentrate on the fact that we'll be in Tampa in just a few hours and you can soak up the sun for a while—do whatever you want."

"And I fully plan to utilize every spare moment doing as much." Her voice lost some of its harshness as she considered the notion. "I can't wait to feel that soft powdery white sand squishing between my toes."

"Yeah . . . "

"I really like Tampa."

"It's nice to visit," he agreed.

"No, I mean, I would like to live there."

"In Tampa? It's so big—impersonal."

Meg looked dreamy as she mentally mulled it over.

"There are things to do."

"There are things to do in Iowa," he interjected.

"There are things to do that don't involve pig calling contests and dill pickle championships." She shot him a look. "I just find Tampa alluring. And the fact that you can get to the beach, well, that never hurt anyone."

"What about the traffic?"

"What about the traffic? We had to wait in traffic to get out of *Jasper Falls* today—Jasper Falls, Marcus." Her eyes widened as she went on. "I don't believe in being in a traffic jam in any city that doesn't at least have better shopping or not more than half an hour away from a sparkling beach. It just shouldn't be."

"The only reason there was a traffic jam in Jasper Falls was because that tractor rear ended that semi hauling all those pigs . . . "

Meg smirked at him and he stopped short.

"Exactly! I rest my case."

"You wouldn't like a big city, Meg, trust me. You have no idea the things they do in big cities." Marcus lowered his voice as he went on.

"What are you talking about? What kinds of things?"

"Hmph—all *sorts* of crazy stuff. You gotta have bars on your windows and you can't hang out your wash to dry, or leave your car unlocked. It's crazy." He grew even quieter. "And their social life is *way* different from what we're used to."

"In what way?" She turned to see him now and waited.

"Well, like the things couples do when they get together, they don't just go get pizza and a movie, let's just put it that way."

"Well, pray tell, what do you think they do?"

"Well, for starters, everybody's a player."

"A *player?*" Now she narrowed her brow and issued him a sarcastic look. "What are you talking about?"

"A *player*, you know, where they have those contests to see who can have sex with the most men or women, depending upon what they're into." Marcus nodded his head as he glanced sideways to be sure no one was listening to their conversation. "And when they swing, well, they're not referring to do-si-do, if you know what I mean."

"Marcus, that is insane."

"No, Meg, I'm serious. Couples get together and they swing, you know, *swap partners* and stuff. Real sick. I know these things. I watch NYPD Blue. No, Meg, the city isn't for decent folks like us. You wait and see."

Meg stared at him in disbelief. Finally she shook her head as she handed her ticket over to the man waiting to take them.

"You've lost your mind. We're on our way to Tampa for a publishing extravaganza—and you're *demeaning* the entire book I've created and talking about purely irrational things."

"No, what's irrational is you thinking that people in big cities don't swing, and that people really do go around shouting out their feelings to each other as if it were as simple as like ordering a cheeseburger at a drive through. I mean, get over it Meg, accept the cold hard facts! Men don't do the kind of stuff like you've got them doing in this book! And people swing!" Marcus handed his ticket to the man at the gate, an older gentleman, and waited for him to mark it. "People *do* swing! They swap partners and all *sorts* of kinky stuff!"

The man handed it back to him, issuing him a glare as he did so. When he spoke, his words were low and firm.

"Please board and take your seats." He released the ticket to Marcus' grip but kept his steady gaze. "We want to get you on your way as *soon* as possible."

Marcus looked at him for a moment and then back at Meg. They both entered the plane.

"What did that mean? What?" He was befuddled.

"I'm sure you just took it the wrong way." Meg muttered as she scooted into the row of seats and made herself comfortable. "Read and be quiet."

"What?" He cocked his head sideways at her. "Are you telling me to shut up?"

"I'm sure you just took it the wrong way."

Meg slumped down in her seat and took one last look at the cold and snow below them as the plane began its slow taxi around the air strip. She closed her eyes to shut everything out and tried to relax.

Chapter Forty

"I thought you said you weren't coming into the office today?" Jan slipped out of her jacket as she stood in the doorway of Nick Carter's office. He'd clearly been there for a few hours already judging from the number of empty coffee cups sitting around. She glanced at her watch. It was only eight thirteen.

"No, you heard me wrong." He answered without looking at his secretary. "I said I never want to come into this office *again*. But here I am, so we can see that I lied."

"What are you working on?"

Just estimating the damages here." He finished scribbling his signature onto something he'd been frittering over and raised his eyes to see her now. "St. John's visit is quickly turning into a three-ring circus and the ringleader is probably only flying over, oh, about, Missouri as we speak."

"What's the trouble?"

"The trouble is, the trouble is that he was going to do an "Inside Tampa Bay" interview on Monday, but now Barnes & Noble tells me that they feel a Monday book signing would be more successful than one on Sunday. So strike that, move Barnes & Noble to Monday, and Chapters Superbook Store wants to see if they can get a visit in before St. John leaves on Tuesday, Kip Kaller from the St. Petersburg Times is doing a book review on *Around the Corner* and would like to include some personal reflections from its author. We still have an issue about where to put "Inside Tampa Bay" on this roster, and then there's a little matter of the King's Court Spectacular on Saturday night."

"Whoa, hold on now." Jan raised her hand at him like a traffic cop. She looked thoughtful for a second before she spoke again. "Okay, when you call "Inside Tampa Bay" ask for Ann, tell her that she needs to work him in on today's program, that's at four o'clock. Amish boy's flight gets here at two, that will work. It runs half an hour, have Kip Kaller on the set for a post show interview, and an evening signing is in order for the Chapters Superbook Store—beggars can't be choosers, they should have called weeks ago. Barnes & Noble will work on Monday, the flight back to the cornfield departs Tuesday morning. Presto."

"Presto?" Carter looked at her with bewilderment. "You want me to call "Inside Tampa Bay" and tell *them* how to run their program?"

"I told you, talk to Ann, I set her up with my cousin, she owes me. Trust me."

There was silence for a few moments as Carter stared at her with one eyebrow arched.

"Are you getting efficient on me?"

"Honey, I've always been efficient. My job is to put ideas into your head in a subtle manner that makes you believe they are your own. That's what a good secretary does."

"You do not."

She nodded with a little smile as she touched her temple knowingly. "I do."

"You didn't just now. You just told me what to do."

"We're short on time. You do what you can."

Carter nodded in her direction. He began to hunt through his rolodex for the number for "Inside Tampa Bay"studios.

"So, are you looking forward to Oswell's big affair tomorrow night?" He asked her as he pulled a card from the file.

"Heavens no, I'm not going. And in the future, never use my name and the Oswell name in the same sentence with the word affair. You're libel to shorten my life expectancy drastically." She glanced at him before leaving the office. "You're going, right?"

"Right, and so are you."

"Do you have wind in your ears? I said I'm *not* going."

"You have to, as my secretary. I'm confident that you won't make me go in there alone, sit alone, and listen to the hoards of *Why hasn't a nice guy like yourself settled down yet?* questions. Am I right?"

"It's never been your style to worry about what other people think."

"I'm not worried. I'm also not interested in offering lame excuses to any pseudo suitors." He picked up his pen and began to scribble away in his book. "That plane had better not be delayed for any reason. Okay, that puts "Inside Tampa Bay" this afternoon, followed by a brief interview for the Times and then a Chapters signing. Saturday is the grand gala and Sunday—what's Sunday again?"

"Day of *rest*, worship the Lord. That kind of thing." Jan rolled her eyes at him. She stood in the doorway watching him with amazement. "You really need to get a life, Boss."

"I'll do that Tuesday afternoon after Marcus St. John is tucked safely away on his flight home. Oops, no-can-do. The Judy Armando meeting happens that afternoon. I'll work it in on Friday sometime." He closed his schedule book and reached for the phone, dialing for an outside line.

"You're scary, Boss." She opened the door and turned again before leaving his office. "I can see you telling the doctor to schedule the delivery of your first child for sometime after five o'clock preferably on a weekend or something."

Carter merely shrugged as he waited for the connection to be made.

"That's what cesareans are for."

Chapter Forty-one

"Live from Mason Intercable Studio 5A—it's Inside Tampa Bay!"

A moderate amount of applause followed the announcer's voice as a tall, toned woman in a red Halston sun dress strode confidently across the stage. She whipped her waist-length platinum hair a few times and offered the studio audience a little playful wave. Her impeccable pearly whites glimmered between ruby-painted lips as she flirted and bowed, flirted and bowed...The applause continued. The set was simple, two stools and a countertop which she slipped behind and sat down. Between sips from a dainty glass water bottle, she gushed to the studio and television audiences about the wonderful show in store for them that day.

Meg watched the show from the green room backstage as Marcus prepared to go onstage.

"I'm so glad you could join us this afternoon! As you know, I'm Michelle Mason, your host."

Meg nearly sprayed diet soda from her nose as she smirked.

"Mason Studios, Michelle Mason. Gee, I wonder how she got that job." She peeled the lid off the top of her drink and fished out an ice cube, popping it into her mouth. "What was on her resume? A good boob job?"

"Today's guest is an exciting, up-and-coming author who is really taking the shelves by storm with his first title, *Just Around the Corner.* Please join me as we welcome Marcus St. John!"

Applause sounded as Marcus nervously sauntered across the stage. He gave the audience a self-conscious wave before shaking her hand, an action that backfired when the hostess used his grip as an means of yanking him toward her. She laid a kiss on him and held him against her, squished to her full busom.

"Oh, I'll bet he's hating that," Meg was barely amused. "Okay, sister, back off now. Marcus, quit staring at her boobs—all right already."

The sound of someone entering the room interrupted her one sided conversation and she was a little embarrassed to see that it was Nick Carter.

"Hey." He handed her a diet soda that she politely declined. He sat down beside her, nodding at the monitor. "He's doing good isn't he? Well, I mean, except for all that lovey-dovey crap Michelle pulls on every guest that steps in front of the camera. She's very *open*."

Meg only glanced at him, focusing her attention toward the monitor where Marcus was rambling on about life in Iowa.

"Her father owns the studios what can I say? Some people need an agent and—"

"Others just need implants?" Meg smirked.

Carter arched an eyebrow in surprise, a mischievous grin coming to his face. Meg shook her head in spite of herself.

"That was rude."

"Actually, that's exactly what I was going to say." Carter laughed but Meg didn't join him. He could see that she'd yet to forgive him for the argument at her home almost a month earlier. He pretended not to notice this though, and sat down behind her where he could look at her without being seen.

Her hair was drawn back in a loose knot secured by an interesting tiny white butterfly clip. Messy tendrils spilled down the graceful curve of her neck and onto the collar of the soft baby blue cotton blouse she was wearing. Her legs extended out of the matching wrap skirt and ended in brown strappy, thick-heeled sandals,and though she was casually dressed, Carter thought she was somewhat elegant as she leaned forward, chomping an ice cube. Elegant and charming, maybe. His eyes returned to the clip in her hair and he studied it. The butterfly wings shown their iridescent hue in the overhead light,and moved ever so slightly as she did when she picked up her drink and sipped from its straw.

"That's an interesting clip," he found himself saying for no apparent reason. And after the words were out, he felt a little foolish.

"Pardon?"She turned to issue him a puzzled look, giving him ample time to squirm as he prepared his save.

"Your hair thing, the butterfly."

Caught off guard, she looked away again.

"Thanks."

Silence.

"So, what's the significance of it? Or do you just like butterflies?" Carter was desperately trying to fill the uncomfortable void that existed between them, even if it meant spewing out something meaningless. And, he thought, he seemed to be blessed with plenty of that kind of stuff today.

"No particular fondness. It's in accordance with an Irish legend." She surprised him by actually answering the stupid question as her eyes remained fixed upon the television, her expression unmoving. "A white butterfly is an omen for good luck, particularly if it's the first one you see in the spring."

"I do believe that is the first one I've seen this spring." He laughed lightly.

She remained staring straight ahead. "Well then, bully for you."

"Yes, bully." He nodded, feeling a little stupid as he replayed the words in his head. The notion of a good luck charm amused him some. "So, you are Irish, then?"

"No, my best friend is. She got it for me."

"Does she have red hair?"

Meg turned to see him, a loathing look upon her face. Apparently her shortness wasn't getting the point across as she'd hoped.

"Mr. Carter, just because we are stuck in the same room together doesn't mean that we have to talk."

Carter raised his hands in surrender. He sat back in his chair again and turned his attention to the interview in progress.

"I don't want to call you Mr. St. John, it's so formal."

"Call me Marcus," he interjected with a schoolboy grin.

"How about Marky?" Michelle was practically drooling over the well dressed man as he sat there quietly. He didn't argue the ridiculous name so she assumed he approved. "Marky, whatever possessed you to create a book written in a first person view—that just happens to belong to a woman? What an ingenious idea!"

"Well, I uh—"

"Were you raised with sisters?"

"Actually, no, four brothers."

"Your mother must be a wonderfully open minded woman to have raised such an objective thinking man."

"My mother's passed away now, but yes, she was a very good woman."

"Well, to teach her son to respect women, to reach inside their very minds and know what they need. How they *want* to be treated, well,I was almost moved to tears when I read the book last night—just knowing that there are a few men out there who *do* understand."

The woman's eyes glassed over as she spoke. Marcus quickly reached behind them on the little side table and got her a tissue which she took graciously.

"See? See there he goes again! He knows what a woman wants ladies!" Michelle laughed as she dabbed her eyes. The audience chuckled

"Yeah, but I'm so sick of him getting my toilet paper when I go to the bathroom." Meg muttered. Carter touched his lips to suppress his laughter. "She's laying it on a tad thick, don't you think?"

"Well," Carter shrugged. "You're going to have to get used to this kind of thing. Marcus has struck a note with the female reading audience—he'll likely have a lot of admirers."

"What's your point?"

"My point being, that if you're at all the jealous type, you better fix that because it's highly probable that he'll have women throwing themselves at him. But I imagine that as long as your relationship is—"

"We have a relationship that is plenty strong enough. *Plenty.* I am crazy about Marcus as he is about me. So, you needn't worry about it."

Just then a stagehand poked his head inside the door of the green room. He stood there, pen in hand, his laminated badge dangling from around his neck, concern all over his face.

"Ummm, Mr. Carter? Your client is dying out there. Anything you wanna do about it? Cause we're going to break in thirty."

Carter glanced back at the screen suddenly realizing that Marcus was stuttering and stammering away. He quickly rose and started for the door. Meg glanced around her, her eyes coming across the envelope she'd prepared for him still lying atop their luggage as they'd come straight from the airport. She retrieved it quickly and lunged for the door, catching the back of Carter's coatsleeve.

"Here—take this to him." She found herself stumbling over her own words now. "It's some, some notes he took for this interview. Maybe it will help him."

Carter nodded and took it from her before he bolted down the hallway toward the set.

By the time the agent reached the set, a two minute break had been called and several stage assistants were flocking around the duo, adjusting clothing and microphones and refilling water in their cups. A makeup woman approached Michelle and brushed a generous helping of powder across her nose and forehead, squashing the little shine that the hot set lights had created. Carter watched the scurried action from the side, waiting to have a word with Marcus. He watched as the pair on set had their heads leaned toward each other, giggling and he decided to make his approach. Handing the envelope to Marcus, he smiled a polite greeting to Michelle.

"I was just giving Marky some pointers on doing this show," she chirped gleefully. Again, Carter smiled at her. "He's doing splendidly, after all, he's never had to do a show like this before. Right Marky?"

Marcus smiled and nodded like a puppy.

"Meg told me you might feel more comfortable if you had your notes." Carter began.

"Notes—shmotes!" Michelle put in. "He'll be just fine, I guarantee it! I'm flattered that we're the first interview that he's done!"

"Thank you Michelle," Marcus mumbled, his face turning bright red. He swallowed hard and adjusted the collar of his red plaid cotton shirt.

"You call me Mitzy. I insist! All my closest friends call me Mitzy."

"Mitzy, then." Marcus sat back in his seat and the set director began to roll the count. Carter quickly backed off the set and waited beside the curtain to watch the rest of the interview which only had about four minutes left.

"We're talking with Marcus St. John, author of the new best seller, *Just Around the Corner*." Michelle continued when the red camera light turned back on. "Marky, honey, can you tell me what kinds of things motivate you to write in such vivid detail?"

"Well, I'll tell you," Marcus drifted off momentarily and Carter held his breath, wondering what his client would possibly say next. "I . . . just love women."

The entire audience oohed appreciatively at this response. Their reaction to his answer gave him the courage to go on.

"I think women are highly instinctual, intelligent, lovely creatures." He nodded with faux confidence as he spoke, realizing that they were eating it up, only adding to his bravery. "Women are to be cherished, understood, appreciated."

"Oh please," Carter mumbled from his place off the stage.

"Oh please." Meg put her hand over her eyes as she slumped in her seat in the green room.

"Oh, that is so, so *sagacious*!" Michelle's eyes were misty now as she leaned toward her guest. "I could cry! That is beautiful!"

"I didn't invent the concept." Marcus continued.

"I'll say." Meg interjected to no one.

"History shows an appreciation for women. Look at the great works of art. The Mona Lisa, for example. Great literature emerged out of the Renaissance era detailing man's affection for women. And although the women's movement was a wonderfully inspiring time, it has, unfortunately, robbed something out of man's heart, replacing it with a certain fearfulness of women. That they are to be regarded with distance and defense." Marcus had Michelle now, along with the greater part of the predominantly female audience, hook, line and sinker. "I have studied women extensively in an effort to look at life from their eyes, to understand they way they understand. I do not have a fearfulness of women. I'm open to it."

"I'll say you are. I will go right along with that statement!" Michelle gushed.

"Romance, commitment. Believing in *the one*. These are things that do exist. As a man, I am not afraid to be in touch with my feminine side."

"I'm not afraid for you to either." Michelle purred.

Meg had both of her hands over her eyes now as she sat with her legs crunched under her in the chair in the green room. It wasn't at all a ladylike position, as she listened to whatever nonsense would fall from his lips next.

"More men should try it!" Marcus quipped. "In fact, I would highly recommend that men flip through this book to gain a better understanding about the life experiences that women undergo. I really would."

"Marcus St. John—Marky—it has been a genuine pleasure to have you as a guest on our show. I want you to come back here every single time you turn out another wonderful book."

"Well, that should be soon then, as I just finished penning two more that should be out by the end of this month and again, the middle of next month. I know you'll like them."

"I'm sure we will! Ladies?"

The crowd burst into cheers.

"Thank you for having me, Mitzy." Marcus kissed her hand rather dramatically before the commercial. "I'm not afraid to tell you what a delightful person you truly are."

"*Cut!* And we're clear!"

"Marky! That was wonderful!" Michelle walked with him to the side of the stage, paying little attention to the stagehands attempting to flock around her with makeup and notes.

"Thank you. I was a little nervous," he stammered, smiling.

"You recovered tremendously! I am so impressed! I want you to promise me that you will send your next book right to this studio so that I can eat it right up."

"I promise. I certainly can do that."

"Marcus?" The voice belonged to Carter who had been waiting for him to finish his conversation. "Mr. Kaller is waiting for his interview for the Times, and *Mitzy*, I believe they want you back on the set. Thank you."

"Well, now there's no show without me, so I'm really not all that concerned." She smirked, shrugging the tanned shoulders that showed out of her sundress. Her long hair wagged along behind her as she flitted back out to her seat on stage. "Bye-bye Marky!"

Marcus watched her go with an odd look in his eye. Noting this, Carter practically pulled him down the hallway toward the green room where Kip Kaller would join them. He pushed open the door and looked over at Meg who was still sitting in a rather uncouth pose. She quickly put her feet onto the floor and straightened her skirt when the men entered.

"Well?" Marcus smiled at her expectantly. "Did I do good or what?"

"Or what," Meg answered in a sing-song voice. She smiled at him as she nodded.

"They loved it! Did you hear those women? They loved it!"

"Okay, well, love yourself a little quieter now, will you?" Meg headed for the door, pushing past Carter as she did so. "Excuse me, I'm going to slip out to the commissary to get some coffee or something."

Kip Kaller nodded in her direction as he prepared to enter the very room she'd just fled from. He closed the door behind her.

Chapter Forty-two

Thanks to the influx of fans that had seen Marcus' interview on "Inside Tampa Bay," the book signing at Chapters Superbook Store was lasting much longer than planned. The affair, originally slated to start at five and end at seven, was still going full swing at eight. Meg sighed as she looked at her watch while sitting just inside the back room door watching over the event. Her stomach was rumbling but the line of people was steady still, something that didn't really bother her considering they were all heading to the checkout before leaving with their signed books in hand.

"Tired?" It was Carter's voice that startled her out of her haze as she sat there.

"Starving, mostly."

"There's a cafe down the street," he offered, but she shook her head. "How about Starbucks? I'm headed there now. This is dragging on."

Meg eyed him with interest at the mention of Starbucks, recalling how colorfully Noel had described it before. She was intrigued. She stood up.

"Okay. I'm for that."

It was a toss up as to who was more surprised that she'd agreed to go—Carter, or Meg, herself. But seconds later she was following him through the crowd of people toward the door, completely unnoticed by Marcus.

They walked out the door and onto the sidewalk of the large strip mall. Carter nodded his head in the direction of the brightly lit Starbucks about a block down and they began their walk. It had grown chillier and Meg was thankful she'd brought a thin cardigan with her, pulling it around her shoulders as they went.

"This surely isn't cold to you? Being an Iowa girl and all." Carter grinned at her as they went but was only met with a little glimpse of a cordial smile from Meg as they continued on. They entered the warmth of the coffee shop a few minutes later where the heavenly scent of Java hung heavily in the air. She stepped inside and paused momentarily. Meg closed her eyes and breathed in deeply, holding it for a moment. Caffeine never smelled so good.

"Anything wrong?" Carter looked at her as she stood there. Only half a dozen other people were seated quietly around this time of the evening. They were mostly studying alone or making small talk. One man seated in the corner was on his cell phone and the woman behind the counter stood there watching them, waiting to take their order. Meg took it all in and committed it to memory before turning to look at Carter.

"Yeah, I'm fine. It smells great in here. I was just enjoying it."

Carter nodded and stepped to the counter.

"What would you like Ms. Laine?"

"Coffee, black."

Hearing this, he turned away from the counterperson briefly to confer with her.

"We're in Starbucks—you're not in Kansas anymore,' he laughed quietly. "Live a little. There's every flavor under the moon here."

"I don't do flavored coffees."

"Cappuccinos?"

"Nope."

"Frappicinos?"

"Nope."

"Mochas?"

"Nope."

Carter nodded slowly and turned back to the counterperson.

"Two black coffees and two apple bran muffins."

He paid the server and struggled with the large Styrofoam cups and the little plates. Meg picked up the two muffins and followed him to a little table that was situated flush against the large front plate glass windows. They sat down.

"Thanks." She took the coffee from him and peeled the lid off, sipping it slowly. "You know, just because *I* don't like fun coffee doesn't mean that you couldn't order whatever you wanted."

"I only drink black coffee. Maybe an occasional drop of almond or vanilla flavoring, nothing fancier than that." He broke his muffin in half and wiped his fingers on a paper napkin. "Cappuccinos are for wimps who can't drink coffee."

"I just don't like flavored stuff. Although the idea of cappuccino is so good. I mean, imagine, liquefied chocolate caffeine. Too bad it tastes so terrible." She took another sip as she looked out the window at the neon lights on the night club across the street. "Tampa's pretty busy on a Friday night."

"I imagine it is. To tell you the truth, this is the first time I've been out for quite a while."

"This is *out* for you?" She laughed a little as she picked a piece of apple off the top of the muffin. She popped it into her mouth. "Wow, you really know how to live."

It was his turn to laugh.

"Life is rich, isn't it?" He paused as his eyes roved along the sidewalk across the way at the throngs of club goers making their route to the bars. "So, Marcus did a pretty bang up job during the interview today, you think?"

"Yeah, super."

Carter folded his hands around the sides of his cup as he studied her quietly. He felt the overwhelming compulsion to apologize to the woman before him, but his stubborn pride made the words difficult. He swallowed hard and forced himself to begin.

"I underestimated you, Meghan." He started slowly. She watched him with growing interest that made him even more nervous. Perhaps she was enjoying his struggle? "We got off on the wrong foot right at the start of things, and, I shouldn't have said those things to you, in your own home, nonetheless. For that, I'm, well, I'm sorry."

"How do you feel you underestimated me?" Meg's eyes never wandered from his face as she waited. She blinked her eyes once, careful not to bat. Heaven forbid that she be blamed for that wrongly a second time.

"What do you mean?"

"I mean, how can you tell that you've underestimated me? What have I done to prove your theory wrong?"

Carter mulled her words over carefully. Actually she was right. As far as he could see, she had only insulted his work habits and even his very personality since the time they'd been introduced. He couldn't tell her that it was just a gut feeling that he had about her. She wouldn't buy that. He mulled it over.

"The very idea that you didn't kill Mitzy today on the set of "Inside Tampa Bay" shows a tremendous amount of restraint and composure on your part." He sipped his coffee to wash the strangeness of his jagged words down. "If I had been in your shoes, I wouldn't have been quite so cool, I'm sure."

Meg didn't dare utter a word relative to what she was thinking, lest she come across as cold hearted as she was feeling at the moment. She watched him coolly.

"Well, perhaps if you possessed some of that super intuitive female persona that Marcus has, you would have been realized the reason behind my lack of action."

They both stared at each other for a minute and suddenly burst into small laughter. Carter nodded his head as he looked down a little.

"Perhaps," he agreed with a smile.

Feeling uncomfortable again once the laughter had subsided, Meg glanced at her watch. She wrinkled her nose as she looked at it oddly. It had quit working.

"What is it?"

"My watch, I think it's stopped." She struggled to remove it with her free hand for a moment. Carter reached across the small tabletop and gently began to work at the fragile clasp of the band. She watched him nervously as he pulled it from her wrist and examined it carefully.

"I think it's just the battery," he offered as he turned it over. "I can get someone to run it to a jewelry shop tomorrow to be sure."

"No, no really that's okay. I'll just take it home with me."

Carter shrugged, sure not to offer a second time, lest she find him overbearing. He reached back across the table and turned her hand over, laying her watch across her open palm.

Meg stared at him as he held his hand there touching hers. She was suddenly acutely aware of a tingling sensation behind her ears and the back of her neck. Her stomach felt strangely light. Her head spontaneously tipped to one side and her lips parted ever so slightly as she stared at him sitting before her. Touching her hand . . .

Carter lowered his chin as he kept his gaze fixed upon the woman before him. He needed to let go, now. Now would be a good time to let go. Anytime.

He slowly folded her fingers around the silvery watch one by one in an effort that he hoped didn't appear too obvious. He simply wanted to touch her a bit longer. To bask in the ethereal energy that he had suspected she possessed but could now confirm as it radiated through her mere touch. He wanted to consume it. Finally, after what seemed like forever, she finished the action of grasping the watch and pulling her hand slowly from his grip. They remained staring at each other.

Carter forced himself to snap out of it, shaking his head slightly.

"Speaking of time," he glanced at his own watch. "It's nearly nine—that's when Chapters closes. Surely the session is nearly over."

"Yes."

"Shall we?"

He rose from his seat and quietly escorted her out of the shop and down the street, back toward the bookstore. He was careful to confine his distance to a safe one, glancing in her direction now and again.

Chapter Forty-three

C arter stared at the Saturday afternoon rain from the sliding glass door that lead out to his balcony. The glass was slightly fogged from the unexpected chillness that the rain had brought with it, seemingly out of nowhere. The local news channel hadn't forecast even a hint of dampness, and now there was a virtual deluge.

He picked up his coffee mug from the kitchen countertop and opened the sliding door just slightly, enough to hear the sound the rain was making on the overhang outside and to feel the little burst of coolness whip past him. He sighed recalling how envious his old friends at home had been knowing that he was "enjoying the good life" in the Sunshine State. Maybe there was no snow in Florida, but this raining once a day business coupled with the downpours that came about during hurricane season was quite depressing. At least the snow, cold and sometimes inconvenient as it was, was pretty. That much he could remember, although he'd not been to his homestate for nearly ten years now. Carter had thought about it more often since he'd come back from his brief jaunt to Iowa, Wisconsin's Midwest neighbor, and he found himself fondly remembering his old home on the drab days that he endured now. Days like this one.

He glanced at the clock on the nearby wall, whose ticking seemed to be competing with the sound of the raindrops all of a sudden. Carter sighed. Social stuff wasn't his strong point, he smirked. *Let me add that to the list of things that aren't my strong points, right up there with love, commitment, and first impressions.*

He drifted off again, his mind eventually making the full circle to Meghan Laine. He fought it ferociously, as if out of fear that someone might possibly be reading his mind. Carter laughed out loud at his own silly notions. Why, he'd never found that he was the fortunate holder of any such ability when it came to women. It was almost as if his purity had been tarnished by the endless chain of meaningless relationships he'd succumbed to. He sighed again, kneading the back of his neck with his fingertips.

Chapter Forty-four

"**M**itzy? Her name was *Mitzy?*" Noel burst out laughing into the phone as she responded to her friend's story. Meg held the receiver away from her ear as the unexpected ragged laugh of the former New Yorker pierced her hearing across the miles. "Marcus, pardon, *Marky* and *Mitzy?* Oh for the love of the gawds. I wished t'Gawd I coulda recorded that! Oh, I'm *crying* here."

"I'm glad you find it funny," came Meg's reply.

"Oh, I don't find it funny Meggie." She could hear her friend gasping for breath as she paused for a moment. "I find it *hilarious!*"

"Well, then you would have died if you could have seen him feeding those women full of, full of *it*." Meg's voice was short as she went on. Her words didn't seem to be flowing properly but she'd needed to speak with her friend. "I was so embarrassed I almost died myself. He didn't even seem fazed. Marcus is adjusting to his role of the Great Pretender just a little too well. It's sickening."

Noel quieted her laughing, and got serious.

"What's sickening, Meggie, is that you don't get the credit for your work. That's what makes me sad, all kidding aside." Her words were comforting. "Not that I wouldn't love the opportunity to see Marcus make a mule of himself. But as funny as that would be, I hate to see you stuck behind the scenes while the Big Schmooze takes credit for your work. It's heartbreaking."

"Don't worry about me, I'm fine." Meg's words sounded less than convincing. "I'm trying to get in the mood to go to this *thing* tonight. I would just about stay home if I thought that Marcus wouldn't stick his foot in his mouth somewhere along the way."

"Or make off with a hot little blonde named Skitzy."

"Mitzy."

"Whatever." Noel smirked. "So, where's Mr. Congeniality now?"

"Down at the spa getting a massage."

"Hope the steam isn't too much for him. Meggie I know you, what else is on your mind?"

"Nothing really," Meg rolled her eyes on her end as she uncapped the lid of her pink polish, preparing to streak it across her toenails as she talked. "Do you remember when we talked about *the one*?"

"Of course I do."

"You said, *twinkly.*"

"Yes, yes I did." Noel's voice sounded anxious. "You're not twinkling there for someone and not telling me now, are you? Come on Meggie, are you twinkling?"

"No." Her voice wasn't as confident as she would have preferred as she polished the last toenail and carefully switched feet. She started again. "I just wanted you to tell me some more about that. It's for a story that I'm trying to write, for some reason the words just aren't flowing."

"Don't you dare write another thing and sign Marcus' name to it! Don't even think about it!"

"I won't, I won't. This is something else I'm working on. A little side project, if you will." Meg capped the polish and looked at the rainwater beating a cadence against the window near where she was sitting. It was rather a depressing day, dreary at best. She watched the little trails the water made as it hit and fell to the lower sill. Little patterns and designs spattered about. Her mind impulsively went to Nick Carter and she hoped her friend would speak again to interrupt what had become her one track way of thinking.

"You know. It's hard to describe. You get a light feeling, your stomach, your head. You might think that you're going to faint or something, but you're fine. *Perfectly* fine. You feel a little tingling sensation, maybe around your feet or your knees, kinda like when you've been sitting too long."

"On your shoulders? Kind of like a chill?" She interjected the question casually as her stare remained fixed on two raindrops that seemed to be engaged in a slow race down the glass before her. "I just want to describe it the right way."

"It can be, that's a possibility." Noel was quiet. "Sounds like you're writing a pretty good story. Anything you wanna share with your best friend?"

"Not yet, I'll let you know how it's coming along later though." Meg watched as same two raindrops stumbled over several others that had come to a standstill. They seemed to make an almost human effort to overcome these smaller ones and get on with their race. Drop after drop was consumed by the persistent duo as they carried on, sometimes slowing and even nearly stopping, but keeping on nonetheless. A large drop that stood strong and fixed between them seemed to be the demise of the little game that Meg had witnessed. Much to her surprise, the raindrops merged into an even larger one and overcame the obstacle. They finished their journey to the sill as one. "I should go. I'm not even ready for this tonight."

"I know. You go and take care."

"I will," Meg smiled lightly. "I love you."

"I love you too." Noel added. "Meg, you'll be perfectly fine."

Chapter Forty-five

"Come on Boss, let's get our table." Jan trudged ahead of him with an attitude that closely resembled dread. She looked around her nervously and he smiled rather sarcastically at her odd behavior.

"Remember why I made you come here?" he asked her quietly. "Could you act like you have some *semblance* of affection for me? And for heaven's sake, quit calling me Boss."

Jan shot him a look and grabbed his hand, her head still down, nearly charging with him in tow across the lavish ballroom adorned with glittery decorations and beautifully set round tables.

"Is this going to kill you?" He yanked her hand back and slowed her hurried pace. "Head up, shoulders back, smile. Yes, yes, there we go."

"I'm sorry, Boss," she whispered through her smile in the crowded large room. "But whenever we get around Oswell, I start getting creeped out. I don't feel right. My feet feel funny, my head feels light—my stomach. Kinda like I'm gonna yak. You know?"

"Sounds like love." He said softly with a teasing grin. He then counted himself fortunate that Jan didn't draw back and punch him square in the jaw. Thankful that she was inhibited enough to avoid acting upon her instincts in such a crowded area, he pulled her chair out at their assigned table and helped her scoot in.

"Bite your tongue, Carter." What started out as a sarcastic laugh turned suddenly charming and witty as she waved to one of their firm's clients across the way. "Yes! *Hello* Mrs. Scarloey, you're looking wonderful tonight as well!"

Carter smiled and nodded in the woman's direction as his secretary greeted her. He was pleased with the job she was doing, looking every bit the part of an esteemed socialite. Her hair was cascading down her back in its natural waves, resting on her shoulders, bare from the strapless red sequined dress she'd selected to wear for the event.

"You look nice tonight. That's a nice dress." He offered her.

"I'm glad you feel that way. I charged it to your office account. I think it's a tax write-off, however. Why don't you get yourself a woman to do this job. Preferably one you're not paying." Jan kept her radiant smile, speaking in a low tone under her breath. "I am getting paid for this, right?"

"You don't simply enjoy my company?"

"I do enjoy your company, that's why I've let you pay me to work there for the past five years. I'm sure there are plenty of other firms that would—"

"Okay, overtime. So pour it on thick." Carter smiled and issued a little wave to some acquaintances a few tables away. Once again his associates were out of state or the country or wherever they saw fit to jet off to this time, leaving him the lone representative of the Bankson, Laughton and Carter Literary Agency. He breathed a heavy sigh, never losing his smile. It was likely to be a long night.

The sound of chairs sliding back from the table drew his attention back to where they were sitting. Carter had been engaged in idle conversation with an older gentleman sitting behind him and turned just in time to see Meghan Laine and Marcus St. John sitting in their places. Quickly he looked at the placecards before them and realized that they'd all been assigned to sit at the table together. There were two more cards, however, and he just might be saved by having someone else to talk to. He looked at the tags. *Ted Bankson and Guest.* Carter sighed. Well, that cinched that. He smiled politely and nodded in their direction.

"Meggie!" Jan was doing her job a little too well now, and Carter turned to send her an unspoken message to stifle some of that excitement. To his surprise, her expression was genuine for the first time that evening, as she was actually glad to see the young woman from Iowa with whom, Carter guessed, she could surely have nothing in common. Meg returned her genuine manner and Jan glanced over to the woman's partner, nodding in a slightly less warm manner as she acknowledged him. "Marcus."

Much to Carter's relief, a publishing house associate immediately recognized the new author, and came right to his side, drawing him into their own conversation. Carter continued to sit there like a statue, with a smile perched stolidly upon his lips.

"Meggie, you look stunning! Where on *earth* did you find something like that?" Jan waved her hand in the woman's direction and then looked at Carter. "Boss, doesn't she look wonderful?"

Carter's eyes roved over the soft baby blue knit dress that fit her closely, its little cap sleeves barely off her shoulders. Its sequin gleam seemed equal to the sparkle in her eyes as she returned the look. Perhaps she was eager to hear how he would answer as well. Carter felt uncomfortable as he stumbled over his words.

"Yes, you are . . . wonderful, looking."

Meg forced herself to look away, her cheeks warm suddenly. She nodded thanks.

"Carter! Nick Carter!" The boisterous greeting came from an old friend in the publishing business and as Carter rose to greet him they exchanged enthusiastic smacks on the back. He glanced back to his date and Meg sitting there before he gratefully made his departure.

"Uh uh—Boss,are you going to get us a drink before you go?" Carter smiled and nodded to the waitress nearby.

"Get these ladies whatever they'd like tonight please, put it on my tab." He lowered his voice a bit before adding. "What the heck, I already bought the dress."

Jan shot him a look that offered no apology. He escaped.

The event was not altogether boring, but was dragging on, nonetheless, for its second hour. Meg was fidgeting in her seat. She hadn't seen Marcus except in passing since their arrival. But he seemed to be faring well, fitting right in with the men and dancing nearly every dance with a different glamorous looking woman. Marcus St. John was clearly the hit of the party.

Meg was enjoying her conversation with her new friend but felt the hoards of peering eyes that wanted to see just who the lucky woman was to be there with the overnight publishing sensation. At last, Jan motioned for Carter to rejoin them at their table. He did so obediently, appreciative of her effort at entertaining Meg. Marcus breezed past them once again, only offering a nod in their direction as he went. Meg smiled with a little embarrassment at his apparent social superstardom, but thankfully didn't have to utter a word about his perpetual absence as J.T. Oswell made a beeline to their table next. He issued a dazzling smile. His wavy blonde hair offered a handsome contrast to his black tuxedo and his eyes sparkled as he nodded a round of hellos.

"Good evening Carter, Ms. Laine, Jan." Jan looked at him with stifled admiration as he spoke. The mere fact that he was walking upright in a dignified manner impressed her some. He looked at Carter. "Are there some great skirts here or what?"

Jan rolled her eyes and groaned.

"You have about as much charm as a peanut butter and caviar sandwich," she muttered with disgust.

"You say that," he smiled as he wagged his index finger in the secretary's direction. "But I know where it's at. I know what a woman wants.'

"Apparently not, you're still here." Jan's eyes never moved from his He persevered anyway.

"Is this seat empty?"

"Yes, and this one will be too if you sit down."

Silence. At last Oswell got the courage to test the theory. He pulled out the chair. At the same time she scooted her own away from the table. He slid the seat back in and she scooted back in as well. He pulled it out once more and she scooted away from the table, never leaving his range of sight. The man sighed defeatedly as he stood there. At last he sat down. Jan rose and tapped the shoulder of the older gentleman that Carter had been speaking with earlier.

"Would you care to dance with me?" she asked the man in her most cheery voice. He nodded eagerly with surprise on his face and they linked arms, making their way to the ballroom floor.

Meg was left with the two men and she smiled in their direction politely before turning her attention toward the band, feigning sudden interest. A woman dressed in a style reminiscent of a gentler era, long, slinky black sparkly gown and heels, belted out her songs backed by the lavish band. They had been performing classic songs, predominantly from the 1950s and 60s. She moved her head slightly in time with the rhythm as she watched the dancers move to a lively tune that was playing.

Their dance moves were calculated and well practiced. Suddenly Meg could feel Oswell watching her and she swallowed hard, praying he wouldn't ask her to dance. Sharing her premonition, Carter had no choice but to offer her an escape.

"Would you care to dance?"

"I wouldn't mind."

She stood immediately, grateful to be away from Oswell's stare, and sauntered slowly to the main floor. Carter spoke quietly to her as they made their way to the front.

"Do you swing?" he asked.

Meg suddenly flashed back to the conversation she'd had with Marcus before their flight out. Her eyes widened as she stared at him blankly.

"Beg pardon?" she asked airily.

"Swing, you know, *swing dance?*"

Meg nodded as she breathed out a sigh of relief. A little casual smile came to her lips as she smirked, internally cursing Marcus for her paranoid behavior.

"Swing dance, of course."

"Then you do?"

"Actually, no I don't." She mumbled shyly as she shook her head. As if taking its cue, the music ended and a softer sound came from the bandstand now, as the dancers flocked to the floor two by two. The woman behind the microphone heartily mustered up a wonderful version of "Chances Are" and Meg's eyes widened with surprise.

It's a sign. No, it's a song. She swallowed hard and looked at her dance partner who was motioning toward the dance floor. She smiled politely and followed his lead.

Once out on the floor, they looked at each other rather apprehensively, trying to decide exactly how one properly holds an acquaintance during a slow dance. Little nervous giggles could be heard by the others crowding around, already dancing, and they hurriedly made the adjustments necessary to carry the project off. His left hand on her waist, their right hands clasping. *Little distance there.*

Meg focused on their folded hands as she moved around the floor with him. Despite the crowd, she decided that it must be slightly cool in the ballroom and she tried to avoid openly shuddering with the chill that rippled along her shoulders. Meg gnawed lightly at her lower lip, raising her eyes to his for a time.

Carter smiled at her. She could swear his look bordered on adoring. but she wasn't sure she'd ever been recipient to that kind of thing before. She knew that now. She moved closer to him, an adjustment that didn't look at all premeditated or unusual as the crowd nearly forced them to do as much. Now dangerously in his personal zone, she felt an odd sense of security as they moved. Her eyes closed, sensing it was okay to do such, and he leaned over her shoulder ever so slightly, his lips very close to her ear.

"Just because my composure sort of slips, the moment that your lips meet mine." Carter sang quietly as he hovered over her. Meg smiled as she continued moving with him. "Chances are you think that my heart's your valentine."

"You like this song?" She finally asked, forcing herself to offer up some space between them before the comfort was overwhelming.

"Hmph, I love this song." He laughed quietly. "I prefer Johnny Mathis, but some skirt singing it a little off key will do."

He leaned back slightly and smiled at his own mockery of Oswell. She returned the favor splendidly. Carter soaked it in. The smoothness of her skin, of her neck with her hair drawn away from it, exposing her like that. Her dancing eyes. He nudged her toward him to avoid having to behold with his eyes any longer that which was not his. That which belonged to a man who could never fully appreciate his good fortune. Carter sighed.

"Guess you feel you'll always be the one and only for me. And if you think you could, well, chances are your chances are, aw-fully good." He quit singing before the last chorus began its repeat.

Meg stopped moving and Carter followed suit, looking at her hesitantly as they stood quiet and still amidst a sea of dancing couples.

"I think we should go back now," she offered, her tone unconvincing.

"You don't sound all that certain." His eyes involuntarily roved along the curve of her shoulders, her smooth cheeks and soft lips.

"Yes," she forced herself. She needed to. Meg felt herself slipping, and did her best to muster false courage. "Yes, just as soon as this song is over, we should definitely go back."

Chances are your chances are pret-ty good.

The two stood there still, his height towering over her as she raised her eyes to look at his face. Neither moved a muscle. The music stopped and the moment of silence seemed to last forever.

"Meghan—" He started to speak but was interrupted by the sound of something unusual. The band began to play again.

Chances are because I wear a silly grin the moment you come into view . . .

Meg blinked with wonder as the song started over. Carter smiled at her. With some amusement, they began to move again.

"That's the strangest—"She started to voice her bewilderment quietly, but was stopped as Carter touched her lips softly with his index finger, halting her protest.

"Don't question a good thing." He smiled and held her close again, his lips lingering dangerously close to her ear as he added in a whisper: "It's a sign."

"A *sign*?"She half spoke,half whispered,as if she weren't aware of the existence of such nonsense.

Never missing a beat, Carter laughed softly into her ear in a manner that she found quite comforting, excusing her own awkward feelings.

"It's a sign we should keep dancing, at least."

Chapter Forty-six

"You want to move to *Tampa?*" Meg nearly slammed her coffee mug onto the countertop before her. The volume from the crashing sound startled her, and she stared at it, thankful that she hadn't actually broken it into pieces. She gathered her composure and started again. "You honestly want to move to *Tampa?* What about the farm?"

"It's something I'm mulling over. You don't like the idea?" Marcus looked at her now in a doey-eyed way that reminded her of a puppy. She only remained staring at him, waiting for him to justify his statement. "After being at that party and speaking to a few of the other Oswell House writers—well, heck, most of them live right there in Tampa or in New York near the branch office there. It's easier because you don't have to fly all over creation and anytime you want to meet with your editor, you've got him right there. I mean, Meg, we've already got enough frequent flyer miles racked up to go to Mars! Not to mention the fact that I have to pay Harve to work the place single-handedly each time we jet out of this place—between that and air fare, I could squash all my profits."

Meg glared at him, wondering if what she would say next would address the fact that he was using the possessive terms *me, mine* and *my* a bit too often for her taste lately, or if she should just skip the preliminaries and tell him how insane the whole idea was. She chose the latter.

"Again, I'll ask, you're wanting to sell the farm? The farm that has been in your family for three generations? The farm that you work with your own hands *daily?*" She waved her hand dramatically as she made her point. "Just sell it? *Vamoose* That's it?"

Marcus was nodding his head as he listened, waiting impatiently to talk.

"I offered Harve a chance to lease it from me—the house, the land, the equipment, the buildings. The works. He's willing to go for it."

"You already talked to Harve about this before you even talked with me?" Her voice was rising with exasperation. "Were you going to tell me before the moving trucks came to the door, or was that going to be a surprise too? Did you pack my bags already?"

"Calm down, calm down." Marcus moved closer to stand directly before her now. He rested his hands on her shoulders and bowed his head to see her stern look. "I thought you'd be thrilled. You're the one who said that big city living would be more exciting. Closer to the beach. The *shop - ping*—any of this sound familiar?"

"I recall a particular conversation, but it was laced with words like wild life, danger. Swingers and other alternative recreational habits. Do you recall?"

"Meg, I thought this would make you happy beyond all!"

"I'm perfectly content to live on a farm in, in Podunk, Iowa." She stammered the words as she shoved a few stray hairs out of her eyes. She didn't want to tell him that she what she really feared most was moving closer to Nick Carter. She swallowed hard and continued. "What's wrong with Jasper Falls?"

"Nothing's wrong with it, if you don't mind humdrum rural living. You're made for more than that Meg, you tried to tell me yourself. And now, looking at the big picture, I think I might be too."

"So when it was me it was a stupid idea, and now that it's you wanting to make the quantum leap, it's a great idea?" She smiled sarcastically. "That's quite a deal, Marcus."

"I know how it seems, Meg, but really, I just didn't understand you before." He ran his hands down her arms and clasped her hands now, swinging them a little as he gazed into her eyes, his own, pleading. "I do see the appeal of a bigger city now, I do. But it wouldn't be good without you there."

"Yeah, and it would be a difficult idea to sell, you living there and me living here, writing books under your name." She rolled her eyes. "You astonish me sometimes."

"You're right."

"You are single minded to a fault."

"I am."

"You are so one-dimensional—you can't see anyone else's view unless you have an interest in it."

"Again, I concede. You're right." He nodded as he clasped his hands, bowing his head shamefully before him. "I guess I'm just lucky to have a good woman like you to show me the error of my ways."

Meg watched him as he stood. She rolled her eyes and chuckled a little forgiving laugh as she did. Marcus raised his own to see her and smiled coyly.

"Let's think this thing through before we do anything rash. Okay? At least promise me that." Meg tousled his hair roughly with her knuckles.

"You know it, boss."

Suddenly Meg's eyes widened as she remembered something important.

"Oh—what time is it? I'm supposed to meet Noel and Reed at the mall at four."

"It's three-thirty. What's wrong with your watch?" Marcus started to touch her wrist, but she drew it away quickly.

"Um, it's not working right,' She mumbled weakly.

"Well, let me take a look at it."

"No, no it just needs a battery. That's all."

"Then why are you wearing it? If it doesn't keep time and all."

"To remind me to buy a battery for it." Meg nodded with confidence suddenly. "And it just keeps slipping my mind. I'll do that at the mall maybe, while I'm there."

Marcus nodded as he watched her peculiar behavior.

"Okay."

She quickly raised up on her toes and planted a kiss on his forehead before bounding toward the door, grabbing her coat from the kitchen chair as she did.

"I'll see you tonight."

"Okay, honey, have a good time."

Chapter Forty-seven

The food court was only barely occupied by a few mall employees on their break or having an early dinner. Being that it was early April and not daylight savings time yet,the large series of plate glass windows let the only a little remaining sunlight onto the seating area. Meg quickened her pace toward the usual little table near the carousel where she and her two friends always sat.

She could see Reed pacing frantically near their usual spot, only stopping to cast a look now and again out the window, and as she drew nearer she was growing more concerned for her friend's odd behavior.

"Reed?"

Her voice held a note of worry and wonder that startled him out of his apparent haze. He stopped in his tracks when he saw her, his eyes nearly glowing red with fury that he dealt straight to the approaching woman. She slowed some, but kept on nonetheless, touching his shoulder lightly with alarm when she reached him.

"What is it, Reed?"

"What *is* it? What is it, Meggie?" His voice sounded breathy. He raised his arms with exasperation, trying to decide where he should begin. "Well, let me tell you what it is. What it is, is this. As you know, I've been having coffee with my friend Perry from the book shop across the way from the studio lately, and he and I have been getting pretty chummy and all and I confided in him your little undercover book venture with *whatshisname* and stuff . . ."

Reed rolled the words off as if he couldn't get them out fast enough. He stopped and closed his eyes for a few seconds to regroup, breathing in deeply before continuing. "So, Perry comes over to the studio during his lunch which hasn't been the same as mine lately—and he tosses a book across the counter at me while I'm sitting there processing the order for those horrid little Mendato twins, and do you know what book it was? *Do you?*"

Meg's eyes were wide with wonder and she shrugged, choosing to remain quiet at this point.

"It was *this*! Do you recognize this? *An Event at Juniper Hill,* which, I might add, is a really stupid name for a book if I don't say so myself."

"That's fine, you have that right." She nodded, encouragingly. Actually, she'd hated it too, but it was one of the numerous changes requested by the Oswell House editor. She'd stayed up way into the night making the recommended changes to send back with Carter. Suddenly she drew her breath in sharply and cringed. The memory of what was contained now between the pages, only a former shell of its original version, flooded her thoughts now. "Oh Reed, oh no—"

"Oh *no*! Oh *really*? Then you do *know* what I'm going to tell you! And it's *not* some fluky publishing decision that was made without your knowledge at the last minute. Well that's just swell. *Super*!"

"Oh Reed...You've got to believe me when I say that I didn't make those changes willingly—not at all! Ask Noel!"

"I will, I *will* because I'm sure she will be plenty interested to know what the hell happened to her character as well! A prostitute! Hmph! And this was the book that was so near and dear to your heart!"

"Reed, *please*! You've got to believe me! It didn't turn out to be a story about us at all! That's the way the business works! I had no say-so in the deal!" She reached out to touch his shoulder but he flinched away violently as if she might contaminate him with some terrible disease. "*Please* Reed!"

"You made me a janitor at some slinky underground night club!"

"I'm sorry."

"You made me some cheap closet transvestite!"

"I'm sorry, Reed."

"You dressed me in low-rent clothing and made me a drug dealer!"

"I *am* sorry, Reed!"

"*Sorry*? This is supposed to be a broad spectrum commercial romance novel! Does any of what I've just said to you sound like a *romance?*"

"Reed, would you please sit down?"

"No! No I won't! My best friend tells me she's created the ultimate book as a tribute to the true and wonderful friendship we have! And on page one hundred nineteen I get killed! And let me quote," Reed immediately flipped through several pages and scanned down some until he found what he was looking for. "Here we go—*bludgeoned to a bloody pulp by the underside of a taxi cab after having stepped off the curb in a drug induced stupor.* Does that sound like a beautiful tribute to a best friend?"

"Reed!"

"And *another* thing." His voice was rising out of control and a few patrons seated across the way turned and stared. Noel had arrived on the scene and was quickly approaching them as she saw what was happening.

"Whoa! Wait! Reed!" She raised her voice above both of theirs and wedged her body between them. "Hold up! Hold on already!"

"You made me pathetic! A disgrace to good gay men like myself!"

"Reed!"

Noel placed her fingers on each side of her mouth, sending out a shrill whistle that got their attention and shut them both up.

"Thank you, for the love of the gawds." She looked at them and then waved her hand over to their usual table. "Now, shall we?"

"But—" Reed began his protest and was quickly stopped by Noel's hand as she raised it before his face in a firm halting manner.

"Hmph! Enough now! Reed *sit*! Meg *sit*!"

Meg never released him from her look as she sat in silence. Reed leaned against the table with his back facing them, arms crossed before him.

"Now, what on earth is going on here? Someone?"

No one said anything.

"*Anyone?*" Noel's eyes were wide and she was growing extremely frustrated with the entire operation. "You all seemed to have plenty to say a minute ago."

"Did you read our little Megan's newest book?" Reed finally began.

"No, no I didn't." Noel answered matter-of-factly. "Meggie, number two hit the stands today?"

"Lucky me," Meg muttered.

"That's *great!*" Her friend was suddenly beaming with pride as she reached across the table and clasped her hands, smiling.

"You say that now . . ." Meg sighed.

"Tell her Meggie! Tell her about the few minor changes you made to it! Go on! Go on!"

"There were a few changes made, you remember Noel? The ones that Carter came to hand deliver back to the publishing house?" Meg's look reeked of desperation. "You know how opposed I was to rewriting the whole thing! Tell Reed about it!"

"It's a discredit to both of us!" He shouted.

"It's a book, Reed, a work of *fiction*, nonetheless." Noel maintained her composure.

"It's a wretched thing!"

"I'm sorry Reed." Meg touched her forehead and lowered her chin in despair.

"You made me look like a cheap transvestite *floozy!*" he spouted off.

"Reed, the editors tend to go with colorful language," Noel defended.

"You made me look like a drug addicted *fool!*"

"*Drugs?* Well, that's a little unusual, but could make for a good story." Her friend nodded.

"She *killed* me off!" he burst out.

"You killed Reed?" Noel looked at Meg now with confusion.

"With a taxi! To a *bloody pulp!*"

"You ran over Reed with a taxi? Ewwe . . ." Noel wrinkled her nose at Meg for a second but quickly recovered as she breathed deeply. "Now Reed, as an editor myself, I can tell you that Meg only did what she had to—"

"Oh, go ahead and tell her what *her* role is in the book now! Go ahead! Go ahead!" Reed waved his hand in Meg's direction. She rolled her eyes and spoke quietly.

"The newspaper editor is now a prostitute."

"I'm a prostitute?" Noel, said her voice rising an octave. She considered it carefully nonetheless. "You didn't kill me off, did you?"

"No," Meg began to knead at her temples furiously. "No I didn't."

"Who cares! You're a *prostitute!*" Reed was at his height.

Noel silently analyzed the situation and began to speak diplomatically.

"Well, now see? That's the way it works sometimes." Noel clasped her hands before her now in an effort to make peace. "I recognize that any changes made are only for the sake of whatever the market calls for, therefore I am not offended. Simple enough."

"Thank you, Noel."

"*You* are not offended? Well, that's probably because *your* facial features aren't plastered on the underside of some taxi cab on the seedier side of town!"

"Reed! I *told* you! I didn't create the changes in the book!"

"They didn't write themselves, sister!"

"I was only doing like I was told!"

"Well, you keep letting them tell you how to write your books and you'll have no friends left! Your pen will have damned them all to fiction *hell*!"

"Reed—" Noel tried to interject.

"Peace, Noel! This really doesn't concern you. It is about Meggie and her creative writing processes that seem to be a *little* out of whack!"

"I'm sorry, Reed."

There was silence as her voice trailed off. Reed turned to look at her for the first time in several minutes. His eyes were misty, only clarifying the hurt behind them. Meg's heart nearly broke as she impulsively rose and tried to put her arms around him, but he backed away suddenly, leaving her standing there alone.

"I'm sorry too, Meg." His voice sounded broken as he spoke. "But for some of us with small lives, seeing ourselves in print is a big deal. Of course, now that you have a life, you'd know nothing about that."

"Oh, Reed . . . "

He turned abruptly and marched down the mall. He was gone.

Meg eyes remained fixed in the direction that he'd stormed off in. She finally turned to see Noel who was gauging her friend's reaction to the incident. Noel reached her hand across the cafe table and patted Meg's hand with sympathy.

"I know ya didn't mean to kill Reed off," she said quietly. "Those damn cabs can come out of *nowhere*. He'll get over it."

"No, he's right." Meg's eyes were tear-filled. "He's right. In an effort to make the editors happy I took a flying leap from my standards and landed right in the lap of commercial publishing. Looks like I took a few people with me on this leap."

"Meggie, you're going to learn that sometimes what things are and what things appear to be are really two different things. I could lay out that *White Christmas* scenario where Betty leaves, thinking that Bob is going to sell out his old military buddy . . ."

"No, spare me, please." Meg rose from her place at the table and Noel quickly gathered her things and followed her friend. They began a slow walk out of the food court and down the vacant wide-open hallway. "It's time I learned that things don't happen like they do in the stupid movies—that real life is a lot less eventful and a lot more hurtful than a handful of mushy Christmas flicks. And that there is no such thing as a perpetual string of happily-ever-afters."

"Not true Meggie! Not *true!*" Noel spoke quickly, realizing how sad her friend had become.

"You know it is, Noel. You've said it before yourself."

"Listen to me!" Noel pulled her friend's arm, turning her around to face her. "You've got something special within you Meg, you make people *feel* good! The reason you've heard so much negative-shmegative out of me over the years isn't because I don't believe in fate and miracles—it's because I tell you so that you will remind me that such things *do* exist!"

"Like what you're doing now?"

"Like what I'm trying to do now. You're much better than I am at it." Noel's eyes widened as she nodded dramatically. "That's just it! People are drawn to you—you have a gift for making them feel good, for restoring their hope and faith in *themselves!* Your own goodness brings out the goodness in us."

There was silence between them for a moment and a few tears escaped from Meg's eyes and streamed down her cheek. She dug into her pocket for a tissue to blot it, but found nothing. Noel quickly handed her friend one of her fleece mittens to wipe her face. Meg laughed.

"Yeah, you see how I just inflicted that gift on Reed. He's feeling much better now, isn't he?"

"Don't worry about it—Reed's got problems of his own too. Getting that bent out of shape, knowing you like he does, only means that there's something else there. Chances are it has nothing to do with you."

"Oh, another one of those right place at the right time deals? Lucky me." She sniffed as she began to button her coat and adjust her collar. "Noel, I hope I haven't let you down terribly. There's so many things—"

"Don't worry about it. Don't give it another thought." Noel sounded very certain of her words as she stood there, patiently.

"This whole charade . . . "

"I know."

"The *damned* book!"

"I know."

"And now, Marcus wants to move to Tampa."

"You're serious?"

"Yes, I'm serious."

"Wow," Noel initially appeared surprised but then quickly spoke so as to not upset her friend any more than necessary. "Well, Tampa's good."

"I don't know that I can do that right now."

"Sure you can. You're *resilient!* You can do anything!"

"And leave you and Reed? What would I—"

"You'd make new friends. And I'd come visit you all the time. I'd love it!"

"But what about the book? How will I ever escape this trap I've made for myself?"

"You'll think of a way."

"There's other things too."

"Tell me, what is it?"

Meg's eyes were glassy and wide as she looked at her best friend standing before her.

"I'm feeling things that aren't right for a man that I can't even hardly stand—"

"Nick Carter."

"How did you know?" She seemed genuinely surprised.

"Meggie, how could I *not* know? I'm your best friend." She touched her shoulder with a smile. "Fate, miracles—you taught me about them. Now recognize them in your own life. Trust your instincts."

"This is crazy."

"It is. But *you're* not crazy. Know that. You've got what it takes to make it, and you will. In life and in love." She nodded at her, speaking quietly. Noel walked Meg a little closer to the door as she continued. "Do you know what a great place this world would be to live in if we'd just dance like there's nobody watching and love like it's never gonna hurt?"

Meg's lips parted slightly and she slowly nodded. Noel smiled at her.

"Go dance, Meggie. You go dance."

The friends stood there for a few moments before embracing.

"What about Reed?"

"You leave him to me." Noel backed away a little and looked at her. "Don't give it another thought."

"As much as you've always claimed I've done for you, you've provided at least as much for me."

"Really? I hear there's more money in counseling. Maybe I should consider a career change?"

The both giggled a little.

"I know that everything will work out between you and Elliot as well, you've got the right stuff. You just need to figure out what to do with it."

"From your lips to Gawd's ears," Noel glanced skyward and then smiled at her best friend. She waved her on toward the door. "You go now before we have a really bad girly moment here. I'm getting all weird."

Meg nodded and dabbed her eyes again, making her way to the front entry of the mall. She turned one last time to see her friend standing there and smiled before pushing the door open and entering into the chilly evening air.

Noel watched her go, still standing in the same place but alone now, feeling rather empty inside as she contemplated the changes that were ahead for the three best friends.

"You glimmer girl."

Chapter Forty-eight

B*uzz! Buzz!*

Meg quickly pulled her cell phone from her purse and punched it on as she hurried down the hallway of the television studio in Atlanta, Georgia. Marcus was on the set of "Good Day Atlanta" discussing the third book which had just been released days earlier, and Meg had been waiting in the wings along with Jan and Carter. She left them there as to not disrupt the stage activities with her ringing phone or the conversation that would follow. She pushed through the double doors before speaking finally.

"Hello?"

"Yes, Meghan St. John?"

"Meghan Laine."

"Ms. Laine, I was given this number to call as soon as I got the test results back from your Labrador, Boo."

"Yes, yes, have you discovered what that terrible rash stuff was all over his underside? It looks awful."

"The bloodwork we performed shows that Boo has a flea intolerance. Put simply enough, he's allergic to fleas."

"So what can you do for him? What's that mean?"

"Well, I've given him a shot of cortisone and put him on a type of steroid that will help amend the situation somewhat. You'll need to help him avoid the elements as much as possible. There are sand fleas all over Florida."

"So, I shouldn't take him to the beach anymore?"

"You should avoid even having him outside as much as possible due to the extreme infestation that this environment has. It's not going to be easy. His rash wounds are so severe that we must handle them much like burns at this point."

"What can I do to make sure this doesn't happen again?"

The vet was quiet for a few moments and she waited, eagerly.

"You have a few options—send him home—"

"He is home! I can't send him back to Iowa, alone, for heaven's sake!"

"You should know, Ms. Laine, that this is a rather inhumane way for a dog to live. You've seen his condition. He looks like an Oscar Mayer wiener. It's not right. The other alternative I would offer would be to have him put to sleep, because all the treatments and medications in the world aren't enough to ward this off. He's miserable. I sincerely hope you work on the first option—he's a good dog."

"Oh God . . ." Meg's voice trailed off as she stood in the hallway shaking her head. Slowly she punched the phone off and replaced it into her purse. She stepped into the waiting area down the way and slumped into a chair with a sigh.

The show was finished minutes later and the sound of approaching talking and laughter drew nearer the room where she sat. Marcus' head popped into the room and he motioned for her to come along with them.

"How did it go?" she asked numbly.

"Tip top!" Marcus' voice was a little too chipper on this particular day. Meg smiled at him weakly as he chattered away with Jan and Carter. "To lunch?"

"I'm starving." Jan didn't waste any time jumping on that one. "Chinese?"

Chinese gives me a rash." Marcus complained. Hearing that word, Meg was sad all over again as she was reminded of her loyal dog back at the vet in Tampa. "How about pizza?"

"I have pizza delivery on my autodial." Carter vetoed that idea. "Let's go somewhere where they actually have silverware."

"Mexican!" Jan gushed with more excitement than Carter had ever witnessed during her employment with him thus far. He laughed lightly at her giddy behavior as she dropped back to walk with Meg.

There was something peculiar about Meg in that she seemed to possess a vitality that was rather contagious to those around her. Now, having seen the transformation come over even Jan, he was more certain than ever that isn't wasn't merely a coincidence, but rather a particular aura she had about her. As wary as he was of it, he liked it. However, he did notice something was lacking from her mood today, but was careful not to appear overly concerned about it. Or perhaps it was nothing, as Marcus, who would naturally have more experience with her moods, didn't seem remotely concerned.

"Atlanta is great! There's *tons* of stuff to do here!" He was exuberant, having pulled off yet another successful television interview. He was dishing it out in heaping portions and the female clientele was lining up for their helping one after another.

"I suppose you'll want to move here next," Meg mumbled. She quickly stifled her comment and made up for it with the brilliant smile she offered her fiancé. Marcus looked at her oddly and smiled back.

Lunch was a colorful experience in the Tex Mex Cafe on Border Avenue in the city. The waitresses wore bright clothing and flocked to their table to get an autograph from their favorite author, either on their order pads or a napkin. It seemed that Marcus St. John was gaining incredible notoriety as an author renowned for his ability to be sensitive with his understanding of the female mind. His numerous television appearances and newspaper review articles seemed to always have his face somewhere where it could be seen, all a part of the incredible publicity push that the Oswell Publishing House was so good at. Marcus smiled at the waitresses in a teasing way, and obliged in their requests to sign anything and everything. As the center of attention, he'd clearly turned their simple lunch into some kind of spectacle. Meg watched with mild amusement, smiling politely. Now and again, Marcus would nod in her direction knowingly, as if to let her know that she was still his *number one girl*. She would scrunch her nose and smile back in her wonderful way in an unspoken reply that said she knew.

When Marcus had slipped over to another table to speak with some fans and Carter left to take care of the bill at the front counter, Jan stood and slid into the booth next to Meg, who'd been noticeably quieter than usual. She smiled broadly and leaned toward the woman curiously.

"What's up, Meggie? I've seen stiffs more lively at their own funerals."

Meg smiled with a little laugh as she shrugged her shoulders nonchalantly.

"Nothing really. I guess I'm just a little tired, that's all."

Jan hesitated before going on.

"What do you say we get away from these guys for a bit? Just you and me, the girls! We'll go get our nails done, or our hair. Shop or something. Leave this drab scene behind."

"But we're all in the same car."

"Hello? Taxi cabs."

"But the workshop this afternoon—"

"Not until five o'clock. We've got all sorts of time! Come on."

Meg looked at her for a moment and then her eyes lit up a little as she nodded her head in agreement.

"Okay, I'd like that."

Two hours later Meg and Jan were laying side by side on parallel tables getting a well deserved massage in one of Atlanta's poshest salons. Never having treated herself to such a luxury before, Meg was thoroughly enjoying the sensation as she closed her eyes and relaxed. She breathed in the clean scent of floral-scented oils and let herself go to the relaxing music that played softly in the background.

"You've been a little distant today, if you don't mind my noticing." Jan's words bridged the little space between their tables. "What gives?"

"I guess that I am just not used to this whirlwind tour stuff. I'm a little ragged out, I guess."

"I'm not used to it either." Jan laughed. "I wouldn't be here if it weren't for you."

Meg's opened one eye at the woman laying across the way in a white terry towel, her hair pulled off her neck.

"Don't you do this kind of stuff all the time? The agency and all?"

"No, actually I don't. I never do. But I had some time off coming and when the boss offered to spring for the trip, I couldn't refuse. You're a ball, Meggie. I like ya."

"Thank you. I guess I just thought that the secretary sort of did this kind of stuff with the agent. Like an organizer, or something."

Jan laughed, her eyes opening to see if Meg was serious or not.

"Heavens *no!* The writers usually do this stuff on their own. The agent gets their itinerary lined up and helps out at the start. But at this stage in the game yo-yo." She clarified herself as she relaxed again. "*You're on your own.* It's really not like the boss to do all this galavantin' around the country and stuff. It's weird."

"Then why is he?" Meg's head was raised now, giving the secretary her undivided attention. Jan opened her eyes again with a coy little smile.

"You tell me."

There was silence as they both lay there.

"I need a change, Jan."

"What? Moving to Florida from the cornbelt and becoming near relative to the trendiest writer in the country wasn't change enough? Geesh!"

"I think I'm in the mood to do something unusual."

Chapter Forty-nine

"Where in the world are they?" Marcus was pacing frantically inside an office at the University of Georgia. The literature department of the college had invited him to stop in during his visit to the city and give a little impromptu workshop—something Marcus knew absolutely nothing about. Thankfully, Meg had made some notes for him pertaining to her writing style. Unfortunately she had them with her now, somewhere in Atlanta. He glanced at his watch again. "Why would she do this to me?"

Nick Carter set aside the magazine that he'd been flipping through and watched him now, no particular concern on his face. He shrugged.

"What's the big deal? They'll get here eventually. Maybe they're tired of sitting through all this kind of thing and decided to meet us afterwards."

"No, no I don't think so." Marcus shook his head as he made another hurried walking lap across the room. "Meg knows how important it is that she be here for me during this stuff."

"You'll be fine this once, I'm sure."

"But you don't understand, she's got some notes of mine."

"It's an impromptu workshop—wing it."

"I can't *wing it*! I don't know how to *wing it*! The whole idea of *winging* it terrifies me!"

His voice was beginning to tremble, Carter noticed, and started taking his anxiety more seriously.

"*Calm down*, St. John."

"Calm down? I can't calm down! I need the damned notes which are in the damned purse in a damned boutique or taxi cab right now!"

Carter looked at him with growing comprehension that perhaps this wasn't just a simple case of stage fright, but rather some kind of phobic behavior that he'd not been warned of. He set the magazine aside now and stood to smack his client's shoulder lightly in a reassuring male gesture that he didn't seem to be buying into. Carter clapped his hands together. The door opened and Marcus turned with pending relief on his face, only to nearly launch back into a panic attack at discovering that it was the professor and not Meg.

"We're ready for you, Mr. St. John." The older gentleman smiled behind his wire rimmed glasses. He nodded and backed out of the office and into the classroom. Marcus caught a glimpse of the room as the door closed. It was a small, brightly lit auditorium and was packed with at least two hundred students.

"Great! Oh my God!" Marcus was definitely coming unglued, forcing Carter to offer him some semblance of reassurance.

"You'll be fine. Don't worry about it! It's just like the television studio audiences! You always do great with that stuff." Carter waved his hand as he rambled on, hoping that his client would quickly get some courage from somewhere.

"Oh God. I can't believe that she'd do this to me! Knowing how important this is!"

"Oh God...I can't believe that we're not there yet!" Meg was leaning forward near the driver of the cab as she sat in the backseat. "Oh. This *traffic!*"

"Calm down Meggie." Jan pulled a nail file out of her purse and began to shape her pink capped fingertips.

"Yeah, calm down lady! Aintcha ever been in a traffic jam before?" The cab driver spoke to her harshly as he rolled down his window and began to holler out to the masses of honking cars. "Shut up your honkin'! We ain't gettin' there any faster by you tootin' your BMW!"

"I have, I have, but not usually at such an *inconvenient* time." Meg mumbled, her brow furrowed with distress. "Marcus is going to kill me."

"He can't kill you, sales would plummet if Mister I'm-in-touch-with-my-feminine-side killed his wife." She giggled.

"Fiancé." Meg corrected.

"Enough already with the honking—redneck! How did a backwoods hillbilly hick like yourself score such a sweet car?"

Meg glanced at the cab driver who was still hollering out the window, and then looked at Jan who only smiled casually.

"Is there some other way we could take?"

"Lady—we're in *gridlock* here! Even the way to the way to the other way looks just like this—as well as the rest of the city right now!" The cabby poked his head back out the window. "If you get any closer to my ass end, you can just latch on and save your gas!"

"I love your hair, Meggie. I can't believe you had the nerve to cut it all off. It's wonderful and daring!" Jan leaned forward and touched the young woman's hair that was flipped up on the ends, layered around her ears and above her neck. It looked rather unkempt and stylish and Meg swallowed hard as she arched an eyebrow.

"Well, I'm not sure that this was such a good day to do this after all." She ducked her head down, analyzing the bumper to bumper traffic they were locked into. Clearly they were going nowhere for a while. "Do you think we should get out and walk there?"

"*Ha!*" The driver belted out sarcastically. "The University's a good ten miles outta here still, sister! If you could walk that far without getting mugged and killed you'd still not be there for hours!"

"Great!" Meg ran her fingers through her hair and made a little face. She looked at Jan. "I guess I'm used to there being hair there still. I don't know about this."

"Don't worry about it! Short hair is sexy!"

"Not according to Marcus."

"Well, I know plenty of men who love a good neck." Jan leaned forward now and spoke near the cabby's ear. "Tell me, sir, do you appreciate the fine curve of a woman's neck?"

"What?" His voice bellowed over the sound of honking horns and people yelling outside.

"Do you like a woman's neck? Do you find it *alluring*?"

"Lady, at this stage in the game I find a *brisk wind* alluring," the cabby muttered. He leaned his head out of the window and barked loudly at the man who was still honking his horn annoyingly loud. "Keep honking! I'm reloading!"

"See? Every man likes the soft curve of a woman's neck. It's sexy."

Jan's thick Eastern accent rolled on as she stuck a piece of gum into her mouth and then offered Meg a stick. She declined. "Why Mr. Carter *him - self* was just telling me the other day how absolutely charming he finds a woman with short hair."

Meg's eyes widened and she shot the secretary a look, trying to read her expression. She came up empty handed at the effort.

"Well, I didn't do it for any silly man. I did it for myself." Meg's voice sounded braver now.

"Then why are you worried that Marcus will hate it?"

"I'm worried that Marcus will never see it! The workshop was set to begin twenty minutes ago!" She glanced at her watch only to remember for the millionth time that it didn't work. Sighing, she pulled it off and stashed it in her purse to resist the temptation of looking at it again. Meg swallowed hard and peered over the cabby's shoulder again.

"Relax, Blondie. Your old man will know you're there when he sees the whites of your eyes." The cabby waved his hand in her direction. Meg didn't bother to answer. Instead she merely sighed heavily and slumped back into the seat. She gazed out the window at the standstill traffic and wondered how Marcus was doing.

"I'd like to do this a little differently today, if you don't mind." Marcus' voice was trembling and his smile weak as he addressed the students sitting at attention in the large classroom. He bypassed the podium and felt his way over to the professor's desk that was situated on the platform there. He pulled the chair out and adjusted the microphone on the collar of his plaid shirt, offering them another smile. "I'd like to conduct this as casually as possible. If you don't mind, I'd rather sit."

He felt it was best that he leave out the part about feeling ready to faint as fear gripped him. He swallowed hard and looked over the rows of eager faces before him.

"I've never done a workshop like this before, so you'll have to bear with me." He continued, his voice crackling somewhat. "I'd like to start by having a little question and answer session. So anyone start and we'll muddle through it. Sound okay?"

Marcus glanced in the direction of the professor and Carter who were sitting in the first row. The professor nodded with a smile that said he must not be doing too horribly so far.

Finally a young blonde woman seated about midway back the rows of inclining desk chairs stood and smiled shyly. She was dressed in a rather revealing way that Marcus didn't at all find terribly appropriate for an educational setting. But she was easy on the eyes, nonetheless, and he felt suddenly uncomfortable as he watched her. Marcus unbuttoned the top button of his shirt and loosened his tie as he waited for her to ask her question.

"I'm a really big fan of your work, Mr. St. John. Can you tell me what your motivation is for your books?" Her voice was quiet and squeaky and she smiled as she watched him.

"I, uh, well, I love beautiful women. And when I write, I try to get inside them." Suddenly, he noted the surprised look on the young woman's face and he reevaluated his statement, quickly amending it, red-faced. "I mean, get inside their *minds*, naturally."

The blonde woman nodded with relief as she smiled even more broadly. She apparently had another question.

"Don't you find that a challenge?"

Marcus nodded slowly, contemplating his words more carefully before speaking again.

"Yes, sometimes it is."

"Do you think you'd could get inside my mind?" she persisted.

"Yes, quite easily."

The woman looked confused as she stood there, her forehead creased. Carter shot Marcus a look of horror.

"I mean, possibly, it's quite possible that I could get inside your mind that is—I would imagine." Marcus was scaring his agent quite a bit now. Knowing this, he quickly refocused his attention and moved on. "Next question?"

"I've got one." A man in his mid twenties near the front row stood up and prepared to speak. "How long have you been writing?"

"For about a year now."

"A year?" The man was impressed and amazed. "How did you get so lucky to be published in one little year?"

"Beginner's luck, I guess." Marcus nodded. "Next?"

A non-traditional student in the very rear of the classroom stood now. He was an older, large man, rugged looking, his expression border-ing on unforgiving.

"I've got a question for ya. Why do you make us look like a bunch of dopey fools in your books? What kind of man would do that to his own kind?"

Marcus slumped in his seat just a little and looked quickly at Carter for courage. The agent was similarly slumped with his hand covering his eyes, which offered no reassurance whatsoever.

"How about we move on and finish up the question-answer session?" Marcus quickly interjected instead of answering. "I wonder if I could first get a glass of water."

Carter took this cue and immediately exited the room. He returned a few moments later with a Styrofoam cup full of water in hand that he set on the desk before Marcus.

"Where the hell is Meg?" Marcus whispered in a panicked voice.

"I don't know. I haven't seen her."

Carter smiled briefly and backed off the platform, standing in the doorway of the professor's office. He clenched his eyes shut with worry once he was out of the author's eyeshot.

"I have an idea, Mr. St. John," The professor stood now from his place in the front row and spoke courteously, and obviously realizing that the man needed some guidance for his lecture. "Why don't you share with the class tonight the way you organize your ideas before you write."

Marcus looked at him blankly, saying nothing.

"You know, the thought process you follow."

Although the professor's kind voice was encouraging and patient, Marcus clearly had no idea what he was talking about and looked at him nodding slowly, hoping for clarity.

"You know, the way you put your *thoughts* onto *paper* before you write. Outline? Brainstorming? Do you know what I mean?"

There was a good chance that the professor was finally growing impatient as well. Marcus smiled feebly in his direction.

"Brainstorming. That's exactly what I do. Before each and every book, I think real hard about what I'm going to write. If you don't think before you write, you might write something really stupid."

"That's very profound." The professor looked at him with growing disenchantment. "What kinds of procedures or exercises do you follow when you are doing this, this *brainstorming*, Mr. St. John?"

"I do some, relaxation therapy, just prior to, you know."

"Perhaps you'd like to share your technique with us then."

"Perhaps I would." Marcus nodded carefully. He looked at the silent curious eyes that seemed to form a wall before him in the octagon-shaped room. He continued to nod as he scanned along each face. His main focus now was getting *their* direct focus off himself. He wanted to hide from the leering eyes and came up with an idea suddenly. "Okay, okay. I think this is something we can all do together. I hope you will find it helpful as I do."

Carter watched on curiously as he rested his cheek on his hand, drumming his fingers as he remained fixed in the office doorway.

"This is a thinking exercise that I particularly enjoy. Close your eyes everyone. Please close your eyes so we can do this together."

The class grew hauntingly quiet as two hundred-plus pairs of eyes shut, preparing to embark on the thinking process exercise as directed by Marcus St. John, famous author. They waited silently.

"Okay, now you'll need to clear your mind. Clear it of everything. Come on." He closed his eyes along with them once he was sure they were following his instruction. "Very good. Now think *story*. Just think about it. *Story*."

Every fleeting hope that Marcus may know what the heck he was doing went out the window as Carter stared on in horror, and some amount of morbid curiosity at the same time.

"Now say it with me, *story*." He continued. The class whispered the word in the same manner he spoke it to them. "Very good, you're doing great. Let's try some tranquillity exercises to go along with that."

"Any more tranquillity and they'll all be asleep." Marcus muttered to no one. He continued to watch the scenario unfold before him.

"Okay, hum with me now. We'll hum four counts and then *stooor - rrry*. Okay, work with me." Marcus breathed in deeply and began. "Hmmm . . . *stooorrrryyy*."

Carter's lips parted at the stupidest action he'd ever been a party to, he was certain. Hordes of seemingly intelligent, normal students were actually following along with the exercise in insanity, the underlying buzz of their humming nearly overwhelming the agent.

He shook his head and rubbed the back of his neck rapidly. Suddenly, the sound of heels rapidly clicking behind him alerted him to the presence of others. With half fear, he turned to see the two women running across the office they'd entered into and toward the agent. Carter's shoulders slumped with relief that he wouldn't have to deal with the outlandish scenario alone any longer and his eyes went from face to face. Something looked different, but he didn't go there right yet.

"He's out there?" Meg wrinkled her nose as she looked past the man standing in the doorway.

"Oh, he's *out there*, all right." Carter rubbed his forehead now. "Did you bring the God blessed notes?"

"Here." Meg thrust them into his hands and Carter immediately marched across the platform toward Marcus, nearly scaring the author right out of his seat when he interrupted his "exercise session" with the class.

"Here's your notes," he whispered into the man's ear. Marcus hurriedly unfolded the sheets of paper, and his confidence immediately returned now that the precious notes were in hand.

"Okay, here we go," he said out loud, his voice more jovial suddenly. The class opened their eyes and ceased their humming. "Enough of that crap."

Carter went back into the office, shaking his head all the way.

"What the heck are they doing?" Meg's brow was furrowed as she peered out the door at the odd behavior of the group that had been humming in unison until seconds earlier.

"Oh, God." Carter began with a smirk. "You missed the really good stuff. What a nightmare that was."

"We were stuck in the middle of the city." Meg rummaged through her purse for an aspirin. Her head was pounding.

"That's fine."

"It was the worst traffic jam I've ever—"

"Meghan," Carter turned toward her. "It was an unavoidable situation or else you would have been here. You don't have to go on."

Meg raised her eyes from the shuffling she was doing in her purse. She nodded slowly. Carter looked at her and narrowed his eyes. He nodded toward her.

"Your hair looks good."

"Your hair looks *horrible*!" Marcus blurted out once the session was over and he entered the office connected to the classroom. "Where did it go? What possessed you to hack it all off like that? Have you gone crazy?"

Meg only stared at him blankly. She blinked her eyes once, then twice and then turned to walk down the hallway of the school toward the exit of the building.

"How could you let her do that?" Marcus looked at Jan helplessly. She only shrugged.

"I know!" She feigned exasperation at the author. "How could she do that without asking for your permission first? I said Meggie, you better ask Marcus first. He is your keeper, after all."

"I'm not her keeper." He weakly defended himself.

"You said it, not me."

Chapter Fifty

"Mr. Carter, Ed Givinchy is here. He'd like to speak with you as soon as possible."

The sound of Jan's voice came through his speaker loud and clear, and he could tell there was something wrong from her guarded tone. He wrinkled his forehead.

"Send him in." He took his finger off the intercom button and spoke under his breath. "Isn't Givinchy supposed to be in LA?"

His office door suddenly swung open and the doorway was filled with the stately figure of the tall fellow in dark framed glasses. His coal black hair was generously lubed with brill cream and peppered with a fleck of gray now and again, as was his mustache. He was dressed in a fine suit, his hands clasped confidently before him. His Rolex watch emitted a blinding gleam as it reflected the sunshine that poured into the window from the pleasant July afternoon. Carter stood to greet him. The man was clearly displeased about something. He bypassed the agent's gesture and slipped into a seat directly in front of Carter's desk. He glanced down at his own still-extended hand that had been ignored and nodded slightly. He sat down as well.

"Good afternoon, Ed. How's things?" He waited to see what wrath he would incur. "Should I ask how come you're not on the sunny West Coast?"

I've decided to pass on the LA Chronicles. LA is filthy and degenerate. I'm not interested in doing the book after all."

"Well, pardon me, Ed, but you were certainly interested when you accepted the hefty advance on the project. What happened to that interest?"

"I just found out that Shelton's doing a piece in London. What's wrong with this picture? We're always at least two beats ahead of Shelton, but he's exceeded us with this last assignment. His chronicle will hit the stands in four months. Now, tell me, do you think that a trashy, well traveled city will sell out, next to the wonder and enchantment of a place like London? Pictorial spectacular versus everyone's been-there and done-that with pictures in their family album to prove it? No, I don't think so."

"Ed." Carter shifted his position in his seat, resisting the sudden urge he had to hurl his entire body over his desk, grabbing the man in a stranglehold. "Los Angeles, the *City of Angels*—it's one of the most beloved cities in this country. Your inventiveness will reveal fresh marvels to old timers and a glimpse into the city life for those who've never ventured there before. We have a word for that in the writing business: *creativity*."

"I have been a faithful client of this firm for ten years, Carter. I think that as one of your star pupils, you could at least be as good as to avoid having my name downgraded to a newcomer like Shelton. It's an absolute embarrassment." Givinchy waved his hand. "A fresh kid like that a world traveler and here's me—a little gray around the face, canvassing a tired joint like LA."

"I'm sure a lot of die-hard Californians would beg to differ with that opinion." Carter rubbed his forehead. "Ed, do you remember when you came into this agency ten years ago? Do you remember what your first pitch was?"

"Yes, I recall it was a photo essay on inner city children's programs."

"In a sense," Carter nodded slowly as he leaned back in his chair some, folding his hands across his stomach. "But it was the worst thing I'd ever seen. Your writing was jagged and your approach was all wrong. Hell, you even misspelled the name of our agency."

"I was a little rough."

"A little? Yes. But as awful as I thought the entire package was, I could see that there was something there. Something that you could convey to the masses within the confines of a few snapshots and carefully worded phrases. And I was right, was I not?"

"What's your point?"

"My point being, I trusted your insight then. When are you going to learn to quit fighting mine?" Now Carter leaned forward onto his desk, speaking in a low tone, his eyes never leaving those of the graying man's before him. "You were a struggling photographer, and now you're a star. Kind of leads me to believe I must have been doing *something* right. Don't you think?"

"It's not like I didn't give you something to work with. Don't go giving yourself too much credit."

Carter smiled and nodded.

"What exactly do you want me to do for you, Ed?"

"I want Ireland. I want to portray the inner qualities. The uniqueness of societies. The joy, the angst. I need freedom, otherwise I'm going to be forced to explore other avenues."

Carter studied him as he sat there. He'd been down this road just a few times too many with Ed Givinchy, and he was ready to call it a day. He eventually leaned forward and pulled open his top side drawer, removing a single piece of paper. Taking a pen in hand he scribbled something onto it and shoved it toward Givinchy, offering him his pen.

"What's this?"

"I'm giving you that freedom with my blessing."

"You're letting me go? Just like that?"

"I am, it's what you wanted, am I correct?" Carter watched as the man glared at him, accepting the pen and forming some scrawl on the bottom of the page.

"It's your loss."

"I'm sure it is."

"You're going to be sorry."

"I'm sorry already."

"You'll be begging me to come back after this next project."

Carter shook his head as he rose and shook the man's hand.

"I don't think so, Ed."

Ed Givinchy glared at him without moving.

"You're a feeble minded fool," he muttered to his now former agent. "I'll show you how it's done, you'll see."

"Good day, Mr. Givinchy. And best of luck on your endeavors."

The man stormed toward the door and opened it slightly, turning once again before he departed.

"I gave you too much credit, Carter. You're nothing but an idiot and a fool."

"Sticks and stones, Mr. Givinchy." Carter smiled still.

"You can kiss my Blarney Stone, Mr. Carter!"

"And you can shove your blarney stone up your angst. Good day." Carter smiled brilliantly as he watched Mr. Givinchy storm across the lobby toward the elevator.

Jan watched the exchange over the top of her magazine. She quickly lowered it and followed her boss back into his office, shutting the door behind her.

"What in the world was that all about?"

"I was just giving Mr. Givinchy the divorce he wanted."

"You *fired* him?"

"We parted ways."

"Okay." She watched him curiously as he shuffled through the piles of paperwork on his desk. "What are you looking for?"

"Are there anymore clients to be seen this afternoon?"

"No. What are you looking for?"

"Is there any reason we have to stay around this place today?" Carter's search grew more harried, but his face wouldn't reveal it.

"No. What are you looking for?"

"An address. I'm looking for an address."

Jan smiled and walked out the door of the office. She reappeared moments later with her purse in hand, poised and ready to go.

"Let's go," she chirped.

"You don't even know where I want to go to."

"Ambrosia Books and Music Store—Marcus St. John's book signing. That's on my side of town. I'll show you the ropes."

Carter looked at her with amazement. He blinked once and nodded. The woman was a mystery to him.

Chapter Fifty-one

Meg paced the floor with the phone receiver wedged between her ear and the crook of her shoulder. This was the third time this week she'd called the vet about poor Boo's ailing skin condition and she was beginning to suspect that she wasn't going to get through this time either. She glanced at the clock on the wall seeing that it was nearly five o'clock. Meg set the phone back on the counter and sighed as she looked at her beloved dog laying before the coffee table.

"I imagine they've all gone for the weekend, Boo." She knelt down and patted the old dog's scruffy neck and he looked at her helplessly. His skin was scaly and red from his midsection down. His back legs twitched now and again, in pain, she suspected. Boo's treatments had begun to work but caused a drying dermatitis as a side effect. It seemed to be a no-win situation. The poor dog was either inflamed from scratching or inflamed from fleas, and there seemed to be no practical way around it or balance to be achieved. Meg lovingly pulled him into her lap and hugged him.

"Oh, Boo, my gramma used to say *what a tangled web we weave.* I never really understood that until now. I feel like this is my punishment for deceiving the public for my own stingy reasons—lonely days and now you, this." She looked at him as he sighed loudly. "Don't worry, I'll figure this out somehow."

Marcus walked through the door just then and tossed his bag onto the couch near Meg. He smiled broadly and knelt to kiss her on the forehead, barely noticing her forlorn behavior. She smiled back.

"How did the signing go?"

"Fine! Great!" He clapped his hands together. "Carter and Jan showed up toward the end. They sent their hellos. Jan wants you to call her before tomorrow night."

"What's tomorrow night?" Meg wrinkled her forehead.

"Tomorrow night—you know," he waved his hand as he mentally searched for the name of the charitable gala that was taking place at the Harbor Island Civic Center. She sighed as she faintly recalled such an event, covering her eyes with her hand as she nodded.

"I remember, the media blitz. Oh God," she trailed off. "Is there anyway I can get out of it? I mean, you're the center of attention anyway. It's not like anyone's going to miss me."

"That's not true Meg! You know that I will miss you and Jan is likely to shoot me if I don't bring along her new best friend."

"Honey, I didn't mean it that way. It's just that there's a deadline to be met with the first draft of this next book and it's not flowing."

"What do you mean? I'm sure you'll figure it out."

"I don't know, Marcus," she shook her head in despair as she wrinkled her nose and rubbed her temples. "The ideas are there, I guess, but it's *jagged* and it sounds—"

"Like what?"

"When I read it aloud it sounds like I'm reading a bad script for a soap opera. It's no good."

Marcus sat next to her now and she leaned her head onto his shoulder.

"Honey, that's what it's all about anyway."

"What is?"

"The soap opera stuff. They never make any sense to me, just like these books didn't used to."

"They make sense to you now?" She tipped her face to see his with a little smile.

"Not really in the way that I'm sure that millions of women would like to think." He paused. "I don't feel like I can relate to some *inner qual -ity* of the female mind, but I understand what kinds of things they're looking for now, I think."

"What kinds of things *are* they looking for?"

"You know, knight on a white horse, romance, flowers, candy. Valentine's day everyday. That kind of thing." He laughed as he went on.

"Well, I guess you're closer than some men ever get then, even if you do think it's a bunch of crap."

"I don't necessarily think it's *crap*, rather, it's an *entrepreneurial* move. Myself? I just don't see the need for playing like that. It's like, it's like— foreplay, leading to one single event and then it's over. Then you have your letdown factor and the seven year itch. All sorts of complications just because all the role playing got in the way, keeping the couple from really getting to *know* each other at the start. They have no idea who they're really in for the long haul with."

"Role playing? *Entrepreneurial?*" She looked at him with an expression that resembled a cross between disgust and amusement. "You think that's what it is?"

"Meg, I know that's all it is. Women want to be swept off their feet and treated like queens, and men, hell, men just want a decent life with a compatible wife. Good paying job, few kids maybe, box seats for the Chicago Blackhawks now and again—that kind of thing." He waved his hand as he went on. "We don't require the high maintenance that you women do. The truth be known, we do the bare minimum allowed by *love law* to keep you all happy."

"Really?"

"Really. All in the wake of the women's movement, we have to angle ourselves a little differently now."

"How do romance movies and books relate to entreprenurship? Give me the tie-in here."

"I'm getting to that part. Hold on. Okay, take this for example—some of the greatest romantic classics were either written by women at the request of a *male* publisher or producer or written by a *man* to impress a woman—screen or paper. You see, Meg. It all leads back to the battle of the sexes. And it's not just books and movies, it's a whole plethora of things."

"Do go on." She leaned away from him now to better gauge his expression as he spoke to her. It was the first time she had ever heard him use the word *plethora*.

"You women wanted control—you demanded it, and we, how can one say? We *lent* you that control. And as a result, you're happy and we're happy. See? So what harm did it do?"

"I see I don't like where this conversation's going."

"No, no listen, really. I'm only being honest with you." He spoke earnestly. "You see, women want to believe that they are the ones to have it all together, and that they pull men's strings and such. But really, it's the men pulling the strings of the women who think they are."

"Wha . . . ?"

"Meg, think about it, why do you think they charge more for women's clothes than men's? Or about the haircuts—it costs me twelve dollars to get a cut and it costs you forty to fifty bucks now, doesn't it now?"

"So, you are saying that men regulate the price of that kind of stuff to make money?"

"Yes, I am. I would ask you this as well, why do you think that they have all those fancy colors for vehicles? Like *seafoam green or salmon*? Huh? Do you honestly think that any man wants to drive a pink truck? Women think it's cute. It sells."

Meg smiled slightly.

"No, some *woman* came up with that name so that she could convince her husband that indeed, the truck wasn't *pink*, it was *salmon*—something entirely different. Now who's pulling the strings?"

Marcus smiled now and shook his head.

"The man did get his new truck, however, am I right? Salmon is a small price to pay in return."

Meg stared at him.

"I'm still waiting to see how this works into the book-movie thing."

"Very simple. Because, when the box offices are dragging, some big producer says get me a chic flick and *bam*! Millions of women drag their husbands, dates and hankies off to the local AMC. As well, the willing significant others who accompany the women look like heroes for obliging to do so. It's a win-win situation for all men involved. The producers make millions, the theaters sell healthy amounts of diet soda and popcorn and the men who take the women get, you know." He smiled coyly.

"You're assuming two things. One being that the producer is a *man*. The other being that the male accompanying the woman to the *chic flick* will likely have said something stupid by the time they reach her apartment anyway to cancel out his chances of getting any *at all*." Meg continued to watch him as he nodded and grinned. Finally she rose from her place on the floor, standing before him. "Marcus St. John, that is the most sexist thing I've ever heard of!"

"But true! But true!" He stood up. "You have to admit that it makes pretty good sense."

"It's insane!"

She walked into the study of their condo, leaving him behind. Meg pulled the chair out before the desk where her laptop was situated and stared at its blank screen. Marcus followed her and stood in the doorway.

"You're mad."

"Yes, I'm a little mad." She didn't look at him. "You think you know everything about *everything*."

"I don't. But I know this much. If men don't control the socioeconomic life of this country, how come they never accepted any of the hundred books you sent in until you signed my name to it? The agent and the publisher both being *men* even?" His look burned through her as she glared back at him, daring not utter something she might later regret. When she regained her composure, she attempted to answer in a civilized tone.

"I would appreciate it if you would not speak to me in that condescending way while I am sitting here trying to fake your very existence." Meg looked at him for a few seconds before he raised his hands in concession before backing out of the room. She turned again to look at the screen. She slumped in her seat and whispered to no one. "He's pretending to have a career and I'm pretending to have a life. I wish I could remember how to pretend to be happy."

Chapter Fifty-two

Nick Carter noticed her right away when she entered the grand ball-room atmosphere of the Harbor Island Civic Center.

He stood a little straighter and away from the wall where he'd been leaning, far across the way from the entry, and now feigned interest in a conversation that was being played out amidst the group of associates before him. He glanced over the gentlemen's shoulders slightly, careful not to be seen.

Her smile was brilliant, its gleaming whiteness complimenting the knit white dress she was wearing, flecked with silver. That still newly cropped hair was not as casually strewn as usual, but behaving rather nice-ly, rather fashionably in fact. *Meghan Laine.*

He laughed lightly because the rest of the little circle laughed and then nodded in the direction of the author and his beautiful fiancée as if he'd just noticed them standing there for the first time.

"Meggie! You look wonderful!"

The voice belonged to Jan who had flounced to where she was stand-ing. She promptly linked her arm through the young woman's, leading her across the room toward their table. "Our seats are over here. This is a fab-ulous dress. I *love* it!"

"Thanks. You look pretty terrific." Her words seemed to float airily between them with no real direction. They reached the taffeta covered table sprinkled with glittery stars and placecards.

"Ms. Laine." Carter bowed his head formally with a little hint of a smile before he approached Marcus who was already socializing a few feet away.

"I tell ya, Meggie, having you at these events is making my job actually somewhat *bearable!*" Jan sat beside her. "I mean, I used to avoid these optional things and now I've hit almost every single one in the past few months. Are you liking Tampa?"

"I am."

"Do you miss things in Iowa?"

"I miss a few good friends I left behind." Meg smiled politely.

"Your parents are there, I assume? Family?"

Meg looked at her curiously now before answering. During the entire time she'd lived in Tampa to this point, no one had asked a single question pertaining to her own life, or whether or not she even had one. Meg shook her head lightly.

"No, my parents are both deceased and I really don't have any family to speak of. Just Noel and Reed," her voice trailed off. "They're the friends."

"I see." Jan leaned across the table and patted her friend's hand.

"Actually, I'm not even originally from Iowa. I just went to school there, the University, and I met Marcus and ended up staying longer than I planned. That's all." Her smile brightened a little as she recalled the day she'd met Marcus. He was getting an agricultural degree there. She remembered his winning smile, and his charming down home ways—how he held the door for her and actually even carried her books! It was like puppy love that didn't go away.

"So where are you from originally, then?"

Meg realized suddenly that she'd drifted into a daze in her recollection and she brought her attention back to the subject at hand.

"Oh, I'm from just outside Madison. That's Wisconsin."

Jan set her drink on the table immediately, staring wide eyed at the impish woman.

A nice quiche, a little snow on the ground. Take the dog for a walk.

"It's a sign," she barely whispered. Meg narrowed her brow and looked at her oddly.

"What?"

Jan shook her head and smiled broadly.

"Nothing. Nothing." She waved her hand a little as she spoke. Jan noticed that the music had slowed and saw that Marcus had taken to the dance floor with the woman from "Inside Tampa Bay." Meg still stared at her oddly. The secretary regrouped and smiled a little. "I said, it's *time*— time to dance,that is. It sure looks like everyone's dancing, having a good time, that kind of thing."

"If you're referring to Marcus dancing with the Mitzy chick,I already noticed it." Meg laughed. "Oh well, as long as I know where his heart's at."

"So, you think you and Marcus will ever really get married?"

"Of course we will. Why would you ask such a thing?" Meg sipped her drink. "We got together, got engaged. The next course of action is marriage. That's the *natural* thing to do."

"I just wondered, that's all. I mean, I've known lots of people who've gotten together and tried each other on for a few years and decided the fit wasn't all that great. But, I'm sure you're right about Marcus."

"Of course I'm right about Marcus. I don't think that marriage is like taking a coat out on approval. You get married and you, you do it."

"Do what?" Jan pretended to be nonchalant. "What do you do?"

"Get married and . . . live happily ever after, I guess."

"I see. I just thought there might be a little trial period there where you tried to discover if the person was the right one to live happily ever after with.I've never been engaged.I don't know how it works." Jan sipped her drink and set it back again, looking around her casually. "I guess I just thought that if he was *the one*, then you wouldn't feel the need to try him on for so many years—that you would have just married him by now. That's all."

Meg's look of bewilderment was apparent and Jan quickly touched the woman's shoulder as she leaned toward her. She wanted to stifle any hurt feelings that she might have stirred.

"Meggie, I meant nothing by it, I told you, I don't know much about these things." She spoke quietly. "Look at me—still waiting to find that *one*. You understand."

"No," she lied.

"You know, the one that makes your walk a little bouncier and your heart a little quicker. The one that you just have to be near to feel dizzy, whose touch sends you."

"Sends you where?"

"Oh Meggie! You're such a character!" Jan laughed and leaned back a little now. "The one that sends you straight to cloud nine! That's the one

I'm waiting for. I just hope that when I finally find him, I'm smart enough to recognize him—like you have with Marcus, you know. That I don't just pass him up because of my own stubborn hard-headedness."

Meg smiled and nodded in agreement. They both sat there quietly for a while, watching the dancers whirl around the ballroom floor gracefully in the large dimly lit room.

"I know that sometimes these things really only happen once. Sure would hate to miss my boat." Jan muttered, sipping her drink nervously, uncharacteristic for her. She glanced in Meg's direction and noticed that the woman was staring at her with an unusual expression about her. "What did you feel like—the moment you knew that Marcus was it for you?"

"I—I felt those things." Meg wrinkled her forehead as she went on. "But that's not what a relationships all about. It's the ability to get along and feel comfortable with each other. Not just the excitement and whirlwind stuff. Practicality is where it's at. Predictability, that kind of thing."

"Practicality? Ha, well, count me out," Jan laughed now. "I have practicality now—only I call it boring. I want someone whose every move isn't premeditated. Who can surprise me now and again just in the course of ordinary conversation. What the heck, you only live once, you know."

Marcus was headed back for the table where the girls were sitting and Meg actually looked incredibly relieved to see him. She was in need of a good saving along about now, and he looked good to her tonight, lonely as she'd felt lately. She smiled wide and patted the space next to her. Jan stood and excused herself to speak with a friend she'd spotted across the way just as Marcus sat down with them.

"Isn't she great?" He motioned toward Jan as she left. Meg nodded, her eyes never leaving his. Marcus leaned closer toward her and spoke more quietly now. "I need to talk to you about something."

"I do too, Marcus, I'm so glad you're here." Meg's eyes were sparkling with hope and delight as she leaned closer to him as well.

"Okay, you first."

"All right." She took a deep breath and gathered her courage to say what she needed to. "Do you remember what we talked about in Jasper Falls?"

"We talked about lots of things, Meg." Marcus touched her cheek with his fingertips. He moved them along her jawline and into her hair where he squeezed a few strands of her blonde hair between his fingers playfully. "Be more specific."

"Okay, I'm just going to say it." She looked directly into his eyes. "I'm ready to do all the things we talked about. I'm ready to marry you and start our family."

Marcus' hand froze and he looked straight into her eyes, waiting for her to add the usual catch. She surprised him by smiling instead and shrugging rather with rather a carefree attitude.

"I'm ready! How's that!"She laughed now. "Oh, I'm so glad I've said it. I honestly don't know what took me so long."

"Meg—"

"I mean, we've always known that this is they way it would work out. I wonder why it took me *so long*? Like I was trying you out to see how you would wear, and obviously you were a perfectly good fit!"

"Meg," he said, his eyes darting between hers, accompanied by his smile."It's such a crazy time right now, though."

"You want to get married and all that still, right? The biological clock and stuff?"

"Of course."

"So, what's the problem? Let's do it! Let's get married!"

"We can, we can," he nodded speaking in his low voice. "I think that we should talk about it later, I mean, we're here and all."

"What's to talk about? We just did." She refused to dismiss his look. "Unless you're having second thoughts."

"I'm not, that's nonsense. It's just, well, we've just moved to a bigger city, for the first time we have so much to do! I mean, let's enjoy it for a while before we go and fill the condo with kids. What do you say?"

Meg felt her insides collapse. She knew then that there would never be any children of the Meg and Marcus merger. In fact, it was now clearly unlikely that there would be any merger.

She watched him, smiling there before her, trying to soften the blow. Meg patted his hand and smiled back. The surrounding sounds seemed to grow louder, overpowering the silence between them.

"What did you want to talk about? You said there was something." Meg finally spoke. Marcus bowed his head, looking rather sheepish.

"Well, Oswell wanted to know when his editor could expect the first draft of the new one. It's not important."

"Of course it is."

"I'll tell him it's in the works."

"You tell him that. I'll work everything out somehow."

"Thanks, Meg," he said before kissing her cheek. He started to leave. "You're the best."

Meg nodded at him with her smile. Her eyes followed him as he went back to the little elite group he'd left in the opposite corner of the room.

Jan glanced over in time to see Meg sitting alone at the table again. She quickly worked her way over to Oswell and grabbed his arm.

"You need to do me a favor."

Wishing like everything that she had stayed home that evening, Meg was having a terrible night. Her fate with Marcus had obviously been sealed with a mere handful of words and she watched on as he danced with a few women, most often, Mitzy.

Smile, back straight. Chin up! And then she recalled her grandmother's words: *You can't lose what was never yours.* Maybe, but it wasn't that pain that hurt so terribly. What stung most was the cruel feeling of abandonment that she felt. Not of being deserted by anyone in particular, but of being untrue to herself. It suddenly became clear that she had forsaken her own dreams to create a far-fetched lie that had quickly spiraled out of control.

She recalled the night months earlier when he'd given her the ring. Her head had been so flooded with thoughts of the book that she'd hardly paid it proper notice. How left out Marcus must have felt, and now it was her turn. Always out of synch, Meg felt that she and Marcus had come full circle. And how she could feel so much wiser yet so much emptier at the same time was beyond her.

"Meggie! You are going to dance with me!" The obnoxious voice jarred her from her sad thoughts. J.T. Oswell was standing directly before her.

"No thank you, Mr. Oswell."

"You call me J.T., and no one says no to J.T." He pulled her hand in an upward motion. "Come on, come now!"

"I can't." She shook her head but suddenly caught a glimpse of Carter approaching—the one person she wanted to dance with even less than J.T. Oswell at that point. She feigned a change of heart before Carter could reach them. Reluctantly, she followed him to the dance floor.

The orchestra played on forcing Meg to hold tighter to her dancing partner. It wasn't desire, she simply feared she would spin dizzily out of control as she thought about it all. She listened to the wordless music, singing along in her head.

Buffalo Bill won't you come out tonight,
Come out tonight,
Come out tonight . . .

It was the song that George Bailey and Mary Hatch had danced to in *It's a Wonderful Life.* She thought of Noel, recalling how her friend had poked fun at her habit of relating everything in life to a Christmas movie.

"Can I cut in?" Jan smiled broadly at the dancing couple. She was very near the duo, dancing of course, with Nick Carter.

"Sure!" Oswell was a little too enthusiastic, and Meg recognized the setup immediately. Carter also knew as much and he rolled his eyes and smiled, newly abandoned by his partner. Her face held no expression when he extended his hand to her. She found herself folding her fingers around his and they began to move slowly.

"That was a well contrived plan," he mumbled with an apologetic smile.

"I'll say." Her tone was not as cordial. She stood taut as they moved, not allowing him into her personal zone so easily this time. She guarded herself carefully, not smiling.

"Are you enjoying yourself?" He prompted her along.

"Not particularly."

Carter touched her chin, forcing her to look into his eyes now.

"What is it? Is it Marcus?"

Meg rolled her eyes and issued a little laugh.

"You'd love that now, wouldn't you?"

Instead of denying the accusation, he answered in a serious tone.

"I'd be a liar if I told you I wouldn't like it a little."

Meg's mouth fell open and her eyes widened at his boldness.

"You big city types have a funny way of amusing yourselves. I'm glad you would find it entertaining!"

"Not entertaining, auspicious maybe." His eyes struggled against conveying any look of apology. He watched her expectantly.

"You and your big words. You are *arrogant. There!* Is that something you can understand?" She whispered loud enough only for him to hear. "Wanting the end of my relationship with my fiancée—*your* client! That is absolutely awful!"

"Call it what you will. But it still doesn't erase the way that I feel. Now, I can be a liar or I can lay the cards on the table which is something I'm not normally forced to do. I find that necessary now, however." He struggled for confidence that he couldn't find, but continued anyway. "I'm strongly considering embarking on some major changes in my life, and I think I'm going to start tonight. I've just decided that. Just now."

"What's so special about tonight?" she asked, pretending disinterest. She noticed the dance floor was becoming more crowded. The ensemble was playing "You Made Me Love You" and smiling couples around them were speaking softly and laughing. She caught a glimpse of Jan and Oswell bickering as they danced several feet away. It was a funny scene but Meg couldn't force a laugh now.

"Quite frankly, I was hesitant, but we're here now, not by our own choice, I'll admit. But suddenly it seemed like a good time. Trust is a fragile thing, don't you think? Something not to be taken lightly."

"I suppose."

"I've never been very good at trusting others. I've been lied to and I've lied to myself ito make me believe it was okay. But, now I find myself in a most unusual situation. For the first time in a long while, I want to trust again. I feel I can."

They began to dance more slowly and the music and voices seemed to soften around his low, steady words.

"Why is that?" Hers was a raspy whisper.

"It's because of you.I know it,and I know you know it. And I was just thinking about how nice it would be if we could stop playing around and just admit it to each other and start living happily ever after."

Meg stopped cold in her tracks and they stood there amidst the others whirling and swirling around them. His arm held tightly to her waist, their hands raised, clasped. No one seemed to notice that they were no longer moving. They stood there for several seconds.

Meg suddenly became aware of a certain tingling sensation, just like Noel had described. Unfortunately, it had begun to resemble a gut-wrenching sickness, and for a moment, she wasn't sure she was going to be all right.

It was ironic that Nick Carter would think that she was responsible for the honest changes in him, worthy of his trust even. The very premise of their entire relationship had been born out of a lie. An all encompassing lie that had consumed her and sucked in poor, unsuspecting fools like Nick Carter. She shook her head absently as she pondered it. There were going to be many casualties thanks to the same craftiness she'd previously mistaken for creativity.

"I don't want to frighten you off. I'm sure you think it's plenty underhanded of me to get you here, like this, and unload all of that on you." Carter looked concerned as he observed her expression, still and quiet. His voice was steady and matter-of-fact as he bravely forged ahead. "But I can't pretend that it doesn't exist when it does."

The lines in her forehead began to relax, her look, distant as she stood there. She blinked once, moving her lips, but no words would come. She stared at him until she found her voice at last.

"Mr. Carter, I'm afraid you've been brought to this point under false pretenses."

He arched an eyebrow, confused.

"I'm afraid being with me would make any deception you've experienced before seem like a mere walk in the park."

Meg barely had to struggled to break free from his grip as she backed away. Quickly she turned and went, weaving through the jungle of whirling dancers. Carter watched as she pushed open the door of the grand ballroom. And then she was gone.

Chapter Fifty-three

"**N**oel!" Meg tearfully blurted into the telephone. She'd run through the courtyard of the condominium complex and up the stairs and was nearly out of breath when she'd dialed her best friend's number. It had rung seven times when Noel answered.

"Meggie? My Gawd! What is it? What's happened?" Noel's voice on the other end sounded as if she'd just been awakened, but was quickly coming to life, hearing her friend sobbing.

"What *hasn't* happened?" She blew her nose loudly before going on. "My life's a mess! I have a horrible case of writer's block! My damned dog's allergic to these freakin' Florida fleas—it looks like someone *boiled* him! And Marcus doesn't want to get married and have any babies with me!"

"Whoa, sweetheart! Hold on, hold on." Noel was quickly analyzing the situation and trying to calm her desperate friend. "Okay, one thing at a time now. Did you and Marcus break up?"

"No, not yet anyway." Meg blotted her eyes. She stretched her arm behind her head and grabbed the dress zipper firmly, yanking it down. She shimmied out of the sleek fitting white sheath and stepped out, standing there in only her underslip. "He is enjoying his freedom, Noel. And the worst part is, I don't *care*! Oh my *God*!"

"Now, now, Meggie."

"He told me he wants to wait on the wedding and the kids until we finish having fun here—"

"Thank Gawd."

"Thank God? *Ha*!" Meg felt a second wave of sobs working its way into her throat. She couldn't swallow it down as it erupted. "I just ran out on the man I love."

"Wait a second, I thought you said you didn't care? You're confusing me with this Marcus thing."

"Not Marcus—*Nick!*"

"Nick? Nick of *Nick Carter* fame?" Noel couldn't help but laugh. "That's *great!*"

"That's terrible! He was just saying how much he trusts me. That's the last thing I deserve after all this and I couldn't possibly bear to tell him."

She listened to Meg's sobbing down the line. Finally Noel spoke.

"You really love him?"

"I don't know . . . I just know the way I feel around him is like nothing I've ever felt before."

"Go on."

"I'm tingly and dizzy even—and he makes me *so mad!*" Her voice found its volume at that mention.

"Yeah, it's love." Noel agreed, sympathetically.

"I just couldn't let him do it. I couldn't let him be deceived like that. I *couldn't!*" Meg sniffed uncontrollably. "Noel, I want to come home."

"And leave Mr. Right on the beach? You've got to be kidding me."

"I've got to get out of here. Away from all this."

"Hold on a second, lemme think about it," Noel went quiet for a few seconds. "I'll be there tomorrow afternoon. Promise me you won't do anything ridiculous before then."

"Are you sure?"

"I'm positive."

"You're the best, Noel."

"No you are."

"No you are."

"Stop it, already. Get yourself a tofu bar or one of those gross snacks that you like. And relax."

"I could go for some Haagen-Dazs chocolate almond."

"Oh Gawd, it's worse than I thought. Sleep tight my friend."

Chapter Fifty-four

J an saw Carter leaving the dance floor alone. Dancing with Oswell nearby, she'd been watching the situation and was surprised to see her boss looking rather distraught as he veered through the crowd toward their table. She wasn't too sorry to break away from Oswell to check the situation out. Steadily, she made her way through the maze of people never removing her eyes from her goal.

"Why aren't you on the dance floor?" She spoke to him with a chastising tone.

"Because it looks a little silly when you're dancing a slow dance with yourself." He snaked a drink from the tray of a passing waitress and downed nearly the whole glass in a single swallow. "People start to stare and point, and you hear the occasional mention of *psychosis* or *breakdown* in conversations around you."

"Where's Meg?"

Carter made an exaggerated comical face and shrugged.

"How should I know? Maybe her carriage was getting set to turn into a pumpkin." He grabbed a second drink from a passing platter and downed it as well. He slammed it onto the table before him, looking rather satisfied with himself. "Here comes—"

"Jan!" It was Oswell.

"J.T . . . "

"J.T?" Carter smirked, surprised that Jan would address him so personally.

"Oswell." Jan corrected herself.

"Carter?" Oswell looked confused.

"Well now that we're all here and accounted for." Carter ran his finger along the rim of his glass as he watched the duo standing before him.

"What happened? We were dancing?"

"I'm helping Carter, here."

"No, you're not." Carter muttered.

"I'm trying, you *ninny*!" Jan was growing impatient with her boss' self pity.

"We were havin' a good time there!" Oswell waved his hand toward the dance floor again. "Can't we carry on?"

"No, no we cannot, I'm trying to *do* something here."

"Jan, go dance," Carter waved nonchalantly at her. "Someone here might as well be with the one they want to be with."

"Come on!" Oswell seconded the motion eagerly.

"No! Boss, I want to be with you. Come on—"

"I don't want you to want to be with me."

"I don't want to be with you the way you want Meg to be with you, *dorkwad*!" She snapped the correction.

"I love those little names she uses." Oswell laughed affectionately at the secretary. Then, his expression changed dramatically as his head whipped toward Carter. "Whoa! Wait a second! Hold everything! You want to be with Meg?"

"Of course he wants to be with Meg! You *nimrod*!"

"Meg wants to be with Marcus!" Oswell shouted back.

"Marcus wants to be with Titsy!"

"That's Mitzy to you, sister," Carter corrected Jan with a little hint of a smile that said he was on his way to drunkenness.

"Lemme get this straight!" Oswell was trying to talk above their nonsense. "Carter wants to be with Meg, Meg wants to be with Carter, Marcus wants to be with *Titsy*—"

"*Mitzy*!" Jan and Carter corrected in a boisterous unison.

"Marcus wants to be with Mitzy . . . " Oswell was at a loss for words. He stopped suddenly, his newly quieted voice directed toward Jan. "Who do you want to be with, then?"

"*Me*? Dream on, brother." Jan laughed at the publishing mogul whose brow furrowed as she slumped into the seat before him. "You've fulfilled your usefulness with me. Go about your business."

"I don't believe I have!"

"Well, maybe you didn't, but you're free to do what you want to now, anyway." She waved at him. "Buh-bye."

"We were having a good time!"

"*You* were having a good time. I was letting you."

"We were having a few laughs!"

"*You* were laughing, I was laughing at you."

"I don't have to stand here and be insulted!"

"Good, cause I can do it better when you're across the room and I don't have to look at those dopey puppy-eyes."

"You're a cold woman." He stared at her, pathetically.

"You're a quirky little man."

"I have many good inner qualities."

"Problem is they're so deep in there we've yet to see them." She coolly lounged back in her seat and waved at the waitress who promptly set two champagnes before Jan and her boss. She nodded appreciatively before continuing. "But just for fun you can apprise me of those qualities. You've got a few minutes to kill before I call security on you."

"Many people have told me that I'm a kind and generous person—a wise man." He looked thoughtful.

"Whoever told you that meant wise *guy*, I guarantee it."

"Why can't you just admit that you were having a good time with me?"

"Why can't you just understand that you don't stand a chance in hell with this girl and bug off?" She didn't look in his direction, for if she had, she surely would have noted his hurt expression. He had nothing to come back with. The game was over.

Carter looked at her to gauge her expression as the man left their table.

"You were a little hard on him, don't you think?"

"Oh *please*, you men are always standing up for each other." She took a long drink, nearly draining the cocktail glass. "Men, you can't kill 'em—and the price of hallucinogenic drugs is outrageous these days."

Chapter Fifty-five

"Meggie!" Noel caught sight of her beloved friend and flung her arms around the smallish woman's shoulders. They stood there hugging in the baggage claim area of Tampa International Airport. When she pulled back to look at her friend her eyes were misty. "Your hair! I *love* it! You! Florida suits you well, my summer blonde friend."

"I'm so glad to see you, Noel!" Meg hugged her again.

"Let's get out of here, look at the two of us, hugging like fools here." Noel was carrying her jacket over her arm as she waved toward the walk-way that connected the terminals.

"Were you waiting long?"

"No, we just got in a few minutes ago."

"*We?*" Meg arched an eyebrow at her friend.

"I told Elliot I was coming here and he told me he'd like to come along if I didn't mind. Can you believe it?"

"No, no I can't." Meg's eyes were wide with amazement. "What about Mother O'Dell?"

"Well, she's keeping my Jeremy until Wednesday when we fly back out. She wasn't thrilled, but the very idea that she'll have my son all to herself to fill with insane notions about what horrific parents we are should be enough to keep her at bay for a few days."

"That's terrific!"

"Well, you know, first I thought it would be good to get away, just the girls and all. But Elliot looked so sad. He was like a small child. And I thought, what the heck?" She looked around them some and then back at Meg. "Where's Marcus?"

"Oh, he didn't get in until late, he's still asleep."

"I see."

"Yeah."

"Well, there's going to be time for all of that. Let's go see if Elliot needs any help with the luggage. I swear, I packed a planeload myself alone. But you know how it goes. I mean you can predict the weather, but who can predict what kind of mood you'll be in that day?"

"Exactly."

Chapter Fifty-six

With Noel and Elliot tucked safely away in their hotel a few miles away, Marcus and Meg finished their dinner in silence. She rose to carry the plates into the kitchen when he reached out and grabbed her arm.

"Meg, that can wait. Let's go for a walk."

She looked at him for a few seconds before she smiled and nodded. Setting the plates back on the table, she grabbed a cardigan and followed him out the back sliding glass door. The duo slipped down the steps and onto the sandy beach below, continuing on until they reached the water's edge. It was a chilly night, as the dark was arriving earlier now and they walked until they came to a large rock before the pier. He climbed upon it and patted the flat space beside him, helping her up. They looked out over the water.

"You know Meg, things are so different here. I would never have pictured myself here even last year, I could have never imagined that I would be a *city* boy." He laughed. She smiled and nodded. "I love it here."

"I know you do. I'm glad."

"I know what they say about city smog, but somehow being here allows me to think more clearly. Maybe it's that cold weather that is always getting in the way in Iowa. Do you think? I think a person feels more alive with the sun on their shoulders and the sand under their feet."

"Maybe."

Marcus didn't waste any more time, his look serious.

"I want to call it off."

Meg looked at him blankly for an instant before relief washed over her. Her shoulders relaxed and her expression softened as he went on.

"The books, this whole thing has gotten . . . so far gone."

"Okay."

"Let's figure out how to retire Marcus St. John, the writer, ASAP." He looked down, his voice softly above the sound of the waves rolling onto the shore. "I don't like living a lie. You are a talented writer, and you deserve your name on those covers—you said so yourself. I don't want to do it anymore, it hurts me—it hurts you. And there are so many other things—" His voice trailed off.

"I know you're falling for Mitzy." Meg stated matter-of-factly as she looked at him through a few wispy pieces of hair that floated into her eyelashes. She smiled and spoke calmly. "I know you want to break up with me."

Marcus' lips parted, wordless.

"It's okay, Marcus." She nodded. "I know things have been different between us and I understand that."

"You have someone, too?"

"No. But someday I may." She watched him for a few seconds before she playfully nudged him with her shoulder. "I just wouldn't want you to settle for hamburger when you can have steak."

"Meg, I've always known you were a filet mignon." He wrapped his arms around her as they sat there watching a few seagulls dive into the water and rise up quickly again. "And you deserve the best too."

"I know."

There was silence between them as they looked out over the pink streaked sky tinged with a blue that seemed to meld into the water in the distance. She leaned back on his shoulder and smiled.

"You know, of all the times I've been here with you, I don't recall the sky being this beautiful."

"What will you do? I mean, now that your ghostwriting career is over?"

Meg shrugged.

"I'll start from square one until someone is fool enough to publish something of mine." She smiled. "And I'll be sure to sign *my* name to it this time."

They both chuckled.

"What about you? What will you do now that you're not going to be penning any more Marcus St. John romance novels?"

"Actually, Mitzy's dad offered me a position at the station as a sort of stage-tech." He sounded rather apologetic.

"That's great! That's great. I know how you used to do some of that kind of stuff at the University—remember?"

"Yeah, I'm counting on those talents to haunt me now. I hope I've got what it takes."

"You've got what it takes, Marcus."

"It's been fun, Meg."

"It's been interesting, anyway." She laughed quietly before they lapsed into a silent spell.

"We've been through a lot together Meg. I hate to just throw it all away—like I've wasted your time."

"Anytime you make a good friend, Marcus,it's never a waste of time.'

"So, are we going to be okay, with this?" Marcus scooted aside to see her. She smiled at him genuinely.

"Yes. We're going to be just fine."

Chapter Fifty-seven

"So, it's over? Just like that?" Noel looked at Meg over a mound of frozen yogurt covered in pralines and nougat. The *TCBY* was nearly empty that afternoon as they sat there, talking quietly. Meg nodded with the smile of a good sport about the whole deal and dove back into her pineapple softserve. "This is good,then. Is this *good*, then?"

"It's right. Whether or not it feels good isn't really the issue. Marcus has a right to be happy, and I've been uncertain for a while."

"I know, I know. I'm proud of you Meggie. All the kooks and schizos in this world who go all Fatal Attraction about this kind of stuff. I think you two handled it in a very admirable way. I hope you feel okay about it."

"I do."

"Good. You're not going to be alone for long, you know." Noel waved her spoon as she went on. "I mean, I don't think you'll obsess over this mutual dumping to the point that Marcus finds a rabbit boiling on his stove one day."

Meg smiled as she shook her head.

"No, I don't think we have to worry about that." She looked contemplative. "I've been thinking about a lot of things lately. I guess that's going around."

"You know this healthy stuff is pretty good when you load it down with the right goods." She strung a strand of caramel to her mouth still hooked to the spoon. Meg laughed. "What's on your mind?"

"I think I'm tired of this whole scene. It's a little too . . . too *escapist* for me. Like,I keep thinking everyday is a day off work. I guess I need the reality of the seasons to make it real for me." Meg squinted at her friend.

"Does that make sense?"

"No, to someone else maybe, but not to me. But I respect your opinion."

"I'm going back." She didn't let the subject die just yet. "I've decided that. Marcus has arranged to sell his farm to Harve, so I guess I'll find someplace. Or maybe you and Elliot will let me camp out with you for a while—be your nanny or something until I figure out what I'm doing with this phase I'm in."

"That phase you're in is called life." Noel pushed her ice cream away. She blotted her mouth and looked at her friend seriously. "Meggie, Elliot and I have decided to move to Tampa. I was going to tell you eventually, but now's as good a time as any."

"Really? You're *kidding*!"

"I'm serious. Meggie, we've had a ball since we got here. Both of us agreed that we hate the idea of going back tomorrow. So we're going to go back, get some things in order, and we plan to be here well before Christmas. I'm so excited!"

"What will Elliot do here for work?"

"Well, you know I've got relatives all over the place here. I was tellin' you about them."

"Yeah?"

"Well, my great uncle Harry has this stained glass shop here that is always booming. Seems they get a lot of call for replacement due to all those hurricanes they get." Noel laughed. "Anyhow, he says he's needin' a manager for his branch office here while he looks over the one in Lakewood, and here's my Elliot with experience in window working! How's that?"

"Great!" Meg reached across the table and clasped her friend's hands. Her expression changed slightly to one of worry as she continued. "What will Mother O'Dell say?"

"Oh, sister, she said it all already on the phone when Elliot told her about it last night. Ewwe, was she steamed. But Elliot told her that if the Jasper Falls Gazette were to continue on as a Jasper Falls tradition, she would have to hire someone that lived there to run it. Then of course she gave him the schmeal about it being in the family, and he told her that in this day and age, she should be flexible to an alternative family lifestyle and hire someone qualified. Then yadda yadda yadda and they hung up. The end! I was so proud of Elliot! That's the *first* time I've ever heard him take a stand on our behalf against his mother."

"Looks like things are working out for you two after all."

"You know, Meggie, it's the craziest thing. But just being here in these surroundings, it's so natural. We've done things here that we never even did when we were dating! Taking walks, holding hands. He even went to the mall with me yesterday morning. This is a side of Elliot that I could really learn to appreciate. I've never seen the man smile so many days in a row before. I'm tickled!"

"I'm so glad." Meg patted her hands and clenched them tightly in hers. "You needed that break away from the Queen Mum I think,and now I know you'll be fine. Looks like the climate does offer a dull clarity of sorts."

"We're all discovering things, Meg. We always do."

There was silence for a moment as Meg sat there looking thoughtful. Finally she asked the question she'd been avoiding.

"So, does Reed still think I'm the evil writer? His machine picks up every time I call."

Noel nodded slowly as she chose her words carefully.

"Reed's got a lot of issues, Meggie. He will get over it."

"But he's not, yet, is what you're saying?"

Noel looked at her sympathetically.

Meg's eyes lit through the mistiness that had grown over them as she laughed out loud suddenly.

"And do you know—it's nearly your birthday! The start of a new cycle!" Meg smiled at her. "It's a sign."

"It's a sign that we place too much emphasis on things that really make no sense whatsoever." Noel squeezed her hands back. "Those were games we played because we needed them. I don't need that anymore. You don't either."

Meg rose stood and sauntered over to stand behind her best friend. She bent at her waist and folded her arms around Noel's neck, pressing their cheeks together. She whispered in her ear as she closed her eyes.

"I love you Noel. You're the best."

"Same here Meggie. You're the best."

"No you are."

"Don't get me started, Megs."

"I guess some things never change, that's reassuring at least."

Chapter Fifty-eight

"Here's the mail, finally," Jan waved her hand in Carter's direction as he entered his office after lunch. "I guess Tampa post was running a *little* late today. I set it on your desk."

"Well, you know," He laughed lightly.

"Yeah, Tampa post sucks."

He stepped into his office and shut the door behind him. Carter removed his suit jacket and loosened his tie as he uncapped the coffee he'd brought back with him and sat down.

The mail was a heaping mound this morning, likely more poor writers pleading for an agent to steer them down the path to success. Carter had that reputation now, so hundreds of unsolicited manuscripts made their way across his desk every month.

He sighed as he began the tiring process of filtering through the stack. He glanced at the office door, surprised a little that Jan didn't come in to join him. This was usually her favorite part of the day—critiquing well-meaning potential clients who'd poured their very heart and soul out on paper for them to brutalize. *Geesh!* Now he sounded like Meg! He put it out of his mind.

Carter divided the stack into three smaller piles—mailers, letters and client letters. He charged into the mailers first. On about his third dive, he narrowed his eyes curiously and held the white cardboard box closer to see better.

Meghan Laine
R. R. #6
Jasper Falls, Iowa

"What the hell?" He studied the battered condition of the mailer. It had three different postmarks on its front, the original one dated November of the previous year. He pressed the intercom button. "Jan, did all of this stuff come regular hell-mail?"

"Yeah, all except for a few things that were forwarded here via carrier. Oswell House, like you requested, and there was a Federal Express package from that Claire Sodey chick—"

"Good enough." He cut her off.

"Hey, it is *rude* to interrupt me like that!" Her voice came back on again. He rolled his eyes.

"Sorry."

"Okay then, I—"

"Did you look through any of this stuff before you put it on my desk?"

"You just interrupted me again! That is rude! And looking through your mail while you talk to me is rude too! No, I did not!"

"Thanks." He released the button and then added to himself. "Never stopped you before."

He snatched a pair of scissors out of his desk drawer and began to diligently work at the heavy shipping tape that someone had apparently added to keep the rough package intact. After a good five minutes he was able to tear the top off of the crude box and he quickly pulled the first page off the stack, holding it up eagerly to read it.

"Dear Acquisitions Editor, I am a writer for a local newspaper here, blah, blah, blah. I have never been published before, blah, blah, blah. Please read my latest book for consideration for publication." Carter's eyes raised for a moment as he savored what he was reading. He immediately lowered them to the package at hand and continued the quest. The agent pulled the manuscript out and flipped past the first few pages of biographical material until he came to the start of the novel. "*Just Around the Corner?*"

With a creased brow, he hurriedly flipped through several pages of it and then slammed it onto the desk loudly as a finale. He sat quietly for a moment before he jammed his finger onto the intercom button.

"Jan, get me Oswell."

"Do I have to?"

"I'd like him here in my office, right away."

Jan must have realized the tone of his voice that it wasn't a good time to wager any protests. She picked up the phone promptly and made the call.

"What did you need? Lemme guess—Claire Sodey's switching imprints and has a hot new one she wants to send the Oswell way?" Oswell was smiling from ear to ear as he unbuttoned his jacket and took a seat before Carter's desk. He slumped casually. Carter only stared at him momentarily before pressing the intercom button again.

"Jan, get our fresh new talent, Mr. St. John, in our office ASAP. And please don't forget to have him bring along his lovely fiancée."

"Whatever you say, Boss." Jan didn't sound at all sure of what was going on.

"St. John? I knew it would be St. John!" Oswell flung his head back happily and applauded loudly. "You got number five out of him—all in one year? Incredible! I am the happiest man alive!"

"Oswell—"

"That kid's got a line of bull from here to Tahiti and I love watching the women line up to buy it! All under the Oswell Publishing House name, of course."

"Oswell—"

"I knew he was a winner when I—"

"J.T." Carter stood up and stared at him in a no nonsense way. Oswell swallowed hard and suddenly began to feel slightly warm around the collar. Carter's expression was not that of shared joy. "Look at this."

The agent handed him the printed copy he'd received earlier and Oswell flipped through it quickly, handing it back with a shrug.

"Yeah?"

"I got this today. I had Jan be sure that everything that came from St. John's address be forwarded directly to the agency as we represent him now. Your courier brought it here."

"So?" Oswell nodded. "It's one of St. John's old manuscripts."

"It's not one of St. John's old manuscripts." Carter thrust the battered mailer before him now and thudded his index finger several times loudly on the return address listed there.

"Oh my God—she *stole his work*?" Oswell looked horrified.

"No, you *ninny!*" He borrowed the word from Jan as he flipped through the stack and literally threw the cover letter that had accompanied the package to Oswell. "Read this. Meghan Laine *is* St. John."

"Oh my God. In thirty words or less, tell me what this means." Oswell lowered the paper looking shaken.

"It means just what you think it means."

"What are the legal repercussions here?"

"I'm his agent and you're his publisher. That's where it ends, I can't see reason for us to take any legal action when it comes down to it, it's not like we didn't make money here. But exposure could mean that we'd look like the laughing stock of the publishing industry. We need a plan."

"Do you suppose there's a chance she could write a few more things for—"

"*Oswell!* Are you out of your *mind?*"

"No, of course there's no chance. That's—"

"*Crazy?* You bet it is!" Carter stood before his desk and pressed the intercom button impatiently again. "Jan, did you get hold of them?"

"Marcus is on his way. I'm still hunting down Meg."

"Thank you." He released the button and glared at Oswell. "You and your brilliant publishing ideas. Do you ever actually *read* any of the stuff that comes across your desk? If you would have, you would have realized that there was something slightly amiss here."

"Look at the postage marks on that thing!" Oswell defended himself fiercely. "I never even saw it!"

"Look at this second line here—*I'd like you to consider my latest book,* meaning that there were more before this—likely on your own desktop! How could we have let this happen?" Carter touched his forehead as he walked toward the window in his pacing.

"What do we do?" Oswell shrugged meekly.

"*What do we do?* How the hell would I know? My involvement with scandal to this point has been strictly within the confines of someone's fictitious espionage or what have you. What do we do, Oswell? You're the one with the fancy lawyers."

"Oh God, the lawyers. *Not* the lawyers!" Oswell shook his head rapidly. "I swear, if I had to one week to make this world a perfect place, I'd kill all the lawyers first."

"Well, what a web we have weaved for ourselves here," Carter went on.

"I've got it!"Oswell slapped his hands together with a growing smile. "We can take joint legal action against *them*!"

"What do you expect to get out of Marcus St. John? A fatted calf and a pair of Oshkosh overalls?"

"No—our reputation! We sue them and the publicity will be focused on their evil deed and away from our screw up here! It's a terrific idea!"

"It's a terrible idea! And what do you propose you do with all those women who want to return their books in the wake of a phony exposé? You want to refund all their money?"

"You're right, that was a very, *very* bad idea."

The intercom buzzed loudly and Marcus punched the button.

"What?"

"Boss? Mr. St. John is here to see you."

"How the hell did he get here so fast?" Oswell furrowed his brow. "What—did he jump in a phone booth and get here by cape?"

"Send him in."

The office door opened and Marcus St. John entered with his usual smile at first. His pace slowed and his smiled gradually disappeared with each step he took as the two men before him glared in his direction.

"Have a seat, Marcus." Carter lowered his voice and breathed deeply for a few seconds before continuing. Marcus took the seat across the desk, next to Oswell. "Is Ms. Laine with you?"

"No. She's packing."

"You're planning a trip?" Carter was mildly amused. Assuming they'd have to wait until she got there, he felt he could afford to listen to his airy tale.

"No, Meg's been staying her last week in Clearwater. I've taken an apartment over in Carollwood. She's moving back to Iowa."

"I see," Carter's voice softened some but then, recalling the reason for the meeting, found his sternness again. He looked at Oswell through narrow eyes and nodded his head that they should begin without her. "I got something very unusual in the mail today. We decided to share it with you and let you help us decide how to amend the situation."

Carter threw the entire package on his desk in front of Marcus. He picked up the manuscript and as he flipped through it, a knowing look came to his face. Clearly, the game was over. He nodded without apolo-gizing and laid it back again. There was silence as the two studied him waiting for any further reaction. Marcus shrugged and made a little face.

"What do you think about that, Mr. St. John?"

"I guess the jig is up."

"I guess it is." Carter nodded as he took his own seat behind the desk, the first time he'd sat down since summoning Oswell to his office. "Yes, I guess it is."

"How do you explain yourself, Marcus?"

"How can I? It's obvious what happened here. What else do you need to know?"

"Why?" Carter slammed his hand on the desk before him. "I need to know why you did it in the first place! Why you would *unlawfully* take credit for something that's not yours! Why you would sign your name away on a contract on behalf of someone else's work! Why you would start something that would perpetuate into a virtual string of non-stop lies and roll with it the entire time like it's *no* biggy!"

Marcus promptly dropped his casual demeanor as he leaned forward suddenly, waving his index finger in the agent's direction with a serious look in his eye.

"Hey, Meg tried for years to get one of you close-minded, stars-in-your eyes jerks to look at even one thing that she'd written! None of you would have anything to do with her—and she's an excellent writer!"

"Well, if she would have got in line and waited her turn, we would have discovered that all in due time anyway." Oswell slumped in his seat a little further and brushed his fingertips along his jawline, looking con-templative.

"In line? Behind *who?* Out of the blue flukes like myself? I lived on a farm long enough to know a load of manure when I smell it!"

"Calm down now," Carter mumbled.

"I'll tell you something! It's people like you that force people to make up angles like that! It's true about what they say—it's who you know or how far you'll go. Well, I'll tell you how it goes. Meg wanted it so badly—*so* badly—that she went well beyond her personal code of ethics to do it. Being the kind of people that all media types are,I suspect you have prob-ably exceeded those limits yourself, but so quickly point the finger at a woman who only wanted to see her life's dream become a reality." Marcus stood and walked around to the other side of his chair, leaning onto it as he smirked and then continued. "Yes, my friends—my *agent*, my *publish - er*. It was an angle. So sue me. But do nothing to Meg. She only took no credit or money for the job she loves doing the most. You'd be hard pressed to find a judge in this land who would hold that against her."

The pair watched as Marcus St. John rose from his chair and began to walk toward the door, neither speaking until finally Carter thought quickly.

"Hold up. Hold on," Carter stood and moved toward the door as well, stopping Marcus from leaving. He walked back toward his desk and leaned on its front, crossing his arms before him. "We need a plan here. You can't just leave before we've come up with a solution to this whole mess."

Oswell looked at Carter hopefully, waiting for guidance for their mission. Finally the agent nodded and looked at Marcus again.

"This is over. The books,the tour. You're retiring from writing. One day you just woke up and decided that it wasn't for you and *bam!* The end." Carter glared at him as he spoke. "Are we clear? We chalk this one up to your ten minutes of fame and never utter another word about it."

"Okay." Marcus nodded solemnly. "Deal."

"Oswell House continues to run the series that is out there so far, the proceeds will be split evenly between you and Ms. Laine. You arrange it, Oswell—make it look like a dispute settlement, no one gets wind of this. Are we straight here?"

"As an arrow." Oswell arched an eyebrow and nodded.

"Then I can see no need to involve any outside people in this mess. Let's clean it up expediently and move on."

The three men stood there quietly. Marcus turned toward the door again. Oswell hurried to walk him out, stopping before they opened the office door. He shook his hand heartily.

"You're a hell of a good guy. I always thought the only thing wrong with you was all that gushy female stuff you wrote about."

"Well, I guess we cleared that up," Marcus smiled. He turned toward Carter. "Mr. Carter, it's been an experience. I think I'll confine my book interests to the library, however. Thanks."

Nick Carter nodded in his direction with no particular emotion behind his expression. The two men exited.

After they'd gone, Carter pressed the intercom button to speak with Jan.

"Come in here please."

In seconds Jan was standing before his desk with a notepad in hand. She looked concerned.

"Are you okay, Boss? You look terrible."

"Do I look like a dupe?"

"No sir."

"You didn't need to answer that." He rubbed his forehead and closed his eyes tightly. "I want you to call everyone scheduled for a book review, signing, anything to do with Marcus St. John and cancel the works. Tell them anything you want. Just cancel it. I'm taking no more appointments this afternoon, and put this in Laughton's pile."

He dug Judy Armando's mailer out of the pile and handed it to her.

"I'm not taking any new clients, not here."

"Can I get you a water or something?"

"If you can't get me a bourbon, don't bother." He waved her away and leaned back in his desk chair kicking his feet up onto the top of his desk. Jan nodded sympathetically, knowing better than to ask anymore questions, and ducked out of the room. She closed the door, backing toward her desk as she went. She turned suddenly bumping straight into a fixed object there.

"*Augh!*" She screamed with a little surprise. Oswell had been standing beside her desk waiting for her, something she hadn't noticed in her quiet pondering. She was angry all of the sudden. "What do you want?"

"Hey! I just thought I'd wait around and tell you hello. I didn't expect full body contact there, don't blame me—that was you." He laughed lightly. "Can't say I didn't enjoy it however."

"Well commit it to memory, cause that'll be as close as it gets for you in this lifetime."

"I don't think you give me enough credit here, little sister."

"I don't think you deserve any." She walked around him and sat down at her desk. She began to flip through her rolodex to find the people that she needed to contact regarding the St. John appearances. "That is, unless you want credit for being an idiot."

"I'm going to tell you something, Jan, Jan . . . " Oswell looked at her with a comedic expression. "Jan, of all the years I've known you, what the hell is your last name?"

"That's none of your business."

Oswell looked at her with a hurt expression.

"I just thought I could know that much about you."

"That's just too much information."

The sound of someone clearing their throat came from a few feet away, and both sets of eyes were immediately drawn to Meghan Laine. She was standing there with a look of confusion on her face.

"Meggie," Jan didn't quite know what to tell her, unsure of what was happening herself.

"I got a message. It sounded desperate."

"Yes, well, Carter wants to see you. Why don't you go on in?"

The secretary and publisher watched as the young woman timidly entered into what they could only suspect to be certain slaughter. She closed the door behind her.

The sound of the door clicking shut jarred Nick Carter out of his solitude. He sat up, watching her quietly.

"Come in. Sit." He nodded toward the seat before his desk. "Marcus just left here."

"He was here?"

"Yes, yes he was." Carter breathed deeply and leaned forward onto his desk, rubbing his eyes in distress.

"What is it? Is there something wrong?"

"By whose definition?" Carter began. "By the definition that says that signing someone else's name to your work is a bad thing to do—or by the one that says lying about it is okay when done in the name of love?"

Meg drew her breath in sharply and watched him, afraid of moving a muscle. She waited for the follow-up.

"You know it's the damnedest thing, this terrible postal system we've got here in the Sunshine State. Sometimes you don't get your mail for two, three weeks. Sometimes you don't get it for months. Case in point." He raised the familiar, though badly beaten, mailer for her to see. Carter nodded knowingly in her direction. Meg's shoulders slumped and she breathed out, finally. That would about clinch it.

"It wasn't any of Marcus' doing. I was testing a theory—I simply wanted to see if I could get published if I put a little spin on things. Marcus was good enough to go along with it."

Carter nodded a little as he refused to release her look from his.

"Not such a good idea?" Hers was more of a statement than a question.

"No."

It was quiet until Carter finally spoke again.

"There will be no legal action taken concerning this. It will be handled internally. As well, you will leave an address with Jan so that we can be assured that you will get your half of the residuals from the product already on the stands."

"That's not necessary."

"*None* of this was necessary, Ms. Laine. But that's the way it goes sometimes." He leaned forward and scribbled a few things into his calendar book. Finally he raised his eyes again with no feeling in his words. "That will be all, Ms. Laine."

She sat still, quiet.

"You're free to go, now."

"Is there anything I can do to fix this, anyhow?" Her voice sounded low and squeaky as she spoke to him. "I'm just, so sorry, that's all."

Carter looked at her carefully. The nerve of this woman! Flaunting herself before him, conjuring up all these feelings within him that he'd been certain had expired after so many years, and then, deceiving him in a most unforgivable way. Could she do anything to fix it now? Surely not.

"I'm sorry too, but not for the reasons you are." He placed his pen softly on the desk before him, giving her his undivided attention. "I gave you more credit than that, Meghan."

"I know."

"No, I don't think you do know. You made me feel things that I thought I'd forgotten how to feel. You dangled yourself there and then made yourself unavailable. And now this." His voice trailed off as he recalled the last night that they'd been together, dancing at the benefit. Her words haunted him now. "I guess you were right. The deception I'd experienced before now was a mere walk in the park."

"I'm sorry. I never meant for it to go this far."

"You made me remember what it was like to be on cloud nine, except you exceeded that—like cloud ten or eleven or something." He stared at her still. "I guess that's why they coined the phrase *too good to be true*. Just a little theory *I* was testing."

Meg's eyes glistened as she watched him, listening intently.

"I guess so," she whispered.

"So, that will be all. And thanks for giving me the business. The book, I mean, of course."

Meg stood slowly and walked toward the door. She paused before leaving.

"You tried to tell me the other night. I couldn't bear to let you divulge your honest feelings to a person who has been anything but honest with you. And suddenly, I couldn't go on with it. Perhaps some day you'll believe that." She pleaded with him quietly. "I swear, if ever I'd have known the way things would be—"

"No one is to know these things, Ms. Laine." He looked at her before he continued with his writing. "I guess that's a good lesson for a little moral consistency in our behavior, now. Isn't it?"

"I guess so." She looked at her feet. "I'm leaving for the Midwest this afternoon. You shouldn't have to worry about being reminded of me again." She turned and walked out of the office, closing the door silently behind her. Carter glanced up and then down again. He began to mumble.

"Sure, after my heart stops and my body hardens into rigor mortis, I shouldn't have to worry about ever being reminded of you again."

"You are the most obnoxious man I've met in my lifetime!" Jan was hollering at Oswell as he stood before her desk. She rose from her seat to meet his height, staring at him eye to eye.

"You are the most nagging shrew I have ever met *as well!*"

"If I'm such a bitch, why do you spend more time here than in your own office? You own the building, for God's sake!"

Meg watched the scene being played out for a few moments after reentering the waiting area. She stuck her fingers to her lips and closed her eyes, sending forth a powerful and shrill whistle that silenced them both immediately. They turned to her at once.

"Thank you!" she started, looking at them each, one at a time. Meg walked toward them. "I've never seen anything like you two before! Why can't you just drop the hard-headed act and admit that you are *crazy* about each other? What the hell are you afraid of!"

She flung her arms about with dramatic flair as the duo stood, quietly watching.

"There's got to be a time in your life when you just say screw this!" She recalled her conversation with Noel in Jasper Falls and found new inspiration to fire her words. "Why can't you just dance like there's nobody watching and love like it's never gonna hurt!"

She marched to the edge of the room and paused before starting across the lobby, calling out to them one last time:

"For God's sakes! *Seize the moment!*"

Jan and Oswell watched as she boarded the elevator. They glanced at each other in silence.

"She was a little moody, don't you think?" Oswell finally spoke. He looked at Jan who had started sniffing. She suddenly raised her hand to shield her eyes as she ran toward the women's restroom. "What? Was it something I said?"

"Yes!" She hollered through her sobs. "You men *never* get it!"

Oswell remained alone in the waiting room, his hands raised in despair. He finally reluctantly walked toward the elevator.

Chapter Fifty-nine

"My Gawd, Meggie. I'm so tired of saying goodbye to you." Noel clutched her friend in a rough embrace. They stood in the driveway of the family's little home before a tightly packed U-Haul. It was November. The air was chill and they trembled with the brisk wind that swept through the vast barren farmland all around. Noel pulled away to see her friend tearfully. "I'm going to miss you so much!"

"Me too." Meg's voice cracked. She swallowed hard, trying to avoid a full scale crying session right then and there. "I know you'll have a great life in Florida. You fit right in there, sis."

"I feel good there, Meg. I hope you find what you're looking for. I'll offer one more time."

"No," Meg smiled. "I don't want to come back to Florida with you. But you can bet my vacations will be booked from here on out. I need to find myself."

"But in *Wisconsin*?"

Meg nodded. Noel reached up and stroked her friend's short hairdo and smiled through her tears.

"Well, you'll be the hippest chick in the dairy state, my dear."

They both laughed.

"Meggie, don't worry about anything."

"I won't." She nodded. "I can't believe how different Elliot seems now. I think that's wonderful."

"I know, it's like just knowing that he's striking out on his own, he's a changed person."

"Well, when forces come together, striking out doesn't seem so scary."

Meg grabbed her friend's hand as they strolled leisurely toward the little car she'd crammed full to make the trip to Wisconsin. "I'm glad we're going on the same day. I couldn't bear to be here without you."

"Me neither," Noel whispered, trying to contain her emotions. "What are you going to do when you get there, Meg?"

"I'm not sure yet. There are some newspapers in Wisconsin I might check into when the Marcus St. John romance novel royalties run dry." She laughed lightly. "What about you? Are you going to do something fabulous in Tampa?"

"I'm not going to work right away, it was Elliot's idea. He had another idea—you'll flip."

"Tell me?"

The girls stopped walking and leaned their heads close together.

"Elliot wants to have another baby. Can you *believe* it?"

"That's *great!*" Meg hugged her again. "I'm so happy for you."

"Of course you'll be a godmother for number two as well, should the project ever materialize."

"I would love nothing more. At this rate, it could be the only little patter of feet I hear." Meg smiled genuinely as she rolled her eyes. "Well, I guess this is my stop."

She motioned toward her own well-packed car with her eyes, and then clenched them shut as they hugged again.

"Oh Gawd," Noel cried. "Meggie, you're gonna be okay, you know that, don't you?"

"I know that. I love you, my best friend."

"I love you too, my very best friend."

They finally broke away from each other and smiled through their tears as Meg opened her car door and Noel reluctantly backed away toward their truck. She waved a little.

"You're the best."

"You are."

"You are."

"You are."

Chapter Sixty

J an picked up another flat cardboard form and punched it into a box, struggling to secure its sides with packing tape. She cursed in a low voice. No one was there in Nick Carter's office, and it was likely that after she finished shipping the last of these items, no one would be for a while again.

"Stop it, you *ninny*, blubbering like some kind of a fool," she directed aloud to herself. Unable to take her own advice, the tears streamed down her cheeks and dropped onto the box she'd just made. Jan continued the chore nonetheless, diligently placing the last of the leftover contents of her longtime boss' desk drawers into the large container.

She reached the bottom drawer and pulled it open. It was the last one and only held a thick Tampa telephone directory which she pulled out and set aside. Preparing to close the drawer, her eyes fell upon a small box. She reached for the pretty thing and slipped it out of the little ribbon that held it closed. Inside was a sterling silver dragon fly. Jan lifted it out and studied it carefully, discovering that it was a hair pin. She swallowed hard.

"Nick Carter, what in the world?" She looked at it for a few seconds longer before gingerly placing it back in the velvet lined box. Suddenly she recalled having seen a similar pin in Meg's hair months earlier during her pre-short hair era. It had been a butterfly or something, hadn't it? A little less delicate and not nearly as exquisite or expensive as this one. Jan smiled and slipped the lid back on it, still holding it thoughtfully. She turned the box over a few times in her hands before setting it atop the desk.

Jan checked the drawers once more and then sat on the floor behind the desk with the last box before her, yet to be sealed. She wondered if she should put the little dragonfly in with these items, or if it would be too painful a memory for the boss she so admired. She sighed, her eyes feeling warm with tears again.

A sudden sound on the other side of the desk alerted her to the fact that she was not alone. She raised her eyes with some mild alarm, as there were to be no clients until after Laughton came back next week. J.T. Oswell stood there running his finger along the top of Carter's old desk, looking rather forlorn.

"Oswell?" She spoke in an uncharacteristically soft voice, nearly scaring him half out of his wits. "What are you doing?"

"Just thinking." He regained his composure and smiled at her. Oswell walked around to where she was sitting and knelt beside her, watching her struggle with the tape. He took it from her hands and worked at it patiently, removing enough tape to cover the box and seal it adequately. They worked silently together. She smiled at him appreciatively when they were done as she set it aside.

"Well, I guess that's that."

"I guess." He nodded. "I'm going to miss him. You were right, I did spend most of my time here."

"So what will you do with your time now?"

Oswell shrugged. He looked saddened but smiled at her anyway.

"I think maybe I should get a hobby." He nodded softly. "What about you? You staying on with Laughton and Bankson?"

"No. I'm tired of trying to put ideas into everyone else's minds, pretending like I don't have onr of my own."

"You have a good mind. I can see where you're cut out for more than that."

They were quiet.

"So, what kind of hobby?" She struggled to keep the conversation up. "That hobby you were going to take up—remember?"

"I don't know. Any suggestions?"

She looked at him through her misty eyes and burst out in a little laugh.

"You're setting yourself up for me to say a lot of really awful things to you."

"But you're not, and don't think I don't appreciate that, cause I do."

They both laughed softly. Jan wiped her eyes and looked around.

"Well, I guess I should get this stuff all downstairs for the mail." She waved her hand at the boxes there. "Not like it will ever get there."

They laughed again.

"I guess. I'll help you, okay?" J.T. Oswell nodded at her. They both knelt to grab the same large box at the same time, nearly knocking their heads together. "Oh, sorry."

"I'm sorry—"

They were nose to nose as they knelt there hovered over the same box. Neither moved a muscle. Jan could feel his breath on her lips as they stayed there, and she swallowed hard as she studied his mouth.

"What are we doing?" she whispered.

Without another word, their lips moved softly over each other's, gently feeling their way around uncharted territory. The apprehensive kiss turned more eager as they gradually pulled each other closer. When it was over, they backed away ever so slightly, still very near each other's faces.

"What did we just do here?" he asked in a haunted voice.

"I think we were coming up with an idea for that hobby you were looking for."

"Ever I'm lucky enough to have a hobby that terrific, I'd definitely have to think about taking it up full time."

Jan smiled almost shyly at him.

"What now?" he asked quietly.

"Let's get this stuff downstairs. Then maybe we can go somewhere to discuss this possible hobby. What do you say?"

"I say okay—an enthusiastic okay at that, lest my odd behavior lead you to believe otherwise."

"If this is odd, Oswell, I could learn to live with your odd." She stopped, turning to see him as she corrected herself. "J.T."

"We could get dinner. Couldn't we?"

"We could."

"Maybe go to a movie or something."

"That would be good." Jan caught a glimpse of the little box still perched on the desktop there and she quickly picked it up. "I, um, need to stop by the Federal Express office before we go anywhere."

"Sure, whatchya sendin' where?"

Jan looked thoughtful for a moment as she prepared her answer.

"I feel good, all of a sudden, and I want to share it." She hastily stuffed the box into her jacket pocket.

"What?"

Jan smiled at him and nodded toward the door.

"I'll explain later."

He held the door for her as they made their exit.

"Jetsum."

Oswell stopped and looked at her oddly.

"Pardon?"

"Jetsum. That's my last name."

"Why didn't you ever tell me?" He hesitated before turning out the office light.

"Because I knew you would make fun of it, like *Jan Jetsum, come and get some.*"

"I wouldn't have." He shook his head. "Okay, I probably would have."

"I thought so." She smiled as he flipped the light out.

"Jetsum. That's poetry."

"You think so?"

"I do."

They walked across the lobby and stopped at the elevator where Oswell pressed the button. They smiled at each other as the doors parted. They stepped inside.

"Maybe after that movie you can come over and meet my dog."

Her eyes widened innocently as the doors began to shut.

"You have a dog? Wow . . . "

Chapter Sixty-one

Meg finished putting the finishing touches on the little Christmas tree in her apartment. The AM radio station was playing a talk show, something she seem to have cultivated an appreciation for as of late. Somehow, hearing someone else's problems for a short time made her feel more human. As well, merely hearing the verbal exchange made her feel a little less lonely.

Blue trundled over to where she was standing at the window, looking out at the cold Wisconsin night. The sky was a particular paleness that forecasted snow with a certainty that she was used to by now, as the ground was already blanketed with an even whiteness.

Meg looked at her old dog as he sighed loudly. She roughly patted his neck. Blue had made a nearly complete recovery upon moving back to this familiar climate. Only few scars showed now and he was back to his normal self.

They'd been lucky to find a lovely apartment in the Victorian style house owned by an older couple. There were three other apartments in the house as well, each with its original wood trim and other antique details of an earlier era, much as the rest of the large homes in this vintage neighborhood. It was sparsely furnished so far, but cozy enough with its fireplace home to a crackling fire each night. She'd purchased a few items for the front room and the old landlady had lent her an ancient sea chest that was doubling for a coffee table before her sofa.

Across the room was a little writing desk where her laptop computer was making itself at home, dust covered and alone. She paid it rare notice, as she had since moving to the home over a month earlier. For the first time, she actually realized what true writer's block was. What alarmed her moreover was the fact that she really didn't care.

A knock at her door drew her out of the daydream she'd drifted into and she promptly went to answer it.

"Who could it be on Christmas eve, do you suppose, Boo?"

She unchained the safety latch and slid the deadbolt away, pulling the door open hesitantly. What she saw next surprised her more than anyone she could have hoped to see.

"Reed!"

Meg lunged toward him as he stood there, wrapping her arms around him as the tears sprang to her eyes.

"Hey, Meggie. How are you?"

"Oh my God! I'm so much better now! So much better . . . " She grabbed his hand and pulled him inside the apartment. "Welcome to my earthy digs! Sit down."

Reed smiled handsomely and Meg studied him carefully trying to come up with an approximation of everything that was different about her old friend.

"No, thanks Meggie. I just stopped in for a minute."

"You look too fabu. What in the world?" Her eyes were wide as she gazed over him. "You are so trim and your hair—my God!"

"I see you freed yourself of those outdated tresses as well." He laughed lightly as she smiled. "Yeah, I finally actually learned to choke down tofu and use a half amount of peanut butter on those rice cakes. You're right, they're not too terrible that way."

"You are a sight for sore eyes, Reed. I've missed you so much." Meg refused to let go of his hand. He was holding something in his other hand that he raised to her now.

"Here, I caught the FedEx guy downstairs. He was bringing this to you.I signed." He offered it to her and she nodded gratefully. "I was on my way to Milwaukee and I couldn't pass through without telling you how sorry I am about everything."

"Don't be sorry. It was me."

"No, it was me." He smiled as he spoke calmly. "I have done a lot of thinking about everything. I was blaming you for a bunch of things that you really had nothing to do with. It was a convenient way of doing things."

"I'm glad you're doing good." She spoke quietly. "What's in Milwaukee?"

"Ronald's parents. They invited us up for the holiday. He's in the car."

Meg squeezed his shoulders impulsively as she smiled broadly.

"Oh, oh, I'm so happy for you, Reed."

"I knew you would be, Meggie."

"So, is he, the one, do you think?"

"I know he is." Reed returned her enthusiastic smile. He looked around her apartment. "I see your one is still in Florida. Sorry, Noel told me all about him."

"Oh, I see." She smiled and then rolled her eyes. "Well, I don't know, Reed. You know these things work sometimes,and sometimes they don't."

"And, sometimes they do."

"And sometimes they don't."

They laughed at their silly conversation and Reed glanced down at his watch suddenly and then toward the window.

"You have to go so soon?"

"Yes,I'm afraid I do. He's an only child and his mother tends to freak a little when we're running late." Reed rolled his eyes and nodded. "I've loved seeing you, Meggie."

"Thank you for coming to see me. You can't know how much it means to me."

He nodded and they hugged tightly again. Finally they parted and he walked to the door, turning to see her once again. He smiled at her as he left quietly. Meg impulsively stepped into the hallway and called to him.

"Reed—" The friend stopped and turned to see her standing in the doorway. She smiled and nodded, her eyes misty. "Glimmer on."

Reed smiled as he nodded and then he was gone.

Meg stepped back inside her apartment and shut the door, replacing the locks. She blotted her damp eyes with her sweatshirt sleeve as she walked to the window to see Reed get into his car and leave. Finally she forced herself to leave it, feeling hollow.

Catching a glimpse of the barren little tree from the corner of her eye, she walked over to it and plugged in its lights. It glowed softly in the corner, and she returned to the writing table where the package was sitting that Reed had brought from downstairs. Meg went to it now, working steadily at the wrap job, tearing it open at last. She dumped it onto the desk. A little black velvet box tumbled out of the mailer. She looked at it curiously. She felt the smoothness of it between her fingers as she slipped her fingernail into the crease and flipped the top back.

Meg tipped her head sideways as she looked at it through wide eyes. She picked up the dainty little clip and held it toward the window to study its iridescent and jeweled wings. Returning to the box, she dug her finger along the bottom and pulled out the holder, revealing a little compartment below it. A small slip of paper was crammed in there that she promptly removed and smoothed flat to read.

Seize the moment—you'll find him here. Merry Christmas, Meggie. Love, Jan

Meg silently read the address that followed and then wrinkled her nose as she looked at Boo.

"He's in Wisconsin. It's a sign."

Chapter Sixty-two

Nick Carter finished chopping the last of the firewood into workable pieces. It wasn't the traditional way to spend a holiday, but it would keep him busy.

"That should do ... " He muttered, stacking them near the house. He grabbed a single slab off the top of the stack as he entered his home.

Boo came to greet him with his bowl hanging out of his mouth. Carter laughed as he smacked the snow off his gloves and slipped out of his boots.

"We're going to have to work on that greeting thing a little." He roughly tousled the dog's thick fur. "First the slippers, then I get you the food. Got me?"

He removed his coat and set it aside, following the dog to the kitchen where he scooped out a few cups of kibble.

"There you go." He patted him again and then turned to fill his kettle with tap water that he placed on the stove top. Next he returned to the front door to retrieve the firewood, carefully tossing it onto the fire in the living room. Carter stood back and warmed his hands.

The sound of the doorbell disrupted his warming session and he sighed as he rolled the cuffs back on his chambray shirt. Smoothing his hair, he walked to the front door. He threw the door open, his eyes landing on a pair of suede boots. He carefully scanned upward to the leggings and sweater that barely poked out beneath a fleecy coat. The neckscarf. Up a little further . . .

"Meghan?" His heart pounded so loudly inside his chest he was sure that Meghan Laine would certainly hear it and see through his cool exterior. He quickly found his composure. "I think you must have lost your way."

"I would like to talk to you."

"Do you think you can do it without an alias?"

Meg blinked hard but continued with what she had to do.

"I'm sorry that you feel like I'm nothing but a deceptive waste of flesh. But I'd be a liar if I said I would take it all back if I could." She waited as he stood there looking less than thrilled. "I might have spent my life as a farmgirl in Iowa, and possibly even married to someone I wasn't meant to marry."

"I don't want to talk to you about this."

"You don't have to." She shook her head suddenly. "I'm here on business anyway—I heard you were doing some book agenting here in the Midwest and thought you might want to take a look at some of my work."

"I'm afraid you won't find the all star representation you're looking for with this guy. I only consider newcomers." His voice was steady and low as she stood there on the snowy steps of his little farm house.

"I've never had my name on a cover."

"I don't think I can help you." He looked away as Meg quickly spoke up, fearful that he may simply shut the door in her face.

"It's a story about a girl who pretended to write a book for the man she loved,the only problem was that she had to deceive a lot of people she cared about in the process and as it turns out,the love she thought she had wasn't even real."

"I'm not taking any new submissions."

"She ends up hurting the one she knew she could fall totally, madly in love with, and he sends her away before she can tell him that . . . that he's the one."

"The one for what?"

"The one and only. The one that she wants to quit wasting time and start living happily ever after with."

Carter stared at her as she looked at him hopefully, nervously . . . eagerly. Silence. His expression softened some when he saw a familiar little silver dragonfly clip peering ever so slightly from below her knit stocking cap. He froze. At last he spoke with a different tone.

"Of course you'll have to rewrite it, and I know how much you hate doing that."

"Just tell me how, editor." A spark of hope was growing within her, but she was cautious of it.

"First, I'd want the cat to be a dog the dog to be a cat—up to be down. Right to be left—that kind of thing."

She stepped closer, her misty breath near him as he remained in the threshold of his warm home. She trembled inside, from the cold winter she suspected. She swallowed hard with wide eyes as she waited with great apprehension.

"Anything else?"

"Yeah," His eyes roved over her rosy cheeks and blue eyes and his voice fell into a whisper. "The one should probably reconsider the writer's offer. Write in some part about how they start living that *happily ever after.*"

His words were stifled suddenly by her kiss. Her nose was cold as it pressed against his own warm one, and when he pulled her back a little, her confident blue eyes had turned to warm seas.

"So, do you think anyone will buy it?" she whispered. He was quiet for a moment.

"I know I would." He playfully raised his eyebrows. They both laughed with their faces pressed to each other still. Carter pulled her into the threshold where he stood. He kissed her again.

"Do you think there's a chance that you could be a farm girl after all?" he asked her as he gazed into her eyes lovingly. Meg smiled and nodded with a sparkle of new life glistening in her eyes.

"I think I just had the wrong farm."

Nick Carter consumed the welcome sight of her, a smile growing across his face. Finally, it erupted into a laugh. He put his arm around her shoulder and led her into the warmth of his house.

The door closed quietly as the snow softly began to fall again, adding to the winter white cover that lay quietly all around. The light from the window of the little farm home glowed brightly from within.

"Chances Are" is a novel from newcomer Meg Carter about three best friends, a writer, a mother and a gay man, whose lives veer off in separated directions, all with the same destiny in mind: to find true love. The story cen - ters around the writer who submits her novel under an alias believing that it will benefit her on her publishing quest, and wildly enough, it does! However,

she falls in love with her agent along the way, and is forced to live a double life. Although incredibly unbelievable, the premise is an interesting one, at least, but the characters in this book are implausible and flatter than the hot - cakes on a Denny's Grand Slam number two. Their airy conversations are loaded with all sorts of symbolism and 'sap' for a lack of a better word, things that I just don't get. But if you're one of those boomer or generation X-er types with an appreciation for an unrealistic piece of fluff and still believe that Johnny Mathis can make people fall in love, then "Chances Are" may be for you.

To me, it was like an appetizer—it put me in the mood for one of the greats, like a helping of Claire Sodey, a side portion of Nona Shipman, or a dessert dish of Marcus St. John. Speaking of which, a valid source says that Claire Sodey has something hot set for release in the fall. But alas, whatever happened to Marcus St. John? Now there was a man in touch with character dimensionality..."

—Gibson Porter, NY Times Book Review